TRANSFIXION

J. GIAMBRONE

Cover Art:

Publisher's Note:

This is a work of fiction. All names, characters, places, and events are the work of the author's imagination.

Any resemblance to real persons, places, or events is coincidental.

Solstice Publishing - www.solsticepublishing.com

Transfixion

by

J. Giambrone

Transfixion

For NIO

One

"Don't read while you eat, Kaylee," said Mom, as she usually did, in her blunt, matter-of-fact manner. This was one of her policies.

Kaylee Colton didn't care about that, as she was too immersed in *Ghostliest*, the third volume in the *Ghostly* series, to concern herself with trivial matters like etiquette or basic hygiene at the breakfast table. She was far more concerned with the potential traps awaiting the two ghost hunters, Jasmine and Kurtz. A transfixion snare could mesmerize their minds until they dissociated. They would see without seeing. This type of hazard nearly imprisoned Jasmine, the legendary ghost huntress, in the final chapter of *Ghostly*. Again in *Ghostlier*, Jasmine and Kurtz were transfixed when they stumbled across the Ancient Fountain, which could easily suck their brains into an infinite void.

"You're going to get milk on that brand-new book." Mom was in one of her usual morning moods. "Sean!" she yelled up the stairs, and Kaylee cringed. "Five minutes." Mom stood tall and commanding, like a blunt force of nature, and she tended to yell a lot.

Kaylee wasn't speaking to Sean since he'd called her an "ugly troll," and she just wanted to find out what Jasmine and Kurtz were blundering into. The two unlikely ghost hunters always wound up at the locus of some inter-dimensional rift. The object they sought could be hexed and potentially freeze their minds for eternity, but that was the ghost-hunting biz.

Kaylee escaped toward the stairs to finish the chapter before school.

"So how is it?" Mom stared over, expecting some kind of elaboration.

"So far so good."

"I want to read it, after you're done. Okay?"

Kaylee nodded. "Five minutes, right?"

Her mother nodded back and then exploded in a bellowing thunder. "Sean! Turn that damned noise off!" Mom huffed in frustration, and she hustled about to finish up. She tended to be more than a little disorganized.

Kaylee ascended the carpeted staircase with her book. From Sean's bedroom at the end of the second floor hallway, a loud screech flooded out from his television set. It sounded weird, like aliens playing with the Emergency Broadcasting System. Repeating endlessly, the turbulence ground out somewhere between an old modem connecting and an obnoxious electric guitar with too many effect pedals turned on. Not even Sean's taste in music was *that* terrible.

Paused before her bedroom doorway, Kaylee felt awkward, and she just wanted to duck inside to escape.

"Dorkus." The noise barrage tugged at her sense of equilibrium, and her body felt queasy and numb, but the last thing she wanted to do was confront Sean. Her brother liked to brag about roughing up other kids at his high school for fun. He lifted weights in order to become an even bigger asshole. The best policy was to avoid, avoid, avoid.

She ducked inside her bedroom and jumped on her bed to finish that *Ghostliest* chapter. Mom had gifted her the book yesterday after she had suffered and cleaned dirty dishes, load after load. That was their deal.

In the book, Jasmine and Kurtz happened upon a secret door buried in the landscaping of the curiously designed gardens surrounding the Metropolitan Museum. Actually, Kurtz tripped over the handle and fell on his face in the wet dirt.

Kaylee's ears still tingled from that TV interference, and so she increased the volume of the words in her eyes to block it out. Reading always helped her ignore her jerky brother. Mom would sort Sean out and maybe take his damned TV away. Perhaps he'd even remember how to read.

Ghost huntress Jasmine was first through the steel trapdoor and down the filthy concrete staircase plunging fearlessly below the earth. Whatever or whoever waited down in that black underground passageway was integral to setting the spiritual planes back in alignment. Jasmine's extra senses tingled with certainty.

Kurtz, the nerdier and more cautious member of the team, felt obligated to follow Jasmine, as he usually did, down into the spider hole. Not least because he was secretly, madly in love with her. But Jasmine was mission-oriented and single-mindedly determined. Because she was the only known medium sensitive enough to do this job, she had no choice in the matter, really.

Thud.

Kaylee heard something from downstairs. It seemed like shouting, an overheated fight with Sean. Snapping from the text, she froze to listen. Mom yelled again, but she always yelled, and Kaylee couldn't understand any of the words.

She glanced over to her bedroom door crinkling her nose. This was a trying decision, and she didn't want to get involved.

Down in the underground stairwell, an overhead, rusty steel door slammed shut on the two ghost hunters. The pair had no option but to forge into the catacombs and hope for another way out. But their flashlights went all flickery due to some electromagnetic anomalies, probably connected with paranormal energy fields.

Crash!

A metallic explosion sounded in Kaylee's house, a real smashing clank from the kitchen. Steel pans bashed. She jumped up on her bed, nervous and disoriented.

Still clutching *Ghostliest*, she carried it to her bedroom door and listened. That cycling noisy pattern masked whatever was happening downstairs. She strained to hear. The TV speakers droned on in a hypnotic rhythm that made her mind feel spacey.

Mom screamed, "Sean!"

Kaylee pulled open her bedroom door. Quietly she sneaked out onto the carpeted hallway. Down the stairs and back toward the kitchen she stepped, surrounded by swirling noise. Along the narrow corridor, she gazed as if in slow motion. The wall opened up on the right.

"Sean, stop!" Mom's voice was a desperate, guttural roar.

"Mom?" Kaylee froze at the edge of the hallway, where the carpet met the ceramic tiling. There she gazed on Sean, who was standing over Mom with one of those long, super-sharp chef's knives raised above his head. Millions of infinitesimally small droplets of blood hung motionless in the air.

There was something about a scream that was so inconsequential, so ineffectual that it couldn't be relied upon. The mist of blood was the last thing Kaylee saw as a colorless wall of numbness overtook her eyes.

She became a marble statue.

Perhaps something happened then, which she couldn't see. Grey liquid had splashed all over their white, newly remodeled kitchen, but large dark blind spots lingered.

Kaylee suspected that she could speak no more, that her voice had evaporated in that strange, lost moment. The screeching television sounded so much louder now, and it confused her such that she didn't know if she was dreaming.

Pulsing and throbbing, the noise blitz swirled around the hallway like dancing ghosts. Buzzing sounds posed oddly in the air to her left and right as if in an insect swarm. The television cacophony carried her mind away on its fog, and it tugged at her like a siren.

Kaylee swayed on rubbery legs.

Sean then turned his head toward his sister, and he noticed her standing there. His expressionless face was splattered with grey galaxies. Wet patches soaked up into his spiked, dirty blond hair. His pale eyes shot right through her. It was as if he didn't know her at all.

But she could see him now.

Sean wrenched the massive knife upward, and he held it in his two dripping hands. Without pause, he scurried directly at Kaylee like some demonic animal from Hades on a mission to destroy the world. He had become a hell-bat turned human.

Kaylee couldn't scream, couldn't say anything at all. All she could do was run back upstairs and slam her bedroom door behind her and lock it. Inside the paint seemed to have faded and the world resembled some black and white old movie.

Her brother's body pounded against the wood. The force strained the steel lock as her door thundered.

Kaylee sat on her floor, and her back automatically pushed back against the door. Sean slammed again, and the shock of his jolt shot through her spine and skull. Now she felt like she must be dreaming, as it was far too strange, and there were gaps in her memories, like in nightmares. The real world was supposed to make more sense.

Sean stabbed into the wood panel just above her head.

She liked her door, and she remembered how Dad had replaced all the hollow ones with solid wood composite versions. Dad said the cheap ones were just garbage, and they didn't block sounds. They certainly wouldn't block a butcher knife.

Dad wasn't even in the country. He was probably flying around over Europe, or it could be Japan? She used to keep a journal of his every stop and write the airport codes, but that was years ago.

All she could manage now was to mechanically push back against her door each time Sean bashed into it. It seemed like the right thing to do. Her brain was operating on auto-pilot.

Kaylee's ears picked up the sounds of gouging, as well as the distorted buzzing from that messed-up TV down the hallway. If this was a dream, it was a really bad one, and she didn't want to play along anymore. It had to be a dream, because there was no other explanation worth a damn.

Dad wouldn't arrive home until the end of the following week, too late to sort this mess out. She was now completely on her own.

Two

K aylee lingered in a bland, grey world of numbness and confusion. Another jolt into the back of her skull from the door and she decided she'd had enough of this annoying game with Sean. It was time to return to her life. As she pressed her back against her bedroom door, she flipped open *Ghostliest*. Calmly she located her previous page.

Sean's knife scraped at the wood behind her.

As she found the proper paragraph, it occurred to her that she might not want to remain in her bedroom at all, given the circumstances. She spied her window. Her room was up on the second floor, and she had been forbidden to climb out on the rooftop. She was certain that her dad had had her best interests in mind, but this time had to be different. She'd never even wanted to climb out on her roof until now.

Sean's bayonet punctured the skin of the door panel an inch above Kaylee's skull. She raised her eyes. The steel edge jutted out just above her scalp. There it stuck, and Sean couldn't free it right away, which amused her greatly. Growling, Sean yanked at the chef's knife.

Kaylee huffed and her fingers bent back the corner of page 174. She slid the volume under her left arm carefully avoiding the knife blade, as she rose up off her floor. The steel weapon squealed back out of the crack.

Sean's eye peered in through the jagged hole. He shook the door's handle. In his blind rage, he attempted to muscle the whole door off its hinges.

Kaylee retreated to her window. Still dazed, she saw the knife slide inside at the side door jamb above the silver knob. It scraped back and forth against the metal strike plate.

Her butt backed into the windowsill just as her bedroom door flew open. Except for the mesh insect screen, her window was open, and she slammed *Ghostliest* into the screen to just knock it right out of her way. If she was going to get into trouble over that, then something was truly wrong with the world.

Sean raced across the bedroom and lunged. His knife extended, he growled like some sick dog.

Kaylee clawed her way out onto the shingled rooftop. Behind her, Sean slashed wildly in pursuit.

She steadied herself on the sloping surface, and she snatched the book. As she did, the knife struck down where *Ghostliest* had been a moment before and stabbed right through the roofing shingles.

There was no way she would leave that book behind. It had been the very last thing Mom had given her, the last hug she could recall. It had been their last moment being happy together yesterday afternoon, and it was all she had to keep from collapsing into a ball.

Sean climbed through the open window as Kaylee tip-toed across the rooftop, trying not to look down. Atop the first level she spun, dizzy at the sight of her neighborhood from above. The roof was slanted like it wanted to knock her right off, and she was deathly afraid of heights. Many neighbors rushed about below, some fist-fighting and jogging past her driveway. Neighbors wielded baseball bats and handguns as they raced by. Cars honked and sped off, tires screeching above the echoes of men's shouts.

Kaylee halted at the end of the roof, lingering apprehensively above fluffy decorative bushes below in her front yard. The long drop looked even worse from her vantage point. The height caused her hands to shake, and she jerked into a tight clump at the roof's edge.

Sean again.

What's his problem?

He stomped across the shingles with that long chopper pushed out in front of him, like a caveman who had found a magic wand. He seemed to have no recognition of her, his own sister, or even of what he was doing. Kaylee backed up to the very edge, flapping her arms above the nine foot drop, which seemed a lot higher. She stood another five feet and an inch above there, and so this was no small decision, except for that knife.

The steel razor edge sliced the air at her cheek. Sean was apparently now some kind of killing machine from an R-rated movie, and Kaylee needed to get away from him once and for all.

She dropped her body down to the rooftop, one leg strewn over the side of the gutter. Attacked by the abrasive shingles, tar, and fiberglass, the skin of her forearm scraped off. The sharp aluminum edge inside the rain gutter was the only place left to grip onto. Kaylee's luck improved when the gutter ripped right off the house from the weight of her body, and she fell backwards into the leafy shrubs below. When she hit the ground, the impact knocked her nervous system and the air out of her lungs. She lay on her back, devastated.

Sean remained standing high up on the rooftop, and he searched for a way down to pursue her.

Kaylee still held *Ghostliest* in her right hand, and she twisted over and up to her feet. Her left hand bled profusely, sliced open from the thin metal edge of the rain gutter. At the sight of the bleeding she instinctively tried to scream out, but nothing came. Nothing but the blood glugging out of her hand.

Kaylee tried to shout all manners of curse words, but her voice had escaped in that other moment, that instant she couldn't remember.

She spun in panic and pressed her hand up against her shirt. Frantic, she abhorred all that blood escaping her, and she certainly didn't want to stain *Ghostliest*. With the book tucked under the elbow of her bad arm she could still use her right hand.

13

Screams echoed from Mrs. Fowler's yard next door. The air roared with anger and shouts, all of it incomprehensible and terrifying. Car tires screeched in the morning air as more people fled as rapidly as they could get away. Metal scraped against metal. Glass from a car's window shattered. The rumbling destruction enveloped the entire neighborhood from every possible direction. Kaylee listened with apprehension as her neighborhood had never before exploded in cacophony. Street fighting was everywhere all at once, that is, if any of it was real. She was in no position to tell anymore.

Meandering down her driveway and through the soft branches of the weeping willow, she heard a primitive grunt from behind. Sean hit the ground and landed in the bushes as she had done.

No time to patch up her bleeding hand. She pivoted left down the sidewalk on Carmelita Way. Their normally pacific suburban street was in the throes of World War V, or whatever number they were up to. Smashed vehicles were strewn along the gentle curve, and several dead bodies lay unattended in the street. A mob of frenetic neighbors brawled with each other behind her. Sean ran out after.

Kaylee sprinted the sidewalk, and she jumped over a pile of garbage from two overturned trash cans. At the next house, she ran right past a yellow ten-speed bicycle lying in the street with no owner in sight. She turned back and awkwardly righted the bike. Her left hand bled onto the foam handlebar grip, but she didn't mind the mess. She fully climbed on and pedaled with desperation.

Sean roared in anger. His twisted, deformed face and his disheveled bloodstained hair made him seem almost comical, like an evil cartoon leprechaun.

Kaylee pedaled hard around various crashed cars, but more neighbors emerged up ahead. Carmelita Way had become an obstacle course of scattered garbage cans and a flame-spewing pickup truck.

Where can I go?

She shot down the street. Without a destination, she lost her confidence.

A pair of rioters homed in on Kaylee. A man in a white shirt and tie and a woman wearing only a fluttering, pink bathrobe ran laterally to cut her path before she could reach the next cross street. These two wanted to ram her over for no reason. Sean kept chasing as well. Right behind he slashed at her back. She turned the bike away and changed gears. Avoiding this new attack, she pedaled faster onto the opposite sidewalk.

Adrenaline suddenly jolted her, and she couldn't feel anything at all: no pain, no regret, nothing. Although Sean snarled and whipped the air with the butcher knife, he couldn't catch up with her. The two neighbors, the business man and the woman in pink, slowed and returned their attentions to those large scuffles well behind her, in some other universe.

Peeking back over her shoulder, Kaylee almost dropped *Ghostliest.* As her bloody hand grabbed at the book in midair, she came close to losing her balance and tumbling end over end onto the unforgiving street. But she recovered, as rattled as ever. Gunshots—rapid fire—filled the air.

Instantly she decided to try for the deserted fields, the cement channel just outside her housing development. She crossed to the next avenue, riding down the middle of the street, and then that screeching sound, that modem pattern from the TV, sang out to her again.

I have to call Mom.

Her heart and blood pressure shot up. Her stomach ached. The street faded out to dim grey lifelessness and blood droplets like rain hung in the air.

To her left, Kaylee rolled past a house with an open front door. The blare from the television set within cycled through its sickly computer patterns and its nauseating, satanic guitar pulsations. This unexpected mental jolt sickened her and rendered her stomach queasy again. It played with her sense of balance.

Still rocketing into a bland colorless world where spatters of faded grey blood stained her vision, a beast appeared, like a charging bull. Not an animal, a speeding pickup truck, and it rushed at her with a horn blast to her face. At the last instant, Kaylee wrenched the handlebars over and crashed into the side of a parked car. Gracelessly, she slammed onto the street.

Mom.

Kaylee hit the asphalt, and she tasted metallic blood in her mouth. Her teeth stung, and her lip began to swell. The slam left her legs tangled up in the frame of the bike. Staring at the dark texture of the roadway she thought of just stopping there and sleeping.

Her eyes closed. She just needed to find Mom, but she hoped her mom would find her instead. Lethargically she turned to check the state of her body on the pavement. Wiggling a bit, her foot became free. It was so much effort to stand back up again, too much effort really.

Then the roar of it all returned with nearby shotgun blasts and screams from several directions at once.

Three

Kaylee Colton, her left hand still trickling, aimed her stolen bicycle onto a rough dirt trail beside the cement drainage channel, a shortcut inaccessible to cars. Her pace slowed, and she panted as she strained to listen. Gunshots popped on the horizon like one-off firecrackers. A boom echoed over town. Then a single plume of smoke rose like a mushroom cloud. This wasn't good at all.

Her crusted-over hand needed attention. She ripped a piece of cloth from the bottom of her T-shirt and tied it around her left hand. The cut began to ache, and she thought she might cry, but nothing came out. No sound, no tears, just anger and a blunt throbbing each time her heart pumped more pressure into the gash.

As she continued biking, the dirt path beside the dry channel became serene. Bird chirps and insect calls replaced the guns and roaring riots. Maybe it was all over by now and time to move along with life. Here among the trees and thirsty weeds it felt normal.

Kaylee pointed her bike toward the street of a friend from school, Blair Corning. Blair lived in a house several blocks outside of Kaylee's neighborhood, and she could at least help patch the bloody hand. She knew that her wound definitely needed peroxide and bandages, potentially even a couple of stitches. Then, maybe, she could finally relax and finish reading her ghost hunter book in peace.

There couldn't possibly be any school today.

A major avenue stood in the way before Kaylee could even reach Blair's house. Martin Luther King Boulevard was a busy artery, and the risk of crossing was great, with all those cars and crazies running amok. Maybe it wasn't such a good idea to ride in that direction at all.

Kaylee peered down the length of the side street. The area seemed quiet. As she glided ahead, a silhouette in a window above her snapped the curtain closed. She listened for them, for anyone. Martin Luther King Boulevard sounded quieter than usual, except for the low rumbling of a diesel engine around the corner. Parked right beside the first building was an abandoned gasoline tanker truck, still glugging and spitting out fumes from an exhaust pipe. The driver's door hung completely open.

Kaylee pulled the yellow bike alongside the truck's vibrating cab. Down the boulevard she couldn't see anyone at all. The tanker truck rumbled in its own world, oblivious to the unfolding apocalypse. She circled the tanker. As she did, an SUV whipped onto the boulevard and ripped past her on the opposite side. Instantly it disappeared again around another corner.

She felt odd, alone with that running truck, sorry for it, all alone in the world like herself. And it was wasting gas.

If people didn't use so much gas, they wouldn't need so many of these smelly tankers.

Kaylee crept up into the truck cab. To reach the key, she needed to climb completely inside and into the driver's seat. She peeked out through the dirty windshield, and she checked the side mirrors for anyone who might approach. With an emphatic nod, she turned the key, and the tanker engine ceased.

She felt momentarily satisfied, but now she had to take responsibility and keep the keys safe. Her fingers slid the key out of the ignition, and she studied them along with the attached plastic whiskey bottle trinket.

Shouts and gunshots returned, low and muffled but a cacophony nonetheless.

***

Blair Corning's front door hung partially open. Kaylee abandoned the yellow ten-speed on Blair's front lawn and poked her head into the foyer. It was dark. She stepped in and closed the front door behind.

Gingerly she tapped her knuckles on the inside of the door to make some sound. A little louder and a little harder, and then she quit before she bruised them.

No one responded. It was too quiet. Kaylee felt creeped out after everything that had happened, and now Blair was missing in the middle of all this. Not just Blair, but her entire family. Talk about unsettling. Maybe they'd left for school already. It smelled funny, permanently pungent, but that was normal. Actually, it felt comforting that at least something was familiar today, and that she could smell again.

She considered pedaling her bike elsewhere, but there wasn't anywhere else to go. Maybe to school. Maybe she would just go in like any other day and see what happened.

Bang. Bang. Bang.

Thunder from a gun discharged. A car squealed in front of Blair's house, some kind of drive-by shooting. Kaylee dropped flat on the floor, her face on the dirty brown carpet.

No one seemed to be shooting at this house. So she stood up again and peeked out the front window for a glimpse. They were already long gone.

Perhaps this was just the new normal, and everything was as it should be. That was a comforting idea, sort of.

Kaylee washed off her crusty wound in Blair's kitchen sink, avoiding a pile of slimy dishes. Blood trickled again down over the plates. From inside one of the kitchen drawers, she grabbed a clean green dishtowel and tied it around her palm.

In the fridge she dug through the leftovers, careful not to leave evidence of taking anything. A chicken carcass hid under some crumpled tin foil, coating her fingers with grease. All that pedaling and running away had given her an undeniable appetite.

If nothing else, she could finally find out what those ghost hunters were up to down in that catacomb.

Kaylee curled up on Blair's sofa with *Ghostliest*. She realized that she couldn't keep her eyes open, though, and her mind lingered in such a fog that her vision could no longer slog through the words. Normally she could read all night with just a flashlight.

Pain stabbed her forehead like that chef's knife had passed through her bedroom door, and she fell asleep on Blair's couch to escape.

By the time she awakened, covered in sweat and dying to pee, it was nighttime. Her torso stiffened. Thoroughly dark, the house was cast with jagged shadows. None of the lights were lit; nobody had come home. Strange shapes gyrated on the wall above her face, projected in from a pulsing orange streetlight outside.

Kaylee couldn't bring herself to flick on the light switch, and she wobbled in the dark toward the hallway, banging the wall. Nature called, but she felt too unnerved.

Stumbling in the dark, her hand knocked lotion containers and toothpaste onto the floor. After locating the toilet, she considered whether or not to risk actually using it. Her body shook, and she didn't want to pee in her pants, but confusion and terror had returned.

Across town, gunfire erupted in fast, automatic bursts.

Kaylee sat on the toilet seat, too balled up with tension to actually urinate. Then she heard footsteps in the house, low at first but each step louder than its predecessor. Filled with dread, Kaylee bit on her lip. The footsteps halted directly on the other side of the door.

She was breathing so hard and so roughly through her nostrils that anyone inside the house could hear her.

"Kaylee?" said a voice.

It was Mom.

Kaylee fell off the toilet and blacked out.

Four

I t was just after midnight when Kaylee stirred again on Blair's bathroom floor.

"I don't think you should stay here, honey." Her mom's voice called to her from out in the hallway.

Kaylee opened her eyes only to see the one-inch square tiles and a grid of shadows cast from a neighbor's light through the shower-stall window. Her arms squirmed, and she scrambled up to her knees. In a daze, she pulled open the bathroom door.

No one stood there. Not Mom.

Kaylee crawled out to investigate. The house felt empty. As she knelt in the hallway she realized there really was no point being on her knees, and so she stood up. Her mom had either left without her or something else was going on.

She searched room to room, methodically peeking into the shadows for some sign of life. After working her way through the cluttered, three-bedroom dwelling, she paused at Blair's bedroom doorway. Her friend's posters showed pop stars up on the walls. Outside the window, a blue flashlight beam streaked.

She froze. Footsteps pattered. Men grunted as they stormed past the window. The flashlight invaded. Its beam, like a sword, sliced through the bedroom across the posters and toward her.

Kaylee slammed herself down onto the floor in the hallway. The blue light raked overhead. Men outside were searching for something. Then she heard the front door open. They were coming.

The flashlight guy disappeared, and she listened as boots stomped into the living room. They turned on the houselights, and they dispersed, charging down the hallway toward her.

Kaylee jumped back into Blair's bedroom and then into the closet. She slid the closet door across, but the slider caught on some shoes left in the track. She searched the closet desperately for something to hide beneath. Then she remembered.

Above was the overhead door to the crawlspace attic. That was where Blair concealed her diary. She faced up, remembering how Blair climbed up there. It wasn't easy.

Strange men flicked on the hallway light, and they marched in deeper.

Kaylee jumped up onto the wire mesh closet shelves. Her left hand was barely usable, and only her fingertips could assist. When her skull reached the ceiling hatch, her foot slipped. Rough metal edges gouged into her cheek.

The monsters entered.

Kaylee kicked aside a board game, and she stood up awkwardly at the ceiling. The top of her head pushed the plywood hatch, and she raised her face into the attic. It was so terrible, black darkness, where the black widow spiders were supposed to live. There could be a thousand black widows or brown recluses or wolf spiders. It was total insanity, but she had no choice. She looked down, and a man flicked on the light in Blair's bedroom. The entire space flared. No time at all. Kaylee threw her arms up through the dusty crawlspace hole, and she pulled her legs up into the attic.

Only there wasn't an attic. There was no floor! Only crossbeams with itchy, dusty insulation stuffed between.

Below, the man threw open the closet door. Kaylee softly lowered the plywood hatch into place. She heard him rummage through Blair's closet, heard thuds as he threw boxes out of his way. She convulsed with each new slam that she felt. Her shoulders jolted, and she crouched silently atop a two-by-four crossbeam.

The intruders tore apart the dwelling. They knocked over furniture, overturned beds, and wrecked the place without a care. Muffled voices spoke at one another, words here and there.

"What you find?"

"Not much."

"Where next?"

They seemed to agree on something. A minute later they all stormed back out of the house. The front door shuddered, and then it was silent.

Kaylee felt the sting in her foot, and her leg couldn't take this squatting down any longer. The crawlspace was low, with wood supports angled this way and that. Water pipes and electrical wires, spider webs and heating ducts—all of them were coated with thick dust. Whenever she tried to move, her sneakers kicked clouds into the air.

A small scrap of plywood rested between two beams. Kaylee reached over, and she slid it toward herself. It was just wide enough to form a floor between the spacing of the joists. She sat hard, and the dust puffed up. She coughed and covered her mouth with her shirt. This had to be the most terrible place of all. The attic's dark angled corners squirmed, probably with nests of spiders.

She thought of climbing back down. From next door she heard a clash. Glass smashed and a lady screamed for her life. The sounds shot through the crawlspace in through the slatted rectangular air vents.

Nowhere was safe, not the house, not the street. Kaylee shivered solemnly. The screams stopped.

Eyes closed, Kaylee wiped dust from her cheek, careful not to get any grime in her eyeballs. When she opened her eyes again, they adjusted more to the near-total darkness and narrow shafts of moonlight angled in through whirlybird vent above. She noticed something move in the corner where the spiders lived. Her eyes made out a shadowy human figure, which slithered across the wooden beams like a shadow wolf. Maybe it crawled, and maybe it was a pattern in the shifting light. Her eyes had gone blurry with dust, and they teared up. It was hard to tell if the wolf shape was human, or if the human was Mom.

Mom!

The wispy shadow, Kaylee's mother, glided silently across the black crawlspace without kicking up any dust. She hovered, half-hidden behind an air conditioning duct at the far side of the crawlspace.

"Kaylee?" said Mom. "I told you not to stay here. When are you going to come home?"

Kaylee couldn't respond. Her head moved about, and she opened her mouth, but nothing came out at all. No sounds, and this disturbed her greatly.

"What's the matter, honey?"

Kaylee pointed at her mouth. Her eyes pleaded with the shadowy form for understanding.

"Well, I don't think you should stay up here," said Mom, "but you never listen."

Kaylee opened her eyes wider, but not enough light entered. She could no longer find Mom in the shadows. Her eyes just couldn't catch enough light at all. The attic was too dark and too confusing.

Mom didn't respond anymore; she'd gone away again. Kaylee climbed deeper into the attic toward tangled heating vents. As she peeked around the octopus-like hub, the old insulation broke apart. Dried-out duct tape peeled off. She touched the duct pipe to steady it, but it dropped right off the hub and slammed, kicking up even more dust everywhere. This choked her with a blast of toxic grit.

Kaylee scrambled back to the plywood shelf, where she waited for Mom to return. For the remainder of the night, she squirmed back and forth in order to stop her legs and her butt from going numb. Lying on one side and then another, atop the plywood platform, she listened intently for any trace of Mom.

Hours passed.

Sirens squealed in the distance. Helicopters flew above town, interspersed with the occasional crash and gunfight. Kaylee felt pretty good about hiding up in her personal nest like a lonely rat. Nobody knew where she was, not even those men who had searched, but especially not Sean Colton.

Eventually the crawlspace seemed familiar. As the sky outside lightened to a purple glow and then some blue, the attic took on a more hospitable aura, golden wood. Kaylee twisted to her left side as sunlight appeared and brightened her hideout a thousandfold.

The attic would serve as her new temporary home, and she set out to explore it from one end to the other. Like a monkey, she climbed toward the bright, glowing air vent on the far wall at the gable, where the most sunlight poured in. It was probably the best place to set up living accommodations.

She peeked down through the horizontal slats of the air vent, and she smiled. Below, her neighbor's yellow ten-speed bicycle was waiting on the lawn for her where she had left it. That comforted her, since she remembered putting it there yesterday, and so it made some kind of logical sense. Not much else did. Blair's front door was directly below her, and Kaylee figured out where she was in the world, roughly.

Like a spy, she observed the street passers-by from above. The neighborhood below seemed peaceful, but every once in a while a figure jogged past from left to right or right to left. Kaylee put her mind to work, and she tried to discern whose side they might be on, but she was clueless as to where they were going.

She climbed across the attic beams and back to the plywood platform above the closet. There, at the hatch, she noticed Blair's diary safely resting in its hiding spot, beside the pink insulation.

She slid the diary into her pants behind her back so that she could haul the plywood shelf back across the attic. With some strain, she maneuvered about the rafters like an ape, dragging the flat piece of wood toward her spy vent. Now she had a purpose. If she got bored spying on the neighbors, she might just have to read Blair's diary.

After thirty seconds, Kaylee turned her attention to the diary. She thought about how prying into Blair's personal journal might be seen as ethically questionable. But Blair was missing; she might even be dead. Holding onto her diary could be construed as keeping her memory alive. Plus, Kaylee had nothing else to read, and she was afraid to climb back down to retrieve *Ghostliest*. Climbing up here in the first place had been ridiculously strenuous. Her body felt sore all over. Her hands were bruised, cut and scraped. She felt like hell.

No sooner had Kaylee opened the diary and paused to read Blair's numerous threats, which told her not to proceed under any circumstances, did she hear a distinct metallic scrape below in the front yard, the kickstand from a bicycle.

She looked down through the air vent. Examining her yellow bike was one teenage boy in a T-shirt, his brown scruffy hair down at his shoulders. He wore faded blue jeans with holes in the knees and old work boots.

When Kaylee realized that he was checking the tires to steal her bike, she let out a loud gasp of a breath. The rush of air into her lungs made a thundering rasp aimed right down toward the thief.

The strange boy spun around to see the house. Kaylee froze, her eyes wide. He dropped the ten-speed to the lawn, and he slid an aluminum baseball bat from across his back.

The boy swung the bat around for effect, and he searched in a circle for the source of the breathing. His face tilted up to the air vent, and his eyes locked on directly into Kaylee's mind like a laser.

She jumped backwards, and she tried to avoid the incoming sunlight from the vent, but it was too late.

Outside, the older boy marched up the stairs, and he opened the front door below Kaylee. She could hear his steps beneath her, and she danced across the wooden crossbeams to escape. Trying to avoid the sounds below, she slipped right off of a two-by-four. Her foot shot straight down through the insulation and through the drywall ceiling, where it dangled down in the living room.

"Hey!" The boy shouted up at her. He ran around the house below, kicking over furniture.

Her foot dropped its sneaker, and she pulled it back up through the hole. With care, she rebalanced herself on the wooden beams. The unseen boy whacked at the ceiling.

"Who's up there? Get down here now!" He blustered like he owned the place.

Kaylee tiptoed around the attic, avoiding his sounds. She had no intention of complying.

The bat pounded the crossbeams below her feet. She could feel the vibrations through her sock. Each step forward caused little creaks in the structure. Crawling over the center beam to the other side of the house, she found that she was instinctively clutching Blair's diary.

The house muted for a minute, and then the ceiling hatch flew up, knocked through the air by the baseball bat. Yellow light flooded in from below and lit up the dust cloud.

Kaylee squatted between the heating ducts.

"Who's up in there?" the strange boy called again in a low-pitched voice, more intimidating than before. "You want some of this?" He slapped the bat around the wood framing of the hatch. "Huh? Do ya?"

27

His scruffy head popped up through the hatch hole, gazing around rapidly.

"Get over here!" He spotted Kaylee in the recesses.

Kaylee said nothing.

"Who are you?" He shouldered his bat apprehensively. "Is this your house?"

She stared back solemnly.

"Hey. You better answer me. You're one a them."

Insulted, Kaylee shook her head.

"Then you'd better say somethin'."

She felt trapped and helpless, and not about to move.

"Say something! You're one a them."

She shook her head, and she pointed at her mouth. Opening it, she tried to signal with gestures.

"Come down here," he said. Kaylee thought on it, but instead she pointed at his baseball bat.

"What?"

She poked her finger, annoyed at the threat.

"Hey." The boy struggled to respond. "Hey, shut up."

Kaylee folded her arms. She sneered back and then retreated into the shadows.

"Where you goin'?" the boy shouted. "What are you doing?"

She climbed back across the attic rafters to her personal spot in front of the outer air vent. Sitting on her plywood shelf, she opened up Blair's diary, ignoring him.

The boy retreated back down through the hole. From below she could hear furniture scraped across the floor. Something was kicked over, and she looked back over to the hatch. It remained still.

Blair's spelling was terrible. After her initial death threats Blair wrote of Nicole's crush on a boy in her school, whom Kaylee didn't know. She learned that Alison's father was sick, and he could be dying of cancer. Blair said she was saving up money for a class trip in June. Nothing about Kaylee at all.

Outside, a car door opened. Footsteps poured out.

Kaylee placed down the diary, and she turned to the air vent in order to watch. Across the street, a maroon van had parked and a squad of young men fanned out. They carried hunting rifles, and they signaled with hand gestures. Four of the guys moved up toward the front door of the house directly across the street.

The grey aluminum baseball bat flew straight up through the hatch, and it bounced around, coming to rest in the fluffy insulation with more dust launched into the air.

Kaylee sprang to her feet and crouched down in the gable point of the roof. She stared. The boy poked his head up into the crawlspace again.

He yanked himself awkwardly all the way inside.

"Shh!" He gazed at her, his eyes wild and desperate, and he squatted. Quietly, he closed the hatch, and he shifted around to find a place to sit. Again he pointed at her.

Kaylee listened, and her ears tingled with that screechy TV signal as it wafted in through the air vent. The volume had been jacked up. The carload of armed militants emerged from the house, along with a middle-aged couple whom Kaylee hadn't seen before. Most of the young men climbed back inside the van, along with the older man and woman.

Two of the guerillas remained behind with their rifles after the van pulled off. These two tapped on their web pads, which screeched with that signal noise pattern. Those two set off on foot together. That's where Kaylee lost sight of them.

Over at the center beam of the roof, the teenaged boy with brown, scruffy hair huffed out his breath in annoyance.

Inside their attic it was starting to swelter. An automatic ventilation fan provided some fresh air through the crawlspace, but as the sun baked the roof just above Kaylee's head, the temperature soared well over one hundred degrees. Her skin sweated uncontrollably. Her mind blurred. She panted involuntarily like a dog, and she looked over to the boy.

He was also panting. "Are they gone?" he whispered.

Kaylee peeked out the vent, and she nodded.

"Good. I'm *outta* here." He wrenched up the rectangular hatch, and he swung his legs over. Kaylee watched him slide from sight.

The boy took a big fresh breath as his head disappeared below. Then his face popped back up through the hole.

"Hey? You're not going to stay up here?"

Confused, Kaylee searched around the attic awkwardly.

"Come on," he said.

She considered a moment, then nodded.

Five

B lair's house was bright and glowed with saturated colors like a dreamy neon amusement park. Kaylee's head had cooled, but only so much. Her shirt was soaked with grimy sweat. Floating along the hallway, she glided into the bathroom where she placed her head under the faucet and splashed cold water onto her hair and neck. When she picked her head back up, she saw the mirrored reflection.

That boy was nowhere to be seen. Good. Kaylee looked a complete mess. Her clothes were filthy. Brown blood stained her shirt and pants. Streaks of brown and black and grey slashed down the length of her outfit. She didn't even want to touch her decrepit shirt with clean hands.

She tiptoed back over to Blair's bedroom. Blair's clothes had been tossed all over the floor, and her dresser drawers were thrown randomly about the room. But the clothes were clean, if too large. These would be fine as long as Kaylee wore a belt to tighten up the waistline.

She snuck back down the hallway in search of the boy with the baseball bat. She found him sitting on the couch, where he watched the street through the transparent lace curtains. Engulfed with being a lookout, he didn't even notice her.

Kaylee backed away, and then she picked up a wooden kitchen chair. She wrestled it over to the bathroom. After locking the bathroom door, she wedged the chair up under the doorknob. Pulling with all her strength, she tested it. The door remained barred shut. This was one of the techniques that she had picked up from a vampire story, or it could have been ghouls.

She tested the chair again. And again. Then she got undressed nervously and took a shower. The cool water blasted off all that dirt. The streaming water felt such a relief that she stayed under the spray until the hot water tank ran out. She didn't care. Blair's bathroom coated over with fog.

Kaylee borrowed a toothbrush, which she wasn't happy about doing, and she scrubbed her mouth clean. Lastly, she dressed in Blair's baggy jeans and a T-shirt two sizes too big. She styled her hair properly and wrapped a small bandage around her left hand, squeezing some lotion onto the abrasions.

It was time to open the bathroom door. But the chair was stuck. The wood must have expanded from all that moisture. Kaylee couldn't believe it. She was locked inside the bathroom from her own doing.

She grabbed the chair leg. With a ferocious growl she pulled as hard as she could. Still it remained stuck. Her palm slapped her own forehead and held her face as she tried to think of a solution.

This chair is going to pay.

She climbed around by the door, where she could get a good arc with her leg. Like a kung fu star she kicked, but her foot bounced off, and she fell down onto the slick ceramic tiles, bouncing on her tailbone. She would have yelled out from the shock wave alone, but her voice couldn't produce any sound.

"What are you doin'?" said the boy out in the hallway. "You been in there all day."

Kaylee turned angrily to the door, and she flipped it off. She had never been so angry at a chair before.

"Look, I'm goin' to Sports Warehouse," he said. "I found me a bike."

Her eyelids popped open. She jumped to her feet, desperate to open the stuck door. The boy lumbered off in his stupid boots.

She kicked the chair sideways, trying to dislodge it from under the doorknob. Flailing madly, the dark wood cracked. Her good hand lunged at the doorknob and whipped the door open. Rushing down the hallway, Kaylee chased after the bike.

In the living room, she found the boy about to open the front door, clutching the handlebars.

Kaylee grabbed the handlebars back, heaving the bike. He turned to her in surprise.

"What the hell?"

She pulled the bike across the carpet, away from him, and into the living room.

"Hey! Give me that!" He stormed after her. He was very tall, and it looked like he might work out. Kaylee cowered, retreating until one of the pedals caught on the kickstand. She stood cornered at Blair's couch, facing off against the brown-haired boy over their disputed ten-speed. She pointed a finger at the bike and then at herself.

"I don't care," he said. His big mitt latched onto the handlebars.

Kaylee repeatedly pointed at herself, and she pulled the bike over to her side.

"Give it," he said. "I'm goin' to Sports Warehouse, and I don't really care what you do."

Her face curled up in confusion, and she threw her hands up into the air in frustration. He was crazy to worry about sports at a time like this. She thought of slapping herself in the forehead just for effect.

The boy dragged the bicycle back toward the front door. Kaylee just stewed on the couch, and she mad dogged the bike.

He turned back. "It's where the guns are. It's right around the corner."

Kaylee caught his eyes, and she became self-conscious.

"I might come back," he said. "I don' know."

She sulked. Her index finger pointed at the bike and then herself.

"Yeah, well, that's life," he said obnoxiously. A brown electrical cord had been duct-taped to his baseball bat's handle. He pushed his arm through the loop, draping the bat onto his back like a sword.

Softly the boy opened Blair's front door, and he peeked out into the white glare. In a flash, he disappeared with the bicycle.

Kaylee's eyes soon rested on her copy of *Ghostliest*. She placed Blair's diary next to the novel. Looking up from the books to the dark television screen, she considered all three possibilities.

There was something ghastly about the television though. Curious, Kaylee rose up and examined it. It was the TVs that made all that cycling noise from the Emergency Broadcasting signal. The thought of actually turning on the power, however, gave her such chills that she sized up the device, careful not to get too close, and then she located the power cord sticking out from the wall socket and unplugged it. Dissatisfied, she went and hunted down a pair of scissors in the kitchen drawer, brought them back and chopped off the plug.

Helicopter blades and sporadic gunfire echoed over the little suburb. Sometimes they drifted closer and other times petered out altogether. Each episode made her queasy. It was so taxing, trying to ignore the chaos intruding in from the outside world.

If that boy didn't return with her bicycle, then she'd be stuck here at Blair's house. That guy obviously thought he was all that. Maybe it was better if he didn't come back.

Kaylee decided that she was hungry. If there was any more of that roasted chicken in the fridge, then it belonged to her.

Blair's kitchen had suffered the same assaults that the bedrooms had. Pans were flung, along with cans and boxes of food from the cabinets. The cutlery drawer was overturned, and it was difficult now to even reach the refrigerator.

Gunshots blasted. A battle erupted outside in the street. Kaylee spun around in the kitchen, and she noticed a dark brown wooden door. With a glance to the front windows, she turned back to this unknown portal and opened it.

It led into Blair's garage. Kaylee stepped inside, and her eyes adjusted to the slivers of light. In the center sat an unfinished, matte grey car with its hood open.

Blair's garage was like an auto shop. There were curly red hoses and spinning tools, red steel cabinets to hold more tools, and a piece of the car's outer skin sitting separately on a workbench.

Gunmen ran past the garage door, and Kaylee squatted behind the nose of the car for cover. The engine seemed shiny new, like it had recently been installed.

The street's gun battle migrated away, and a ping ricocheted off the concrete of the driveway just outside.

Kaylee opened the Mustang's driver's side door and the interior light popped on. Sitting down, she made herself comfortable. Then she poked around the dashboard and in the glove compartment. There were no keys. She felt the floor mats, and she twisted back to check in the rear seat. Then she got out.

At the workbench, she searched for the keys as if she were now on a quest. She flicked the light switch. The garage brightened from the glow of a sickly yellow light bulb hanging directly above the car.

"Kaylee!" said Mom in a muffled echo. "What are you going to do?"

Kaylee gasped. She spun around. She couldn't see anyone, just the eerie emptiness of the garage. Outside, a shadow flickered hypnotically at the edge of the door. She stared at the dancing sliver, but she retreated a step.

"Just hot-wire the sucker," said Mom through the bright slit. Her presence evaporated.

Kaylee nodded. As in the shape-shifter story, the car could be hers if she wanted it. All she had to do was play with some wires from inside the steering column. She poked her head back into the car. The plastic column covered everything, and she couldn't find any wires. Maybe it would be easier to just look for the keys, so she trudged back inside the shambles of Blair's kitchen.

In Blair's parent's bedroom, she dug through the overturned drawers. Jewelry, cufflinks, photographs, and every kind of clothing were just tossed there rudely by the unseen men who had rampaged through the night before.

With all that key hunting, Kaylee's stomach turned hungry again, so she returned to the refrigerator and checked the freezer. Mocha mint chocolate-chip ice cream, and nearly a half-gallon of it was left for her. She pigged out for half an hour until she couldn't stuff anymore ice cream into her body.

Kaylee washed up, and she saw the sunlight fade swiftly away outside the front window. She tensed, knowing that she needed to read a book right away, especially if it was going to go completely dark, and she couldn't use any lights.

Blair's journal was primarily blank. Kaylee found a pen on the floor, and she cleared off a section of the kitchen table to write. Her pen steadied above a new clean page, and she wrote:

Blair, I'm sorry for stealing your diary, but I really need to write some things down right now. I'll buy you a new one if you're not dead. And if you are, I'm really sorry.

I know you're probably not dead, so you're going to want to read this. I had to do it because if I don't, I'm going to go crazy and be bouncing off the walls like in a cartoon. And that's not good.

My mom keeps appearing. Maybe not appearing so good, but I hear her voice telling me stuff. By the way, I'm not sure if she's dead or alive. It's a long story. I'm not sure what's happening.

Angry bangs thundered from behind Kaylee. The front door rattled.

She turned slowly, her hands shaking.

The door pounded again.

That caused her to pee in her jeans, right on the kitchen chair. Slowly she slipped down and hid beneath the table. In the orange glare of the front window a shadow bobbed back and forth. Glass rattled as knuckles tapped hard. Dark hands forced the window, but it was locked.

Kaylee followed with her eyes as the shadowy form passed across each curtained window like the Grim Reaper. The gate outside squeaked open, and it clanked shut again. She crawled backward all the way into the kitchen's corner, still below the table, where she curled up into an inconsequential ball.

The back door bashed in. A sharp kick echoed throughout the house. Footsteps slapped louder, marching toward the kitchen.

Kaylee saw familiar work boots and ripped jeans rush past. Her face twitched uncontrollably, and her body tingled.

The legs stormed out to the living room. Above them was a familiar form. It could be that scruffy-haired boy with the baseball bat.

Kaylee's shoulders drooped, and instantly she relaxed. She hated acting so dramatic. This was embarrassing. She needed to change her clothes before he noticed her, and so she slid forward on her knees until she could stand unimpeded. After reaching Blair's bedroom, she grabbed a new pair of pants and underwear.

The boy jumped out suddenly, filling the hallway. He wore a massive compound hunting bow across his chest now.

"There y'are. You're still here."

Kaylee hid the fresh clothing behind her back and nodded with a bit too much emphasis.

"They took all the guns," he said. "But I know where to go."

Kaylee cocked her head.

"Jefferson High. It's the headquarters of the resistance, I guess you could call it."

She nodded.

"The streets ain't safe though."

She shrugged.

"So I don't know what to do, right now." He paused.

She nodded again, and then she pointed and pushed her hands in the air for him to get out of the way. After sliding past, she strolled nonchalantly to the bathroom. There she locked the door behind, and she let out a massive gasp of tension. Changing out of the wet pants, Kaylee buried the old jeans at the bottom of the hamper. With care she scrubbed her face, wetting some disobedient hairs in order to get them to stay.

When she emerged from Blair's bathroom again, it was almost dark outside. She located the boy in the kitchen picking at what was left of the chicken carcass.

The boy looked up at her. "Hey, you want some a this?"

She stared back, disgusted and eyed Blair's journal next to the boy. So she floated over and snatched it up.

He looked at her oddly but quickly carved off some more meat with a steak knife.

Kaylee grabbed her pen, and she tore out a new page from the back of the diary.

There's a car in there.

Pushing the note in front of his face, her finger pointed at the garage door.

"Huh? What? A car?"

She nodded.

He jumped to his feet. Together they entered the garage.

Six

"Hey, you got the keys?" The boy lumbered into the garage like a tourist.

Kaylee shook her head. Then she grabbed the flashlight that she had previously left on the roof of the vehicle, and she clicked it on so that she could scribble another message.

You could hot-wire it.

He laughed. The boy wasn't so bad looking either, when he wasn't swinging a baseball bat around like a Neanderthal.

"Like I know how to hot-wire cars," he said.

She pointed below the steering wheel, and she made a hand motion like pulling it apart.

He laughed more loudly. "Why don't we just find the keys?"

She scratched out another response.

I already looked.

He frowned. "Gimme the light."

Kaylee handed him the flashlight, and she stepped out of his way to write again.

The boy bent down over the steering wheel and scrutinized the dashboard.

If you take it apart, I'll tell you how to start it.

She tapped on his back as he continued to poke at the car's innards.

"Quit it," he said. "What you want?"

She presented the note, and he examined it under the flashlight.

"Yeah, right. You know to steal cars."

Kaylee nodded briskly.

"Get outta here!"

She shook her head and called for her paper.

I read about it in a book.

When he had finished reading, she gestured for him to rip apart the steering column plastic cover.

"Look," he said, "I don't see how it comes off."

Kaylee grabbed the flashlight, and she skipped over to the workbench. From the wall she snatched a hammer and a sharp wood chisel.

"You're really serious!" he said.

She presented the tools with a hammering motion.

He took the tools from her hands and turned back to the car. She held the flashlight and directed him to destroy the steering column's plastic covering. The boy paused to size her up.

"Man, I hope the guy whose car this is doesn't come back."

After the hammering, Kaylee found the wires leading from the ignition switch, and she selected several. The boy cut the wires and twisted copper from the two red striped ones together. The dashboard lights started to glow, and the Mustang awakened as if from a deep sleep. Kaylee's had him rub the bare wire from the brown lead across the red connection.

The boy paused in place, not entirely convinced. He peeked back over his shoulder.

"You're sure?"

She shrugged. In the overhead interior light of the car, she noticed his deep blue eyes.

As he flicked the wire toward the others, a spark jumped. The motor revved and died. The boy poked at the connection again, and the car engine turned over until its mechanical magic fired up with a surprisingly loud roar. It vibrated like a concert, so strong and determined, spewing exhaust gases into the garage.

The boy dropped the wires.

"Yeah! I did it." He seemed pleased, nodding to himself.

Kaylee frowned.

The boy played with the radio controller, and Kaylee retreated from the humming car. Radio frequencies sounded either like static or that hypnotizing noise, the electronic brain jamming. The boy looked at her. "We gotta grab all that stuff. Get the food," he said.

Kaylee nodded, and she returned to the house, leaving the Mustang running by itself in the garage. She dashed into Blair's bedroom, and she stuffed clothes into a black garbage bag. Underwear, jeans, shirts and a hat, she felt so guilty now that she was just taking and taking.

Lastly she wrote out another note to Blair.

Hi, it's Kaylee Colton. I took some of your clothes, Blair, because I really needed them. I'm going over to Jefferson High School, and maybe I'll run into you there. We took some food also. Thanks so much. I owe you. Hope you're okay wherever you are. Sorry again.

Neglecting to mention the part about stealing the car from the garage, Kaylee closed the diary. Jamming a chair into the closet helped her climb up onto the steel wire shelves. She despised those shelves for repeatedly digging into her hands. As she struggled to return the diary to its hiding place she hoped Blair wouldn't be too angry with her. It was the apocalypse and everything, mitigating circumstances and such.

Back in the garage, Kaylee saw the boy load a large box of hunting arrows for his compound bow into the Mustang. The two of them grabbed all the cans and boxes from the kitchen, and they stuffed them into the back seat and trunk.

The boy rushed about, appearing jumpy. When he dropped himself down into the driver's seat, he affixed the ignition wires to the steering column so that they wouldn't fall and zap him.

The garage air clouded thick with engine fumes, and Kaylee scavenged a few more items. Meanwhile, the boy fidgeted behind the steering wheel, eager to drive, and he grew more impatient each second.

"Come on, come on, come on! Open the garage door, will ya?"

Kaylee twisted in place beside the car. Noxious fumes stung her eyes and lungs, discombobulating her.

"Let's go!" the strange boy barked from his seat.

Kaylee froze before the massive aluminum double-door, unsure whether to go with him at all or to stay right there. As she stepped toward the door, fear squashed at her, and she couldn't decide whether to trust him. Suddenly, she didn't want to go anywhere. Her mind entered such a haze that she was unsure about their entire plan.

She suddenly coughed uncontrollably as she retreated back away from the passenger side door.

"You got a better idea?" he said.

She held her nose and gazed about the garage.

"Look." He stood beside the driver's side. "We can't wait here. They'll come and get us. There's dozens. Hundreds, maybe. You haven't seen it out there, man. It's crazy!"

Kaylee frowned, motionless, damned if she did, and damned if she didn't.

"Fine! *I'll* open it." The boy scrambled around the car door.

Her body trembled, and she shook her head.

"Okay, you know what?" he said. "You stay here. And I'm goin'. Later."

Kaylee yanked at his arm as he began to lift the door, but he wrenched his arm free.

"You want to stay here? Okay. Stay here. Whatever."

She gasped, lightheaded.

The boy rolled open the door, and suddenly fresh air rushed in. After a couple of breaths her head cleared. She drifted out into the crisp night air toward the streetlamps. A dog barked from down the block. A single gunshot echoed about a mile away. The breeze carried the fresh scent of blooming flowers from the front yard. Kaylee's nose operated again.

That strange boy sat back into the driver's seat. Then the car crawled up alongside her.

"Are you comin' or not?"

Kaylee reluctantly reached for the door handle, nodded, and climbed into the seat beside him.

"You know we can come back, if it's too messed up?"

She looked into his eyes, still somewhat in a confused daze. She didn't know why she was going with him, but there weren't many other places for her to go.

His foot eased off the brake, and the car rambled down the driveway and onto Blair's street. He jammed the steering wheel to the left and hit the gas. Their car shot off into pure darkness. The boy hadn't turned on the headlights.

Grey mist slid past. Kaylee watched the road, and she braced her hands against the dashboard.

The boy laughed nervously to himself. "I flunked the written exam. I'm not supposed to drive, you know."

She bit her lip. Their car sped straight into the downtown area, where streetlights aided. Random figures scurried along the sidewalks and streets.

Kaylee saw the group first. Straight ahead, at the end of the dark road, a collection of forms congregated in a sprawling mob. She pointed wildly at them.

The boy slowed the car, but he didn't stop. The Mustang rolled forward.

She grabbed at his arm.

"All right. All right." He braked in the middle of the poorly lit suburban block. The two of them gazed ahead at the human wall.

A gang of teenage boys piled out haphazardly to block off the street. One pointed at Kaylee. They talked with each other in jerky body language. Several reached into their belts and produced handguns. The gang opened fire on the car.

Kaylee dropped down low in her seat. As she did, a bullet ripped through the windshield above her head and shattered the rear window.

The boy floored the gas pedal, and their car spun one hundred and eighty degrees. Rounds pinged off of the metal body as the car bounced up off the asphalt and over the curb, scraping the undercarriage. Its tires peeled, and they sped away from the shooters.

After the gunfire had receded into the distance behind them, Kaylee finally raised her head.

The boy was too consumed with steering around the obstacles abandoned in the street to even notice her. She braced herself, her mind fixed on the bullet hole in front of her face.

They zipped off into a dark, unlit part of town. Then he slowed the car, searching in the darkness.

"Where is Jefferson High, anyway?"

Kaylee scribbled frantically onto a page from a notebook.

Don't you go there?

"Naw." He flooded the gas, flattening her back against her seat. The car crashed through an overturned shopping cart.

She lowered her hands from in front of her face, and she wanted to scream at him but couldn't. Her gaze darted around the side streets. Street lamps whipped by with the blurred streaks of parked cars.

A woman stood at a corner ahead, covered top to bottom in dark blood. From her stomach protruded a black knife handle.

It was Mom. She pointed for them to turn right.

Kaylee's mouth hung open, and she twisted her head around to locate the figure passing behind them, but her mother had disintegrated into the air. She turned to the oblivious boy as he drove recklessly. Pointing to the right, she pulled at his hand.

"What!" he yelled. "Stop grabbin' at me!"

She persisted, pointing to the right until he accepted the message.

"You sure?"

She nodded.

"You better be right." He turned onto the next street, a dark suburban side street with several lit homes up ahead on the left. Everything seemed still in milky black shadows. Their car crawled along until it reached a stop sign. Ahead lay a desolate Grand Avenue, four lanes wide but empty.

"Yeah, yeah," he said. "This is it. Grand turns into Jefferson." Kaylee sighed and shot him a frustrated glance. He pushed the accelerator and they chugged forward toward the high school.

Kaylee clutched her copy of *Ghostliest*. She needed to keep it close by no matter what else happened.

The Mustang finally emerged onto the empty, four lane-wide Jefferson Avenue. They coasted past tall stone-textured concrete walls, which surrounded the school's grounds. Kaylee didn't care for Jefferson High, and it wasn't her school. It seemed dark, mysterious, and intimidating, and that was before any of these troubles had even begun. The front of Jefferson High School was deserted, but several shafts of light slipped out from inside the buildings. A yellow school bus blocked the driveway across the entrance gate.

She watched the dim sidewalk opposite the school through her window. On the sidewalk was a long brown smear, blood from some unknown person who had been dragged away. Apparently their car was right in the middle of a former battlefield. Shiny bullet casings littered the sidewalks and the street by the hundreds.

The boy honked his horn impatiently, and the note pierced the still night air. Kaylee jumped in her seat. Terrified, she put up her hands awkwardly to try and signal him.

He honked it a second time, and then he yelled out of his window, "Hey! Y'all. We're here!"

Kaylee felt exposed and vulnerable. Her gaze dashed about the street and to the dark collection of houses with bullet-ridden siding and shattered windows. With *Ghostliest* clutched in her hands, she shivered down into the passenger seat and ducked below the glass. Lightheaded, she spied on her side of the avenue for any signs of aggressors.

Flashlight beams penetrated the interior of their car. Above the school bus, several spotlights shot out. An unseen teenager of unknown gender clicked on a megaphone.

"Who's there?"

The driving boy pleaded with his hands while blocking the glare from his eyes.

"Hey, man, we want to join up!"

"Who's in there with you?" asked the bullhorn.

The boy checked on Kaylee. "It's just some girl. She's one 'a us. She's all right."

Light beams searched the avenue and lit up the houses. The school compound people took their time. Their megaphone squawked out again.

"Hold on!"

The big yellow bus gate across the entrance suddenly started up with a thick *vroom*. Clanking old gears, and the bus reversed. As it slid to the left, a fat grungy man in a dirty-white wife-beater tank top appeared in the opening. With sinewy muscles, a hunting rifle in his hands, and a couple of pistols strapped to his waist, he gawked around the avenue cautiously. He appeared to be in charge. His long ponytail whipped left and right, and he slunk toward the wall.

The boy called over, "We need to come in, 'cause we want to join up."

The overweight armed man talked with his lieutenant, a blond-haired apprentice who watched the Mustang through binoculars.

"Well?"

The apprentice said, "I don't see anything."

The hefty, pony-tailed man nodded and marched forward several steps, his lieutenant trailing right behind him.

The big man barked, "Nice job honking your horn, genius. Who's in the car?"

Right away, Kaylee disliked him. He seemed mean and repulsive. She sat brooding, wondering if they should race away before it was too late.

"She wants to join up too. She's cool."

Kaylee's eyes popped. No one had ever called her "cool" before. She didn't understand why she was cool, or if she really was cool, or if he was just saying it. She didn't really get the definition of cool anyway. At least it was probably better to be cool than un-cool. She felt a sense of urgency, but about what she wasn't sure. She stared back toward the boy, trying to glean something from his tone, but the gorilla man holding the rifle seized her attention.

"What you bring?" He scrutinized their supplies in the back seat.

"Oh, we got a bow and arrow–"

"You bring guns?"

"Naw. Couldn't find any. But we got food, cereal. We got cans."

"Uh huh." The man stepped closer, filling the driver's side window, and bent down. "What's your name?"

The scruffy, brown-haired boy looked up and smiled. "Dustin Hafstead."

Dustin. Kaylee studied him. He didn't look like a Dustin.

"What's her name? You. What's your name?"

Kaylee pointed at her mouth and her throat, and she mouthed a few silent syllables.

I can't talk.

The boy, Dustin, answered, "She can't talk."

"Why not?" The man jolted back. "What do you mean she can't talk? What's wrong with her?"

"She just don't talk."

The man stroked his finger along his rifle near the trigger. Kaylee gulped, suddenly with an excess of saliva to deal with.

"All right, we don't need her," he said. "You ready to fight?"

"Hell yeah."

"Well, we don't need her."

"Uh." Dustin glanced back to Kaylee.

"So, she's gotta *go*," said the man. Kaylee reached and grabbed the dashboard for security.

The leader pointed at Kaylee. "You, out of the car."

Kaylee shook her head vigorously.

"Go somewhere else," he said. "This is a military base now, under my authority. And I say soldiers get to be here. Little girls not needed. Don't need mouths to feed. Go find your parents, kid."

Kaylee refused to move, more adamant than ever.

"Hang on, man," said Dustin. "She's like, sorta with me. I brought her here, so I said she could be here already. Or else she wouldn't a come along. You know?"

"Pssh!" Suddenly the fat man exploded like a rabid grizzly bear. With a gust of breath he jumped back and aimed his rifle into the Mustang.

"Get out of the car!" he said. "Out of the car! You both can go to hell. I'm takin' the car."

The blond lieutenant boy behind him jumped to attention and aimed his own rifle at Dustin, and then at Kaylee.

Dustin raised his hands up off the steering wheel. She raised hers similarly. Cautiously he stepped out, leaving Kaylee alone on the passenger's side.

Just then, the supersonic pop of a bullet echoed off all the concrete and stone like a firecracker. The pony-tailed man took the hit in his belly. He doubled over as blood oozed onto his white shirt. Grunting and growling, he covered up. Gunshots rang out from both directions. Kaylee ducked down onto the floor of the Mustang and covered her head, her eyes tightly shut. The thundering pounded around her, and she was helpless.

The car slammed and revved, twisting about in space. Opening her eyes, she saw Dustin wrench the steering wheel as they sailed around and bounced up into the air.

Bullets zinged back and forth between the houses and the school.

The rifle battle raged. Shots deafened Kaylee as she huddled on the floor. Once she realized that they were inside the high school walls, she sat up.

The lieutenant boy helped the pony-tailed man stumble back inside the gate. As they rushed in, the school bus driver rolled the bus back across the front opening.

Kaylee and Dustin panted, awaiting their fate, as the battle outside the car simmered to a few sporadic blasts.

Several high school boys assisted the big injured man and rushed him inside a building through a metal door. That door slammed, and the schoolyard was left mostly deserted.

Kaylee's heart churned and stabilized as the minutes ticked away. Nothing happened. No one came over to their car or attempted to talk to them at all.

Dustin spoke up. "I guess we're in."

Seven

Kaylee shrugged. Dustin stepped out into the yard. Finally she summoned up her own courage. Reaching for the handle, she stepped from the car. Looking around the schoolyard, she saw a couple of teenage guards staring out above the concrete wall at various positions, which had been built up on flimsy perches. None of these guards noticed her presence or seemed to care.

Kaylee carried in supplies from the Mustang with Dustin. Dustin located an empty cot in the gym, where beds were sloppily strewn all over the basketball court. She claimed another empty cot, and she left *Ghostliest* on it while she helped haul their food to the kitchen.

Other teens watched them but remained distant. Kaylee saw them spying on each trip inside, but they turned quickly from her gaze. In the gym office near the front, by the outer door, teenagers performed surgery on the wounded, gruff ponytail man. His shouts shook the rafters while the young medical team attempted to remove the bullet. His swearing echoed across the gym, and he guzzled from a bottle of whiskey.

Those on their cots in the gym tensed at each painful howl. Kids sneered at Kaylee. Gazes dashed away like spooked forest creatures.

The basketball court was already littered with filthy clothes, shoes, paper cups, and backpacks.

Kaylee lay back on her new cot, closing her eyes. Instantly she fell asleep, but she was next awakened by cold metal jabbing at her cheek.

She opened her eyes. A tall, angry brunette hovered in the wispy shadows and jabbed at her face with a loaded revolver.

"Who the hell are you?" said the girl. "Answer me right now." She moved the barrel onto Kaylee's forehead, her finger on the trigger.

Kaylee gasped emptily for words, suddenly terrified and very awake.

"What are you doing in my bed? Answer, bitch!"

The handgun still pressed against her forehead, Kaylee held her hands uneasily at her chin.

"She's one of them!" said another girl with long red hair and pale, freckled skin. Three of them pointed their guns at Kaylee, and they surrounded her on the cot. They kicked at the metal legs.

Kaylee shook her head rapidly.

The tall, dark-haired girl, who wore a green khaki jacket, shouted, "We got a spy!"

Dustin Hafstead ran over in Kaylee's defense. "Hey! She's not a spy. What are you doin'?"

Kaylee grabbed the barrel of the revolver and pointed it away from her head. The two wrestled and jerked at the gun.

"Get off it!" the tall brunette barked, but Kaylee wouldn't let go, instead pointing it up and away from herself. "Little bitch! You better listen."

Dustin said, "Be careful! Stop it!"

Kaylee jumped up, still fighting for the revolver.

The ruckus must have awoken the injured, pony tailed man, who was lying on another cot at the front.

"Cut it!" he thundered.

The girls stopped in their tracks. The brunette seemed to acquiesce. Kaylee glared, ready to gouge out the girl's eyeballs. The two others lowered their guns and relaxed.

"Assholes," said the overweight man, wrapped in bandages. "Come over here. Everybody."

The entire gym meandered closer toward him in a semi-circle. Kaylee claimed a different cot, which seemed empty, while the brunette girl sat cross-legged on her own cot, guarding it smugly. Dustin approached the man but swiftly sat down on the gym floor behind a bunch of others.

"Dammit!" The man grabbed at his belly, and he reached for his bottle of whiskey. It took him a minute to work the cap off. With his pockmarked face and thick, drooping mustache, he looked like some anachronism from the age of heavy metal.

"Listen up," he attempted to shout but coughed harshly. Then he whispered, "Listen up."

Most of them leaned in to hear. Kaylee listened to the two girls sitting out at the periphery chattering away, oblivious.

The janitor pointed at his lieutenant, the blond, spiky-haired one whose name, Kaylee learned, was Lucas. He was about seventeen, taller than six feet, and moderately good-looking. Lucas stormed to the two chatterboxes and blasted, "Shh!" with a hiss of finality.

Kaylee tried to memorize all their faces, all these strangers. She couldn't trust a single one of them. And she wouldn't allow herself to trust Dustin, either.

The janitor sat up with pillows wedged in behind his back, which obviously caused him discomfort. Then he stared out at the group.

"Everyone keeps their assigned areas clean and organized, at all times," he said. His hand clutched at his torso. "Y'all want to survive?"

The entire gymnasium looked on tensely. Kaylee rolled away on the coarse, musty blanket draped across the cot. The stale odor permeated the fibers.

"You keep your utensils and plates and your hands as clean as possible, so you don't invite disease."

Kaylee looked at her hands, which were grimy and smeared.

"There's no doctor," said the injured man, "no nurses, no antibiotics or any other medicine. Lucas?"

"Yes?"

"You're in charge of making sure everybody does their part keeping things spotless. Bathrooms—you kids get to do my job, ha ha—kitchen, beds, everywhere."

Kaylee studied Lucas and the man, who was the janitor. The younger one sported a rock band T-shirt, baggy pants, and expensive-looking sneakers.

Lucas scurried to the janitor. "How am I supposed to make them all clean?"

"That's easy. You're in charge of the food distribution. Nobody eats until they pass your inspection."

A look of satisfaction spread out across Lucas's face. Kaylee located a clean page in her notebook, and she took account.

Why does he get to decide everything?

She didn't like that janitor at all. He was the one who had wanted to leave her outside to die. She still seethed, and she scribbled furiously about how he was the wrong person to keep them safe, and how her mom or dad would have done a much better job.

"People need to write this stuff down," said the janitor. Then he saw Kaylee on her cot, scratching away at the page.

"You!"

Kaylee snapped backward, staring at him across the silent collection of cots. The others turned to assess her.

"You like to write in that book a yours," said the janitor. "You can be my personal assistant. Keep notes."

Kaylee couldn't believe it. Her face deformed into a quizzical retching, something so negative the janitor was amazed at her visceral response.

"What?" he said. "You don't want to help? You're not sure you want to survive this ordeal?" He slumped back down, having exerted too much strain on his torso already just in keeping his head elevated.

She scribbled a quick note sideways, and she held it up. Lucas marched over to act as an intermediary.

Lucas read, "I'm not sure about being near you."

The janitor nearly spit out in frustration. "Shoulda left your ass outside the wall!" He turned faint with fatigue. "Will anyone at all write down these life-saving survival instructions, goddammit?"

A petite girl in librarian glasses raised her hand politely.

Indignation swept over Kaylee. She rolled away on her new cot and looked down on *Ghostliest*.

The janitor strained to continue. "Everybody with a gun, you get a partner. Partner who follows you around, carries stuff for you, so you're ready to use your weapon at a moment's notice. Your partner learns how to properly discharge the weapon, learns what caliber, how to load, how to unload, how to clean it, how to store it, how to carry it."

The entire gymnasium perked up, everyone searching for their would-be partners. Kaylee peeked back around, unable to find her page in the ghost hunting book. She noticed Dustin Hafstead. He sat alone, cross-legged on the hardwood. Kaylee whipped out her notepad, and she snapped to a blank page, but she didn't know what to write. Maybe they were already partners. She couldn't risk being presumptuous. Dustin might want a boy partner instead. He could reject her, or he could reluctantly accept her, secretly wishing that she was somebody else. Her pen circled in a black mess at the bottom corner of the sheet.

That janitor droned on like some big Buddha surrounded by a mesmerized cult. "And that partner—should you face the unfortunate possibility of gettin' shot by the enemy—your partner takes the gun and keeps on returning fire, in the event of a battle, a crisis, you understand?"

Lucas interjected. "What do you mean? We need to babysit someone?" It was obvious to Kaylee that Lucas felt superior to the rest already, and detached from the population.

"You need to apprentice someone," said the janitor with more vigor. "You're now soldiers. You have trainees to carry your stuff and learn. And follow you around, make sure you both got water and food. And if a battle starts, when you're attacked, your partner takes cover, stays out of the line of fire. And in the unfortunate event that one of you gets wounded, he drags you to safety, takes your weapon, and keeps on fightin'."

The assistant girl in librarian glasses scribbled frantically, sitting on the floor just beside his cot. Blood dribbled out from his gunshot wound, and his bandages were soaked in a dirty red.

Most everyone nodded along silently.

Kaylee's face contorted, and she hadn't yet written a single word. Her teeth grabbed at her lower lip. Instinctively, she kept looking up at Dustin, but he thankfully never turned around to catch her.

Everyone paired off, an explosion of social trial and error. Kaylee scooted up from the cot to close in on Dustin. She waved to catch his attention. Eventually he noticed her in the crowd, and he nodded. He seemed less-than-certain at first. She held up her palms in an exaggerated shrug.

Dustin walked over through the chaotic crowd as the rest of the teenagers tried to buddy up with one another. Then they both walked to the line to be accounted. He held up his compound bow, and he pointed back at Kaylee. "I'm sorta with her."

The janitor assessed them. "He's got a bow? You're gonna have to learn how to use that bow, little girl."

Lucas, beside the janitor's cot, shook his head. "She can't pull that bow. It's like eighty pounds."

"Yeah. You're right." The janitor sized up Kaylee. His condescending stare infuriated her.

"She could be a second assistant then. She could just carry stuff. See why I didn't want her? Another mouth."

"All right," said Dustin.

Kaylee hated that hideous janitor more than anyone else in the world. She was glad that he had gotten shot, and she thought maybe he would die, which she wasn't supposed to do, of course. She felt terrible wishing for his death, but still, the next person they put in charge couldn't be worse than that a-hole. Things could only get better if he was too sick to order everybody around like a dictator.

People grouped in twos, and the noise subsided. The janitor's eyes remained closed, and he lay gritting his teeth, breathing hard.

"There's all manner of improvised weapons that we're gonna go over," he said. "In the meantime, you can eat your dinners and make sure we got everyone on lookout who's supposed to be there."

Kaylee followed Dustin into the hallway with the group and toward the doors of the cafeteria. Behind them, the janitor kept on. "And Lucas will try and connect us to somebody out there..."

The bus driver turned out to be a middle-aged, hard-working woman named Caroline Anderson, who was busy in the kitchen cooking up a large pot of soup for everyone. Kaylee and Dustin stepped along the line and filled their bowls. Chatter fell to a constant level, and the cafeteria started to feel like an actual school again, except for the dimness and the time of night. Kaylee stuck close by Dustin as they chose an empty table in the back corner of the dining hall.

While she sipped at her beef broth, she noticed the brunette in the khaki military jacket who had attacked her, two tables across. Their clique traded catty quips and sneered back at Kaylee in between giggles. She couldn't be sure if they were plotting some move against her, and she started to jitter. The brunette caught her eye, and Kaylee looked away.

"It's good," said Dustin, breaking the tension. He gobbled down his own soup.

She nodded, still on edge from the three girls and their gossip.

The tall brunette caught Kaylee's glance again, and she flipped her middle finger, along with a devious grin. Kaylee returned to her own soup, and she took her notebook. Scratching out a message, she asked Dustin, *Are you going to teach me how to use the bow?*

"Yeah, sure. I have to."

Kaylee nodded rapidly, and she returned to finish her soup.

After they had eaten dinner, Lucas arrived at the cafeteria doors. "He's ready to tell you guys some more."

Everyone rose up to return to the gymnasium. Most left their bowls and utensils on the tables, and the cafeteria was abandoned in a disheveled state.

Kaylee caught up with Dustin, who was sitting near the janitor's cot with a circle of students. The injured janitor rattled off more orders, which the scribe dutifully notated.

"As of now we are one hundred percent an island in a sea of hostility, you understand?" He coughed, which jolted his wound, and he doubled up for a moment.

"As far as we know there are no friendlies outside these walls, at all, *anywhere*, on earth. I pray to God that I'm wrong on this, but just goin' on what I see and hear with my own eyes, with my own ears, I'm not in a hopeful situation of sunshine and lollipops, children. I don't like it one bit. Not one bit."

The partnered-up teens formed a line in twos, waiting to get their orders from the prone commander.

When it came time for Dustin and Kaylee, the janitor couldn't decide what to do with them. He finally said, "Give her a whistle. She can still look out on the wall. She's gonna pull her weight like everybody else. There is no alternative. Understand me, little girl? No alternative."

Kaylee sneered back, emotionless. From the gymnasium office, Lucas snatched a coach's whistle, and he twirled it around on its rope as he rejoined them. Kaylee took the silver device in her hand, studying it.

"Now, you're a lookout," said the janitor. "You see anything weird outside or inside this compound, blow that whistle."

She nodded back but remained fixated on the several large caliber pistols laid out on a table beside the janitor's cot.

He whipped his head to the side, and he began to chuckle. "What? You want me to give you my American Eagle .50 cal revolver? Are you outta your little mind?"

Kaylee nodded at the pistol, unamused. Lucas and several of the jocks behind her joined in the laughter. The janitor lay back, incredulous.

"First of all, the whistle is better than the gun, 'cause guess what, honey? You blow that whistle, you get ten or fifteen guys with guns. Now you got ten or fifteen guns. Get it? Don't be silly. Get outta here. You're gonna check in with Anderson for your watches."

Kaylee stepped back, right into Dustin. They repositioned themselves awkwardly.

"And you be on those shifts, awake, at all times. Anyone I catch asleep during one of their watches is out the gate. *Sayonara*. Find somewhere else. You all get me?"

Eight other teens remained in line behind her, four pairs of inexperienced fighters. They agreed with the janitor, naturally, and vied for his approval.

"That's where we're at. Go. Relieve whoever's on duty. Tell 'em come see me."

The girl with the librarian glasses scratched down everything he said into a notebook, a running log of whatever was supposed to help them survive this incomprehensible siege.

Eight

The sun shone brightly and an ethereal glow washed over the suburban streets. Kaylee floated to the front door of her home, and she sailed straight inside without pause. The windows of her house on Carmelita Way beamed with pure white light, which enveloped everything and bathed it in an alluring, diffused softness. She felt optimistic again as she returned home, like she could talk, like everything was all right after all.

Around the living room corner the walls seemed a dim purple, and then brownish. The bright sunlight disappeared, and she spun about searching for what was wrong.

"I'm back," she announced, as if that would erase any lingering negativity. Her mind tried to remain hopeful, and she proceeded further in toward the kitchen.

Kaylee's mom pulled herself up off the kitchen floor, a steel knife still wedged in her abdomen. She seemed well enough as she planted her two feet in the blood puddle, one splash and then another.

"Mom, we have to get you to a doctor," said Kaylee, increasingly concerned.

Mom seemed casual about the whole ordeal. "Where the hell's your father? I need a beer."

Kaylee shivered, cut off from any memory of her dad at all. All she remembered was that he wasn't there.

Mom bickered at the walls. "He's always late, with his stupid, stupid job." Her face wrinkled up. "Where is he?"

Mom seemed unfamiliar and distant. "Probably dead," answered Kaylee. "I don't know."

Mom stepped closer, suddenly angry, and she flew past Kaylee off into the living room. Kaylee stood alone in the darkening house.

"Can you sense if Daddy's... dead?"

"Sure," said Mom's voice. "No. I don't know." Her shadow snaked across a wall. Then she reappeared wearing a floral-print summer dress. All cleaned up, she seemed fine, vibrant even. Her hair had been curled and tied up smartly. Their house was airy and lit-up once more. Perhaps things were going to be okay.

Mom reached out and stroked Kaylee's hair. Warm fingers glided across her scalp.

Her eyes glowed unnaturally green. "What about you, Kaylee? Are you dead?"

Kaylee froze like a fish in an ice chest.

Isolated in her cot, she awoke inside the high school's gymnasium, barely breathing. The cavernous gym was so dark, with only a single overhead light burning near the entrance door. She managed to turn her head and move her tingling hands. Other cots held snoring co-inhabitants. The space, impersonal and bouncing with echoes, felt frigidly foreign. She sat up on her cot, throwing her feet over onto the chilly basketball court floorboards.

Passing the sleepers, their rifles, baseball bats, and knives within reach, she tiptoed softy by each cot and into a black hallway that seemed like the mouth of a cavern.

In the bathroom the lights weren't working, and Kaylee fumbled about in the narrow shafts of moonlight. Her toilet stall felt desolate and solitary, something from a different life. Again she felt seized by nervousness and unable to pee. As she listened to the faint scrapes and echoes from beyond the lavatory, the wisps built on top of one another. Two feet shuffled across the tiles toward her stall, skidding to a halt. Below the stall door danced a shadow, enhanced by an even darker, undulating blackness.

"Kaylee Irene Colton!" yelled the voice. It was Mom, and she was livid about something.

Kaylee sat motionless on the toilet as the amorphous shadow dodged to and fro below the door of the stall.

Mom's voice warbled, "You need to find your father."

Kaylee shivered, holding her face involuntarily.

"You've got to find Daddy," said her mother again. Then her voice receded into the echoes.

Kaylee nodded to herself.

"So find him!"

The bathroom fell silent.

***

Early at sunrise the yelling began.

"Everybody up!" Lucas banged on a metal baking tray with a steel spoon. The janitor was already awake, and he seemed to be directing from his cot. Everyone hustled from their beds and threw on shirts and shoes, grumbling.

Kaylee quickly dressed herself in another of Blair's oversized outfits, the belt pulled tightly and the jeans all baggy and puffed out. Her eyes adjusted to the sun streaking in through the dirty windows above the basketball hoop. She felt thirsty but had no water.

"Everyone come up front here," yelled Lucas, standing near the gym's entrance.

"Sergeant Jaworski, who most of you might know as our janitor, wants me to direct you in some training-"

"All right, Lucas," the janitor called from behind the group. He was alive, but still bedridden and slowly rotting.

Everyone turned back to Jaworski.

"And you all can call Lucas Corporal for now on," he said. "Everybody sit down so I can see ya."

Kaylee sat beside Dustin, who seemed half asleep, and she tried to remain inconspicuous. They nodded at one another.

Jaworski grumbled. He instructed his note-taker to keep a record. "Anyone who's been in martial arts training, raise your hand."

The tall brunette who had taken Kaylee's cot and almost killed her kept her hand raised. She answered, "Tyretta, Tae Kwon Do. Green belt."

"Excellent. You're the new Tae Kwon Do instructor. Need you to turn 'em into green belts by next week. Give 'em the basics."

Tyretta said sarcastically, "That's not possible-"

"Don't tell me what's possible!" He jerked himself about sharply and winced.

Lucas leaned in and whispered in his ear.

"No, no. I'm fine."

"You don't look fine, Sarge."

Jaworski brushed him off. "You know what's possible, people?" His voice attempted to mask his pain with aggression. "Surviving to tomorrow. If that's possible, everything's possible. Don't contradict me. I don't care if it's possible or not. You're gonna try. Understand?"

"Yes, sir," said Tyretta.

"Well, don't call me sir, neither. If you're gonna say somethin', say, 'Yes, Sergeant.'"

"Whatever." Tyretta rolled her eyes and sat back down.

"Next!"

Kaylee had taken three classes in kung fu two years ago. She didn't want to volunteer, but she didn't want to remain an ornament either, so she decided to raise her hand.

"You? Huh." Jaworski laughed. When he jolted from the pain, Kaylee felt an amused sense of satisfaction.

She scribbled out a quick note, and she passed it forward until it traveled to the janitor's hands.

"Three classes in kung fu,'" he said. "What they show you? Let's see what they showed you. Come on."

Kaylee stood up, and the whole group turned to look at her.

The janitor smiled with his own satisfaction, which she wanted to kick right off his face. She crouched down into a fighting stance.

"Go!"

She kicked to the front and returned her leg to where it had started. Then she looked for approval.

Jaworski just snickered. "So. We need teams for training! I need weight trainers. I want running, and use them stair steppers, and every other machine. When you're not on watch, you get down there and get in a training group. If nobody's training, you start a group."

Jaworski held his belly, his breathing harsh. "Shit!" He grabbed his bottle of whiskey and took a large gulp. "Uh."

The others seemed to grow edgy and fearful as the janitor's pains dragged on. No one knew what to do for him, or if they should leave him be.

Nine

Watching out over the top of the wall was uneventful. On a hard plastic chair perched atop the trash dumpster, Kaylee found the stink inescapable. Eventually she put it out of her mind, if not out of her nose. Dustin Hafstead stood on an adjacent platform fifty feet down along the perimeter wall. Occasionally she watched him. He rested for periods of time, but his eyes were too low to see over the wall if he sat down. In a way she was lucky, able to sit the entire time. No one else coveted her spot, however.

She twirled her whistle on its rope, listening for the passing of a distant car, or the occasional firefight that popped out from the other side of town. The battles gave her hope that people were fighting back outside their walls somewhere, off in the distance. They probably would lose to the *dupes*, which was the name Jaworski had given them. Anyone who wasn't all there was called a dupe now, and the dupes were the clear enemies of those inside the school walls, attacking the school repeatedly. Everyone was saying it, except Kaylee, who couldn't say anything. She just listened.

She schemed to bring *Ghostliest* up on her watch the next time, but she knew that might get her into some kind of trouble. Supposedly, she was to watch through a pair of cheap little binoculars as the sun beat down on her skull. Tedium made her drowsy and irritable. At least she'd grown used to the stench. She continually checked her wristwatch, waiting for ten p.m. to roll around, and she took some consolation in the sunset, although it arrived at a glacial pace.

Kaylee didn't know what she would do if the dupes attacked the school again. Dupes weren't seen alone anymore, but always in groups, always with that horrible screeching, which throbbed in the background like hornets massing.

She wondered what they wanted, and why they had to be so violent about getting it. Also, she worried about her father, and not hearing from him since the total meltdown of society. She had no way of contacting him. Their walkie-talkies were useless for making real phone calls, and all the phone systems and connections were still dead.

Finally ten o'clock came, and Kaylee's replacement shuffled from out of the steel gym door. This pimple-faced boy stepped reluctantly toward the trash dumpster. It was obvious this skinny freshman was just as low on the totem pole.

"Damn!" said the boy. "You gotta be kidding me!"

Kaylee jumped down off the dumpster, and she confidently strutted back inside the gym.

Enough, enough, enough.

After supper, Jaworski held court, a boy's club to decide what they were all going to do. They stood around His Majesty's cot, obscuring the view for everyone else. His words resonated low.

Kaylee took an interest mainly because she wasn't invited, and she stepped closer into their circle. The main issue concerned how little food remained at the school.

As she took her seat on the hardwood, the boy beside her sniffed the air and formed a horrified face. The vexed guy slid away on his butt. Behind her, gossip and giggles struck up. Kaylee tried to ignore them.

"We need to take out their command and control," said Jaworski. He seemed dizzy. "How the hell do they coordinate all those dupes?"

Lucas said, "We can raid the food warehouse out on Highway Forty-One." He and a couple of football player types encircled the cot.

Jaworski shook his head. "We don't have the vehicles for it, unless you count the bus. And that leaves the front door wide open." He spaced for a moment. "But I want to know how they're communicatin'. How does one dupe most of the population?"

Kaylee remembered that grating, screeching, hypnotic, trance-inducing signal. It dawned on her that Sean had been watching television when he had flipped out, and that the television had played the entire time. Not what was supposed to be on, but something strange and alien. Surely the others must have noticed it too? She watched their confused faces as the boys chattered about two or three different topics simultaneously. It hadn't occurred to her to come right out and say it before.

She returned to her cot, and her hand swiftly ripped a new sheet from her notebook. There she studiously wrote a careful note, checking her spelling and crossing out a phrase she didn't like. When finished, she stood up, waving at the oblivious boys' group. They didn't notice her, still guessing about making a food raid of some sort, until she marched over and Lucas smelled her behind his back.

"Oh damn," he said.

The boys parted and gave her a wide swath to the janitor. Kaylee wafted her note around so the janitor would notice.

"No. Not you," he said. His clammy face drooped further. "We're talking serious matters here. Get lost."

Kaylee grimaced, and she shoved her note into Lucas's hands. She pointed at it, jabbing her index finger madly, until he acquiesced and looked at it.

Lucas stepped back, and he raised the note. "It's the TVs," he said. "Uh, she says they make some kind of pulsing modem signal that puts people in a trance."

The janitor froze and thought, as did the others. A little wave of recognition fanned out around the teens sitting on the floor.

"The TVs? You sure?" he asked. The boys seemed swayed, enough to take her information seriously and consider it.

"The TVs." The janitor slouched down on his cot, and he seemed stuck in a cold sweat. The gym fell silent. Jaworski turned to Lucas. "You got any more of that chocolate pudding left?"

"One more can."

"Can I just get a little? Please." He looked over the faces of the teens who sat patiently around the disheveled gym. "And for them too. Let's finish that pudding."

The kitchen detail, consisting of five students, brought out the bowls and spoons. The population enjoyed the remaining gallons of chocolate pudding, which came out of a large silver canister. Jaworski slowly ate his portion, and he ensured that everyone took a break from plotting and strategizing. "Ahhh."

"If it's the TVs," said Lucas. "How are we gonna?"

Jaworski ate slowly and with purpose.

Kaylee finished her bowl, and she decided to go run and take a shower before anyone else had a chance to make fun of the way she smelled.

"Listen up," gasped the janitor, suddenly loud and determined. "You shitheads are gonna have to fight the dupes without me."

Kaylee froze in a crouch.

Bowls slammed down across the gym floor.

Lucas rushed over to Jaworski's cot. "We gotta get you to Mercy."

The janitor shook his head reassuringly. "Guess what they got at hospitals?" He chuckled.

The crowd tightened around him.

Lucas said, "The doctors and nurses."

The janitor considered his words. "No."

"Emergency room, surgery."

"No. They got big screens on every God damned wall 24/7 churnin' out that river a sludge... television."

Caroline Anderson escorted three of the wall guards back inside the gym door and over to Jaworski's cot, where she interrupted the gathering. She said, "They're ill. I can't have them out on the wall tonight."

"Oh, crap." The janitor clenched his mouth shut, and he surveyed the ranks of the students on the floor. "How sick are they? What do they got?"

The janitor consulted with the bus driver quietly, as nearly everyone seemed to make efforts to appear just as ill as the other three. He caught Kaylee's eye.

"You, Colton. Whistle girl. You're all right for another six hours."

Kaylee nearly screamed. She wanted to strangle him, but Jaworski had already moved on to choosing two others from the floor. She had never felt so betrayed and abused in her entire life. She loathed that fat janitor more than she hated Sean. More than she hated the dupes outside. More than anything. There was no way she was going back out there on that dumpster.

But the skinny, pimple-faced freshman was one of the allegedly sick teenagers, and they wanted Kaylee back up on the dumpster because she was short, and it was a taller perch for little old her. It was lucky for them she didn't have a weapon, because this was it. Jerks. And a whole lot of other words she didn't feel comfortable saying, or thinking, but she was ready to change that policy and let loose like she had never gone off before.

In defiance, Kaylee grabbed *Ghostliest* off of her cot on her way out to the elevated dumpster platform.

Maybe she would be better off alone back at Blair's house. Maybe she would go find Dad and take off with him on a jet plane somewhere. It couldn't be so messed up everywhere. Dad would know where to go. He was an international airline pilot, and he had all kinds of radios and computers on his planes. They talked to the flight controllers and the Air Force defense systems. Dad was practically the best person in the world to save her and get her to a safe haven, away from this disgusting, festering, maggot-ridden dumpster!

* * *

The two ghost hunters, Jasmine and Kurtz, were still trapped inside the subterranean catacomb, and things were looking quite bleak for them. Their flashlights had flickered out, and they were now stuck in total darkness, blind to everything. Even Jasmine seemed less than confident that they would ever find a way out again. Jasmine told Kurtz to keep moving forward, slowly, and to shut up for God's sake.

They each slid their hands along the rock walls, attempting to feel for anything out of the ordinary. The stone rubbed their hands like sandpaper. Soon the skin on their palms was raw and ready to peel right off.

Kurtz found it, a spider, and it bit his finger in the pitch blackness. He screamed at the top of his lungs.

Jasmine called back, "What is it?"

"Something bit me! I think it's a spider! Oh my God! Oh my God!"

"Calm down," she said. "Is it poisonous?"

Kurtz's voice had risen in pitch like a soprano. "How am I supposed to know that?"

"Suck out the poison, quickly! Suck and spit." Jasmine bumped into him from behind, and Kurtz shouted.

"It's just me, goofus."

As Kurtz tried to suck out the poison, he became dizzy. In the blackness he began to see colors, swirling clouds, hazy shapes. It was all looking very misty.

The secret catacomb passageway beneath the Metropolitan Museum lit up then. Kaylee found herself inside there with Kurtz. She blasted his face with her flashlight, and she could see that Kurtz looked familiar, like someone at that high school, but she knew it had to be Kurtz because Jasmine was there too, somewhere. All three were locked in below the earth in some trap, which they had stumbled right into like ghost-hunting newbies. Egyptian hieroglyphics were carved all along the tan walls.

Torches burned and flickered and tickled the wall paintings. One of the hieroglyphs showed a big trash dumpster. Another featured a bow and arrow. Kaylee could glimpse them for only short moments, as the flickering flames danced chaotically. The cave drawings changed and disappeared in wisps of ghostly ether. With no signs of any spirits, or of any exit doors, Kaylee wandered into the dark away from the wall torches.

She desperately wanted to help Jasmine and Kurtz find their way out of the catacomb deathtrap, but she wasn't scared for herself... until the earthquake hit.

Slam! Slam! Slam!

Bashing on the dumpster awakened Kaylee. She fell out of her chair and thudded onto the steel lid. Two boys below struck the dumpster repeatedly with a crowbar and a wooden rifle stock.

She scrambled to her feet. The strange boys yelled and growled at her:

"She was asleep!"

"She's sleeping on watch!"

Kaylee composed herself, still entranced like a porcupine in the headlights. More teenagers charged out of the gym door. Word filtered back inside what she had done. She started to tremble as more and more of the boys brought their weapons and formed a semi-circle around her dumpster platform.

Lucas marched slowly out of the building. His somber expression seemed new to her; she didn't know what to make of it. Standing atop the dumpster, she feared moving.

"Come down here," said Lucas, his voice conflicted.

She climbed down with *Ghostliest*, and she planted her feet on the concrete once again. The tall boys towered above her, six of them with guns. A skinny, aggressive ginger, the boy with the crowbar, poked it at her. Dustin Hafstead stood back at the rear, not saying anything.

Kaylee shrugged pointedly.

Lucas emphasized his words for everyone to hear. "Grab your stuff. The sergeant wants you out the gate."

Her mind soared in a light daze. They escorted her back inside and over to her cot, swarming her. They made sure she gathered some food and water into her backpack.

She slid the load of supplies onto her back. They all marched her back outside toward the bus at the front gate. Stopping before the bus, Lucas said, "I'm sorry. It's the way it's gotta be."

Kaylee shook her head defiantly. But the gang stared back even more menacingly.

"Can you just slide under the bus?" said Lucas.

She shook her head again.

"Miss Anderson!" Lucas called to recruit the bus driver into assisting in the banishment.

Caroline exited the gym and scurried over to assess the situation. "Oh, come on," she said. "She's just a kid! And they gave her a double shift. Puh-lease."

Lucas shuffled over to discuss it with Anderson covertly. "I gotta enforce the rules."

"Oh, screw your rules!"

"You don't mean that." Lucas became agitated and defensive. All the others stared on with apprehension.

Caroline looked to the gymnasium building. "There's gotta be some leeway here."

"Not with the watches."

She turned and marched inside to do battle with Jaworski. Kaylee stared on at the gym's doorway, still floating in and out of a dream state. The big boys shuffled uncomfortably on their sneakers, waiting for some kind of signal. This agitated them and made them unpredictable.

Inside the gym Caroline stormed off, shouting, "Son of a bitch!"

It was down to Lucas, now, as the ranking person in the yard. He said, "Somebody move the bus. Rory."

The red-haired boy with the big crowbar jumped at the chance. Soon the school bus belched to life and jerked backwards. The exposed hole was sufficient for Kaylee to slip through, but she wouldn't budge.

"Come on, Colton." Lucas grabbed her by the upper arm, and he prodded her out and toward Jefferson Avenue.

Kaylee turned back and stared at Lucas. Terrified, she begged for forgiveness in her own way. Cast out, she had no plan whatsoever about what to do next.

"Go find a place to hide," he said abruptly. "And be quick."

Kaylee just shook her head.

"Bus!" He waved to signal Rory. The machine sailed across and shut Kaylee out on the sidewalk in front of the school.

Once the bus engine quieted, Kaylee breathed uneasily. Over her shoulder, the houses on the opposite side were splattered with bullet holes from the recent battles. No house lights or streetlights were working. Everything was shot up. The neighborhood was desolate and still. Shadows floated across the ground and swayed with the breezes.

The boys above, searching over the wall, urged her to move on. "Get outta here, useless fool," said Rory. He had taken an interest in personally taunting her.

She wouldn't leave, though. Instead, she sat on the curb, and she slid off her backpack to relax.

"What the hell's she doing?"

"Get outta here, Colton," shouted Lucas from somewhere unseen behind the wall.

"This isn't right," said Dustin. "You guys suck."

Kaylee looked back to the pockmarked stone wall, but she couldn't see him.

Rory responded, raising his voice. "Yeah, you want to say that to my face, boy?" He bashed his crowbar on top of the concrete wall behind her.

"What for?" said Dustin. "You know you suck."

Kaylee sat calmly on the hard curb, supporting her chin in her hands. Her butt went numb and stiff. Her thoughts drifted haphazardly. She didn't know what would happen next, and she wasn't sure that she cared anymore. Everything was so messed up now that she didn't even know whom she was supposed to be fighting or why.

Why should anyone want to attack me? I didn't do anything to anybody.

The abrasive cement dug into Kaylee's backside, and so she leaned on her lumpy backpack. Night sounds whispered, soft and reassuring. Thousands of stars visible above, few of the city lights glowed nearby. The sky was more alive than ever.

Then she heard Dustin's voice behind her, up on the wall. "Kaylee, there's movement."

She jerked to attention, watching the cross street, which ran perpendicular to the front of Jefferson High.

"I see two shadows, maybe more," he said. "We got movement!"

Her hands jittered. She slowly moved them to her backpack, and she searched about in confusion. With no weapons, just the stupid whistle hanging around her neck inside of her shirt, she froze powerless. Slapping footsteps clamored from inside the school grounds. Chairs and tables scraped across the ground and slammed into place.

Fifty feet down, she spotted a lone red fire hydrant jutting up. She crawled slowly along the curb, dragging her backpack behind her. The nylon scraped loudly on the cement.

Bullets rained horizontally. Flashes of gun barrels erupted at the cross street. The concrete wall above her shattered, spraying shrapnel out all over the sidewalk.

Kaylee scrambled the last few feet to the fire hydrant, where she hid with her back up against it. Curling her arms and body into a tight ball, she ducked as the dupes blasted away at her, bullets pinging off the hydrant and exploding into the cinder block wall in front of her face.

She grabbed for the silver whistle, and it screamed at full blast. This did not stop the hail of gunshots. A bullet shattered when it impacted the valve of the fire hydrant sending a lead fragment into her cheek and slicing a thin cut across her face. Fingertips patted at her wound, and she saw the smear of fresh blood. All she could do to save herself was to blow the whistle louder.

Finally, Kaylee heard someone yell above the whistling, "Shut up, stupid!" The shooting had stopped. Quiet again. She wiped her cheek with her shirttail, soaking up the excess blood.

The school bus engine roared to life again. A minute later, Lucas appeared at the school gate. "Come here!"

Ten

Kaylee stood up from the fire hydrant, and she jogged back over to the front gate with her backpack. Standing before Lucas, she could see his demeanor had softened. He seemed disturbed and confused, but relieved and energized all at once. She trembled, staring up at him.

Lucas shuffled uneasily. It wasn't clear what he wanted or why he was having trouble spitting it out.

"The sergeant's dead."

Kaylee snapped back, surprised. A couple of red droplets dribbled from her chin.

Jaworski, dead?

Then she remembered wishing he would die over and over. She had wanted him dead, actually, but the others could find out about her wish and shoot her next. They might discover she was against the janitor. They could hold a trial or something. She would certainly be found guilty. They'd hang her, like Sir Henry Poltergeist, and she would be doomed to haunt Jefferson High School. Unless some ghost hunters figured out how to free her soul.

"Get yourself cleaned up," said Lucas.

In a haze she strolled into the compound. No one opposed her or took any interest. The boys along the wall celebrated their combat victory, and they joked with bravado and bluster. Like just another chapter in her strange dream, Kaylee reentered their world and absorbed back into their little society, which was starting to seem more than a bit insane.

Lucas roared, "Bus!"

Kaylee passed clear through the gym dormitory and continued on left through the hallway toward the cafeteria. Inside, it was dark now and deserted. No one said anything to her, and she stormed right into the kitchen and procured a serrated knife. She held it up and examined the blade. The steak knife featured a long wooden handle, much like the knife that Sean had used. But that other one had been smooth. Like a sword, she whipped it back and forth. Her palm wrapped around the worn down, molded handle and she crushed her hand to hold it tighter.

A footstep down the hallway echoed, and she hid the knife quickly inside her backpack. She spun and marched on through the school, back to reclaim her cot. Her eyes remained stuck open, and she gazed furiously. At the cot she slammed her backpack down, and she looked back and forth at the other inhabitants. Their group seemed sad and quiet.

"Your face is bleeding," said a little voice, a girl whom she had never seen before, only about five years old wearing a dull, faded beige dress.

Kaylee whipped back. This girl was new. Her curly blond hair sprung up in disheveled tangles, and she gazed at Kaylee innocently. "Your face."

Kaylee nodded, and she calmed herself.

"You should get first aid," said the little one.

Kaylee ignored the girl, and she returned to her own plan. From inside her backpack, she retrieved her remaining clean clothes and a bath towel. She held up her palm to dismiss the persistent kid, and then she took off toward the showers.

The stench of rotting food and coffee grounds eventually washed from her hair and skin. Dried crust scrubbed off her cheek. Grime had built up on her hands and under her fingernails. The school's shower ran unlimited hot water, and so she decided to stay there a long, long time, just thinking and becoming as clean as she had ever been in her life. The gash in her hand had opened up again, and she pressed on it until it stopped bleeding.

Now that she was back inside the encampment Kaylee needed to be on guard at all times. It wasn't just the dupes outside the walls, but the rest of them too. Except maybe Dustin, and of course that new little girl. She was determined to make real changes. She would put a stop to all that getting pushed around. She had had enough of being afraid, and she had just as much right to be here as anyone else, no matter what they said about her.

As she stepped out of the shower and into the partially lit girl's locker room, a strange, dark blur of a figure jumped out and ran across her path. Kaylee stood stunned.

They could be dupes launching a surprise attack. She didn't even have her whistle around her neck. Dripping wet and wrapped in a bath towel, she dodged back behind the cinder block shower stall and hid at the corner. Figures moved among the benches and lockers. A hand grabbed at her towel. Kaylee instinctively jerked and pulled herself back to cover up. She recognized who they were.

Tyretta's friends.

Tyretta, that girl who had pointed the gun at her, scooped Kaylee's clean clothes from the bench.

Still dripping wet, she saw Tyretta flee out of the locker room door along with that third girl, laughing. Tyretta cackled like a chihuahua that had lapped up tequila. Luckily they had failed to snatch away her towel.

Kaylee composed herself. Then her anger ramped. She peeked out into the hall. It was deserted and dark, as usual at night. She realized that she had left her backpack vulnerable on her cot. It contained all her remaining possessions. She jogged down the hall, holding her towel so it wouldn't fall off.

At her cot, Kaylee found her backpack. Her previous clothes remained, and she needed to wash them somewhere. Keeping vigilant watch, she slid on her pants beneath the towel and fixed her hair.

What are they doing to my clothes?

It dawned on her that rigor mortis had set in across the population. All the girls were crying, about ten of them.

All the boys were sitting back quietly. Occasionally, they would glance up toward the front of the gym.

Kaylee peered over to see what they were all looking at. It was Jaworski's cot, a large lump covered by a blanket. Below the cot, a yellow liquid dripped from the mattress. A puddle of it spread slowly.

She secured her things and stuffed her comb into her backpack. Lugging it, she stepped toward the janitor's cot for a better look. He was still there, lying beneath the wet blanket. The group watched her, but none of them spoke. They had all gone mute now, like her.

Lucas and several of the large boys burst through the steel door with shovels. "All right, let's get him to the football field. Carefully."

Four of the boys carried Jaworski's remains off into the hallway, trailing a small drip of pee as they bounded along. Lucas followed behind them, carrying three shovels. "Somebody clean this floor, please."

The scribe, Melanie, went off to search for tools to clean with, returning with paper towels and a large rolling garbage can.

Kaylee watched several and gauged their reactions. These ignored her, not making eye contact. Apparently, she was a kind of pariah. No one would interact with her at all.

Then Tyretta and her two accomplices strolled back into the gym from the direction of the cafeteria. Joking with one another, they pranced to their various cots and plopped down in a group.

Kaylee couldn't believe it. They didn't even notice her glaring at them like a rabid pit bull. Oblivious to her, the three girls bantered and gossiped. Kaylee slid off her backpack and rested it on her cot. Her fists squeezed into tight balls of rage, and she clenched her teeth.

Tyretta was lying back, still cackling at the ceiling, when Kaylee raced over and pounced on her. Fists flew, and they both tumbled onto the hardwood floor. Rolling, she pounded Tyretta's face as the crowd roared to life and swarmed them.

Tyretta knocked her off, and she climbed back up on her knees. Kaylee, undeterred, rammed her head into her chest. The taller girl fell over onto her back. Kaylee battered her with a hail of brutal blows until the other girl punched Kaylee's face and sent her down onto her back.

Kaylee couldn't feel pain anymore. She shook her head and jumped right back up.

Tyretta called for her friends. "Get this freak the hell offa me!"

Her two friends, however, seemed less than enthusiastic. Kaylee rushed back over to grab at Tyretta and attempted to tackle her. People yelled out indecipherable words and cheers like a tornado swirling around the two fighters.

Kaylee punched at Tyretta's ribs and wrestled with her on the hard gym floor until Lucas suddenly yanked her into the air. He seemed truly shocked and at a loss for words. Other boys ran in behind him bearing rifles. The room quieted.

"What the hell is wrong with you two?" said Lucas. "We got a thousand lunatics outside who want to shoot us, and you idiots are fighting with each other? Are you for real?"

"Little freak jumped me!" said Tyretta. "She's crazy!"

Kaylee was not to be railroaded. She gestured with her hands for a writing pad. The scribe girl in the glasses immediately delivered her a notebook as Tyretta argued her case at a shrill pitch.

Kaylee scratched out her own case.

Lucas looked at the note and turned back to Tyretta, incredulous. "You stole her clothes?"

For a moment she looked guilty, caught in the act. "No, that's—she jumped me, attacked me like maybe she's a dupe? You ever wonder that?"

Tyretta's two friends, however, remained guilty-looking, and they stepped back to hide in the crowd. Lucas turned to the two co-conspirators.

"You all took her clothes?" He almost laughed, but caught himself.

Kaylee nodded.

"No!" said Tyretta. "She's psycho. She should be outta here. Why is she even back in here? Huh? Lucas?"

Kaylee flipped off Tyretta with both hands.

"Give her her clothes back," said Lucas. "What are you, five?"

The boys holding the rifles laughed.

As Tyretta stonewalled, Lucas singled out Tyretta's friend with the long red hair braided down her back. "You. Where'd you put her clothes?"

"They're –" began the red-haired girl.

"Nowhere!" Tyretta interrupted.

"– In the cafeteria garbage can, under the crud."

Kaylee was livid.

Lucas shook his head. "Okay, you? What's your name?"

"Joanna," said the redhead demurely.

"Joanna what?"

"Joanna McAvoy."

Lucas cleared his throat. "You go get her clothes out, wash 'em in the sink, and hang 'em up to dry."

Joanna nodded, and she scampered off.

Lucas peered down at Tyretta, who had become quieter, if not completely subdued. "You? Liar, what's your name?"

"Tyretta. And I'm not-"

"All right, Tyretta. No breakfast or lunch for you. Somebody write that down. Melanie?"

"I'm here." The scribe, Melanie, shuffled over beside Kaylee.

"Can you do that for me? Keep notes?"

"Of course," she said with enthusiasm.

Kaylee handed Melanie back her notebook.

"Thank you."

Lucas announced, "Tyretta skips two meals. And since you've got so much time on your hands, you can come help dig that six-foot hole for Sergeant Jaworski. It's a lot of fun. Come on."

Tyretta whined and fussed as she was marched out ahead of Lucas.

***

Sometime later, Caroline Anderson called everyone who wasn't on watch to gather and say something at the janitor's gravesite. The school's population trudged out to the football field, where a freshly dug plot sat at their feet. The body had already been buried and the grave marked with a sign. People searched each other's faces and waited for someone to talk. Kaylee stood quietly at the back, on the diametrically opposite side from Tyretta, who was now covered in grime and sweat.

Lucas said, "Sergeant Jaworski made me sergeant before he passed. Said it was a battlefield promotion. I'm supposed to pick my replacement, too. So I think I should pick Miss Anderson, 'cause she's the only adult left."

Caroline nodded. "Wait a minute." Anderson stood as tall as Lucas, and her voice carried. "As far as who's in charge, nobody put you in charge in the first place-"

"The sergeant," Lucas responded.

"The janitor, you mean? No one put him in charge either!"

"Look, you don't want me?" He spun around to see the other teens respond.

"I didn't say that," said Miss Anderson. "But this is still America, isn't it? It's not a military dictatorship!"

"All right." Lucas considered. Everyone stepped back a bit as he and Miss Anderson claimed the ground near the janitor's grave. Two dozen teenagers were present, and the new little girl, Sara. Everyone wanted to hear; nobody wanted to interrupt. Kaylee maneuvered around a lug in front of her so she could see.

Lucas used his crowd voice. "What should we do then? Are you still gonna be the corporal?"

"I think," Caroline said, "we all should vote on the things that affect everybody, and discuss it first. That's democracy."

"Okay," said Lucas. "But there's eight people out on the wall all the time. How are they gonna discuss it?"

"We could just go talk to them," said Caroline.

"Sometimes there's no time to have a meeting."

"That's why you're in charge of military affairs."

Lucas shook his head impatiently. "I don't think it's gonna work." He shuffled about with frustration.

"Tough!" said Caroline. "Since we're all stuck here for what could be the rest of our lives, we all have rights, and we all have a say. I never agreed to make anyone king, Lucas. Little man."

Lucas breathed several times. The muscular boys who were usually seen with hunting rifles stayed back with the others, all of them waiting for events to work themselves out. The mood of the crowd swayed and ebbed like the waves of the sea.

"Fine," he said. "Everybody votes then. Even that little girl? What's her name?"

"Why not?" said Miss Anderson. "Sara's got a right to stay alive too. If you can't convince a five-year-old that what you're doing is right, I mean..."

The crowd looked to little Sara, lost in an ocean of giants. The pixie seemed embarrassed, as she snuck back behind a large boy. Most everyone laughed.

"Whatever," Lucas shot back dismissively. "Here's suttom to vote on. You ready?"

All ears perked up.

"We got about two days' food left at this rate. What are we gonna do? You tell me!" Lucas postured arrogantly, somewhat in the demeanor the janitor had employed.

Caroline said, "We'll... we'll need a plan."

Eleven

The following day, the general mood inside the school remained tense and depressed. Without the janitor, Jaworski, the only adult remaining was Caroline Anderson, but she didn't know anything about warfare, except what she had seen on TV. The only person who seemed confident was Lucas. Most everyone followed Lucas's general plan. Watches continued around the clock, but food was running out fast.

Kaylee and Dustin commandeered the school's auditorium, which was otherwise abandoned. The stage featured tall crimson curtains, which stretched up to the rafters. These were thick and flexible enough to shoot with arrows, as long as the tips were removed. It became Kaylee's job to unscrew the razor-sharp steel points and to keep them organized and accessible in case of surprise attack.

Dustin pinned a stained white rag from backstage to one of the curtains and began shooting arrows at it. After he had shot his quiver, Kaylee ran up and gathered them. This was her assignment, and so she wasn't bothered, at first. Dustin shot arrows for a full hour, over and over. Then it got boring. Instead of running, she sauntered up slowly, and she kicked the arrows into a pile. Upon returning to Dustin, at the row of seats halfway back from the stage, she gestured for him to hand over the bow.

He shrugged.

The compound bow felt heavier than she thought it would. Her arm rattled as she tried to pull it back, but she could only get it halfway there. The steel cable dug into her fingers. Her left hand pulsed with pain where her sliced cut healed slowly. Unable to pull it all the way back, she felt instantly defeated.

Dustin grabbed back the bow, and he took a look at his own hands. Blisters puffed out.

"Let's quit for today. What time's our watch?"

She held up two fingers.

"A'right, we gotta go get some lunch. Good job, Private Colton!" He laughed, and he handed her the bow to strap across her back.

Kaylee rolled her eyes.

Dustin trotted off toward the exit doors.

"Oh. You gotta put the tips back on. Procedure. You know?"

Kaylee huffed and slammed down the quiver.

"I'll save you whatever they're servin'."

Her tongue wagged out sarcastically, as she dug into the sack of arrow tips. Her finger poked onto the first one, of course.

The following day Dustin shot practice arrows from farther distances near the back of the auditorium. They struck the curtain with a soft pat and bounced back down with a second tap. Some of his arrows hit the rag target, but most didn't.

Kaylee gathered up the arrows and dumped them beside Dustin.

"And you see that last one?" he said.

She shook her head, preferring to remain bored. She couldn't pull back the cable no matter how hard she struggled, and she resented Dustin for being the one with the weapon. Stewing in her seat, she felt indignant toward people like him for making this violent, crazy world where everyone had to fight with everyone just to get by. It was always boys.

"Watch this, watch this" he said. The arrow flew pretty near the target. "Bam! You see that?" He seemed to brag a lot now, like the others.

Kaylee disliked that, too, as she was still unable to say a single word. Half-heartedly she nodded and then flopped back in her seat and yawned.

The next arrow that Dustin pulled back splintered as he released it, wooden fragments exploding into the flesh of his hand.

He started to cry; Kaylee found it fascinating. His hand was a mess that hurt her brain just to look at. A jagged wood shard impaled right through it.

"Ahhh!"

Dustin seemed no longer like an adult but a little boy, the way he moved. With his other hand he slid the wood splinter out, and a gush of blood released. He pulled the wound in tight and squeezed it as he curled into a ball and closed his eyes.

"What are we doing here?" he said to himself. "We gotta get outta here." He contorted his body in his seat, faced away from her. "I miss my mom."

Watching him, Kaylee couldn't remember an older boy like Dustin crying in front of her. Sean hadn't cried for years that she could recall. She couldn't even remember the last time she'd cried. It had been so long. It must mean she'd run out of tears or something. Everyone was crying around the school except for herself, and maybe Lucas. Perhaps Lucas had run out of tears too.

Dustin sniffled softly, and it appeared he might drift off to sleep in his chair, but he suddenly opened his eyes. Kaylee stared back, afraid to move. Without a word, he jumped up awkwardly, and he stumbled out of the auditorium.

Had she permanently changed?

Would she cry no more, forever?

Robotically Kaylee finished up the last of her assigned duties. The more she thought on it, the more she wondered what she really wanted. She didn't know why she was even fighting alongside these school kids. The only thing she knew was to go find Dad somehow, and that he was due to return home in a week on Thursday at six p.m. He was so reliable, never late for anything, unlike Mom, who was late for everything. They fought like cats and dogs because Mom always left late and made him tardy when they went out together. She spent so much time getting ready that she didn't seem to care if they made it on time, anywhere, ever.

Dad would make snide jokes, always pushing a new angle to shame her into leaving earlier so that they could just once get to a place on time. He would sit in the car by himself out in the driveway, and then he'd storm back inside, madder each time, because she refused to leave. Mom drove him crazy.

Kaylee lifted the compound bow, which felt very heavy. She tried to pull back the cable again. It hardly moved at all, only three or four inches this time.

She brought the bow and the arrows down to the weight room, where some of the bigger boys pumped away on the machines. In here they acted tough and grunted a lot. Like cavemen. She daintily placed down the weapons on the counter, and she slid off her backpack. The crashing of iron plates stung her ears, but she decided not to be intimidated, no matter what. She was never going to be intimidated again.

One of the muscle-head boys pulled a handle connected to a long steel cable across his chest. She stopped to watch him.

A normal-sized boy with tightly curled hair fiddled with the stereo system behind a desk. Over the speaker blared the screeching dupe noises, then scratches and hisses as the radio stations turned. Again the screeches returned. One of the cavemen slammed down a dumbbell.

"Turn it off! What are you doing?"

The noise broadcast on every radio station. The curly-haired boy attempted to hook up his MP3 player into the stereo.

Kaylee was more interested in the pull weight, as it was just like pulling back the bow and arrow. After that first boy moved on, she inspected the machine. The guy had been pulling sixty pounds. She figured she would start with thirty instead and work her way up. That was how they did it. When she set the steel pin for thirty pounds, and she tried to pull the cable, nothing happened. Maybe it was stuck.

She decided to scale back and try twenty instead. Again, it wouldn't move. Then she went to ten pounds, and that managed to move about two inches and drop back down. Unbelievable. She huffed out and removed the pin completely, leaving five pounds. Even that was hard to pull. But, she did manage to get it across her chest, once. Then it was time for the other side. Her left arm felt a little stronger for some reason, although she was right-handed. She got it to pull across twice before her healing hand alerted her to stop. The entire exercise felt demoralizing. At this rate she couldn't possibly get up to the right strength, and her left hand throbbed beneath its bandage.

Kaylee sulked away and over to the stationary bicycles. They were more her preferred kind of workout. Sitting comfortably she began to pedal, and she kept on it for quite a while continually looking back over at the cross-pull machine, which had humbled her. After she started to sweat, her lungs got a second wind, and she steepened the digital bike hill.

The stereo crackled with dance music, but then it cut out. It scratched and danced, one side of the room, then the other. The muscle boys shot dirty looks over to the stereo boy.

Kaylee saw Tyretta prance in through the room's main entrance. Suddenly she felt confused and a bit trapped. Her eyes on the other girl, Kaylee imagined the types of things Tyretta might do next. The girl cheered for the music as it started playing finally. Stepping toward one of the beefy weight-lifter boys, Tyretta danced without a care, shaking her butt like it was normal. The boys in the room all looked over at her curiously.

Kaylee pedaled her stationary bike faster until she could feel her heart banging to leave. She wanted to get stronger as fast as possible. Glancing back at her inanimate nemesis, the pull machine, she was ready to attack it again. One more try.

She pulled at the cable, and she got it moving, twice on her right side and then once more. Then once more after that. Her torso felt stronger already.

Another boy performed pull ups on a nearby structure with handles, and she thought that was a good idea too. After he moved on, she went in and gave that a try as well. For another hour she remained in the weight room, trying out the various stations.

Tyretta inhabited the opposite side of the expanse, where all the boys pumped iron with free weights. She didn't seem to try very hard, but was more interested in talking, posing and laughing loudly with them.

Eventually Kaylee was so tired and covered in sweat that she snuck out through an emergency door near the aerobics machines.

***

"Volunteers!" Lucas yelled in the gymnasium. "We gotta try for the supermarket on Lincoln."

Fear spread like lightning across the teenagers' faces. Subconsciously, they shrank back and stepped away from the call.

"Come on, people," he said. "You like to eat?"

"I will drive," said Caroline Anderson. She sounded cautious but not too scared. It made sense, because she was the bus driver and had the most experience with cars. She strolled over and stood next to Lucas.

To Kaylee's surprise, Dustin then raised his bandaged hand. "I'll go with y'all."

Her jaw flapped. She hadn't seen Dustin in the room, but now he was volunteering to go outside the walls, and it could be suicide. Nobody knew how many dupes were out there, where they were, or what they planned.

"How's your hand?" Lucas asked.

"It's all right," said Dustin.

"Really? Can you use that bow?"

"Oh yeah. Expert."

"Expert? All right. You're in."

Now there were three.

A muscle-head boy holding a shotgun joined them, the caveman from the weight room who liked to drop the giant dumbbells and roar at the walls. He had brown skin and black hair, not very tall but quite wide.

Now there were four.

Caroline asked Lucas, "Is that enough?"

Lucas shook his head. "Couple more."

The room froze, none willing to volunteer. Kaylee clenched her teeth together, and she raised her hand.

Twelve

Colton?" As no one else was forthcoming, Lucas held his decision for a minute. "Anybody else?"

The other teens' shoulders slumped, and they slouched. The entire gathering held statue-like, afraid to twitch.

Lucas said, "We're taking the Mustang."

Caroline nodded and they moved out. Their squad gathered up materials for the raid. Kaylee stuck close to Caroline. The schoolyard was quiet as they loaded up the Mustang's trunk with a few weapons.

"Not sure how much we can haul back this time," said Lucas. "It's just a test run."

They piled into the Mustang. Kaylee found herself sandwiched between Dustin to the left and the muscle boy, Ruiz, on her right. Lucas signaled for the school bus to move.

Caroline started the Mustang.

"Come on. Seat belts, people."

Everyone squirmed to get their straps into place. Lucas and the large muscle boy, Ruiz, held handguns. All their faces stiffened with dread as the car eased toward the gate. Only Caroline had control from here on, and Kaylee's stomach dropped. The car hesitated halfway out the gate, and Caroline quickly made a sign of a cross with her right hand. They slid out of the schoolyard and into the world.

"What about Kaylee?" asked Dustin. "What's she gonna do?"

"We'll find suttom," said Lucas.

Caroline whipped the car to the left and gave it a surge of gas. They sped off down the avenue, the lone car on the road. Jefferson Avenue was beaten up and blown over with trash. Abandoned cars sat along their route, some with their windows smashed, others with doors left open. It seemed uncannily quiet.

Kaylee peered out the window, and she saw the town streak by at a quickening pace. The auto jerked right, and then stopped abruptly with a skid.

"Who's that?" said Caroline.

"Back the other way!"

The car reversed and spun about with tires skidding. Kaylee felt sick, like she had been on a roller coaster when she was eight. Blurry figures scrambled out of houses down the blocked-off street.

The Mustang raced off, pinning everyone back. Caroline remained on Jefferson for several more blocks before she attempted another path through to downtown. They crawled to a stop at a corner.

"Use the binoculars," she said. "What have we got?"

Lucas spied down the street for several moments as everyone sat tensely.

"Looks passable."

Caroline chomped her fingernails each time she stopped the car.

"You're sure?"

"No, of course I'm not *sure*." He postured in his seat. "The whole town's a red zone."

Caroline gritted her teeth together.

"Yes or no, Lucas?"

He bobbed about with the binoculars. "Go. Slow. Be ready."

The Mustang crawled around the corner, and they rolled gently along the tree-lined side street. Caroline whispered, "Have we ever considered we might find *friendlies*?"

"Screw that," answered Ruiz.

Dustin said snidely, "You guys are real hospitable to strangers."

They jerked to a stop. Again Lucas reconned the street before proceeding. After several more blocks, they approached the Supermart parking lot. Empty, a couple of stripped junk cars at the periphery. The market interior looked dark and silent. Shattered glass doors were left wide open. Caroline drove straight to the entrance, and they bounced to a halt.

Lucas jumped out.

"Dustin, Ruiz, with me. Ladies, stay with the car." He pulled the seat forward to allow the others to rush out.

"Fine by me," said Caroline.

They piled out, jostling Kaylee around in the turmoil, and they held up their firearms. Lucas spied with his binoculars into the food store through the front windows. After making his decision, he turned back to the car.

"Colton, come take the binoculars."

Kaylee jumped out of the back seat, relieved to stretch her legs. Lucas handed her his binoculars as the other two boys stalked closer to the Supermart.

Lucas tested his walkie-talkie. "Caroline, radio check?"

"I'm here."

"Colton, you look out for anyone approaching. You see anything, you signal Miss Anderson."

She nodded confidently.

"Let's go." The boys hustled inside the Supermart. Kaylee spun about, searching the street.

"Anything, honey?" Caroline sat biting her nails while the engine purred softly.

Kaylee stepped around the car to get a better view of Lincoln Street. She scrutinized the row of storefronts until it made her dizzy.

The radio squawked. "How's it looking out there?"

Caroline grabbed her receiver. "Hurry up."

"There's nothing here. We're trying."

Kaylee's stomach sank from some obscure sensory perception. She knew instantly that something terrible was about to happen.

A strange green car turned the corner and rambled down Lincoln Street toward them. She found it in the binoculars. It was real.

Immediately, she banged on the door. Caroline jumped. Pointing and signaling, Kaylee flopped back into the front passenger seat. Caroline pushed the car into gear, and they sped forward around the corner of the market.

Caroline took the radio.

"We've got a car approaching in the front! Don't go out the front!" The Mustang screeched to a stop. "Lucas, are you hearing me? Get out the back now. We're at the loading dock."

Kaylee saw a black pistol lying beside Caroline on the seat. It tempted her. If that green car appeared and chased after them, she could shoot at it. But Caroline might get mad.

Suddenly Caroline snatched the gun herself.

"Get in back, Kaylee, quick!"

Kaylee nodded, and she tumbled over the seat and into the rear. Landing with a thud, she squirmed on the floor of the car, almost upside down. Her brain felt disoriented, and she flailed to right herself from the contortions.

The rear door of the Supermart exploded with the three boys. They bashed shopping carts full of various bags and boxes against the rusty steel rails and bounced them down four cement steps. The boys loaded up the trunk, slammed it, and jumped back in all wild-eyed and crazed. Caroline tore up the pavement, rocketing off down a completely different side street. No one trailed behind, and they appeared to be in the clear.

Ruiz's oversized muscles squished Kaylee against the side of the car, so she shoved him back. He responded by waving his revolver in front of her face as he aimed out the side window. She smacked at him to back off, and eventually he slid back over to the center a couple of inches. Meanwhile she couldn't help but stare at the dull-brushed steel gun barrel hovering right in front of her eyes.

Their matte grey Mustang sputtered in through the school's gate and finally came to rest. All breathed easier. A crowd of curious teenagers formed, those who had not volunteered.

Lucas stood beside the car, and he called back to Caroline, "S-Mart's dead. Not worth it."

A kitchen detail unloaded what noodles and beans had been pilfered. Dustin and Ruiz stretched, posturing about like badasses. Ruiz slid his revolver back into a leather holster with an exaggerated style.

Caroline pushed her door closed. "So, what are we going to do to feed the school?"

"Don't worry," said Lucas. "Sarge said we should try going house to house. And I've got some other possibles."

Kaylee exhaled more easily, as she glided back toward the trunk to see what they had obtained: a sack of rice, condiments, pickled jalapeños. To the side of the car, she saw a burgeoning group of sycophants surround Ruiz and Dustin. No one noticed her, though.

She trudged to her cot to lie down. It had felt so harrowing, and now she needed sleep.

"Hi!" said a little voice. It was Sara. "Did you go outside with them to the store?"

Kaylee nodded.

"Was it scary?" Her cherubic face leaned in with wide eyes, inches from Kaylee's nose.

Kaylee nodded again.

The girl smiled. "Okay." Sara walked off alone, carrying a soft plushy doll.

Kaylee grinned, and she turned to her side to scrunch up in her pillow.

***

That night, after Kaylee was relieved from watch, she went to wash herself in the girl's locker room. Not ready to try another shower, she kept her backpack with her at all times. She scrubbed up in the sink without incident, packed her toothbrush, and trotted back to the cafeteria.

Rows of lockers lined the dimly lit hallway on both sides. Up ahead a pair of girls stopped in a particularly dark spot, discussing something.

That's when Kaylee heard the tinny squeal from a muffled speaker. The repetitive grinding noise was unmistakable. It was that sickening computer modem sound, a hypnotic wave that drew you in and played tricks on your mind. It came from where the two girls ahead stood, slithering out from inside one of the lockers.

Kaylee floated hypnotically forward. One of the girls pointed her gun at the locker door. The other girl argued for her to open it up and have a look inside. It could be something important, some way to communicate. Maybe it could get them rescued.

Kaylee found it extremely difficult to think as she approached closer and closer. Her feet seemed to dance above the hallway floor, carrying her. That noise formed pictures inside her brain, now that she was familiar with the cycling patterns, having heard it so many times before. Like colorful swirling tunnels, the sounds drew giant corkscrews through the air. She feared the deception behind the noise, and so she wanted to warn the two girls, whom she didn't really know at all. Though she couldn't speak, she needed to signal them in a different manner. She stepped nearer and nearer to the two, whether she wanted to or not.

One of the girls suddenly yanked open the locker. Flickers of blue light pulsed out from the open hole and onto their static faces. Kaylee stopped in her tracks, and she grabbed the whistle from around her neck. Without delay she blew a piercing shrill signal as loud as she could, until the whistle blast hurt her ears. The two girls were transfixed on the locker light as if staring into the sun. Their faces flashed with stroboscopic patterns, and the swirling noise filled the hallway.

The girl holding the handgun turned toward Kaylee and took aim. The revolver wobbled in the hypnotized girl's hand. Her blank face seemed devoid of human personality.

Kaylee ran for it, back into the dark hall as fast as her legs could move. The girl fired, and the bullet shot past and exploded into the wall at the end of the hallway. She whipped around madly at the corner and dashed down another hallway, still blowing her whistle. Explosions echoed through the school, as a barrage of gunshots rang out.

Silence returned, a creepy, terrorizing stillness. Kaylee hid inside an empty classroom. For several minutes she stared at the glass window in the door wondering what had happened and if it was safe to emerge.

Footsteps charged into the classroom. Boys with rifles and pistols invaded, and they flicked on the lights. She put her hands up, remaining in place.

"Don't shoot!" Lucas pushed their gun barrels away. "It's just Colton." He rushed over. "Are there any more dupes?"

Kaylee held up two fingers.

"All right, we got 'em." Lucas relaxed again, and he breathed a hearty sigh.

She hung her head. The two girls must have been killed. They'd transformed into dupes after looking into that locker. She rushed to the board at the front of the classroom and grabbed a piece of chalk to scrape out a message.

It's in the locker, a screen.

"We know," said Lucas. "We shot it."

Dustin arrived at the classroom's doorway.

"It's so screwed up, man! We shoulda tried to capture 'em."

Lucas answered, "They were armed and already shooting."

Dustin apparently felt really bad. "They woulda run out of bullets, right?"

Ruiz stepped over to him.

"Yeah. After putting some in you and me." He continued past without pause, and he marched off down the hallway alone.

"They were just little girls," said Dustin.

Lucas whispered, "I know."

Kaylee stared at the cloudy, forest-green chalkboard, feeling conflicted. She scraped out another message.

I should have run over and stopped them.

The classroom went cold.

Two more graves were dug that night alongside the janitor's marker. Kaylee helped dig, and she stabbed into the rocky clay soil without regard for blisters, which formed on her palms. These three dirt rectangles were misaligned, not quite symmetrical.

Blood had splattered all over that hallway and into some of the lockers through the slits. A cleanup operation commenced, consisting of Melanie and a close-knit squad from the kitchen detail.

The school's surviving inhabitants remained absolutely terrorized, on the verge of psychological breakdowns. Caroline Anderson was inconsolable over the killing of the two teenaged girls, both of whom she had known from her bus driving route. She set up her own personal living accommodation in the school's administrative office, cut off from the rest of the people. There she holed up alone for long stretches of time.

Kaylee felt guiltier at not acting sooner, and with more force, to stop the girls before the situation got so out of hand. As she dug into the earth at the bottom of one of the graves, she imagined what she would do differently next time, how she would be decisive, how she would make a difference somehow and not have to dig any more graves.

Thirteen

During another long night in the gymnasium, two dozen cots sitting silently, Kaylee awoke in bed after hearing little noises, wet snapping, light smacking somewhere in the room. Mice, maybe. Or rats. She shook her head and opened her eyes. The rustles sounded faint.

Across several cots in the direction of Tyretta the noise emanated. It seemed like Tyretta's cot was bigger than the others, a large amorphous blob. Someone else lay there with her.

Kaylee's heart raced uncontrollably. She peered over and saw Ruiz reposition himself on the cot beside Tyretta. They kissed each other repeatedly, grunting as they realigned themselves on the tiny bed with accompanying squeaks from the old springs.

Kaylee flattened herself down, her breathing beyond control. Hoping they wouldn't spot her, she stared at the two.

Ruiz jumped up suddenly to his feet, and he yanked Tyretta all the way up to hers. Then they snuck off together into the darkness.

Kaylee watched Tyretta and Ruiz disappear around the hallway corner. She felt so weirded out that she didn't know what to think. Everyone else slumbered oblivious. Only Kaylee witnessed their departure. Her mind raced, and she couldn't force herself back to sleep. So many ideas popped in at once. She kept thinking about them, where they may have gone. This could only lead to trouble, and now that she was a witness, she was part of their little conspiracy.

She tossed for an hour. Finally she grew tired of being awake and was just starting to drift off again when the two returned to the gym. Separately, Tyretta snuck back to her cot, while Ruiz circled around to the far side of the gym and climbed into his own bed.

***

In the morning, someone shook Kaylee by her shoulder, and she slowly returned to consciousness. It was Dustin.

"Come on, Kaylee. Why you sleepin' so late?"

Kaylee smiled, and she stared up at him. Everyone was already out of bed and busy, except for her. She held the sheet over her body, just below her neck, and she waited for him to turn away.

"Come on, come on. Before they run outta chow."

She nodded, and she climbed up to her feet and grabbed for her hairbrush. Raking it though her tangled hair, she pulled at her scalp to get it done in a hurry. Dustin plodded off to the cafeteria, and she wanted to catch up.

In the cafeteria, she spotted Tyretta laughing with her friends, and with Ruiz. They sat closely together, and Tyretta rubbed up casually against his arm as they ate.

Kaylee loaded her plate with some ramen noodles and an apple. The fruit was just about depleted, and they would have to go out scavenging to find more. Dustin sat at a busy table with some of his friends, as well as with Lucas. When Kaylee sat down, the mood seemed to soften, and she listened to them gab about where they desired to venture outside the walls next.

Lucas said, "I think we're going to want small teams to start going through the closest houses. Right across the street. See what's there. Haul it back."

"I'm down," said Dustin. He seemed to deliberately act tough around the other boys. Kaylee thought she knew a different side of him, but this was troubling. Dustin almost seemed like he was playing a part in a movie. Tension was fixed in his face, his jaw, the way he kept it flexed and ready to snap back with a sarcastic response at a moment's notice. This version was a lot more like Rory, that skinny,

104

red-haired guy who carried a crowbar everywhere and never shut up.

Lucas finished eating, but he wasn't yet ready to head off. "All right. Sarge said we need to keep assessing the big picture. What's our strategy? How are we going to win this thing? The end game."

He was met with blank stares and trepidation. Dustin shrugged.

Kaylee thought about the war so far and the behavior of the dupes. They were regular people like Sean, but the TVs seized control of their minds and had them acting very strangely, like puppets. Cruel marionettes. She played with this idea for a bit, and then she reluctantly produced a little yellow notepad and a felt-tip pen.

Turn off all the TVs.

When she was done, she waved at Lucas gently. He pretended not to see her at first and instead looked off the other way. Kaylee waved more enthusiastically. Lucas exhaled without turning toward her.

She slapped the notepad down on the table, and she ripped the page out to push it along a human chain. Lucas was obliged to have a look, which he did. Then he laughed.

"Yeah, right. *Turn off all the TVs.*"

The boys busted up with laughter.

"Turn off the TVs?" They babbled like chimps with a new banana.

"Why didn't we think a that!" said Rory. "Why don't you build a super remote controller, little mute?" Rory fashioned himself some kind of comedian, but this was no comedy show.

Kaylee growled back, infuriated. Then she jumped up and flipped off the whole table with her middle fingers. She even stuck out her tongue for good measure before storming off in a fury.

"Colton! Colton, wait!" Lucas called. "Come on. Come back!"

Kaylee stopped, and she put her hands on her hips in an impatient posture reminiscent of Mom.

"Okay," said Lucas, trying for a conciliatory tone. "It's a good suggestion. But how are we supposed to do that?"

Thinking fast, Kaylee responded only by pointing her index finger at her own skull, her own brain. Then she shuffled out of the cafeteria. Brooding on her cot, she noticed the boys pile out in a bunch and walk through the gym to the front exit door.

Lucas spotted her on her cot, and he came over alone.

"Hey?"

She looked up, waiting.

"Look. I'm sorry. They're a little stupid sometimes." He stepped about uncomfortably. Kaylee just stared noncommittally.

"If you want to tell me something, just write me a note. Okay? Forget about them."

Kaylee breathed in and nodded.

"Okay. Good. Keep up the good work." Lucas waved back nonchalantly as he floated away.

**

Dustin missed as many targets as he hit with his arrows, and Kaylee started to study him and how he was doing it. She excused herself, and she took a hike over to the school's library to see if it had a proper book about archery. There was one book written by an Olympic gold medalist. Her competition bow featured sticks with weights pointing out from it. When she pulled back the bowstring, she seemed very relaxed and natural, unlike Dustin, who tended to have his elbow up too high and sticking out. He strained to keep his arrow from moving around, and his arm vibrated with tension. His face too.

Kaylee snatched the book, and she took it back to the auditorium without checking it out. She felt a little unsure about just removing a book, and she knew that she'd have to remember to return it to the library, which wasn't always easy. So many times before she had racked up massive fines, which her mother had been forced to pay. Then the scolding. Then the chores and the punishment, giving up her library card for months at a time. There were bad memories associated with libraries and late books.

That was all history now. There weren't any more fines to worry about in the world, just getting killed, or turned into one of those *pups*, like Rory had called them. Short for puppets. Everyone started saying it now. Rory also tried to push *deefs* on them, short for defectives, but everyone already had a "d" word, with *dupes*. So that didn't catch on.

Kaylee flipped the archery book pages to find the photos. The text didn't say much about how to shoot arrows. It was all about struggling and overcoming and psychology and growing up and stuff like that, but the photos seemed to be all that were needed.

She waved at Dustin after he'd shot his last arrow.

"What?"

She pointed at the Olympic archery pictures, gesturing at the gold medalist's hands and where she held the string back, right up against her chin.

"Yeah," he said, and he turned away. "Go get my arrows."

Insulted, Kaylee stood up with the book and tapped him on the shoulder. When he turned back she pointed at another Olympic picture, the one with the medal ceremony.

"What?" said Dustin. "Just get the arrows, dude."

Now she was *dude*. Kaylee placed the book down on her seat, and she took off to collect the spent arrows from the stage. As Dustin stood to accept them, she pulled them away and placed the quiver down behind her on the seat.

"Now what?" he said. "Stop bein' a pain in the ass! Look, that's a chick, okay? Guys are different. Just gimme my arrows."

Kaylee frowned, and she gave up the quiver. Dustin resumed his shooting, exactly as he always had. She returned to the book, and she read from the beginning, hoping to find something about men and women archers being different, or not.

***

More and more dupes were spotted over the walls. The enemy had marked out a territory, and they held their own patrols along the side streets leading to Jefferson Avenue, where they monitored the school.

On a day watch Kaylee spotted a pair of dupes coming perpendicularly up the sidewalk near her table perch. Before she could place her whistle, the next boy over yelled, "I see 'em."

She watched them, and she also monitored the boys along her own wall. Two more defenders scrambled to observe the dupe patrol. Soon enough, the dupes walked off together, and the area quieted again.

Kaylee thought much about the dupes, and how they received their orders and carried them out without needing to stay in touch constantly with their TV masters. *How long would they remain dupey without recharging their brains on that pulsing hypnotizer?*

Maybe they would just wake up and be normal human beings again. If it was possible then maybe she could do that with Sean and save him from his psycho robot self. It was an alluring idea, to win the war without killing anyone at all. She brainstormed what she would say to Lucas, and if a plan was feasible.

Kaylee no longer spoke to Dustin openly, not even through notes, since he had turned into such a block-headed dolt. Although she was still his partner, technically, and she followed him around, she wasn't all that excited to see him anymore. Dustin got on her nerves. Even the way he ate his food annoyed her to no end.

She was so over him. Why had she ever considered even maybe liking him in the first place? Now she had much more important things on her mind, like how to win the war and save the dupes without killing them, and how to find her dad and start life over away from all these lunatics.

Now that the food was just about gone she was hungry all the time. Rations were slashed to one meal a day. There weren't any snacks. No sugar. No fruit. No ice cream, that was certain.

Finally Kaylee was ready to join the scavengers. These raided the neighboring houses during the day. She overheard how the scavengers stuffed themselves first. None of the best stuff ever made it back to the school. Kaylee was wise to the situation and sick of being chronically hungry.

That day she volunteered to venture outside the walls, not for the good of the school, but to find something delicious and keep it to herself. Of course, she planned on sharing some of her booty with Sara, the only person here she actually liked enough to care about.

"Be careful!" Sara pleaded.

The youngster tagged along, terrified for Kaylee as she marched out of the gym with the rest of the raiding party. Dustin, Lucas, Rory, Ruiz, and a couple of others would keep in contact with the watch commander back at the school over the walkie-talkies. But this was only in case of emergency.

Lucas told them before they left, "Dupes can hear everything we say. Radios aren't secure. So don't transmit unless you're sure they're coming our way. Okay?"

The wall watchers stayed on high alert. Kaylee crawled beneath the school bus with the others so as not to draw attention or waste fuel. They pulled their gear through with ropes, and they assembled on the sidewalk on the other side of the bus.

"Okay, let's go, quick!" said Lucas.

Everyone jogged down Jefferson Avenue in pursuit of him. Kaylee jogged last, slow but also in no hurry to run into a dupe ambush. She kept pace behind Ruiz, who lumbered more slowly than the others. He carried a shotgun and a ton of supplies in his pack, just in case.

Still running, Lucas pointed left, and they shot across the avenue and onto a side street.

"Second house," he said. "Ruiz out front."

The squad stormed inside. Kaylee panted and looked around wildly. It was smelly and stagnant, like no fresh air had come in for a week. She dropped her backpack in the front hallway, and she took her steak knife in hand. Then she followed after the boys into the kitchen where she found them tossing the cabinets. Below the island in the center, she dove in and rifled through. Oatmeal, rice, canned tomatoes, olive oil—it kept coming. Kaylee threw everything into a sack.

"What else, man?" shouted Rory.

Lucas thought a second. "Look for guns, weapons."

Rory dashed off down a hallway toward the bedrooms. Kaylee spotted a door leading to the garage. Inside the finished space, purring dutifully, was a large horizontal freezer. She flipped it open. Inside was meat, chicken, fish, pork, beef, sausage, and imported dishes. Immediately she ran back in and banged on the wall with her hand. Lucas and Dustin peered over.

Kaylee's face said it all, and she started pointing madly into the garage. Inquisitively the boys followed.

"Oh yeah, doggie!" said Dustin.

"That's the one!" said Lucas. "Come on, grab this stuff. Get sheets to tie it up, and let's get the hell out of here!"

Most of their group stormed the garage freezer, having already cleaned out the kitchen. Kaylee was weighed down with fifty pounds of meat and cans.

The march back to school was grueling. Kaylee thought she would collapse if she had to go any farther. Her vision blurred from the strain. Luckily the school stood right around the corner. Luckier still, no dupes had spotted them. It was a clean raid, and what a haul they had stumbled on.

The entire school feasted that night. It was the first sign of joy that anyone could remember since they'd arrived at Jefferson High. That house had even provided beer and wine, which was divided amongst the older teens. It seemed that life was possible again. Kaylee was accepted at the head table where no one tried to insult her. They were too busy enjoying the respite and the tangy grilled meats.

Later that night, after her very first glass of wine, Kaylee Colton wrote out a lengthy master plan to present to Lucas. In page after page, she explained that they could win the war by capturing test subjects and deprogramming them somehow. Then those people would join the fight and expand their numbers until the freedom fighters outnumbered the dupes, and the whole town was converted back to normal. As for TVs, they could destroy the big antennas that broadcast the enemy signal, and maybe smash all the TVs too. She also wrote to Lucas that her father was scheduled to return this upcoming Thursday, and that she needed to go home and wait for him there. Her dad was an airline pilot, and he could probably fly everyone to safety if the situation was too bad.

After the plan was laid out on paper, Kaylee read it over. Her smile drained. It was full of sloppy sentences, which she scratched out in a huff. Eventually she gave up on the first draft and started writing the plan all over again. It was taking forever. Her nerves were on edge and unsure if Lucas, and especially the other boys, would take her plan seriously. This was clearly what they needed to do. It was obvious.

***

On another food run, farther from the school, Kaylee kept watch outside while the group rummaged through the house. Soft rustles from the bushes, and then a tiny creature leapt out. It was a kitten the size of her palm. Instantly she went for it, creeping down the stairs. The baby cat gazed up at her and began to meow. Once it started, it kept on meowing over and over with a high-pitched squeal. The animal seemed hungry, skinny, and apparently abandoned. Kaylee held the cat to her chest and wished there was some food to provide.

This kitten sported tiger stripes in its grey fur, with splotches of white, and it had wide blue eyes. Kaylee needed to get it some food and water right away, so she entered the house. Dashing straight to the kitchen, she met up with the over-muscled Ruiz as he tore through cabinets and loaded dry goods into a sack. She pushed the cat into his face, smiling.

"What? Get that *gato* outta my face." Ruiz shook his head, and he sighed. "Chicks."

Kaylee searched for cat food, but nothing presented itself. Then Lucas marched in, taking inventory. She quickly presented the kitten, which meowed desperately.

"Colton? Aren't you watching the front?" Lucas ran to the front door. With his handgun aimed out at the world, he checked the porch.

"Colton! Come here!"

Kaylee trudged down the hallway with her newly found friend.

Lucas's face reddened.

"When I tell you to watch our backs, it's not optional. I mean, what were you thinking? We need to be able to rely on you. Dammit, Colton."

112

Kaylee moped, and she tried to seem apologetic. When she figured that he had chewed her out enough, she pointed at the kitten and then at her own open mouth.

"Like I don't have enough problems keeping you from getting us killed." Shaking his head, obviously annoyed, Lucas pushed her out onto the front porch, and he returned back inside to conclude the raid.

Later in the gymnasium, after Kaylee had fed the kitten evaporated milk and chicken leftovers, she carried the beast to the cot where Sara lived. When Sara caught sight of her, Kaylee held up the tiger, who peeked up at the cavernous gym.

"It's a kitty!" Sara sat up in her cot, where she had been coloring with crayons. Kaylee set it down.

"It's so adowable!" Sara cooed and stroked the kitten's fur, and she nestled it with her face. "Is it a girl cat or a boy cat?"

Kaylee shrugged. Inquisitively she reached and picked up the furball to take a peek. There didn't seem to be anything sticking out. On her pad she wrote a message.

I think it's a girl.

"Oh my Gawd. She's so cute. What are we gonna name her?" Sara bounced rapidly and wrestled with the kitten's paws.

Kaylee thought, and she wrote an answer.

Meower?

But Sara had already decided. "Little Paws. She gots little tiny kitty paws."

Kaylee crumpled up her note. Together they played with the kitten for an hour. Then Kaylee needed to find a box to keep Little Paws in.

Fourteen

In the sticky heat of the crowded gym, Kaylee awoke with her face stuck to pieces of notebook paper. She had fallen asleep writing, and now she felt dehydrated. Her teeth were in severe need of a brushing. As she sat up, she peeled a page off of her face. Movements rustled in the dark over near Tyretta's cot again. Ruiz and Tyretta sprang up and scampered off into the dim recesses of the school together.

Toothbrush in hand, Kaylee took off down the hallway. She progressed cautiously, listening for any sign of them. Her heartbeat thumped faster as she spied into the window of the door to the next classroom. Empty. She considered what she was doing, and what might happen if they caught her.

As she turned back, a misty figure shot at her face from the black. It looked a lot like Mom, formed from swirls of air particles.

"Hide!" Mom pointed her wavy arm into the nearest classroom, and she disintegrated.

Pattering footsteps approached. Many pounding feet rushed toward her. Kaylee jumped inside the nearest classroom, and she closed the door softly just in time. Figures charged past the door's window, shadow after shadow, storming in. These were strangers, dupes—at least six of them—invading the school!

Kaylee flattened herself back against the classroom wall, where a protruding metal box dug into her head and neck. The dupes passed by, leaving her standing alone just on the other side of the door. Behind her was the fire alarm, and she wondered what would happen if she pulled it.

Screw it.

Her fingers yanked the handle downward, and the school suddenly roared with bell chimes. Soon thunder echoed through the hallways. She couldn't decide what to do or where to go. She was supposed to be partnered with Dustin carrying arrows.

To avoid the hostile hallway, Kaylee fled to the row of windows. Outside, it was the middle of the night and deserted. She tested a window, and she climbed over and out. The bells rang ceaselessly. More gunshots popped. Some came from inside, but others shot outside in the schoolyard somewhere. Along the outer wall of the building, in the hedges, she spied up over the leaves, and she crept along. After she'd circled around to the front, she saw the gym. Her people held onto the walls.

Dustin shot arrows over the front wall from his perch to the side of the school bus. Bullets returned from outside.

"Turn that damn alarm off!"

He grabbed another arrow, and he searched over the top of the wall with a car mirror.

Kaylee stumbled into the yard, but no one noticed her. Back inside the gym, the scene was chaotic. A gun battle raged through the hallways unseen. She watched wounded people bleeding from bullet holes. Some of the girls treated the injured with first aid.

On the gym floor near the exit to the hallway was a pool of blood. Beside it lay an abandoned black semi-automatic pistol. Kaylee snatched it up. The gun belonged to her now. But she wasn't sure how to work it or check if it had any bullets or not. She spun around, trying to figure out which way to go next. Finally, the bells stopped clanging. She wasn't sure what was happening outside, but at least she could think straight again.

Sirens. The fire department was coming. Trucks raced closer, right toward the siege and the clouds of sulfur.

Kaylee ran outside and saw Lucas near the gym door. He called to Dustin, "How many out there?"

"I don't know, man. Twenty?"

Lucas spoke on the walkie-talkie. "How are we doing inside? Come in."

The response came back. The last dupes fled back out the way they had entered. They were probably regrouping.

"Fall back to the kitchen. Hold the kitchen and the gym."

"Got it." It was Ruiz on the other end of the radio.

Kaylee felt baffled from the concussions pounding the air. She snuck forward and climbed up onto Dustin's platform.

"Kaylee," he said. "What are you doing?"

She shrugged. Then she showed him the handgun.

"Oh, excellent!" Dustin held out his hand to receive it.

She shook her head and pulled back the weapon.

"You don't know how to shoot that damned thing!"

Kaylee decided to climb back down in a hurry, as this wasn't helping at all. There was no way she was giving up the weapon she just found. Dustin gave her a dirty look, and he returned to his bow with a fresh arrow.

She decided to hang out with Lucas instead. She waved at him as she jogged over. He stood with a long rifle strapped across his back, a shiny revolver in one hand and a walkie-talkie in the other, talking to the wall guards and ignoring her.

"Yeah, Colton. What?"

Kaylee shrugged, and she showed him that she was ready with the new black plastic covered pistol.

"Oh, please don't hurt yourself." He turned away, and he raised his walkie-talkie, "Talk to me. What's going on?"

The red flashing strobes of the fire truck washed over the stucco buildings. A ladder rotated into position atop the school's outer wall. In the glare, a man with an ax bounded forward atop the ladder. His silhouette stepped along the ladder atop the wall, and he surveyed the schoolyard.

He wasn't dressed in a fireman's uniform, but he acted like a fireman. Behind him followed another muscular man. Their blank, robotic faces made it almost certain that they were duped.

The first fireman dropped down inside the schoolyard. As he rose with his ax swung back over his shoulder, he jogged down along the inside of the wall toward the nearest defense platform, a cafeteria table with a chair on top and a boy standing on it.

Kaylee searched about. Lucas had disappeared back inside the gym. She took her whistle to alert the boy on the platform.

A second fireman dropped down, also bringing a large steel ax.

Kaylee blew the whistle madly. The boy on top of the platform spun back. He had been firing a rifle over the wall, but now the fireman was running at him. She scrambled toward them, blowing the whistle in a harsh staccato pattern. The boy on the table pulled his trigger, but the rifle was empty. The fireman chopped the legs out below the table platform and it crumbled, the boy along with it.

The second fireman approached with similar aggression, and then a third could be seen on the ladder above the school wall. Dustin let an arrow fly. It struck the first fireman in his shoulder. He fell back, dropping his ax. Dustin took aim at the second fireman.

Kaylee too took aim with her new pistol. As the second fireman ran up to the prone boy, Dustin shot his arrow, missing.

By this time, the knocked down boy had scampered away along the wall. The second ax man pursued at full speed. Kaylee took a breath, and she raised both hands to support the handgun. The ax man ran too fast, and she couldn't get him in the sight for very long. He was too far away.

Kaylee's finger stayed on the trigger, but the gun wobbled. The boy ran past Dustin's platform. The fireman turned his attention from the escaping boy to Dustin. As the ax-wielding man arrived and pulled back to swing, Dustin shot again at point-blank range. This arrow impacted the fireman in his belly, and he doubled over. Kaylee's hand still shook.

Lucas suddenly shouted, "Molotovs! Colton, come with me."

Instantly the two were inside the gym and running toward the coach's office. Lucas ripped open a cabinet, where bottles had been filled with gasoline and left waiting. He grabbed six of the glass bottles and a couple of cigarette lighters.

"Grab all you can."

Kaylee rested the pistol on the coach's metal desk, and she gathered up five gas-filled bottles. Lucas had run halfway across the gym and out, and she raced to keep up. Outside, Lucas stopped within throwing distance of the ladder truck. Already the third fireman was dead. Defenders had gathered along the front wall to repel the invasion. Kaylee brought her cocktails to Lucas, who began lighting them and tossing them at the fire truck. The second bottle landed on top of the ladder, setting a fireman's blue jeans ablaze. He fell right off the truck outside the wall.

"Colton, get those ready."

Kaylee shrugged.

"Put the rags in the top, open them up." Lucas lit another Molotov and threw it over the wall at the fire truck.

Teens hauled a cafeteria table toward Kaylee. She handed Lucas another bottle. He yelled to the others, "We gotta get that truck out of there!"

Rory, who shared the new platform with another boy, yelled back, "Shit's on fire, bro."

"Good." Lucas climbed up to see for himself. Their people fired back over the school walls and kept the dupes at bay. Several dozen pups amassed outside, mostly hiding in the houses across Jefferson Avenue.

Lucas thought a moment. "Who wants to drive that thing?"

"But it's burning," said another boy.

"It'll go out in a minute."

Kaylee tried to pass another bottle of gasoline, but Lucas declined. Gunshots continued to crater the school walls, launching jagged chips of concrete around the yard. The school's force fired back, although no one was hitting anyone else now. On the fire truck the splattered gasoline had all but burned out.

Lucas said, "Come on. Who wants to get us that fire truck? I need a volunteer."

No one was forthcoming. The air above the concrete wall was alive with lead.

"I gotta do it myself?"

Dustin Hafstead shouted back, "I'll do it. But it'll cost ya."

"Huh?" Lucas and the others turned and spotted him down below in the group.

"What? What do you want?"

"I want that thirty-aught-six rifle." This was Lucas's mint-condition weapon that Jaworski had gifted him.

"No way."

"Why not? You're not even usin' it. The middle of a battle, dude."

Lucas suddenly found himself in the spotlight. Everyone turned and waited for him to respond. He couldn't come up with an answer.

"Fine. For the rifle."

"Shake on it," said Dustin, his hand extended up at Lucas. The two shook hands quickly. Dustin grabbed a chair and shot off down the wall.

"You guys better shoot cover fire, and don't stop, man!"

Kaylee turned and ran back to the gym. As fast as she could, she sprinted into the coach's office and snatched that handgun back off the desk. Running back out again, she looked for a platform to climb up on.

On the ground lay two dead firemen in pools of blood. She cringed, her face twisting at the sight of them. Up onto a table, where Dustin had originally been stationed, she balanced on the plastic chair, and she kept her head low at the top edge of the wall. Down the line, Lucas gave his go-ahead, and the action resumed. Their side fired out over the wall into the houses across Jefferson.

Dustin climbed up onto the end of the overhanging ladder.

Kaylee popped her head up to look out. Ready with the handgun, she rested it on top of the wall to steady it. Suddenly two bullets exploded below her chin into the cement. She dropped down right off her chair and fell flat onto the table. Checking herself, she found no blood in sight. She picked the handgun back up and slowly stood.

On the table beside her sat Dustin's car mirror. Kaylee contorted her body to spy with the mirror out into the world. A couple of shadows passed on the perpendicular side street, and she could see them, but she couldn't aim at them.

Eventually, she decided to just try pulling the trigger. When she yanked back the tight lever, the gun exploded violently out of her hand. Her hand stung from the blow, and she felt so useless and stupid. The pistol was down in the dark somewhere in the dirt. Now she had to climb back down and find it.

The school bus roared, and the fire engine jolted into gear. Kaylee scrambled to find the handgun. Everything sounded louder and crazier all of a sudden. Her hand throbbed. She didn't think she could even squeeze the trigger again. Now she had to use her left hand, which didn't feel right at all. But the school bus moved, and the fire engine raced around Jefferson in an arc to enter the schoolyard.

Dupes roared in unison like a primitive choir as they fired shot after shot into the fire truck. Kaylee rushed to the school bus and hid behind it with her weapon.

Dustin raced the fire engine through the front gate and inside the school grounds until the extended ladder impaled the gym building and smashed a hole through its face.

The dupe mob swarmed through the gate.

The bus skidded into position, and Kaylee could hear the swarm outside bash into the side of the bus. Like a river of rats, they slithered in underneath.

Kaylee dropped behind the bus tires to see them, Both of her hands gripped the handgun. Then she closed her eyes and fired. Her face twisted up in unknowing horror as she pulled the trigger again and again. She didn't know whom she was shooting at, or why they were even attacking. She was too scared to do anything else.

Fifteen

Kaylee fired ten bullets blindly under the rear of the school bus, not seeing where they struck. Then the gun was empty. It just clicked instead.

New bodies forced their way through underneath the bus carriage. With hypnotized, staring eyes, the dupes didn't seem part of the real world anymore. Not even gunshot wounds deterred them from crawling inside past the corpses of their compatriots.

Dustin charged with his bow, attempting to nock an arrow as he jogged. Kaylee ran away from the bus down along the wall. She passed Dustin in transit, barely noticing him. At the table platform where she had previously delivered Molotov cocktails, she halted. Three of the gasoline bottles rested on the ground. A cigarette lighter sat adjacently on the cafeteria table.

She ground her teeth together. The melee at the school bus had worsened. The dupes threw everyone at that spot now. A dozen more on the outside rocked the bus back and forth, attempting to tip it over.

The Molotovs sat idly at Kaylee's feet. She was out of bullets and running out of options. Carefully she bent down and gathered up the three bottles of gasoline. With the bombs, she snuck back along the dark crease of the wall toward the bus battle.

Gunfire gushed from both sides. Dupes bashed into the bus *en masse*.

She stepped closer. Unsure if she was going to be able to do anything or not, Kaylee looked around the yard for someone else to pass the Molotovs.

Her plan was dangerous, as the dupe mob could see her skulk closer. Each time the bus rocked inward it opened up a sliver. Thirty feet from the bus Kaylee stopped. She circled to where they couldn't see her. Acrid smoke fouled the air.

Cautiously, she arranged the bottles on the ground. Rattled by the incessant explosions from the firearms and the screams and shouts, which hovered over the tumult, she took the cigarette lighter in her hand. If she didn't do something quickly, the dupes might storm inside and kill everyone, just like Sean. Molotov cocktails were horrible if they hit someone. Their fireballs pushed people back, though. Dupes were no exception.

If she could just throw one of the bombs over the top of the school bus, maybe they would all run away. The way things stood, everyone was going to be shot in this senseless bloodbath.

Kaylee lit the rag protruding from the top of the bottle. Once it caught flame, she shivered. It was too far to throw. Time was up.

She ran at the bus before it would explode in her hand. Her arm launched the bottle up high, where it bounced off the roof of the bus, and rolled off down on the other side. The flash and yellow glow shot up.

Everyone paused their shooting and howling for a moment. Flames caught onto some of the attackers on the outside of the school bus, and they rolled around on the sidewalk, trying to put their clothes out.

Kaylee ran back to the other bottles, and she looked back over her shoulder. The gunshots resumed. Kaylee fumbled to grab the second gas bottle, and likewise ignited it. This time her arm threw it clear over the top of the bus, and into the middle of the dupe mob at the gate. Shrieks pierced the night as fire spread in a mini-mushroom cloud. The outside of the bus glowed.

Kaylee raced back for the third bottle, but when she arrived there and took it up into her hand, the world had gone silent. All the shooting had ceased. The dupes retreated rapidly. Everyone lowered their weapons. The flames beside the school bus petered out, and the thick black smoke dissipated.

Their eyes stuck open like owls, Lucas, Dustin, and Ruiz stepped toward Kaylee together. She hovered there, exhausted, with the final Molotov in one hand and the cigarette lighter in the other. Her mind was blank. She felt hypnotized by it all, and she couldn't even be sure if it was over or not.

"Holy," said Ruiz. "*Loquita*, you're all right." He gently punched Kaylee's biceps, bobbing his head like a tourist.

"Colton, that was outstanding," said Lucas in his unconscious mimicking of Jaworski.

"Kaylee's badass, man." Dustin giggled.

Kaylee wasn't sure whether to smile now. She felt weak inside her core and completely out of control, like someone else was guiding her mind. She couldn't even remember much of what had just happened. Only that she felt like a puppet herself, controlled by fate. The only thing that she knew for sure was that she wanted to put the gasoline bottle back down. She felt relieved that she didn't have to light it and throw it like the others.

"Hey, Lucas, gimme my rifle," said Dustin.

"Saved your ass with this rifle," said Lucas. He looked on it lovingly, with disappointment.

"Thanks, man. Still mine. Gimme my gun. I earned it." Dustin snatched the rifle away and slung it over his shoulder.

Kaylee didn't feel comfortable leaving the Molotov in the middle of the schoolyard, lest Sara find it. She remembered the coach's office with the locked cabinet. Her feet trudged back toward the gymnasium, leaving the others arguing behind her. Delivering the gas cocktail back to where it had come from was her new mission. Her mind fantasized, trying to make sense of what she had done, and if she'd done the right thing or not, or if she was evil.

***

Under the harsh illumination of the morning sun, massive pools of dried blood stained the schoolyard. They had lost four of their own people, but five more refugees had recently shown up outside the gates.

The bodies of the dead, mostly crazed dupes who had dug underneath the school bus, numbered in the upper teens. The health hazard of it all became a major concern for Lucas and Caroline.

Kaylee still felt hypnotized and weird. She had been wrangled into helping dispose of the corpses, but they couldn't possibly dig so many graves on the football field. The situation was terrible no matter how one looked at it.

"Oh my God, oh my God, oh my God," Caroline Anderson chanted as she surveyed the carnage.

"We could burn 'em," suggested Rory at an *ad hoc* meeting in the front yard.

"We can't spare gas," responded Lucas.

Gas?

Kaylee suddenly thought the term familiar and positive. There was something she knew, and she could swear that this was true. She darted back inside the gym and to her cot, where she kept some personal effects beneath it, and located the strange key chain. She also grabbed her notebook and scribbled down a message for Lucas.

Outside, she rejoined them, and she presented her note.

"Huh?" Lucas took the message, and he gave it a cursory glance. "For real?" He stared down at her, bewildered.

She held up the key chain and jingled it.

"Uh," Lucas announced, "Colton says there's a gas tanker truck on M.L.K. Boulevard, and she has the keys."

They all turned to her, astonished. Kaylee nodded, trying to appear nonchalant, but she was very excited how everything had turned around for her so radically. They all took her notes seriously now. They even seemed jealous of how she had stopped the invaders with the gas bottles.

While they pulled the last of the bodies out from under the school bus, Kaylee decided to clean herself up. Covered in filth and soot, and probably blood, she was a stewing horror. Now that the night's assault was over—but it wasn't over. It was never going to be over. She felt spacey again, scrubbing her face and arms clean in the locker room. As she stared into the smeary mirror, her face appeared unfamiliar and surreal. She barely recognized herself. It was like watching a movie of her older self suddenly, something from the future, like she was aging rapidly.

Back at her cot, she gathered up her sheets of paper with her master plan written on them. The pages had scattered all over the floor during the scuffle. Whatever it said was going to have to be sufficient. There wasn't any time to redo anything now. She had to pass the words on to Lucas, because she had figured out the strategy. For a final touch, she stapled the pages together on the coach's stapler on her way out the door. She also smoothed the crinkles. Cleaned up and feeling more down to earth, Kaylee finally felt ready.

Lucas stood alone in the courtyard, and when he saw her, he called her over.

"Colton, we need you. You have to show them where this gas truck is."

Kaylee reluctantly nodded, but she was more concerned with her master plan, of course, than any of that gasoline business. She pushed her manifesto up at Lucas.

"Uh, now what?" He accepted the presentation without looking at it. "I'll try and get to it later."

Kaylee peered up at Lucas like a wounded animal.

"Hey, seriously, are you seeing this?" He pointed at the stack of dead bodies, bullet-ridden, drenched in a sickening brown fluid. Guys yanked at a stuck corpse beneath the bus's axle.

"Priorities, Colton."

Kaylee turned away.

Lucas called back, "We need you. Go with the raid party. You're positive there's a gas truck there, right?"

She nodded on her way around the fire truck to where they had parked the old Mustang out of sight.

Dustin spotted her first. "Kaylee? Are you sure about this?"

She nodded back.

Ruiz added, "You're totally, absolutely one hundred percent, right?"

Kaylee was sick of nodding all the time, and she felt like her head would eventually just fall right off and splatter on the concrete. Maybe then they'd be happy.

The car waited for the school bus to start. All of the bus's tires were flat. Most of the windows had been reduced to jagged edges, and the entire right side was charred. The bus frame wailed as it rolled backward on its rims.

Their grey Mustang pulled to the gate, but another dead body lay in its path just outside on the sidewalk, a disfigured heap toasted to a black char. Kaylee saw this corpse, unidentifiable, and she wanted to vomit. Her breathing ceased as she smooshed her eyes into her arm. The gory, mangled image remained in her mind though, sprawled out and twisted on the concrete, a grim reminder to everyone.

"Move that body, will ya!" Dustin shouted out the passenger window. It took a minute for the cleaners to come.

Caroline gunned the engine. They jetted out of the yard and down Jefferson Avenue. She raced around the big corner, barely slowing, and she floored it on Martin Luther King Boulevard.

"How far?"

Kaylee held up five fingers.

"Five," said Ruiz.

Caroline barked, "Five what? Miles? Blocks?"

Kaylee nodded.

"Blocks, blocks," said Ruiz.

Swiftly they homed in on the massive fuel truck. Caroline skidded to a stop beside the rear of the tanker.

"Somebody come with me."

Caroline pushed open her door and she jumped out, key chain in hand. She sized up the tanker.

"Come, quickly."

Dustin and Ruiz climbed out and searched around with their guns drawn. It was quiet, for the time being.

Caroline climbed into the cab of the tanker truck. Kaylee kept watch along the boulevard. Seconds dragged like hours.

"How you doin'?" asked Dustin.

Caroline turned the key and the truck rumbled to life. The engine pumped, revving several times.

Dustin lowered his rifle.

"We're good." He jumped back into the Mustang before Ruiz had a chance to grab the driver's seat. "Let's get, *hombre*."

In the side mirror Kaylee spotted them. Two cars, each full of dupes, raced up the boulevard behind them.

"We've got problems!" said Ruiz. "Go! Get, dude!"

Dustin jerked the car into drive and pulled forward. Kaylee could hear Caroline struggling to work the gears of the tractor trailer. It was too late. The enemies arrived at the fuel truck, shooting out of their windows.

Ruiz fired back. The second dupe car rushed around to intercept them.

Kaylee crouched down low in the back seat. Bullets zinged up overhead as hell unleashed. Dustin floored it, and Kaylee was thrown about.

The four vehicles chased down Martin Luther King Boulevard around garbage cans and abandoned cars. The tanker truck whipped over and crashed into the first dupe vehicle. The persistent car kept pace with Caroline, narrowly escaping smashing into a telephone pole.

She had the truck really moving, but they were all headed in the exact wrong direction, away from the school. They had to turn the whole crazy caravan around and hopefully not run into any more armed hostiles along the way.

Ruiz fired his handgun continuously as they jerked around obstacles and abandoned cars, which littered the boulevard. Dustin whipped the Mustang a hundred and eighty degrees. Ruiz reloaded another clip of ammunition, and he climbed halfway out his window in order to shoot across the roof at the pursuing dupes.

Caroline slowed the fuel truck, and she ran up over the curb and through an abandoned lot in order to turn around towards the school. The tanker leaked a steady stream of fuel from bullet holes. A trail of gasoline dribbled out as she bounced up over a second curb.

Dustin wrenched his steering wheel left and right, and the Mustang snaked around hazards.

The pursuing dupe car came up alongside them. Dustin slammed his car into their front end to try and knock them to the side.

Caroline raced the tanker down M.L.K. Boulevard as the whole parade approached Jefferson at high speed. Ignoring the cars abandoned in the center of the road, Caroline plowed through them without even slowing down.

Kaylee felt so helpless again, like a rag doll instead of a puppet, like she had in the attic crawlspace.

Right behind, pursuing dupes raced up and crashed into their rear bumper. Her head flew back, hurting her neck, which she grabbed with both her hands. All she wanted to do was scream, but she couldn't even do that.

"Shoot him, Ruiz! I'm gonna hit the brakes."

Dustin jammed the brakes, and the other car rammed them hard. But Dustin kept the brakes on, slowing everyone down to nearly a stop. Ruiz jumped up and twisted out his side window. Then he fired four bullets back into their windshield. Blood could be seen on the spider-webbed glass behind them. The Mustang shot forward again like a rocket, while the pursuing dupe car stayed put where it was. They were free, and they turned right onto Jefferson Avenue unmolested.

Caroline and the big tanker also made the wide arc onto Jefferson, pursued by the second dupe car. The tanker outclassed their little Honda by thousands of pounds. The dupes had no chance of forcing past. Caroline wrestled the wheel back and forth, daring them to try. The pursuing dupe car braked abruptly and snuck off like a reptile up a side street to melt back into dupe-controlled suburbia.

Kaylee saw that Lucas had planned two steps ahead. The bus gate was already open for them. Dustin drove the Mustang back to the end of the courtyard, and squeezed between the school buildings. Plenty of space remained for the tanker truck to hide in the courtyard. Lucas immediately spotted gasoline streaming out the back of the tank. He raced over to plug the holes. A group went to work patching the truck and cleaning the pool of gasoline that spilled out as they worked.

Kaylee instantly became a star celebrity. For now. When word passed around the school of her deeds, an air of legend spread. It seemed like she had done so much, so fast, and she couldn't even talk. It was quite the story, which occupied almost everyone's attention and took their minds off of the daily horrors of the war. Each had to decide whether they liked her or not, and to justify their reasoning about her, because everyone just suddenly seemed to like her.

Kaylee took a much-needed rest, as she could remain awake no longer. Dead to the world of Jefferson High School and its machinations, she slumbered through the entire day.

Kaylee tried repeatedly to recover, on her cot. She couldn't wake up, even though her dreams were dismal, suffocating, paralyzing. Her entire body felt like a sack of wet mud, or a charred corpse. She pressed her face down into her pillow, afraid to awaken. Chilled at what she had become now, she despised this world and everything about it. Nothing was worth this kind of insanity.

Most of all, she was sure she was losing her mind. Her visions of Mom, they couldn't be real. A deep black chasm stretched out before her, too vast and too monstrous to face.

So she slept, hoping that possibly, in some unlikely reality, that it would all just float away. If she just stayed asleep long enough, maybe the horror would vanish. Maybe it was all just a bad dream after all.

Sixteen

A squeaky little voice wafted in, "Kaylee? You want some dinner?"

Kaylee opened an eye just enough to see little Sara gawking down at her through the blur.

"Hi. There's food."

She flopped her face back down and closed her eye.

"Huh," said Sara. "She's a flumpy-head." The plate was left on the floor below the cot, and Sara stepped off alone.

Gentle pulls back and forth on her arm, Kaylee stirred again. It was Caroline Anderson this time, and darkness had fallen.

"We need you, Kaylee. I pushed back your shift, but we're short on the walls."

Kaylee yawned.

Caroline helped her sit up straight and find her bearings.

"Are you okay, dear?" Caroline sat beside her on her cot.

Kaylee looked around the disheveled gym, depressed.

"You didn't eat, did you? There's food here." Caroline bent down and grabbed the rice plate. She offered it to Kaylee. The dinner was cold and soggy, but she realized how weak and hungry she had become. Rapidly, she vacuumed up the rice.

"Are you better now?"

Kaylee inhaled a couple of gusts, and she shook her head back and forth, feeling nauseous and ready to lie back down.

"What's the matter, honey? Do you want me to get you a pencil and-"

Kaylee reached over and extended her arms around Caroline's torso. Closing her eyes, she squeezed tightly.

Holding Caroline felt odd and different, much stockier and more muscular than Mom, not even a close substitute. Caroline petted her hair momentarily, and then Kaylee pulled away.

"All right. Come on." Caroline stood. Kaylee braced herself and rose. The pair started off toward the coach's office.

"We captured a bunch of guns and some bullets," Caroline said as they walked. "Pick yourself one that's small."

Kaylee's eyes opened wide, and the gym brightened. A cache of firearms was laid out on the coach's desk. Among them was the black, square-looking handgun she had fired yesterday. She took it into her hand. Pointing at the bottom of the handle, where the bullets were supposed to go, Kaylee looked up to Caroline, who shrugged.

Kaylee searched around. Several boxes of bullets sat in a pile on the coach's desk. She tried to make sense of the caliber numbers. She remembered how the clip slid out from the black handle, and she carefully ejected it, relieved that someone had filled it back up with more bullets already.

"You like that one?" Caroline stepped over. "That's a very good gun. And it has a safety switch. Here, let me show you."

Caroline took it, and she slid the long steel clip back inside. Then she pulled back the rail on top and it clicked into place.

"Look," she said. "This switch, if you can see the red dot, that means it's ready to fire. If you flip it up, then it won't go off." She moved the switch, and she tried to pull the trigger, but nothing happened. "You see?"

Kaylee nodded.

"All right, there's no holster to hold it in. Maybe you could make one when you get some time?"

Kaylee shrugged.

"We gotta get out on the wall, now, Kaylee. Come on, honey. You can do it."

Kaylee still wanted to know about the bullets. She jerked her wrist free, and she pointed at the several boxes of rounds.

"Ah." Caroline returned to the desk. "That one is a nine millimeter."

There were 9mm bullets in several large boxes. Hundreds of them or more, which provided Kaylee some measure of comfort.

Caroline rushed out toward the exit. Calling back, she said, "They've been testing us all night. Come on. Come on."

Kaylee stuffed her front backpack pocket with bullets. Zipping it up, she turned and plodded off toward the schoolyard.

***

Breakfast was paltry. Already food was scarce and the offerings sub-par. Faces in the cafeteria reflected the diminishing resources, and none were too happy with the situation, except for Sara, who never seemed too concerned about anything. Sara concentrated on playing with her kitten, Little Paws, and she ignored the grown-up chatter.

Kaylee carried her mushy creamed corn and boiled turnips to the honcho's table, where Lucas and the others ate together daily. After she placed down her tray, she tapped Lucas on his shoulder.

"Yeah?"

Kaylee made hand gestures about reading papers.

"Oh yeah. That." Lucas nodded back to her. "Colton's got some ideas that are interesting. You guys, quiet down."

The table chatter dropped to a minimum. Ruiz and Tyretta continued on softly, together at the far end, with pointless gossip from her and patient endurance from him.

Dustin peered up momentarily, and then continued eating his portion of the same gloop. Rory glanced over and smiled at Kaylee, his crooked face staring oddly, like—was he trying to flirt?

"We could take out the TV stations and dishes and stuff when we go out," said Lucas. "There's just so many dishes, it's probably counterproductive to try and get them all. And cell phone towers. They do video, and what about the Wi-Fi?"

Kaylee felt deflated.

"I mean, it's worth doing, but I don't know if it's going to work."

Dustin peered up from his food again.

"Sounds like a good idea."

Kaylee was jolted, thrilled that Dustin agreed with her master plan. She beamed as she caught his eye.

"All right," said Lucas. "So who thinks we should try and take out the TV signal wherever we can?" He searched around for a consensus. Everyone raised his hand, except for Tyretta. But when Ruiz raised his, he elbowed her to join in. Reluctantly, she flipped up her hand for a second, sneering at Kaylee.

"Okay." Lucas stood up to leave, but Kaylee remembered all the rest of her master plan. She waved rapidly to catch his attention.

"Oh. There's more." Lucas sat back down. "Colton wants to try capturing the pups and deprogramming them."

Tyretta and Ruiz burst into laughter. This levity spread down the line to Rory and even to Dustin.

"No! No." Lucas objected. "It's actually a good idea, if they're not armed and trying to take your head off."

"Dude," Dustin said, "that one the other night didn't have no weapon but he still tried to bite me. Crazy, they're crazy outta their minds! You can't capture 'em."

"Yeah, well, maybe we could work on that problem," said Lucas. "There's got to be a way to do it."

Kaylee gauged their responses. Deep down, she knew that her brother was out there fighting on the other side. If there was a chance at saving him and taking him away from the dupes, she wanted to hang onto that possibility. She didn't want to hate Sean, and she sure didn't want to kill him. Actually she didn't want to kill anyone. There had to be a solution to win without becoming just like them.

They debated the merits of Kaylee's master plan. Word spread to the other tables. They thought about it, and they would make a point of finding all the cellphone towers and the TV station antennas, and the giant satellite dishes that sent the signals up into space, and, more importantly, brought them back down. There were so many pathways for the dupes to infect minds and grow their forces.

They also discussed telephone lines and the underground cables and assigned a team of researchers to look into possible targets. Melanie was the most studious and meticulous researcher they had, and so she was put in charge of the working group. She would have her team scour the telephone books and the library sources for information about the locations of all the local media facilities.

Caroline Anderson sauntered over, somber and cryptic, to interrupt their discussion at the leader's table.

"Ahem!"

The table quieted.

"That was the last can," she said. "We are empty."

Lucas smiled casually.

"Looks like we're going out and get some food. I assume everybody's on board?"

Most of them were happy to oblige.

"All right," he said, and he checked his watch against the clock above the cafeteria door. "One hour, in the yard. That's it." Lucas jumped up with energy on display, and he marched out the door.

Kaylee saw that Lucas had left her master plan papers sitting beside his tray. She rushed to grab them back. Caroline strolled toward the kitchen. Kaylee scrambled to catch up with her and tugged at her elbow.

"What!" Caroline jumped back. "Oh, Kaylee. Don't sneak up on me. Ever! Ever."

Kaylee cowered momentarily, and then offered up the plan.

"All right. All right." Caroline perused the first few lines of it. "I'll read it later."

Kaylee nodded, and she started off.

Caroline called back over Kaylee's shoulder. "And you, you be careful out there."

Kaylee procured her 9mm pistol from her backpack, and she tenderly laid it on her cot.

Maybe some practice was in order.

If I have to load the pistol again, what then?

It was daunting to think of loading it from scratch, especially in the middle of a crazy attack.

Carefully, she plucked out every single bullet from within the spring-loaded clip. After a long breath, she began to insert them back into the magazine, the way the boys did it. The first few bullets snapped in easily, but then it became stiffer as it filled up. When she finished that task, she slid the clip into the handle of the handgun and snapped it into place. By now, she felt very self-satisfied. Her finger clicked the safety on, and off. And she grabbed and pulled back the slider to cock it, like Caroline had done. Once it was ready to fire, her body rattled with extreme nervousness. She wanted to just place the gun down and leave it alone, but she couldn't.

Time ticked. Kaylee looked to the gym's round wall clock above the outer door. There was still time enough to try it again, the whole routine from the start. The little machine took all her concentration, and she put everything else out of her head.

Slide out the clip. Cock the slider thingy and pop out the other bullet. Remove all of them, and line them up on the bed.

She added a new step to the routine. When she was pretty positive that it was empty of rounds and as unloaded as it could get, she pointed it up at the roof. Squinting, she clicked the trigger.

Kaylee loaded the clip and pushed it back into the gun's handle, moved the safety lock switch into position, and zipped the gun up into the petite front pocket of her backpack.

***

Their raiding party moved from house to house, just around the corner from the rear of the school. They soon found that the dupes had already cleaned out all the houses near Jefferson. It was a fruitless quest.

After the fourth house, and after smashing a couple of small TV dishes, the squad turned restless. Apparently the enemy was smarter than they had anticipated.

Kaylee could see in Lucas's face that he was genuinely scared. The tranquil side street was lined with cars. Lucas took an interest in them instead. He strolled to the curb, assessing a particularly attractive red sports car.

"Who knows how to hot-wire a car?"

Kaylee demurely raised her hand.

"Colton, come on. Seriously?" He stepped back, shaking his head and laughing.

She smiled. Lucas kept his eye on the slick red sedan, which looked lonely with no one taking care of it any longer.

"Here's one. Can you get it started?"

She shrugged. The car was locked, and that posed a problem. While Lucas and Rory contemplated how to get into the car without damaging the finish or breaking the windows, Kaylee spotted an ancient white pickup truck across the street, its driver-side window half open. She pointed at it.

Lucas seemed disappointed, but he considered it anyway. "Yeah, whatever. Will it work?"

Kaylee strolled to the truck, and she went to work inspecting the pickup's steering column. After a minute inside, she called Lucas over with her hand.

"Did you get it?"

She shook her head. Her fist punched at the plastic covering over the steering column, and she gestured for him to break it off.

"We gotta? Oh." Lucas leaned in, crowding Kaylee, who was twisted and wedged down in the seat awkwardly. She scooted over to the passenger side, and she hammered down at the column to make her point.

"A'right, a'right. We need a tool." Lucas dug behind the driver's seat and produced a tire iron. He went to work busting into the plastic housing and cracking it apart. Kaylee rifled through her backpack and found the serrated knife. Once Lucas ripped the last of the plastic covering off, he took a step back, curious.

Kaylee bent down close to the wires, and she tried to make sense of the colors, and which directions they ran. She tried to look cool as she sliced through them and started shaving at the plastic ends, which covered the copper.

"Which wire's which?" said Lucas.

Kaylee's palm went up for patience. Ruiz and his crew exited a house across the street, and Lucas shouted to them, "Anything?"

"Nah. It's all dry."

"Dammit!"

Tyretta shouted back, "Where we gonna find some food, Lucas? You're the one who brought us here. You know what the hell you're doing?"

With that, Kaylee sparked the starter motor, and it revved.

"Whoa!" Lucas whipped around. "What did you do?" He shoved his face back in beside Kaylee. She felt nervous and strange being so close to Lucas, with his breath hitting her right on the side of her neck.

She sparked the starter again, and she pressed the gas pedal down. The truck coughed to an ugly-sounding start. The others in the raiding party looked over.

Lucas seemed fascinated. "Is it going to stay?"

Kaylee twisted a pair of wires tightly together, and she stuffed them back up into the column. She felt moderately confident in them, but she really needed tape to be sure.

"Let me in. Scoot over." Lucas jumped down into the driver's seat, forcing Kaylee back to the passenger side. He revved the engine and situated himself, jamming the stick shift into reverse. She grabbed at her seat belt instinctively. The parking brake was still on, and Lucas figured out how to release it with a jolt.

The pickup truck rolled backward down the driveway.

"Colton, you should get a medal. Damn, you keep surprising me."

She grinned back, and Lucas yelled out to the party, "Get in. This area's dead. Let's go a few blocks over."

Everyone piled into the back bed of the truck, except Rory. He yanked open Kaylee's side door when she wasn't looking, and he tried to squeeze in beside her. Kaylee, in abhorrent disgust, pushed him back out.

"Aw, come on," said Rory. "I call shotgun."

Kaylee wasn't having it, and she wrestled the door away from Rory's hand and slammed it back shut.

"Dumb bitch!" Rory stormed off, and he climbed aboard in the back bed with the others, running his mouth the entire time.

Lucas couldn't help but snicker.

"Is everybody in?"

They shouted back. Lucas moved the white truck out. Their old pickup crawled slowly around the first corner. Tensions ran high as the crew in the rear aimed their weapons at the silent houses.

"Colton, are you armed?" Lucas looked over momentarily. He seemed apprehensive.

Kaylee dug into her pack, and she carefully slid out the 9mm.

"Open your window," he said. "Keep your eyes sharp."

She did so and grasped tightly at the pistol handle, watching the houses float dreamily by.

"What do you think?" said Lucas. "Another block?"

She nodded back, and Lucas turned the wheel. This new street overflowed with dupes. Everywhere, organized, training, at least a hundred of them. The dupe forces had cars, supplies, food—and they were bunched up in rectangular formations like military units.

Lucas jammed the brakes. The pickup truck whipped around, but not before the barrage of shooting commenced. He steered up onto the curb and turned them around. Kaylee could feel the incoming bullets impacting the truck's metal skin. These dupes were well-armed, and about five guns fired simultaneously.

She pushed her 9mm out of her window, and she pulled the trigger, but nothing happened. The damned safety was on. Then she clicked it off and tried again. Nothing happened. She kept pulling the trigger, but it was dead.

The truck jerked and rocketed, and Rory flew off down onto the street, tumbling on his back. Those in back shouted for Lucas to stop the truck. He had already gunned the engine, intent on getting them out of the line of fire. Rory lay abandoned in the street controlled by the dupes.

What's the matter with this thing?

Kaylee pulled at the trigger, over and over, but nothing was coming out at all. Then she remembered the slider on the top. She grabbed the top piece of the handgun and yanked it back to cock it.

Dammit! Dammit!

She felt so stupid. By now they were safely around the corner and parked beside the nearest house. Dupe forces were massed just around the block behind them.

"Is Rory still alive?" Lucas couldn't see back to where they had dropped him.

Ruiz yelled, "Yeah! He should be!"

"Well, get him!"

After several dammits, Kaylee could hear them arguing.

"You go," said Ruiz.

"Hell no," said Dustin. "You go."

Tyretta yelled over the both of them, "Ruiz don't even like that fool! Needs to learn how to hold on for his self."

"Hurry up, stupids!" Lucas pounded on the steering wheel. Kaylee opened her door, and she jumped out with her own gun extended. It was Rory, whom she wouldn't let sit beside her. She felt empty in her stomach. This was sort of her fault. She might just have gotten Rory killed.

The other boys ran back toward the shooting to go fetch him, and maybe they'd be killed too.

Kaylee's hands jerked with confusion, not wanting to point the gun at her own guys. All she could do was watch the boys rush toward the corner of the house ahead of her.

As Dustin and Ruiz converged at the corner, Rory crashed into them at top speed, screaming like a girl and fleeing from the tsunami of dupers. Hysterical, the gang charged back to the pickup truck and piled in on top of one another like the Keystone Cops. Lucas floored the chugging engine and burned the tires as they shot off ahead of the stampeding army of puppet people.

The jittery old pickup carried Kaylee and her team back to Jefferson High School. They had found zero supplies, no food or drinks, just this truck. The squad was demoralized, worried sick about the massing number of armed dupes, who were gathered about five blocks away. They needed to warn the school, and they needed a new survival plan in a hurry, a safe place to locate enough food to feed everyone.

Lucas dashed out of the pickup as soon as it skidded to a stop in the schoolyard.

"Where's Melanie? I need the maps..." He ran off, searching.

In her seat Kaylee tried to calm herself as she stared down at that red-orange dot on the side of her handgun. Her mind felt light again, and she felt out of her own body, like some ethereal witness, a ghost hovering in the air of the truck's cab. That little red dot, or it could be orange, it meant *something*. The handgun was loaded. It could go off. It could expel a deadly bullet at any moment. She decided to click the safety back on. She stowed the killing machine away inside of her backpack, along with her hidden cache of bullets and her serrated steak knife.

Rory limped away from the rear of the pickup on his own power. His leg seemed sprained, his back hunched. As he glanced back at Kaylee, he sent her a frosty, bitter look.

Kaylee turned, content to ignore him. After Rory disappeared inside the gym, her guilt festered. Clouds rolled and a breeze kicked up. The air in the schoolyard felt chilly all of a sudden. Food was harder to come by, and the situation was worse than any of them had imagined.

"You didn't get no food, Kaylee?" Little Sara peered up, trailing behind Kaylee like a puppy dog.

Kaylee shook her head, and Sara's face instantly fell sadly morbid.

"Should I go with you next time?" said Sara, whose little hazel eyes welled up.

Kaylee shook her head.

"I want to do something." Sara stopped in place to think, peering down at the ground, lost in her worries.

Kaylee turned back to watch Sara brooding at the center of the schoolyard and peering randomly around.

"I'm hungry. What are we gonna eat?"

Kaylee sat down cross-legged on the pavement. Her backpack dropped behind her, and her shoulders were rubbed raw from the weight of lugging it everywhere.

Sara poked at the backpack. "Do *you* have some food?"

Kaylee shook her head.

"Me neither."

Kaylee smiled. She opened her arms, and Sara rushed in to give her a crushing hug.

"We'll find some food."

Kaylee nodded.

"Colton, you might want to get in on this." Lucas marched past, leading Melanie and a couple of others, including Rory, still limping. Kaylee reached for her backpack to follow them inside and to the cafeteria.

Lucas spread out their maps. These were colored over with marks and codes. The additional markings attempted to make sense of the surrounding town. Melanie sat silently with a pack of colored, thin-tipped markers, and she consulted her notes.

Kaylee found a seat at the table, and Sara plopped down beside her with Little Paws.

"People, people, come on, quick." Lucas jerked about uneasily. "We're screwed as of right now."

The cafeteria deadened with silence. Everyone cringed, twenty-two of them in all. Caroline Anderson spoke from her seat, "What happened out there?"

"School's gonna be surrounded any minute."

Gasps. Terror passed through most of the teens in attendance.

Lucas spun about, and his facial expression lost its hard edge. He looked more like a small boy and less like the barking Sergeant Jaworski.

"We're out of food, and they're going to attempt to trap us."

Dustin said, "Where do we go, man?"

"I don't know!"

Caroline said, "This is no good. We have to do something."

"What?"

"I don't know." She looked across their faces. "How did you get that truck?"

The insiders turned to Kaylee.

"Colton hot-wired it."

"Kaylee?" said Caroline. "You know how to hot-wire cars?"

Kaylee nodded back.

"Can you write it down? So everyone can do it?"

They pushed notepads across the table at her. Kaylee grabbed a pen and scribbled away.

Ruiz stood up, a sawed-off shotgun still in his hands. "But where the hell can we all go? Would somebody tell me that?"

Lucas pulled the town map closer. "We go where the food is. Right?"

"Where's that?" said Dustin.

"Here." Lucas brought his finger down on a blue square.

"What is it?"

"Colton, you done with that yet?"

Kaylee looked up momentarily but returned to her scrawling. There was a lot to remember.

Sometimes the steering wheel is just locked in place and won't move, and really old cars are probably better. And sometimes the shifter is stuck, too, and won't go into drive at all. And it would be technically illegal if there were still laws working. And the wires have different colors sometimes, so you can't tell right away which is which, but you should never touch the red to the black directly or it is really bad...

"Colton! Come on, somebody have a look at it," said Lucas. "Melanie, you read it."

Caroline said, "How do you know it's not worse over there than it is right here?"

"I don't."

Caroline huffed out, and she sat back down, flabbergasted. "Jesus, Lucas, you want to have us all drive right into a trap?"

Melanie tapped Kaylee's shoulder. She was about a year older and very polite. Her head sported neatly combed brown hair and bangs. She also wore eyeglasses and kept her skirt and her top crisp and clean.

"May I read it, please?"

Kaylee nodded.

"Thank you." Melanie carried the papers back over to her own spot, and she began correcting it, crossing out parts, and then transcribing the instructions onto a pristine sheet of white copy paper.

Kaylee gawked. Little Sara sat excited beside her, and she grinned broadly, bouncing the kitten on her knee. The older ones argued about the tentative plans being cooked up for their survival.

"We gotta hit this food warehouse, Right now!" Lucas shouted.

When finished transcribing, Melanie whipped the paper up. She handed it to another studious-looking boy beside her, and he copied it onto a second sheet of paper. The two of them churned away and made multiple copies of Kaylee's one-sheet car hot-wiring manual. The two worked together very quickly and efficiently. Kaylee was amazed at how well they cooperated.

"What about you, Colton?" Lucas gazed back at Kaylee as the other fighters slipped out the cafeteria door to prepare themselves.

Kaylee considered as she looked back at the remaining teens, and at Sara. This was a different kind of mission, and she had no idea if the people left behind were doomed. If all those dupes arrived outside the school's walls, they might not be able to hold on.

She needed to ask Lucas one thing first. On her notepad she wrote out a question.

Are we coming back for them?

He turned somber. "Probably. I mean. We don't know if we're even gonna make it into the food depot, Colton. We're gonna do what we can and hope for the best. What more can I do?" He marched back out toward the gym alone.

Kaylee stood at the cafeteria door between the two worlds. There she turned back to see a few of the faces that had recently become familiar. Inside the Jefferson cafeteria, the mood became like that of a funeral. Caroline Anderson cried, and several of the girls attempted to comfort her. The sadness was virulent.

Seventeen

Lucas marched back in, and he called out to them, "We've got room for three more."

"Me! Me, me, me," Sara squeaked and ran over to Lucas.

"No, Sara. Not this time."

Sara stormed off with her cat, cursing Lucas. "Jerky, jerk boy..."

Three more teenagers, two boys and a girl, jumped at the chance to escape the school, perhaps permanently.

The vehicles were gassed to the maximum. School defenders employed every old container on the premises to fill gasoline bombs from the fuel truck. Their school bus started again, and it twitched back on its flat, torn-up tires. In the distance, the dupe forces could be heard, and their electronic pulsing noise wafted in on the breeze.

"We'll try and come back with supplies," said Lucas from behind the wheel of the white pickup truck. Dustin drove the Mustang.

Kaylee rode behind Dustin in the back seat, as usual. Two of the new kids, a boy and a girl, crowded in beside her. Ruiz rode in the front seat shadowed by Tyretta in the middle.

Their vehicles sped around the blocks and toward the highway on-ramp. All their nearest enemies seemed to have gathered at that previous sighting, on the far side of Jefferson. The roads were deserted. The highway was clear up to the horizon, and their two cars raced along unimpeded.

Kaylee spotted a large antenna and a building with satellite dishes arrayed in a line. She banged on the driver's window beside Dustin's head, and she pointed to the left.

"What? What the hell?" Dustin looked around, and Ruiz leaned over to better see across him.

Ruiz said, "Looks like a TV station."

Dustin slowed their car, allowing the old pickup to catch up to them. After a second, he clicked on his turn signal. Everyone searched near the off-ramp for any signs of suspicious activity.

Lucas pulled up beside them. "What are you doing?"

Dustin yelled, "TV station."

"All right. Let's check it out, fast."

They pulled around and through the underpass. That antenna structure shot up a couple of hundred feet. The parking lot was seemingly abandoned.

"Looks nice and quiet," said Ruiz. He pointed his handgun at the car's roof.

Kaylee saw the two new faces quivering in terror beside her. She whipped back to her window, her own handgun at the ready. Heart pulsing faster, she suddenly realized that she wasn't so afraid as before, like she used to be. The two new teens seemed too scared to even function, but Kaylee felt ready and able, like she was starting to get used to it.

They parked at the far edge of the television station's parking lot, highly suspicious of the place. The building was a one-story office, relatively small and secluded. Dustin and Ruiz bolted out of the car, their guns trained on the glass entrance doors. Kaylee, too, climbed out. The boys from the pickup truck flooded across the parking lot, and they all closed in on the station one step at a time. It seemed too quiet. No one home at all. Perhaps the TV workers were part of that huge gathering they had witnessed near Jefferson.

Lucas said, "Maybe it's abandoned?"

The group stormed in through the front doors. Inside, everything was running, all the lights, all the computers, all the monitors. As Kaylee stepped toward the broadcast booth, that screeching pulse noise grew louder. It came from inside the machines and was broadcast out constantly.

Dustin stopped.

"Wait. You hear that? Stop! Stop!" Their platoon froze in place. Several kids brought along Molotovs. They produced them and got ready to light them up. The sign on the door said "Editing," and a sickly blue glow throbbed out from inside the dark chamber.

Lucas decided, "Torch it. Torch it all."

They nodded. Everyone backed away. Down the hallway, Kaylee could see a lunch room and part of a refrigerator through the doorway. She tapped Dustin's arm. Pointing at the end of the hallway, she gestured, appearing famished.

"Let's check down there." Dustin, Kaylee, Ruiz, and Tyretta snuck along the station's hallway as gasoline bombs exploded back around the corner.

The station's lunch break room was clear until everyone raced each other to be first at the refrigerator. Pushing to rummage through, Kaylee knelt down low on the floor and ducked beneath the others. Grabbing fiercely, they seized the old stale lunches and a few pieces of birthday cake left over from the previous week. Kaylee managed to hang onto half a tuna fish sandwich and a red apple, which she stowed inside her backpack for Sara.

They cleaned out the lunch room before any of the flames spread too far from the broadcast booth, but the black, toxic smoke set off the fire alarms and sprinklers. Their group dashed out of the emergency exit, and they found themselves in a small, weedy field where the tall antenna jutted up toward the sky.

"Everyone out?" Lucas jammed his hand down into a box of cereal, and he chewed as he spoke. "Count. Count everybody."

They tried to figure out the total number. Rory's face featured vanilla icing smeared across his lips and nose.

They next focused to the antenna. Dustin charged over to look at the massive steel cables, which stabilized it on three sides.

Lookouts watched the road. The whole TV station caught fire pretty well, but the sprinklers fought back.

"We gotta deal with this antenna," said Dustin.

"And we need to do it quick, too," answered Lucas, on edge.

Gigantic bolts secured the steel cables. The antenna itself was mounted on concrete and steel. Plus, there were signs warning about high voltage and death by electrocution. As they investigated the other electrical structures at the side of the building, Rory shouted, "I'll do it!"

Rory jogged off awkwardly to the parking lot. Lucas and Dustin tried to force open the padlocked metal door on the housing of the electrical components.

Suddenly the pickup truck roared, and everyone perked up with concern.

"The hell's he doin'?" Dustin ran to see.

Rory jerked the truck toward them, and he crashed right over the four-foot high chain link fence at the edge of the parking lot, dragging it forward.

"Rory!" said Lucas. "What are you doing?" He marched toward the plowing pickup, but he was too late. Rory bounded the vehicle over the curb and toward the massive antenna in the middle of the dirt field.

"Oh no." Lucas stood frozen, watching as Rory crashed into the steel support cable. The entire height of the antenna jolted with the shockwave like a dancing spring.

Those on foot retreated in a hurry. The pickup truck stuck. The cable gouged into the front bumper and hood. Rory reversed, and he backed up, ready to hit it again.

Smiling like a naughty two-year-old, he turned to the group and gave them a wishful thumbs up. Everyone gawked and wondered if he could do it or not. Rory revved the truck engine, kicking up dirt behind him in a brown cloud, and he slammed into the supporting cable. The impact twisted the truck around, spinning it out. With the steel cable deformed, suddenly the antenna structure buckled in the center and started collapsing in the direction of Rory's pickup.

Everyone shouted at him, and he jammed the wheel over. The truck zigzagged clear of the support cable. The antenna crunched to the ground in almost slow motion, jolting the earth with high voltage sparks and sizzling crackles. Rory whipped the truck across the sand and weeds, aiming for the hole in the fence. As he pulled it up beside the group, he said, "That's how you do it, boys and girls."

Kaylee rolled her eyes, unimpressed. Rory could have been zapped like a bug, and their truck, which they all needed to get away, could have been toasted.

They took in the death of the TV station and decompressed. Lucas looked back at Rory.

"Don't ever take that truck again without asking."

"Hey, *pukas*," said Rory. "It worked. You're welcome very much, Supreme Leader."

"Don't start with me."

Ruiz had heard enough.

"Goddammit." He stomped over to Rory, grabbed him by the shirt, and yanked him around like a toy. "We all need that truck to get back, *stupido*. You want us to leave you here?"

Rory squirmed. "All right, all right! Gorilla."

Ruiz flung him back a few feet and turned his attention to Lucas. "Where now?"

Lucas seemed overwhelmed and at the edge of confusion. "I think I know where this warehouse is. We have to park four or five blocks away and try and sneak over. Stealth, you know?"

They waited respectfully for the plan to unfold. Kaylee checked the gun in her hand. The safety was off, so she clicked it back on and relaxed.

Ruiz seemed agitated. "Hey, this is a great party and all, but that smoke could bring the pups any second, you know?"

"Right, right." Lucas searched for his bearings. "Dustin?"

"Yo?"

"Bow and arrow boy, expert right?"

"Uh, what about the rifle?"

Lucas lowered his voice. "We want to sneak up to this warehouse. No noise."

Dustin smiled cryptically. "Ninja style."

"Exactly," said Lucas. "We don't want gunshots so we can get inside and see what we're up against. Quieter we do this, the better."

"No problem," said Dustin. He seemed convincing enough, but Kaylee remained skeptical of his accuracy with the bow.

Lucas nodded with confidence. "You and Colton, with the bow. I want a professional mission, with skill, okay?"

Kaylee looked to Dustin, and he looked back. Apparently disliking the expression on her face, he whipped away and marched off toward the parking lot.

"Let's move out! Blockheads are probably at the school by now." Lucas climbed into the driver's seat of the white pickup.

Everyone scrambled for a spot in the vehicles. Kaylee and her people jogged back together across the hot asphalt and to the Mustang. Lucas's pickup rolled out of the field and back to the pavement.

***

Although the highway stayed clear for several minutes, suddenly an eighteen-wheeler appeared on the horizon, coming at them from the opposite direction. Ruiz grabbed the walkie-talkie. "We got a truck coming."

After a few moments, Lucas responded over the radio, "Ah, we're screwed. He's already seen us."

Dustin said, "There's an exit comin' up."

Kaylee reached for her handgun again, and she stared down at it. With so much danger this far from the school base, the helplessness of being strapped inside a speeding car as they shot at top speed toward unseen hazards weighed on her mind.

It didn't help that the other two in the back shook nervously every time anything happened at all. They were getting on her nerves, and she wondered if they were even possibly dupe spies, since they didn't say anything.

The Mustang's air conditioner didn't work, and Kaylee was baking. Enough hot air blew in through the damaged windows to keep it just at a survivable level.

"Try for the exit," said Lucas over the radio.

The large rig raced at them. There was no way its driver could miss noticing them. Their two vehicles whipped around the bend and off the highway, pinning Kaylee against the side of the car.

"Did he see us, man, you think?" said Dustin.

"Of course he saw us," Ruiz sneered back. "We saw him."

Dustin grabbed the walkie-talkie from Ruiz.

"All right, Lucas, now what?"

"Radio silence," Lucas growled back in a low mutter. "Just pull over."

Lucas and Dustin held a conference at the side of the road. With the map, they worked out their final route to approach the food depot. A couple of miles up the road, they parked within sight of the next on-ramp.

"This is it," said Dustin.

Kaylee stretched her legs, and they prepared for the final walk over to the food warehouse. The sun dropped low, and she wished she had sunglasses to fight the intense glare. Their squad marched straight into the sunset. Zigzagging, they cut down an alley between some abandoned, rusted-out warehouses with arced roofs like airplane hangars. Weeds infiltrated the cracks in the concrete. Their army circled another corrugated warehouse and stopped. Once the orange glow of the food distribution facility appeared, everyone froze and hid in the crevices of the structures.

Kaylee carried arrows in a quiver, all with razor tips. Dustin held his bow at the ready, an arrow already nocked. Lucas crouched down by her face.

"Are you ready for this?"

In her right hand she held her 9mm pistol, in the left a bunch of arrows for Dustin. Kaylee shrugged, unsure.

Dustin stepped in close to whisper, "So, how we gonna do this?"

"Stay out of sight," said Lucas. "Do whatever you need, but don't be seen."

"Just me and her?"

Nodding, Lucas handed Kaylee the walkie-talkie. "Colton-"

"She can't use that," said Dustin. "She can't even talk, dude. What are you thinkin'?"

"Be quiet. That's what I want. Kaylee?"

Kaylee accepted the hand radio, pulling it against her chest with the arrows.

Lucas spoke quickly. "You click the send button once, and we can hear the click. Count to five. Then click it again. That means you found a spot with cover for all of us to move up. If you click twice, fast, that means it's not safe, and we won't come. You get it?"

Kaylee nodded, and she slid the handful of arrows back inside the quiver so that she could hold the walkie-talkie instead. Dustin jerked about like a neglected *prima donna*.

"So what do I do?"

"All right," said Lucas. "You are on the binoculars finding out how many meat-heads are in that damned place. See if they got surveillance cameras, too. And where to get in without being seen."

"Yeah. Fine."

"Don't rush," said Lucas. "Take your time. We can't just run in and get massacred."

Kaylee mulled over every word Lucas said. Trailing along after Dustin, the two marched out toward the warehouse complex beside a long, curving road and through the artificial golden-orange glow, which flooded out from all the industrial lights hanging from the buildings. Rig trucks and other large machines were heard inside pushing pallets. Workmen somewhere clanked metal and slammed wood, and the echoes danced through the massive complex. The bright-orange, pulsing glare coated everything in a surreal, foggy haze. Dustin darted around the corner and right out into the open, dashing toward something that Kaylee couldn't even see. She was overcome by the scope and the scale of the warehouse facility on the other side of the road. Dustin slid to a stop behind a sign and waited for her to arrive.

She bounded awkwardly to catch up, and she stumbled into Dustin. He grabbed her to hold her in place. They both sat behind the cover of the narrow building sign.

"Havin' fun yet?" he said.

Kaylee gawked around in confusion. The facility spread down along a tall, razor-wire fence for blocks and blocks. The air smelled of diesel engine fumes and industrial chemicals. A pervasive grinding from within enveloped them.

Dustin scoped out the target. Security cameras sat up on poles thirty-feet high along the fence. These pointed inside, rather than outside where they were hiding. In the compound, they glimpsed a car drive along a road between the warehouses. Then an eighteen-wheeler drove in the opposite direction on that same interior road, disappearing inside the array of rectangular storage buildings. Two other tractor trailers sat backed up against loading docks. Men stuffed them full by driving forklifts and pallets of stacked boxes into the trailers. Each time a forklift entered, the entire trailer bounced from the weight.

Kaylee watched Dustin as he spied on the activity across the road through the chain link fences. As she stared down at the walkie-talkie, she tried to remember what they were supposed to be doing. Where they were now it was sparse and bare, open to the street. Not enough room for the rest of the group to hide. She felt lucky that they hadn't been spotted yet.

Inside the fence, a pair of guards and a German shepherd stepped along, carrying small machine guns. The dog smelled the air, and it momentarily peeked over at Kaylee and Dustin.

Dustin yawned, and he swept the binoculars left and right.

"All right, we should do this after those guards leave."

Kaylee shook her head and pointed around for cover. There was none.

"We'll just go right in, take what we want," said Dustin.

She shook her head again, and she pointed at the fence.

"Dammit, Kaylee. Just gimme the radio."

Kaylee shook her head a third time, now frightened of what was happening. She took a step back. Dustin grabbed at the walkie-talkie, but she pushed his hand away.

Dustin managed to get hold of it, but Kaylee still held her thumb near the transmitter button. She quickly tapped it twice, and then again as they struggled over it. She kept tapping it until Dustin ripped the transmitter away.

"What the hell'd you do that for? You're gonna screw this up."

Kaylee put her finger up to her lip to silence him. The workmen weren't that far off, still loading a truck within sight of them. Her temper livid, she was unable to express her frustration. There was no cover here for the group to gather, and she was trying to do her job, unlike him. Dustin just wanted to rush in and shoot up the place, but he didn't even know how many guards were inside.

He's going to get us all killed!

Dustin sat with the walkie-talkie. He tapped once, counted to five, and then tapped it again.

"There," he said smugly, and he sneered back at Kaylee like a snotty child. After a minute Lucas ran out around the corner and sprinted to them.

Dustin poured on his attitude. "Where's the rest?"

"What the hell's going on?" said Lucas. "You guys said there was danger. Let me see the binoculars." He scouted around the facility nervously, his body pressed up against the big sign post. There wasn't much to see aside from the dull grey corrugated walls of the outer buildings.

Dustin said, "We'll go right in through the fence. I'll do it myself."

Kaylee pointed around the area, trying to indicate something, but the boys were too busy arguing with each other to notice her. As usual.

"All right. Stop. Stop," said Lucas, to shut Dustin's mouth. "How many guards are in there? Do you know?"

He hesitated. "I only seen two."

Lucas looked along the fence. Finally he dropped the binoculars. "It's too big."

"It ain't too big," said Dustin."What the hell are you talkin' about? Food's right there."

"There could be a whole army inside."

Chain link fences with barbed wire on top stretched as far as they could see, with tall, corrugated warehouse walls behind.

"Where's the cover for everybody?" Lucas noticed Kaylee shrugging sarcastically.

A slam echoed across the expanse. A trailer truck had loaded, its roll-down door shut by the unseen workmen. Lucas knelt on one knee, and he stared through the binoculars at the truck.

"I got a better idea," he said. "As soon as this truck pulls out, we run for it."

"To the fence?" asked Dustin.

"No. Back to the cars."

"What?"

Kaylee swiftly packed her stuff into her backpack. The big rig roared, turned on its headlights and pulled away from the loading dock, grinding along through the facility and out of sight.

"Go!" Lucas sprinted back to where they had come, Kaylee and Dustin behind him. As the three of them raced past their large, bored group, Lucas called for them to follow. The whole force sprinted to where the cars were parked. Kaylee panted, keeping pace with the bulk of them as they all ran terrified together, most not knowing if they were being chased. The platoon crashed back into their seats, and the cars shot off toward the highway ramps.

Ruiz and Rory were now in the front seat of the Mustang in front of Kaylee. The cars whipped crazily to make the highway on-ramp as the loaded truck crossed above on the overpass.

"There he is. It's south." Ruiz pointed, and the Mustang raced ahead of the slower pickup. "What are we doin', Dustin?" said Ruiz. "How we gonna do this?"

The Mustang rocketed ahead, lights off, flying to catch up with the big eighteen-wheel truck. Kaylee didn't know what to do other than hold on. Managing to finally click her seat belt, she could only watch as they closed in on the unsuspecting tractor trailer.

"We'll get in front!" said Dustin. "Then I guess we gotta shoot him."

Rory held Dustin's rifle pointed at the roof of the car. Dustin wasted no time sliding beside the truck in the right-hand lane and continuing past.

The truck driver came to some awareness too late. They were out in front and speeding well ahead. The velocities were nauseating the two new kids in the back seat, and Kaylee felt surreal again where time slowed down. Suddenly she saw all the colors and the textures so vividly that they dazzled her eyes.

"I'm gettin' in back," said Dustin as he turned to inform them. "Somebody's gotta come up front. And Rory, you gotta drive."

"Oh yeah, man! That's no problem, *broheim*." Rory grabbed the steering wheel from Dustin and readied himself. Dustin fumbled with the barrel of the hunting rifle. Ruiz twisted back around.

"Kaylee, come up here." He reached his hand back to grab her by the arm.

She unhooked her seat belt, and she tried to dive over Ruiz and the seat. It was a mangled mess, and she landed upside-down and flailed about to try and flop over properly.

"Ahhh!" Rory jerked at the wheel, nearly flipping the car over.

Dustin grabbed it back. "What the hell? You gotta keep it smooth and straight. What's the matter with you?"

Kaylee ended up on Ruiz's lap, waiting for people to shift over. Ruiz yelled at the other kids, "Slide over, get outta the way!"

Well behind their Mustang, in the white pickup truck, Lucas attempted to pass the eighteen-wheeler as well. The driver of the truck slammed them off the road into the shoulder. The pickup crashed against the guard rail and spun out, lost behind them as the big rig kept rolling.

Dustin saw the impact as he was about to climb into the back seat. "He hit Lucas. Son of a bitch."

Ruiz jerked back to see. "Tyretta's in there!"

The car fell silent, nothing but the rushing wind and angry engine. Kaylee tried to see out through the cracks of the rear window. All that was there were the blazing headlights of the big truck a few hundred feet behind them.

Dustin made his contorted climb over his seat into the back seat. Rory scooted into the driver's seat, and Kaylee took his former spot in the center.

Dustin adjusted his rifle and scope, sliding the barrel out through a bullet hole in the rear windshield.

"Okay, okay. Okay, okay, okay."

They waited tensely to see what he would do next.

"Let him catch up. Slowly, not obvious. Okay, man?"

Rory nodded. "Who's the man? Who's your daddy?" The Mustang began to slow.

"Okay. This scope is hard to set right," said Dustin.

Ruiz snapped back to attention. "You gots to take out that driver. Just do it."

"I know, I know, I know." Dustin stared into the scope. "It bounces around a lot. The road's bumpy, you know?"

Rory looked disturbed with the headlight glare reflecting off his side mirror. "He's getting pretty close. Why don't you pull the trigger?"

"He's too close. Can't see him. Step on it!"

The truck attempted to ram into the rear of their car just as Rory stepped on the gas again, sending them racing off around a long, wide curve prior to entering their suburbs.

"You know how to shoot that thing?" said Ruiz.

"Yeah, shut up, man!" Dustin adjusted the scope again, the truck fifty feet behind them and changing lanes erratically.

"Dude, stay in front of him. I can't get that angle."

Kaylee located her pistol from her backpack, and she took it in her hand. They sped at a hundred miles an hour with Rory in control of the car. If anything was a cause to be concerned or nauseous, it was Rory behind the wheel of an automobile.

Suddenly the air pounded with a blunt concussion, and Kaylee went momentarily deaf. The rifle had fired into the truck's front windshield. The eighteen-wheeler continued plowing after them. Dustin snapped another bullet into the rifle's chamber.

"Okay," he yelled. "One more time for good measure."

The truck suddenly veered down an off-ramp, fooling them all. It smashed through several of the big yellow crash barrels before correcting itself and staying on the ramp.

"Stop!" Dustin yelled at Rory. The car skidded to an instant freeze in the middle of the freeway.

"Back up. Back up."

They reversed and followed down the off-ramp in pursuit of the wily beast. Half a mile up the avenue they found it, and they rushed to intercept. The truck had torn through a tree and scraped to a stop against the side of an office building, its engine still running.

The Mustang pulled up ahead of the truck. They gawked at the crash to get a handle on the situation with the driver.

Kaylee stared down at her handgun, wary of where they were now and who might be nearby. The boys piled out to take control of the captured tractor trailer. She remained in the passenger seat, her foot hanging out onto the pavement. She tried to think but had little luck doing so.

Outside on the shoulder of the road, the two newbies vomited together. Kaylee felt dazed and tired, so exhausted like she wouldn't make it to Thursday. It was Tuesday night, but so much bad stuff was coming by the minute now that she couldn't get her hopes up any more.

Apparently, the truck's driver was deceased. Dustin had shot him right through the windshield. This truck was now theirs for the taking, but no one knew how to actually drive an eighteen-wheeler. Lucas and his squad were missing, perhaps dead. The school was probably taken over by the dupes, and everyone either killed or flipped against them by now. Maybe saving that apple for Sara had been a waste of time. It was all so sad, so pointless, and so frustrating.

A strange girl shuffled past the Mustang, holding a long hunting knife with jagged teeth on one side. Her clothes were shredded, like some feral homeless person.

Kaylee blinked.

The boys watched the front of the truck, joking and discussing their predicament. This strange girl with the large knife sneaked up right behind them. Kaylee wanted to shout something, but she couldn't. Immediately she jumped out of the car and ran up behind the knife girl. In her own hand, she pointed the 9mm, first at the girl's back, then at her legs. Kaylee didn't know what to do then, but the girl made a sudden move like she was going to lunge forward at Dustin's neck with the hunting knife. Kaylee lunged first and she poked the girl in the shoulder with the barrel of her handgun.

The knife girl whipped around, and the steel blade sliced past Kaylee's face, cracking the air before her eyes, much like Sean had done on that very first morning. Kaylee stumbled backward, lowering the gun, and she fired. Everyone dove and scattered. The knife girl dropped straight to the road, blood spurting into the air, pulsing from an artery in her upper thigh. It coated her bare legs and her light blue shirt, even as she thrashed on the pavement.

Everyone in their party surrounded her. The bleeding girl lay on the asphalt, still whipping the big blade at them as they stepped closer. Gushes of blood spread out across the asphalt and sputtered through the girl's fingers as she tried to hold it inside. Her petite face contorted. Kaylee threw her gun down in the dirt, and she held her own face in panic. She wanted to stop the bleeding, but the wounded girl growled like an animal, jerking the knife. Her strength poured out onto the roadway.

Kaylee grabbed a T-shirt from inside her backpack, and she took it to the knife girl, where she tried to get close enough to tie up the leg. But the duped girl remained belligerent, attempting to stab her.

Kaylee pointed at the boys, egging them to hold the flailing arm still, but none would assist. Not Dustin, Ruiz, or Rory. They backed away, disgusted.

"Forget it, Kaylee." Dustin leaned against the bumper of the big truck. He watched the road for more dupes, his rifle in his hand.

Ruiz similarly kept watch. "Who's gonna drive this thing?"

"I, uh, never drove stick," said Dustin.

"I did." Ruiz sized up the monster. "I'm doin' it." He climbed up, and he dragged the truck driver's corpse out and onto the dirt shoulder of the road.

"This *gordo*'s heavy. Come on, gimme a hand, fools."

The knife girl eventually weakened, her arm flopping over beside her. Kaylee struggled with whether to try and stop the bleeding now that the girl was so weak.

Kaylee couldn't bring herself to touch the dupe girl, as she might jump up and stab Kaylee through her face like some slasher-movie psycho villain cliché.

Worst of all, none of the others even cared. Or they pretended not to. The unconscious girl's face smoothed. Her dirty-blond curls seemed doll-like, but now she was lying in her own blood, dead.

Kaylee had killed her.

Kaylee's mind remained in serious pain. If she'd entertained any doubts about herself, they were no longer doubts. She was dangerous. She couldn't be trusted. Kaylee was just like the dupes, no matter how hard she tried to fight it. She wanted it all to stop, but it would never stop, ever. It was part of her now.

Rory sauntered over and handed Kaylee back her handgun, which he had found in the dirt at the side of the road. Smiling, he said, "Nice shot, Mutey. I just adore a girl who knows how to handle a weapon." Snickering, Rory stepped back away, leaving Kaylee to her silence.

Her mind entered a permanent kind of daze, where she finally accepted the world the way it was with little desire to do much of anything about it. Her desires seemed futile, and her life insignificant in the face of such a massive onslaught.

When Lucas's white pickup truck squeaked over to their spot, mangled but still in one piece, Kaylee didn't care. When Ruiz ran up to Tyretta and hugged and kissed her in front of everybody, spinning her about in a circle like a doll, Kaylee didn't care. She didn't have anyone at all, and she didn't want anyone.

When their force pulled out again with the tractor trailer packed full of food to keep the whole school going, their three vehicles returning to home base as triumphant heroes, Kaylee didn't care at all. She just stared blankly out the side window of the Mustang, numb to everything and everyone.

When their convoy arrived at Jefferson High School, a veritable cavalry smashing through the dupe lines, chasing dozens of their shock troops away from the front gate and taking up positions to repel the whole demonic plague of them, Kaylee didn't care about that either. She didn't even participate.

Instead, she stumbled out of the Mustang, ignoring the charges and shouts, the shooting, the Molotov cocktails, the incoming gunfire. She trudged inside the gymnasium by herself, abandoning the chaos outside to all of the shrieking lunatics. At her own cot, she dropped her backpack in relief, and she procured for herself that red apple she had stolen from the television station.

Gazing across the field of cots, Kaylee was about to take a big bite for herself when she heard sniffles and shudders across the gym. She snooped closer and listened for more clues. The cries originated from beneath a cot, from inside a little fortress made of draped blankets. She lifted the edge of the dull grey emergency blanket, and she found five-year-old Sara sitting with her kitten, terrified.

Kaylee cared about that.

Eighteen

After Kaylee and Sara shared the apple, the games began. Kaylee wrote "monkey" on the small yellow pad, and she held it secret. Sara jumped about, scratching her armpits and hooting. Her squeaky voice strained to drown out intermittent gunshots. The kitten, Little Paws, jerked nervously at each bang, and she was scared enough for the three of them.

When Kaylee turned over the note, Sara read it. "Mon-kee. Monkey. That's right. Your turn."

Kaylee smirked. Down on all fours, she crawled slowly around the cot. Then she hung her arm from her head like a long trunk, shaking it about.

Sara stared down, dazzled. "Is it a elephant?"

Kaylee nodded.

"Ooh, can I ride on your back, elephant?"

Kaylee thought it over, and she nodded again. Little Paws studied them. Marching in a circle around Sara's bed, Kaylee lumbered with Sara on her back.

"Go that way, elephant."

Kaylee marched on, but abruptly the hallway door slammed open. Caroline Anderson marched, through trailed by Melanie and her lieutenant, Benjamin, a tall, thin boy with short brown hair and metal-rimmed glasses. Kaylee thought that Benjamin might have a crush on Melanie.

Caroline seemed shocked to find her inside the gym playing, and she jolted to a halt.

"Kaylee? What are you doing? Gotta get outside, on the east wall. Now!"

A busybody, Caroline lifted her right up to her feet by her arm, and then she yanked Kaylee back to her cot.

"Is your weapon in here?" Caroline carried the backpack for her and pulled Kaylee off into the bowels of Jefferson. "They've moved away from the front and they're testing us to see where we're weak. Do you understand? We cannot let them in."

Kaylee nodded half-heartedly, yawning and watching the ceiling float past as they stumbled out toward the football field.

"There, there. Take that spot." Caroline pointed to an empty table nestled in the corner. Kaylee nodded gratuitously back at her, but she wasn't really concerned. She flirted with the idea that it was about time to go to sleep.

"I'll be back around later." With that she trotted off at the quick step.

Kaylee sat up on the table, her back against the rough stone wall, and she thought about sleep. On the other side of the football field, she saw a couple of girls at their stations rustling about. On the gym roof, boys strutted around with rifles slung over their shoulders.

She rummaged through her backpack, wishing she'd grabbed more food from that fridge in the television station. From her handgun she slid out the clip to count the remaining bullets. There were eight in there, and more rounds jumbled inside the front pocket of her backpack.

Standing up on a desk chair, Kaylee peeked out over the top of the wall. On the shadowy side street she heard the dupes gather and scurry in the darkness like big cockroaches.

Fine.

Her hand slapped the clip back inside the pistol, and she sat back down. Holding the gun up high over her head, she fired all nine bullets in a row, straight up into the night sky. Her finger clicked the trigger again for good measure, just to be sure, and she grinned to herself. All the bullets were gone, far away, and she wondered where they might come down, and when. Maybe they would never come down and head off into space.

Whatever.

When her hearing returned, she stood back up to check over the top of the wall. Everything was clear now. Silent. Nodding to herself, she slid the handgun back into her backpack and zipped it.

Approximately one hour later, Caroline Anderson returned, beaming with a plastic smile. She and a couple of teen mules carried microwaved macaroni and cheese dinners in black plastic dishes. Renewed with vitality, Caroline celebrated each plate she handed out to the troops on her rounds.

"Kaylee!" she said, offering the hot meal. "You guys did it! Oh my God, that truck is worth its weight in gold."

Kaylee snatched it and wolfed it down without any regard for smearing the cheese across her face.

"Take it easy, honey. There's plenty more."

Kaylee couldn't remember the last time food tasted so good. Lost in the trance of the mac and cheese, she silently proclaimed it her favorite food of all time. She felt she would soon enter a food coma, which was just fine with her. If she lay down in her cheesy food comatose heaven and let the rest of them kill each other off, she might finally be happy.

***

By sunrise, Kaylee huddled against the scratchy sand-textured wall, curled up in a ball to keep warm. The sun poked from the night, and she was truly sick of it all. Fighting off the relentless glare of an impending day seemed impossible. She remembered it was Wednesday, which was supposed to mean something, although she couldn't remember what.

The lanky, brown-haired boy, Benjamin, marched out from the double-glass doors to relieve Kaylee, followed by Caroline Anderson and her ever-present clipboard. Kaylee's face felt icily numb, her body stiff with cramps. The hand-off made, Kaylee managed to stand, although she lurched forward. Her backpack weighed her down just a bit too heavily to straighten up.

As she stumbled off away from the inside corner of the school's wall, she heard Caroline behind her.

"Your gun, Kaylee."

It didn't matter. She kept marching off toward the kitchen in search of more macaroni and cheese.

"Kaylee? What's this? Are those bullets?" Caroline must have noticed the brass casings shimmering in the grass. Kaylee had tossed all her spare ammunition onto the overgrown lawn below her platform. Her corner of the field was littered with live rounds, where she had flicked them away in her boredom. As she reentered the school hallway, she heard confused shouts outside from Caroline, which echoed across the field. It didn't concern her anymore and was already out of her mind.

Kaylee arrived at the gym dormitory to find Sara curled up on her side, staring straight ahead from her cot and unresponsive. She tapped on the girl's shoulder.

"Ohhh." Sara groaned but made no effort to move.

Kaylee took an immediate interest, and she tapped again. Her hand shook at Sara's arm.

"I ate too much macaronis and cheeses."

Kaylee's mouth hung open. She almost laughed, but instead covered her face quickly and turned away. Nodding with an air of concern, she snuck off to go find some more sustenance for herself.

Boxes piled to the ceiling, the school's kitchen overran with new supplies. A small crew opened cartons and inspected their contents. Another worker team delivered boxes to the cafeteria from outside, and they piled them categorically.

Kaylee read the cartons. One interested her, as she didn't know what the word meant. Standing up on an orange lunchroom chair, she dug the box out from a tall stack. At a table, she wrestled open the cardboard. Inside were colorful, shiny bags of pistachio nuts. She couldn't remember how pistachios tasted, but they seemed to have already been freed from their shells and were supposed to be organic. Mom had insisted on organic foods whenever she could afford them. They were better somehow.

She stuffed the pistachios in her mouth, and now she needed a quick drink to wash down all that saltiness. Off she went in search of new boxes through which to rummage. This was better than Christmas, better than a birthday. Their cafeteria was crammed with goodies just waiting for someone to rip open. She eventually stuffed her belly almost as full as Sara had. With her own personal gallon of apple cider, she carried the bag of pistachios back to her cot.

The day quieted. Mornings were when the dupes all retreated. It was like they were on a clock, and it was quitting time for them, time to all sleep together somewhere.

Maybe they're like vampires and vulnerable in their sleep.

Whatever.

Kaylee didn't care about that silly war anymore. To prove it, she went to sleep, covering her head with a pillow to block out the sunlight that sliced across her cot.

Later, when she awoke, she felt much the same, her eyes weighed down and numb. A strong image had appeared in her dream. There she wore a golden necklace with a pendant dangling. When she examined the glowing ornament it was much larger than she had thought. Gigantic, really, in the shape of a Y inside a circle. The mysteriously expanding trinket was a peace symbol.

That day, Wednesday, seemed almost normal. People strolled and performed standard chores. People cleaned the floors. People organized stacks of supply boxes. All of them seemed relieved and happy. It was a little unnerving to Kaylee, the falseness of it all. In a moment it could all wash away. Instantly, the entire school's population could be killed.

Taking an old, frazzled paintbrush and a cup of green acrylic, Kaylee located Sara again and woke her up. Sara's hazel eyes flickered to focus, and Kaylee waved the painting supplies back and forth in front of her face.

Sara quickly caught the idea, and she became interested.

"I have to pee," said Sara.

Kaylee nodded, and the two left together.

The art room at Jefferson was stocked with every manner of paints and brushes, an old ink printing press, clay, and a kiln. Ribbons and scissors, Styrofoam balls, balsa wood shapes, glue, and tape were all abandoned. Paintings, crafted by the previous art class, hung about the room on wires.

Kaylee decided to move her painting supplies out to the hallway, where a large white patch of wall stretched ten feet from floor to ceiling. Sara wore a blue oversized smock, her face already streaked with green.

The two painted the hallway. Sara focused her abilities on stick figures and animal shapes down near the floor level. They resembled cave paintings from a prehistoric time. Kaylee listened in as Sara drew larger shapes, and a family standing before a crude house.

"That's Mommy, and that's Daddy."

Kaylee inspected the stick figures, and she nodded with approval.

"They're gonna come and get me, when they find out I'm here. Right?"

Kaylee paused a sharp moment, and she smiled down at Sara and nodded enthusiastically.

"They... They don't know where I'm at." Sara painted her parents onto the wall, adding colors to their torsos, a yellow smeared shirt on the father and a blue-black smeared dress on mother.

Kaylee dappled green grass along the bottom of the wall, intruding on Sara's space. She then set her mind to mixing the proper shade of orange-yellow. The two of them painted for hours. Kaylee's large circle stretched to within a foot of the ceiling tiles, and she climbed on a ladder to work at that height. Unhappy with the shade of gold, she decided it would have to do. Her mural took the form of a massive golden peace symbol in the center, streaks of golden light emanating from it like the sun. Behind it, she painted a field of green and clouds in a light blue sky.

People wandered by occasionally to investigate. They stayed for a few seconds or a minute, and then they strolled on, usually toward the kitchen. Kaylee didn't care about the spectators. Mindful of not infringing on Sara's space, she pursued her vision. The lawn and the sky remained implied. She left the background space mostly clear for a different purpose.

Behind her giant peace sign, she began with black and maroon, slopping on gory-looking corpses. In between the branches of the peace sign, goopy red and black mounds sat in the grass. The background filled with ugly charred and bleeding figures with little form to them at all, just chunks of dead meat. Happily slopping on her piles of gore, Kaylee mixed up another batch of gut-splatter color. The wall filled with her masterpiece, while Sara tired and took off to play elsewhere. Still Kaylee found new spots to improve upon while up on the ladder, scrutinizing and surveying her wall canvas.

She heard them gather behind her from the whispers and the murmurs. Caroline and Lucas chattered conspiratorially in hushed tones. Dustin, Ruiz, and Tyretta also looked on with curiosity. Others gathered too, once the big names had taken an interest. Melanie, Benjamin, and some of the quieter teens arrived. It was now quite an exhibition, but they all seemed baffled and disturbed. That was fine with her, and she smirked as she dabbed on another severed head.

Kaylee climbed down in order to take in the entire mural from ground level. She could tell they wanted to bother her again and interrupt her project. The painting looked okay, for now, and maybe she would just leave it be and start another one directly across the hallway. Tomorrow.

Caroline coughed artificially.

"Uh, Kaylee, hey? Hello?"

Kaylee turned, dumbfounded by the size of the turnout. Caroline held up Kaylee's 9mm semi-automatic handgun in her hand, and she stood beside Lucas with that obligatory air of concern, which adults were supposed to show most of the time.

Lucas said, "Are you okay?"

Dustin followed. "What's up?"

Caroline shushed them, and she stepped forward to take the lead role.

"Do you want to talk?"

Kaylee shot her back a sarcastic look, the one that said she was too annoyed to answer.

"I mean –" said Caroline. "I know you can't talk. Obviously. But, do you want to tell us something, write it down or something?"

Kaylee just shrugged, and she pointed her hand over at the painting.

Lucas said, "She's all right. Good work. I like it." He nodded and walked away from the mural. Kaylee smiled, surprised that Lucas of all people would respond so positively to her art. She was still a beginner and the circle wasn't completely round. It was difficult judging giant shapes from up on a ladder like that.

Dustin took the cue as well. "All right. Cool." He too walked away. The crowd thinned.

Caroline stepped into Kaylee's personal space. "Honey, I brought your weapon for you. Okay? Don't throw the bullets away like you did-"

Kaylee pushed the gun away. Shaking her head, she turned to deal with the brushes and the cups of paint strewn all over the floor.

"Kaylee, you have to listen to me."

Kaylee instead pretended to poke her fingers into her ears and she bobbed around playfully.

"Dammit." Caroline turned and marched off down the hallway. "Lucas! Come here. We need to talk."

Kaylee cleaned up the paint cups, and then she rinsed out her brushes in the girl's locker room sink. She examined herself in the mirror, covered in paint, much like Sara had been. Dropping her clothes right there in front of the row of sinks, she strolled off into the showers. Her towel had been left to hang dry inside a nearby locker, and she was all set.

Of course Caroline intruded, and she made a new attempt to talk to Kaylee, this time in the shower.

"Kaylee? We want to have a serious talk with you."

Kaylee kept scrubbing, and she tried to ignore Caroline's calls. But Caroline soon appeared at her shower stall. "There you are. Lucas is outside. We really need to know what's up with you, okay? So hurry up and finish."

Kaylee took her sweet time, and she wondered if there might be a back door to the locker room where she could sneak out. Caroline stayed close, however, minding her, remaining vigilant until Kaylee finally dressed and was prepared for more chatter. It was all talk around here, twenty-four/seven. She preened herself in the mirror, particularly to waste time and to annoy Caroline. When Kaylee tired of tussling her hair and posing, the two of them stepped out into the hallway, and they met with Lucas and Ruiz.

"Keep the chunk-heads back away from the walls," said Lucas. The two boys discussed plans for new defensive measures. If they could make barbed wire or put spikes in the ground when the dupes weren't attacking, they could create a second line of defense, or something like that.

"Here we are." Caroline interrupted the males.

Lucas turned quickly. "Colton, where's your gun?"

Kaylee performed an exaggerated dance gesture, like she was free of all that now.

Ruiz snapped back in surprise. "Little one? You *loca*?" He smiled, unsure.

"See what I mean?" said Caroline. "She doesn't care."

Kaylee waved playfully and started to take off down the hallway.

"Hey!" Lucas, grabbed her and yanked her back by her upper arm. Then he barked into her face, the way he did with the boys sometimes, the way that nasty janitor had talked to people.

"This is no joke. We need you, you know? With your head all working right. You know what we're saying?"

Kaylee snatched her arm back from Lucas's aggressive grip, and she stuck out her tongue right in his face.

"Kaylee?" Caroline fumbled with her own supplies in a bag. "Where's that paper?" She retrieved a note pad and pushed it at her. "Tell us what your problem is so we can fix it."

Kaylee reluctantly accepted the pad and pen. Waiting for the right moment of calm, she tossed the papers and pen high in the air and then sprinted off in the opposite direction down the hallway.

Lucas said, "You've gotta be kidding me." All of them bounded along after Kaylee. She could hear Ruiz laughing as he jogged.

"This is a serious problem," Caroline said, already out of breath from the short run.

Kaylee emerged into the next school corridor and she found herself running right toward Dustin Hafstead, who dove and tackled her, stopping her in her tracks.

She panted, and they all caught their breaths. Trapped like a feral animal, she wondered if they were going to start treating her like the enemy now, like a dupe.

Then, from the echoing depths of the school hallways, Rory screamed, "The puppies are massing outside!"

Everyone jolted back to reality, except for Kaylee.

Lucas and Ruiz straightened up.

"Let's do this," said Lucas. They were already on the move.

Caroline shouted after them, "What do we do with her?"

Lucas shook his head, annoyed, before he stormed around the corner. "You babysit her. I don't need this now."

Dustin smiled, and he offered a hand to help Kaylee back onto her feet. But Kaylee just glared.

"Come on," he said. "I'll make it up to ya."

Kaylee's gaze whipped up inquisitively.

"You should see what I located in the cafeteria."

She tilted her head, still weighing her limited set of options. Dustin extended his hand again. This time she took it and stood up.

"She's your partner," said Caroline. "Watch her."

"She's fine. What's the problem?" Dustin chuckled. He hadn't shaved in days, and he was growing a grizzled beard.

Kaylee studied his fuzzy face, and she reached the point of her finger to touch his chin.

Caroline handed Dustin Kaylee's 9mm handgun. "This is hers."

"All right. Take it easy." He slid the gun into his pocket, and they walked away from Caroline. "Come on, pardner."

Kaylee smiled with amusement at this new turn of events. They all treated her so oddly. They made her the center of the world for some reason when all she had done was painted a big picture. Art had that kind of effect on people, it seemed. It got inside them and did its job. Kaylee decided to continue her explorations with color and themes. This kind of success could be addicting.

Jefferson High School tumbled into complete turmoil as the noise outside grew louder and more frenetic. Dustin slammed open an emergency door, and Kaylee instinctively followed him. That electronic cycling trance sound was amplified over loudspeakers, blared into the school as a sound weapon. The screeching noise was dangerously seductive and tried to hypnotize them once they stepped around the corner to the front yard. Vibrations erased thoughts, making it difficult to know what to do next.

Dupes collected at the street corners adjacent the school, surrounding it from every side. They really meant business this time. Over the walls, dupes could be seen using radios, coordinating movements and trying out new tactics.

The yard grew dark at the tail end of twilight, and the purple sky fell away swiftly to black. Kaylee vividly felt the trance wave, just as on that morning when she had stepped out of her bedroom. That enigmatic dissonance confused her again. The schoolyard rippled like gelatin. Her feet sank into the rubbery ground. Although she followed after Dustin, it became harder to step forward with her feet tied up in stickiness, captured in a heavy gravity field.

Dustin didn't seem to be affected as badly, but he too showed signs of assault. As they rounded the front of the gymnasium, in search of Lucas, Dustin paused. His fuzzy face twisted, and he shook himself hard as if to eject the sound cannon from his head. Kaylee gasped and feared the worst.

In anger, guns fired out over the walls. Most of the dupes hung back behind cover, and they weren't offering themselves up as targets. Shooting was sporadic and ineffectual.

And then it happened.

Nineteen

Kaylee noticed the boy on the rooftop above the gym suddenly lower his weapon and stare ahead motionless. Then Tyretta, up on a tabletop at the front wall, did similarly. Down beyond her, another boy lowered his weapon and stared out over the wall, frozen in place. It seemed oddly out of character. Kaylee strained to think, and she suddenly grabbed Dustin's arm to call his attention to them.

"What do you want?" He turned to her, his face strained. Kaylee's finger pointed up at the statuesque boy on the roof. Dustin acknowledged him. Then she tapped him again and pointed at Tyretta. Then the third one, and a fourth one on the same wall near the school bus gate. They stood up on their tables, transfixed over the wall together like monuments.

Ruiz broke off from his position at the gym doorway alongside Lucas, and he rushed toward Tyretta. "Hey, Ty! Get down!"

Kaylee could see blue flickering off the face of the gym building above. Light beams bent down to claw at her eyes.

Tyretta descended from her perch, and she rushed toward the school bus. Ruiz intercepted her at the back emergency door as she yanked it open. The two exchanged words, or at least Ruiz had some words for her.

Tyretta pointed her handgun and blasted into Ruiz's chest. The front schoolyard panicked.

Tyretta shot Ruiz down to the ground, and she jumped up inside the school bus. Next, the boy on the rooftop started firing rifle shots onto the defenders in the front yard, and these wounded two of them. Lucas turned to shoot back up at the boy atop the gym. They played cat and mouse around the obstructions in the architecture.

Dustin yelled, "Come on!" And he took off for cover. Kaylee looked about in confusion, now that dupes were right inside the yard, and some of them were their former friends.

Tyretta started the school bus engine. Instantly she was blasted from Dustin's rifle as well as by Lucas and Rory. A barrage of destruction at the driver's seat of the school bus, and the machine remained purring in place. At the back of the bus, Kaylee found Ruiz groaning.

"Tyretta, why?" Blood oozed from his mouth. Kaylee stepped back as if in a dream. Ruiz struggled up to his knees, and he too pulled himself up and into the back of the school bus. Crawling up the aisle, Ruiz slid forward to the very front, and to Tyretta's shot-up body. He pulled her from the driver seat, and they landed in a tight embrace, covered in each other's blood. Kaylee just watched the two of them die together, powerless to intervene.

She formed an idea then, and she needed to talk to Lucas. She jogged right up and snatched a clipboard, which he held at his side.

"Colton? What?" It was clear Lucas's mind had also blanked out.

Kaylee flipped the top page, and she wrote.

They must have a screen.

"Tell me suttom I don't know!" Lucas shouted, "Nobody look over the wall! Everybody down!" He pointed at the boy at the left corner of the front wall. "Get down. Come over here!" Lucas watched the boy carefully in case he had already been infected.

Kaylee scrawled out another note.

We could shoot the screen.

Lucas read it dismissively. "How can we shoot it without looking at it?"

Kaylee wasn't finished.

By blurring the scope on the rifle.

"What do you mean?" His face froze. "How are we – ?" He stopped in mid-sentence. "Dustin! Bring that rifle over here!"

Dustin snapped back, looking confused. Everyone languished under the pulsing effects of the noise weapon, which lowered blood pressure, instilled seasickness and a sense of impending doom.

"Rory!" said Lucas. "Come here!"

"What, dude?"

"Run the whole perimeter. Nobody looks over the walls until we take care of the video screens. You hear me? Nobody looks."

Rory nodded quickly, and he raced off to deliver the message.

Lucas looked down to Kaylee. "Colton, this better work."

Her pen had already composed another note.

Just the screens. Don't shoot any more people.

"Right." Lucas rolled his eyes as he took off to intercept Dustin. Kaylee jogged behind.

Dustin and his rifle met with Lucas, and they considered the ergonomics.

"We need something," said Lucas. "We need a mask or something to hide where you can only see the scope."

"I dunno," answered Dustin. "Cardboard?"

"Yeah, cardboard. And find duct tape, the most magical stuff on earth. Quick."

Dustin disappeared into the gym.

Kaylee stepped back with the clipboard, contemplating a poem. Looking up at the dark, cloudy sky, she tried to imagine a catchy first line, tapping her pen on the metal clamp of the clipboard. She thought up a rhythm that was close to the pulses in the air, that swirl which scratched the colors off of surfaces. What an opportunity this was for a new song, maybe.

Dustin sprang out the door.

"All right." Lucas grabbed the supplies. "You cannot look unless your scope is totally blurry. Okay? No detail."

"How am I gonna hit anything?"

"It'll be the bright spot. Just shoot out the bright light. I'll make sure you don't get duped."

"Great."

"Colton," Lucas called.

Kaylee looked up from her pad of papers, smiling.

"Uh, never mind."

Kaylee nodded, and she returned to writing her new song, her head bobbing up and down with the beat.

*　*　*

Five dead. Six more wounded. The morning came finally, and Jefferson High lay within a hair of being overrun. The dupes adapted each night, losing fewer of their members and trying new creative tricks to deceive. Progressively their siege improved, and the high school was losing all its best defenders.

After the nightly terror episode clicked off like a thrown switch the gym became serene. Kaylee scraped her cot across the basketball court to beside Sara's. There was vastly more space now than before, with all the deaths. The two girls slept peacefully. Wounded teenagers moaned and cried up in the coach's office, which was coated in dry blood. Their bullet wounds were severe, and medical supplies were non-existent. No anesthetics, no sterile environments. The holes would likely swell up with infection and death, just as had happened to the janitor, Jaworski. The injured cried to themselves until they finally passed out from the pain.

The sun glared in brightly from above, and it seemed such a nice day when Kaylee awoke. She smiled, thinking of which type of art project to embark on and if Sara would help paint some more on the blank walls. It seemed there was something magical in the air today. It was a special day. It was Thursday.

Kaylee instantly realized the significance of it all. Dad was coming back home. She was saved. All she needed to do was get back home and meet up with him. Maybe they would fly away to paradise on a private plane. People left those aircraft all over the little airports just sitting next to the runways. If she could hot-wire a Mustang, she could probably hot-wire just about anything. But then again, she had to get home first and find Dad. This was another mission, a big one.

First, she wrote out a new note.

I have to go home and meet up with my father.

With that, Kaylee left Sara snoring gently to herself, and she scurried out of the gym in search of one of the gatekeepers. It wasn't long before she crossed paths with Caroline trudging down the hallway, coffee in one hand and her clipboard in the other. Kaylee flagged her down and made a fuss, waving her note about.

Caroline read it cursorily, never slowing in her lumbering forward momentum. "That's nice, dear." The older woman held up her hand to dismiss Kaylee, and she turned the corner.

Kaylee felt confounded, and she read the note again.

I have to go home and meet up with my father.

She flipped it over to the back against the nearest wall, and she scribbled in large, scratchy letters.

Today!!!

Kaylee thought through the required trip. It needed planning, and she needed to figure how to get there smoothly. It had been a while since she'd been home on Carmelita, and the location was a little foggy, so she stepped briskly off to the library.

Melanie and her crew had set it up as their headquarters. It was stocked with notebooks and paper, pencils, markers, whiteboards, and filing cabinets. Of interest to Kaylee, it also held the maps. She found Melanie with Ben, just hanging out and amiably socializing.

She helped herself to a sheet of paper and a thin marker, and she wrote requests. Demands, really. She needed to find 535 Carmelita Way and get good directions so she could find her way back to the school again.

"So you're on the north side of town," said Ben as the three of them studied the map around a large, darkly-stained hardwood table.

Melanie traced the street lines with her finger. "You could take Jefferson Avenue to Martin Luther King Jr. Boulevard and then make a right on one of these streets that go through-"

"Or," interrupted Ben, "take the highway." He pointed down, and he studied the lines and curves. "Go up one exit and get off on Imperial Way."

Melanie scrunched her mouth curiously. "She wouldn't want to do that."

"Why not?"

"Because it's longer."

Ben held up a single finger. "Yes, but that doesn't mean it's not safer."

"Ah. Good point."

Kaylee's eyes swelled dizzily from the lines and curves of the map. Her brain felt like it could overheat, and she wanted to understand the map, but it was unfamiliar territory. Her eyes blinked to focus, and she shook her head in frustration.

"Kaylee?" Melanie looked up. "There are a few ways to get over there."

"Hey!" said Ben. "I know."

"Yes?"

"We could make her copies. The copy machine is still functioning."

"Huh!" Melanie held up her palms with exaggerated flamboyance. "Excellent idea, Ben. Yes, let's do that."

They carried the map over to the copier, and Ben pressed the appropriate buttons to get it chugging. He smiled as the light sliced across back and forth. The photocopies emerged on four separate sheets, and they taped them into one big sheet, like the real map.

Melanie highlighted the preferred routes for Kaylee to get back to her house. "When were you going to go back there?"

Kaylee remembered her note. She dug into her pocket to find it, and she flipped the back side to them.

Today!!!

Melanie smiled. "Well, glad we could be of help." The two looked on with amusement.

Kaylee shook their hands in relief, and she smiled finally. With her new town map in hand, she marched off to put her plan in gear.

Lucas looked a mess, as if he hadn't slept in days, and his clothes were ripped, his tank top covered in somebody's dried blood and grease and all manner of ick. All the boys started to smell pretty bad, and their leader was no exception. Sweaty and resembling a scraggly, blond caveman, Lucas stared down and said, "Colton, are you still outta your melon? Or what?" He handed her back her note dismissively.

Kaylee tightened her jaw into her signature growl. As Lucas tried to turn, she stepped to the side and blocked his path.

"You want to go somewhere? Yeah, I'd like to go to Hawaii and camp out on the beach and do some surfing. So?" Lucas laughed to himself, as if he was funny.

Kaylee wasn't amused, and she kept pushing the back of the note toward his face.

Today!!!

"Your father... Look, Colton. I don't want to have to-" Lucas composed himself.

Kaylee wrote out a second message.

"Look. Your father ain't coming home today. Okay? Those plans are from the past, and they're just not happening. Get it?"

Kaylee's new note read: *I just need someone to drive.*

"You're not going anywhere!" Lucas shook his head, and he wiped the sweat from his cheek. "Jesus, we were almost completely overrun last night. Aren't you seeing this?" The front of the school looked like the aftermath of World War II. Bullet holes had smashed into all areas of all walls. Firebombs and the resulting smoke had charred most surfaces. Spent cartridge casings and debris littered the ground. The few teens who remained on watch resembled the walking dead in need of intensive care and a spa resort vacation.

Lucas jerked to walk away, and then Kaylee yanked his arm to keep him in place. She wasn't taking no for an answer.

"Colton, forget it." He ripped his arm free. "Your father is either one of those robots out there, wherever the hell he is, or he's probably dead. So there. That's what you have to deal with. I'm sorry." Lucas stormed off across the wasteland, leaving Kaylee motionless.

Devastated, she breathed uneasily. The yard's asphalt seemed wobbly, the courtyard larger than it had appeared before, or maybe she felt smaller.

What if Lucas is right?

If Dad really was dead or was duped, she would be alone for the rest of her life. She wasn't sure she could handle anything like that, so she refused to believe Lucas. Whatever he said, he didn't know either. Nobody would know until she went home and found out for herself.

Kaylee decided that she was going back to her own house today no matter what, and nobody was going to stop her, even if she had to walk the entire trip by herself with her newly copied town map.

Dustin lay on his own cot, twisting and unable to sleep. Kaylee spotted him, and she got to thinking. Instead of going right up to him, she turned around and worked out a new idea. Then she wrote out a different note.

Softly, she stepped to Dustin's cot. With some acting on display, she tried to appear interested in talking with him.

"Oh. Hey, Kaylee," said Dustin. "Man, I can't sleep. I got such a pain in my head."

Kaylee nodded sympathetically, bit her lip, and delivered her new note.

"What's this?" He accepted the paper. "Today? All right."

She smiled broadly.

"I need chow." He yawned, and he flopped out of the cot, trying to work the kinks out of his shoulders and neck. "Damn, I hate these damned cots." Standing, he stretched and looked about the gym. Wounded boys were stuffed in the coach's office, and Dustin paused as he glanced past. "Let's go see if those guys need suttom."

Kaylee nodded enthusiastically, and the two of them made for the coach's office. It smelled of blood and bile, urine and disease. She wasn't familiar with any of the injured boys, but they were human wreckage, at death's door. The sight was terrifying.

Dustin stepped inside, careful to avoid waking the sleepers. "Hey," he whispered. "Anybody need a drink? Some breakfast?"

The two injured boys who remained conscious were in no mood to eat. They squirmed slowly in place and groaned.

"No?" Dustin took a step backward into Kaylee. "Y'all just say somethin' if you're hungry. We've got lots of food now."

One of the injured boys managed a nod, and that was all.

***

Kaylee had to fill the Mustang's tank from a gas canister, carting one gallon back at a time. The pungent fuel splashed repeatedly onto her hands, souring them. The gasoline supply inside the tanker truck seemed to be holding up pretty well, and so their fuel needs were well taken care of, for now.

Dustin loaded the Mustang with his hunting rifle, bow and arrows, pistol, knives, food and drink, as well as Kaylee's backpack.

When they finally revved the Mustang, Dustin seemed wide awake and ready to roll. Kaylee strapped herself in beside him in the front seat, and they pulled off around the gym building toward the bus gate. Of course the bus was barely in one piece, and shrapnel and broken glass were scattered all over the area. All its tires were flat, but that was okay, as it made it harder for dupes to crawl underneath.

Dustin drove the Mustang up to the bus, and he shouted, "Somebody let us out, will ya?"

Kaylee's gaze darted about nervously. In her side mirror she saw Lucas emerge from the gym building behind them.

"What the hell are you doing?" Lucas rushed over, as angry as she had ever seen him. "Dammit. Turn that car off!"

"What?" asked Dustin.

"Get the hell out of the car. That's what!"

Dustin looked to Kaylee, whose face twisted up with guilt.

"Oh no," he said. Dustin slammed open his door, and he stepped out to face Lucas.

Lucas spit on the ground.

"I told her no. Over and over." The front wall guards took an interest in the conflict. Rory climbed down from his tabletop perch to investigate, stepping over curiously with Ruiz's shotgun held out in front of him.

Dustin shrugged innocently. "Hey, I didn't know."

As they worked out the blame and anger issues, Kaylee finally had enough. She slid into the Mustang's driver's seat, and she put the car into reverse. It jerked back, nearly running over Dustin's foot. He jumped out of the way. She tried to figure out why it was moving so fast toward the fire engine behind her. Her short legs stretched to stomp the brake pedal.

Figures ahead scrambled in confusion as Kaylee took a moment to watch them through the cracked front windshield. The car skidded to a halt, and then she clicked the lever into drive. Her foot let off the brake.

The Mustang jolted forward at Dustin and Lucas, and she jerked the wheel to the left. Whenever she pressed on the brake it jammed to a stop. Her chin smashed against the steering wheel, but she didn't mind, as she needed to keep moving.

The Mustang scraped some of the grey paint off in the narrow corridor between two of the school buildings, on the way out to the football field, where there were fewer obstacles to crash into. She snapped her seat belt into place. Turning onto the lawn of the football field, she was driving.

Lucas, Rory, and Dustin ran behind to catch her. Kaylee quickly made it to the end of the field, and she turned around to go the other way. She found herself facing off against the three boys, and suddenly Rory raised his shotgun and aimed it right at her face.

Kaylee stopped the car.

Dustin shouted at Rory, "What are you doin'?" He grabbed the barrel of the shotgun and pushed it up into the air. The gun blasted up at the sky.

"Stop it! Everybody!" Lucas tried to take charge, pointing madly at Kaylee. "You stay right there!" He scooted around to the driver's side door. "Put it in park. Park."

Kaylee relented. Lucas ripped open the door to eject her from the vehicle.

They all held court at the front of the car. An exit door back at the school burst open, and Caroline Anderson rambled out hysterical, trying to piece together what was occurring.

"This is unacceptable," said Lucas with a barking dog quality.

"Hey, man," said Dustin. "What the hell's the big deal? So we go for a drive?"

"We're completely surrounded, you moron."

Caroline rushed over, out of breath. "Is anyone hurt?"

"No," replied Rory sarcastically.

Kaylee shook her head.

"Oh, thank God." Caroline joined their circle, and they repositioned themselves in front of the little silver horse.

"Turn the damned engine off," snapped Lucas.

Kaylee nodded submissively, and she stepped over to disconnect the wires. The car engine silenced, and the midday sun beat down on their heads.

"Would somebody explain?" Caroline's gaze darted from one teen to the next.

Dustin started. "Kaylee wants to go meet up with her pa. I thought it was cool. Actually, why ain't it cool?"

"So she wants to go home?" said Caroline. "She told me something like that. I didn't know what it was." She looked to Kaylee, who had hopped up to sit on the front hood of the Mustang. Kaylee yawned.

"Her father isn't coming," said Lucas. "It's a fantasy, people. Would you get real?"

"Ah." Rory nodded and flipped his shotgun back up onto his shoulder.

Dustin glanced back to Kaylee. "You're sure he's coming?"

Kaylee shrugged demurely.

"Oh damn." Dustin softened to a Zen neutrality.

Kaylee grabbed her notepad from her pocket, and she wrote down another note, this time with total conviction.

This is my car. I found it. I hot-wired it. It's mine.

She thrust the paper at Lucas, and she stood contemptuously, daring him to disagree.

Lucas read it and hesitated. "Um."

"What does it say?" Caroline snatched the paper. "Oh."

"What she say?" Dustin held his hand out. They passed the paper to him. "Yep. That sounds about right."

Kaylee glared back smugly, standing at the front bumper.

Twenty

Dustin guided the shot-up car forward toward the mangled school bus for the second time. Kaylee sat beside him, feeling optimistic for a change. As Caroline Anderson climbed into the driver's seat of the bus to try and get it started, Dustin turned to Kaylee.

"So we're partners?"

Kaylee nodded. Dustin held up his fist, and she bumped it with her own. She'd never done that before, but it seemed natural.

"Don't go writin' any more lies." He seemed uncomfortable saying it.

A bit ashamed Kaylee shook her head vigorously, and she exhaled with some relief.

From out of the gym's door, little Sara sprinted to intercept their car, slamming her hands down onto Kaylee's door.

"Kaylee! Are you comin' back?"

Kaylee nodded purposefully. Sara's face tensed with distress. "Be careful out dare." Her eyes bugged out as the school bus exploded to life in a crunchy cacophony.

Kaylee smirked and she kissed the tip of her own finger to deliver it to Sara's nose.

"Can't I come too?" Sara pleaded with her eyes to finally escape this dismal compound.

Kaylee shook her head sternly.

"I can never go anywheres!"

"This is it," said Dustin impatiently.

Kaylee pushed her hands at Sara to push her back away from the car. Sara hunched her shoulders and retreated a couple of steps, as if not entirely convinced of Kaylee's return. As their car shifted into gear, Sara blew a kiss. Their car then shot out through the blackened, crusted-over gate opening and streaked into the hostile town.

Kaylee fiddled with her street map. Dustin dodged left and right down the center of Jefferson. "All right, highway or M.L.K.? Left or right?"

Rounds pierced the skin of the car behind them into the back seat as the dupes opened fire from the side street on the left.

"Damn!"

The Mustang flew faster and evaded, around the nearest corner, toward the highway. Kaylee gauged their progress on the map, tracing along with her finger, when Dustin slammed on the brakes.

She gasped, her chest pinned against the seat belt. More dupes. More gunshots, from the front this time.

The car lurched into reverse, backtracking, spinning, peeling out, careening around as trees and houses blurred. Kaylee dizzied and became disoriented. She couldn't tell which direction they were facing. Bumps up into the air. Up onto the curb. Down again. Then around the next corner. They were still only a couple blocks from the school, but they kept getting turned back around, heading in a wide circle through the neighborhood.

"I gotta get us outta here," Dustin said. "Which way?"

Kaylee pointed to the left, and they took the turn violently, nudging a parked car. The street seemed clear up ahead, as far as the two could see. Dustin floored it, speeding dangerously fast through the narrow suburban side street. Kaylee read the blurry street signs as they whipped by. She found them on the map, and she looked for blue highlighter lines. One was coming again in a couple of blocks.

"Looks okay. Looks okay," said Dustin. He slowed down a bit to keep control of the car. "Now where?"

Kaylee held up her finger to alert him.

One more block. Then she pointed right. *Right.*

***

Carmelita Way stood silent and abandoned, like some dead world in the distant future of some dystopian, black-and-white TV show. The road was littered with debris, and their Mustang crept with understandable suspicion.

Kaylee studied her street as if seeing it for the first time. That rotting corpse had been abandoned since that first morning, then another body. Several cars were strewn awkwardly with their doors hung open, left to rust.

She instructed Dustin to pull into her driveway and to park the Mustang out of sight, hidden by the willow tree. As they arrived, she stared up at that broken rain gutter and the dried blood baked onto the contorted aluminum trough. Expecting Sean, Kaylee involuntarily spied around.

"Should I shut it off?" Dustin held his hand on the ignition wires.

She nodded. The car silenced. Sitting there, Kaylee had not considered what she was going to do next besides wait for Dad to arrive.

Dustin pushed open his door, catlike. His thumb cocked his revolver, and he pointed it up at the blue sky.

"You know? We could grab some supplies, pardner. All these houses are just for us."

Kaylee gazed back dreamily, filled with doubts. Creeped out and unsure about a lot of things, including her entire plan, she felt peculiar in her stomach. Unsure if she could stand up or not, or if she might throw up, Kaylee refused to move. Her hands braced against the inside of the car door and the dashboard. She was not herself, and she wasn't sure which version of herself she wasn't. It was all too perplexing, like the clouds were crushing her.

Dad was nowhere in sight. Mom was still inside the house.

"What do you think, pardner? You got any good stuff inside you wanna get?"

Kaylee swayed.

No way. Don't go in that place. Absolutely not.
"We could try the neighbors?"

Kaylee's head screamed in pain. Her arms covered her eyes. She grabbed her head. While she attempted to recover, she heard Dustin retrieve more weapons from the back seat.

"Hey? Hey?" he said. "Shouldn't we at least go look? What's the matter with ya?"

All Kaylee could do was breathe, too fast. Her body hyperventilated to the point of dizziness.

"You need some water?"

Pain pierced her cortex, and she thought it might poke out through the top of her skull and leave a gaping hole in her head. Her hands crushed her face, and she didn't know how to stop.

Dustin took a walk to scout the yards in case they weren't alone. He seemed interested in all the pristine houses just waiting to be plundered.

After some minutes Kaylee calmed back down, and she felt increasingly accustomed to sitting in her own driveway. The trees and the decorative flowers felt familiar again. Her house seemed comforting with its pastel colors and wooden siding. The shiny windows seemed familiar, like she had never even left. Maybe the Jefferson High part of her life had been the dream, and her true reality waited here.

She kept looking back up to check on the bent rain gutter drooping down at an unexpected angle, where it had twisted up and crumpled. Her own blood stained the outer face.

The urge to step out of the Mustang grew, and soon it was unavoidable. Kaylee was home, and she had important business to attend to. That's why she had come. This was her only chance to reunite with Dad, and she had a responsibility to see it through.

As she climbed from the car, she saw a dark figure rustle in the hedges out by the street. She dropped and hid behind the front of the Mustang. When that shape moved again, she discovered it was only Dustin, and she breathed easier.

Dustin marched back to the car, amused.

"So this is where you live?" He smiled.

Kaylee felt so rattled that she didn't know what to do next.

"Shouldn't we see if your dad's home?"

Kaylee froze. She couldn't go inside. No one could go inside her house. Mom was inside. Mom was in there.

"Come on, Kaylee," Dustin said. "What are we doin' here?"

She dragged her eyes up to face him. His patience was eroding. She had to seem like there was some kind of a plan and that the plan was working, even though the only plan she really had was to get here and hope for the best.

"I'll check the back door," he said. "Come on."

Kaylee slogged behind Dustin as he invaded her backyard. He tested a couple of the locked double-pane windows. The sliding glass door was similarly locked. He rapped on the glass, and he stuck his face up to the door. Kaylee refused to look inside.

"Let's try the other side."

Her house had been sealed, which was fine by her. She couldn't go in. After Dustin knocked on a few more windows and doors, they arrived on the front porch. The doorbell chimed, and he squirmed about to try and see through the geometric patterns in the front door glass, which distorted the view in prisms.

"Guess he ain't here."

Then he looked out at the neighbors' houses, practically salivating. "Why don't you wait here, and I'll just go poke around a bit?"

Kaylee shrugged back.

"Just stay outta sight."

She nodded, and she sat down on her bricked front porch behind a column, wedged in among the fluffy bushes at the side. Dustin skulked off quietly. Then he was gone.

Kaylee waited alone for the remainder of the afternoon. Periodically, Dustin would carry his plundered treasures back to the Mustang: a TV, a DVD player, a game console, boxes of movies, and music discs. From the house next door, he produced an electric guitar, then an amplifier and a bunch of effect boxes. This perplexed her.

The sun receded, and Dustin showed up again on the front porch with a full carton of ice cream sandwiches.

"You want one?"

She held out her hand, and he handed her two chilly bars. Vanilla had smeared his chin. She pointed to his mouth.

"What? Oh." Dustin wiped his mouth with his sleeve.

Kaylee rolled her eyes, and she wanted to confront him about all his stealing. Stylishly, she posed and she pointed back to the Mustang, with an inquisitive face.

"Huh? They ain't comin' back. So I wouldn't worry about it. All's fair. Fair game." He nodded, self-satisfied.

Kaylee turned away to hide her anger.

Of course they're coming back.

Everyone was coming back, like her father. Dad was on his way right now. He had to be. She retreated to the end of the porch again as Dustin tromped off to find more toys.

A coil twisted in her gut as she returned to her brick seat, which had numbed her backside all afternoon. Like she hadn't felt in a long time, she was so sad she wanted to cry, so lonely that she couldn't relate to anyone. Kaylee knew that she couldn't cry anymore, and she would have to muddle through this the way she had always done, for as long as she could remember, like a machine.

Someone moved inside her house.

Kaylee whipped back and peered through the decorative glass panels. The prisms, like stained glass rainbows, scattered the light into various shapes and colors. It was difficult to tell what exactly was on the other side. A shadowy human figure shot past and then darted back in the other direction. Kaylee stared, entranced. She blinked repeatedly to clear her eyes.

When the figure inside finally approached the front door, she knew instantly who was there. A translucent, ethereal form on the other side of the light-scattering glass filled the door panel. It was Mom, and she pressed up close to the glass, even though Kaylee could see right through her into the living room behind.

"Who is that boy, Kaylee?"

Mom sounded curious yet concerned, her voice a bit muffled. "You never brought a boy back to our house before." She sounded surprised and a bit in shock.

"He gave you ice cream, too." She sounded displeased. "They do that. It's one of their tricks, you know. To get you to let your guard down. Don't let your guard down."

Kaylee stood motionless in her haze, trying to focus on Mom more clearly through the door panels. Mom's shape altered constantly, a floating partially-formed specter.

"You be careful with those boys," said Mom. "They're not all forthright and honorable. Do you understand, Kaylee?" Her face solidified.

Kaylee was certain it was really her, and she nodded.

"Listen to me, honey. I don't want your father coming in here, okay? Under any circumstances. He cannot see me like this."

Kaylee felt sadness welling up inside her, like she would cry, although she couldn't.

"Tell him I'm not to be disturbed. I'm perfectly fine without him coming in and seeing me and messing with everything. You tell him, no matter what, he does not come into this house."

Kaylee nodded, and she noticed little liquid droplets bouncing around on her own cheeks.

"Oh, Kaylee. I know how you like talking with me like we do, but I can't keep doing this."

Kaylee's eyes glazed over with salt water. Her hands slammed onto the glass. Her head shook wildly to try and communicate with her limited range of signals.

Mom appeared more amorphous, less tangible. Her transparent, misty form receded from the glass, back into the foyer. Kaylee tried to call her back with her hands, but she felt like a trapped prisoner in an evolving nightmare.

"I have to go now," said Mom. "I have to move on from this world. You understand, better than anyone."

Kaylee could only plead, shaking her head violently until it felt like her brain was being bruised and bashed inside of her skull.

"It's the way it works, honey. I love you so much. But I have to go. I'm so sorry."

Kaylee mouthed the words back, but no sound would come. She could barely see a thing through her tears as she collapsed against the front door. There was no longer any sign of Mom's presence. It felt icy, blue, and empty. The sun had descended. It was too dark to see her inside anymore. Her vision was so distorted that she eventually stopped trying to see at all. Instead she succumbed to the darkness as she covered her face with her arms on the doormat. She shivered against that door for some time, although it seemed like only an instant.

"Psst! Kaylee?" Dustin called from up at the sidewalk.

She raised her head, and she wiped her tears with her sleeve. Her nose was running, and she needed to wash off thoroughly just to look presentable.

"Bring your binoculars. I think I see somebody."

She wobbled as she attempted to stand. Her legs buckled, and she braced herself with her arms. Now she had to shake it off and be like the others, keep going even if she felt like dying. Dustin was excited about something.

Kaylee stumbled down her porch stairs, and she tensed up at the walkway.

"Come on, hurry! Move!" Dustin readied his arrow from the draping cover of the willow tree.

She quickened her steps rushing to Dustin, where she reclaimed her bearings.

He pointed his index finger down Carmelita Way. "There! Who the hell's that now?"

Kaylee raised the lenses and she fiddled with the dial to try and focus the thing. Finally, she saw a dark form trudging up Carmelita Way. With some tweaking, she managed to clear up the view, but it was dark. As the figure passed beneath a street light Kaylee thought he might resemble her dad.

Twenty-One

Suddenly Kaylee jolted from a flood of emotions she couldn't contain. The figure walked toward them, about a football field away down the sidewalk. Kaylee turned to Dustin, who already had an arrow pulled back. She grabbed at his arm and moved the bow to the side, and she jerked maniacally and elated.

"What? Is it him? Is that your dad?"

Kaylee nodded, almost sure. She returned to the binoculars, and she stepped out from the tree onto the sidewalk to see better. Behind the lone figure, something odd bounced about. It looked like a car that moved oddly. With no headlights, it stalked forward up the street around the obstacles.

She pieced it all together. The car was coming up behind her dad.

It's hunting!

The dupes had found him.

Kaylee ran along the sidewalk toward the figure, seeing the car creeping closer behind him. All she could do was scream at the top of her lungs, "Dad! Get out of the way!"

The man whipped about at the last moment as the car revved up onto the curb. He leapt off of the sidewalk and dove up onto the nearest yard. But the front bumper of the assaulting car smashed into his legs and flung his body across the lawn, sending him twisting like a doll.

The car raced forward right at Kaylee. Plowing up the sidewalk, it smashed through the garbage cans and trash bags like a bulldozer intent on mowing her down next.

Dustin appeared beside her on the sidewalk, and he let his arrow fly. It bounced off of the hood and windshield, up into the air, but not before cracking the glass and leaving a million spiderwebs. Dustin nocked a second arrow, and he threw Kaylee over onto the lawn out of the way. She tumbled sideways, rolling over and ending up dizzy beneath the willow tree.

Dustin's second arrow penetrated clear through the windshield. The car zipped past him as he similarly dodged behind the safety of the willow.

The attacking car drifted in an arc across to the other side of the street, where it impacted a parked car and spun out. The engine glugged away. Dustin readied a third arrow.

Kaylee leapt up to her feet, and she dashed down the sidewalk.

"Dad! Are you okay!" Sprinting to the figure lying on the grass she stopped to confirm that it really was him. It had to be.

"Oh my God, Dad," said Kaylee. "Are you hurt? How bad is it?"

She dove down and hugged him on the lawn. When he wrapped his arms around her, she couldn't believe how her life had come full circle. Maybe it was all going to be okay now, like a miracle. Burying her head in his chest, she felt so warm that everything else disappeared, and nothing else mattered.

Her dad finally spoke, in some amount of pain. "My feet got banged up pretty good."

Dustin arrived on the sidewalk, keeping watch and looking for more trouble. "It's him? It's really him?"

Kaylee pulled her face from her dad's chest long enough to focus on the world outside.

"It's my dad."

"Holy-" said Dustin, looking stunned. "You can talk."

"I can talk," said Kaylee. "I can *talk*."

Her mouth and throat felt so strange, like an iron pipe had been removed. Everything worked again, and she didn't even know why.

"Well, we better hightail it." Dustin searched about nervously. "If that dupe radioed more, we ain't got much time for reunions."

"Are you okay to walk, Daddy?"

Kaylee's father felt down to his feet, and he winced. "Let me have a second." He rolled up his pants, and he removed his shoes and socks. "Ow. That bumper got me pretty good. Ha."

Dad's calves were darkly bruised and swollen, and his feet had swelled up.

Dustin moved in with an extended hand. "Here, sir, try and stand up. We gotta bounce."

"All right," said Dad. He took Dustin's hand, and he rose. "And you don't have to call me sir, son. It's just Paul."

"Cool, Paul. I'm Dustin, a friend a your daughter's. Like partners. Let's get the hell outta here."

"Can you walk?" Kaylee helped steady him on the opposite side, and they took two short steps down to the sidewalk.

"I need my shoes!"

They had left them on the lawn. Kaylee quickly retrieved them, and she returned with a smile to assist him back to their car.

On the slow trek back down Carmelita to her home, Kaylee's father looked astonished.

"Is your mother ready to go? And Sean? Are they packed? And where is the safe area?"

Kaylee drooped. Her mind retreated. She now had no conceivable way to pull everything together, everything that had happened, now that Dad was so completely in the dark.

With each labored footstep toward her house, she longed for the distancing and the detachment that the Jefferson High School base camp had afforded. Her shoulder braced her father up on his right side, and they struggled forward together, Dustin assisting on the left.

Dad reached into his pocket, and Kaylee could hear the metal house keys jingle together. She had no explanation and no words that could undo what had been done to their family. Her dad limped forward casually, as if nothing was wrong.

The noise from the crashed auto's engine raced, and it served as a distraction. Kaylee needed badly to think. She wished she had remained mute and cut off from verbal exchanges. The three turned into her driveway together, and she watched her father take the front door key between his fingers.

Dad smiled down at her. "Oh," he said. "Is it locked? I'm not even thinking."

Her head felt airy. "You can't go in."

"What?" Dad continued lumbering forward, undeterred.

"Mom said you're not allowed to go in the house. Let's just get in the car before they come."

"No. I need to pack my own things," said her father tersely. "I don't even have any clothes." Without slowing, he marched on toward the inevitable horror inside. They all arrived at the steps, and the sensor-light flicked on. Dustin twisted nervously, still ready with his compound bow.

Without a pause, Dad ascended the brick stairs.

Kaylee stepped out in front, blocking the key. "You absolutely cannot go in. We'll find you different clothes. Everything's for free now."

Dad gazed disbelievingly down on her.

"Kaylee? Step aside." His tone turned stern quickly, and the pain from his damaged feet likely didn't help the situation. The two stood in a momentary standoff, Kaylee blocking his entrance, and her dad determined to ignore her pleas.

"It's a giant mess," said Kaylee, shaking her head nervously.

Her father wasn't having it.

"I don't care about a mess. I want my clothes and my things. Get out of the way!"

Kaylee, frantic and desperate, shouted back, "Mom said no!" She teared up and breathed faster, less assured and less whole.

"What the hell? Kaylee? Just calm down."

Dustin chimed in, spinning with the bow left and right. "People, can you keep it down? Am I the only one who's got his head screwed on straight here?"

Dad's hand reached to her shoulder, partially for comfort, partially for stability, and partially to maneuver her out of the way.

"It's Armageddon out there. I don't care about a messy house. Would you just please get out of the way, angel?"

Tears fell and welled at the bottom of her eyelids.

"It's not that kinda mess."

His big brown eyes wide open, he stared over Kaylee's head and into the dark shadows within.

"What are you saying? Sean? Did something happen to Sean?"

Kaylee turned away, nodding. Defeated, she slouched out of his path. Her strained voice had spoken too many words already, and it was too strenuous to continue. Each syllable she formed cost her more and more energy. Over her long ordeal, she had almost forgotten how to speak. Now she just wanted to sleep.

Leaving Dad to his key and his deadbolt lock, Kaylee collapsed down onto the porch and rolled away to rest her eyes. Her head swirled full of fog, and she remembered Mom and how Sean had stabbed her mercilessly. She remembered Mom's scream. She remembered Sean stabbing right through her bedroom door and how he chased her off of their roof. She remembered accepting *Ghostliest* and hugging Mom for so long, swaying back and forth together. Then she remembered her father.

She shouted, "Daddy, come out! Don't look."

Her father made no sounds from within the house. It remained still and quiet. Dustin stood by the Mustang, tapping his boot impatiently.

Kaylee snapped to attention, and she sprang back up to her feet.

"Dad?" As she stepped inside the dark foyer, the air filled with an unbearable stench. She guardedly slipped inside. "Mom?"

When no one appeared, she stuck to the edge of the living room, peering across in the direction of the kitchen. A dark form rose slowly in the twinkling shadows. It wasn't Mom. It was Dad looking a lot like he had seen a ghost.

Kaylee never imagined that Dad could appear so devastated. He stumbled into the recliner, and he shook.

"Dad?"

His eyes tracked up and he located Kaylee in the dim open arch at the foyer.

"Don't come in here." He was crying, and he stopped in place at the center of the living room. "Go. Go wait outside." Dad dropped down onto their couch, and he supported his face with his palms.

Kaylee turned back to the open front door, and she escaped the house. Outside, the sound of that racing car engine continued mindlessly churning. Dustin was nowhere in sight now, and she assumed he would be checking out the dupe vehicle for intel about the enemy. That's what they were supposed to be doing, anyway. That and procuring weapons. It was standard procedure.

She fled her porch, shaking off the smell and the thick soup of terror inside her childhood home. She found a new purpose in searching for clues in that noisy-ass dupe car and shutting off the damned engine so it wouldn't draw any unnecessary attention. She marched down her driveway and she located the wreck across the street. No sign of Dustin. Selfish hick was probably raiding more houses for video games.

Kaylee stepped around the driver's side to see the dupe who had tried to kill her father and her. As she swung to the side of the car, she could see the smashed windshield and the red-feathered aluminum arrow plunged through the driver's chest. Reflections and darkness obscured the dupe's face until she moved in one step closer.

"Oh my God."

The dupe was Sean. He sat motionless. The aluminum arrow pinned him to the driver's seat. Blood flooded from his chest. Kaylee ceased breathing. Unable to get past that moment, she stared at Sean's face through the car glass. As she did, she wondered how he could have been programmed to kill their mother and run over their father, and how he could try to kill her with a knife and chase her off of their roof.

Sean wasn't even the only one. It was a pandemic. It was everywhere. It defied everything that they taught in school.

A rush of discomfort, and Kaylee gasped for her next breath. She had to turn off that damned car now. The noise ground and whined ridiculously. Dustin should have taken care of it already.

Kaylee yanked open the door, intent on bravely reaching across Sean's corpse to silence the car's engine. That's when she looked past his body.

A small, propped-up computer pad was glowing, spinning, swirling. The engine had masked the noise, but now she could clearly hear the computer modem signal. She only heard it for a few moments. Then it was clear that the computer's video screen held the real secret to understanding what was going on.

Gazing into that little display, Kaylee suddenly found the world much brighter in intensity. The yellow-orange streetlight coated everything with a shimmering, soft glow. Sean's blood became candy apple red, a monument to his efforts. Sounds muted and dissolved as the wisdom of the universe poured into her head, words, paragraphs, that feeling of invincibility, encyclopedias of knowledge.

Her mind felt soothed and relieved. She wondered why she hadn't investigated the signal before. It was extremely beautiful, actually, the way it swirled right into the mind and provided much-needed answers. A river of information, a tsunami even, flooded her entire being and awakened her to the hidden realities of the world.

Kaylee realized that she had been fighting on the wrong side all along. The signal's wisdom gave her the strength and the purpose to correct everything that was wrong, and to finally achieve peace and complete victory. It was so clear that the winning side was theirs, and that the signal was unstoppable. Anyone could see that if they just accepted the new world.

Kaylee finally accepted this reality. She knew that she would be a great soldier. Together, she, with the masses of other soldiers, would achieve the complete rebirth of society from the ground up, and make everything right in the end. It was practically completed already, and she was so lucky to have come aboard at this opportune moment.

All she needed to do was to join forces with the others and kill any of the enemies who stood in her way, like Dustin or her dad. They were on the wrong side, clearly, and sacrifices needed to be made. It was the price of progress and of building a perfect society, which was now inevitable.

Everything made perfect sense. She was so relieved to fight for the right cause that she didn't mind any of the casualties either side had sustained. Her brother was a valued piece of machinery, but now she would take his place and execute instructions as they were given.

That was her assigned role in life, and she knew that she was going to be damned good at it.

Twenty-Two

"Kaylee?"

Behind her, Dustin said something, his voice suspicious. Kaylee accepted this challenge, and she knew that Dustin possessed tactical weaknesses. These she would easily exploit and take him out, and then move on to her father. Since her dad was already injured, it would be an easier task than Dustin, who was still armed and now seemed apprehensive. It was time to jump.

Kaylee turned from the signal, and she sized up Dustin quickly.

"What's goin' on?" He retreated a step, but he was too personally attached to strike first.

Kaylee knew of his softness, and so she leapt directly at him. Although she had no weapons of her own, Dustin's pistol hung from his belt, and he carried a quiver full of razor-tipped arrows on his back. Either way could neutralize him if she acted with enough raw speed.

She rammed him with her head, in the middle of the street, and the two wrestled on the asphalt. Kaylee growled and clawed with her fingernails at Dustin's neck. He seemed reluctant to hit her hard, but he tried to grab her arms and restrain her. She kicked his legs and screamed unintelligibly in his ear.

"Dammit! Kaylee! Quit it!" He elbowed her hard in the ribs.

She tumbled away in the street, rolling over and over.

"What's going on here?" came the voice of her father.

Kaylee rebounded and sank her teeth into Dustin's forearm, trying to rip the flesh off like a tiger shark. She growled, punching at Dustin's head and kneeing him in his groin.

"Ow! Damn!"

Kaylee might have beaten Dustin, or even killed him, if her father hadn't grabbed her and pinned her down onto the pavement. She flailed beneath the pressure, howling and shouting indecipherable screams.

Dustin whimpered and nursed his wounds, while Kaylee struggled to free herself. The two lifted her up.

"What about that car?" Her dad paused momentarily, snapping back.

"Stay away," said Dustin. "It's booby-trapped, man."

They then dragged Kaylee down the driveway to the back seat of the Mustang, where they tied her hands behind her back with an electrical cord from a guitar amplifier.

All the while, Kaylee jerked to and fro to free herself. She needed to devise a plan to kill them both, with or without her hands. She was squeezed in between the guitar, cardboard boxes, and the side wall. Kaylee's wrists pulled against the cables that bound her. In animalistic grunts she shouted at them, and she kicked and flailed to try and work herself free, to no avail.

Dustin started the Mustang, and they shot backward toward the street.

"Oh man, I don't know. I don't know what they're gonna want to do with her at Jefferson."

Kaylee listened, as Dustin debated with her father in front, in the hope that it would help her escape later.

"What do you mean?" said her father, incredulous. "We have to help her until she recovers."

Dustin shook his head with exaggerated disbelief. "They ain't partial to dupes."

"She's not a *dupe*, for God's sake. She's my daughter."

Dustin shook his head dismissively. "Every dupe's got a family. I'm tellin' ya. We gotta be cool, man."

"Oh, Christ." Her father turned back to watch her as Dustin whipped around a turn.

Gazing out, the streetlights swam past, and Kaylee quietly fiddled with the knotted cord behind her. It felt tight and stiff, and she tried to calculate which loop needed work in order to unknot the binds. Her hands manipulated the cable as the car cruised rapidly toward Jefferson Avenue.

If she could only work one hand free, she could use the cord to wrap around Dustin's throat while he drove. That would force him to crash the car and give her a reasonable probability of escaping or of killing them both. Kaylee enjoyed this tactical challenge. One of the loops slid free, and she pulled it out of the knot, ready to continue deeper into the coils.

"What she smilin' about?" Dustin stared back through the rear view mirror, and he elbowed her dad. Dustin's voice grew uneasy. "Hey, guy... Paul? Check on her. I don't trust her. She's a full-blown dupe."

Kaylee's dad swung back around momentarily, and he gave her a once over. "She's okay."

"No! Man, we're ridin' with a damned dupe right in the back seat. Get with the program."

Kaylee continued smiling absently, remaining relaxed each time her father twisted back to check up on her.

"She's not doing anything," he said.

"Aw! There they are!" Dustin jammed the brakes, and he peeled out in the other direction. Everyone slammed to the right, and Kaylee banged into all the boxes. The nearer they got to the school, the more obstructions they found, and the more squads of dupes became involved in the big siege.

Kaylee took this opportunity to work the knot behind her back, watching them carefully.

"Do you have a license, son?"

"DMV's closed, Paul."

"Oh great." Her father fought the g-forces as they slammed around to the next side street. "Slow down! I should drive."

"Too late, man." Dustin bounced them over a corner curb and they straightened out alongside the back wall of the school, outside the football field. "Glove box. Grab the radio."

Her father found the walkie-talkie, and Kaylee heard a click as he turned it on.

"Give it." Dustin snatched it from him, driving with one hand. "Yo, Lucas, open up. It's us! Move the damned bus!"

After several seconds, Lucas came on the radio. "Yeah, yeah, I got ya."

The Mustang fishtailed out onto Jefferson Avenue as several rifle shots ricocheted off the street. Yet the school bus was not moving out of the way. Their Mustang skidded in front of the gate as dupe snipers took pot shots at them. Dustin shouted out his window, "Come on, come on! Assholes!"

More bullets arrived. Dustin and Kaylee's father ducked down low in their seats, while Kaylee seized the moment to work on the next loop of her knot.

As the charred school bus jolted backward on its disintegrated tires, their Mustang exploded forward and through the opening into the schoolyard. Dustin parked, and he hopped nervously out of the car.

Kaylee's father turned back to face her. "Honey, you're going to be okay. Don't worry."

She could only stare back, frozen, temporarily prevented from working her hands free.

"We'll take care of you," said Dad, and he stepped out.

Lucas and Caroline approached the Swiss cheese Mustang together. Dustin leaned back inside to help lift

Kaylee from the back seat. "You best behave yourself," he said, "I swear."

"What you bring us?" said Caroline.

Dustin winced, still facing away from them.

"Trouble. Oh, and I found some first aid and bandages, peroxide and pills and stuff."

"What? What trouble?" Lucas was in a jovial mood, Kaylee could see. She worked her body awkwardly out of the back of the car and up to her feet. Then she sized up the security situation. Lucas's pistol was holstered. Same with Caroline's. Her father was unarmed, and Dustin had carelessly left his pistol and bow on the front seat of the Mustang. A sniper sat on the rooftop above the gym to her right. A couple of spotters hung out on either side of the school bus gate, lazing away on tables. That was it.

Kaylee could feel her knot giving way behind her back, yet she remained silent and motionless. Like a coiled cobra she bided her time to strike with maximum impact.

"It's Kaylee," said Dustin.

"Who the hell is that?" Lucas pointed at her dad.

"Oh damn, I forgot. It's Kaylee's pa."

As Dustin introduced Kaylee's father, she managed to slip one hand free, unnoticed. She improvised a quick plan to incapacitate one of the boys and take his weapon. She was, however, surrounded, with Dustin standing directly in the doorway of the car between her and the most readily accessible gun.

Kaylee thought of striking Lucas with the cable knot, across his throat, giving her a chance to take away his sidearm.

"Are you serious?" said Caroline, perhaps starting to comprehend the situation.

"Colton?" Lucas peered down into Kaylee's wide, staring eyes, astounded. His face twisted up with suspicion. "You in there?"

They all took a nervous step away from her, suddenly unsure of which side she might be fighting for. Kaylee reassessed her options. She could run for it and try and slide under the school bus and out the gate before they stopped her. With her extensive knowledge of the compound, she could help with a successful incursion and quickly take over the school.

Since Lucas and Caroline had retreated back a step, she figured that Dustin would have to be her target. She needed to take him down before her father completed his limp around the back of the car.

Just then, five-year-old Sara skipped out the gym doorway. Spotting Kaylee among the others, Sara jogged toward them happily.

"Kaylee, Kaylee, Kaylee!"

Kaylee needed only to let her arrive.

Lucas turned with exasperation. "What are we gonna do with her? Dammit. A *dupe*?"

She watched every step as Sara approached. She loosened her shoulders and grabbed hold of the black power cable. Crushing it in her palm behind her back, she readied it.

"Kaylee, you're back!"

Sara ran straight through their circle to hug her around the waist. Smiling innocently, Sara rammed right into Kaylee's legs to hold tightly.

That's when she struck. With the electrical cord, she snatched Sara around the throat, pulling the cord across her tiny neck. The others gasped helplessly as Kaylee whipped the child around, and dragged her backward off of her feet.

Sara screamed and gasped as Kaylee yanked her about like a dog's toy, away from Dustin and the Mustang.

"Ow! Kaylee! What are you doing? Ow!"

The others all froze solemnly. Kaylee's father called over, "No, no, Kaylee! Just let her go!"

Dustin put his hands up softly. "You don't wanna do this."

Caroline barked, "Dammit, let go of her!"

Lucas reached for his gun. "Colton, you better let that kid go, right now!"

Kaylee retreated swiftly, pulling Sara back along with her. The rest of them stepped after, one careful footstep at a time.

"What do we do?" Caroline advanced with the others as Kaylee eyed the school bus behind her.

Dustin retrieved his bow and one arrow from the Mustang.

"Kaylee? I'm scared!" Sara rasped, but Kaylee maintained an iron grip around her neck.

Dustin crept forward after Kaylee.

Caroline appeared as if she might run at her in a mad dash. Kaylee stared back knowingly and squeezed the cord so that Sara would gasp. Sara's tongue hung out, and she couldn't breathe.

"Stop it!" Caroline cried out.

Kaylee's dad moved alongside Dustin. "What are you going to do? Don't you shoot her. Don't." Dad tried to interfere with Dustin's aim, and he put himself in the line of fire.

The sniper and the wall guards turned and raised their own weapons. Sara continued to cry and struggle.

Kaylee pulled her until she banged into the school bus with her shoulders. She sized up her opposition, and she forced Sara all the way down to the ground so that they could both slide backward underneath the bus and escape the schoolyard.

Suddenly, Kaylee was knocked off her feet, a sharp pain in her back. Dustin's arrow bounced off of her, without a tip. Kaylee rolled on the ground. Everyone rushed forward to pile on top of her. They freed Sara and restrained Kaylee, who flailed like a wounded cat.

Sara cried continually. Her face was white with fear. She held her throat, which had rubbed red, swelling with bruises.

Caroline and her father wrapped the cord around Kaylee's arms and torso. Then they raised her to her feet again.

Most of the school flooded out into the yard to witness. Melanie and several other girls surrounded Sara and picked her up, petting her head and comforting her.

Most scowled at Kaylee. They now had a dupe prisoner, something unprecedented at Jefferson. Since she was tied up and helpless, the more timid teens were emboldened to come closer and to examine her for themselves. An angry mob formed around Kaylee as Lucas prodded her forward toward the door.

"This is great," said Lucas. "How the hell did they get Colton?"

Dustin shook his head. "Shit happens, man."

Lucas shook with frustration at the surrounding crowd. "All right! Everybody back off!"

The mob loosened, and Lucas pushed Kaylee toward her father. "You. You can babysit her. I've got a siege to worry about."

"Yes. Of course." Kaylee's dad limped forward in a daze. "I'm sorry. I'm so sorry for her. I just can't understand."

They escorted her inside the door of the gym and marched her through to the hallway. Things quieted substantially once inside.

"Okay," said Lucas. "I know one room that locks from the outside. Downstairs."

Kaylee plotted and schemed her next escape attempt during the trek. Even as they transferred her to a holding cell, she knew she would certainly be more successful next time and would take out as many of them as possible. She maintained a lofty, arrogant smirk as she stared ahead down the stairwell and into the basement hallway. It seemed they had a fuel-powered generator and a big tank, which might come in handy for setting a fire.

Her father could barely walk. Kaylee saw that she could easily outrun him. He braced himself against the cinder block walls as they marched, falling well behind.

Lucas unlocked a storage room door and flicked on a switch. The closet was concrete with a thick steel door. A small air vent on the ceiling was unsuitable for crawling through. Many boxes and shelves took up space.

Lucas calmed himself, finally. "Okay. What's your name?"

"Pau-Paul. I'm Kaylee's father."

"Yeah, yeah, I got that."

"I'm just?"

"What?"

"I haven't eaten today, is all." Her dad leaned back weakly.

Lucas nodded. "I'll have somebody send down food."

Her father collapsed. "She'll need something to lie on."

Lucas rubbed his neck. From an overstuffed key chain he slid off the storage room key, and he pointed his finger sharply. "She stays locked in there till I say she's okay to come out." Lucas handed the key over to Kaylee's father. "She's gonna try and use whatever's in there to kill you and get away. You know that."

"I understand."

"Hafstead."

Dustin yawned. "Yeah, dude?"

"Help him get this room stripped down so the prisoner can't pull any more crap, okay?"

"Yeah. Got it."

Kaylee stood hunched forward and to the side. "She's hurt," said her dad. "That arrow." He stood up again, reeling. He lifted Kaylee's shirt on the back and groaned. "Oh God. We need ice, please."

Kaylee growled back like a feral rodent. The pain momentarily overwhelmed her inclinations.

They tied her to the shelving unit with several pieces of electrical cord, and they remodeled the cell. A boy arrived with food and an ice pack. Taking the ice, her father stalked closer to her.

Kaylee's hands were restrained, but her legs were still nimble and ready to lash out. Everyone used utmost caution approaching her. Like with a poisonous snake, it wasn't smart to get too close.

When the cold wave hit, Kaylee wrenched and pulled at the shelving unit, dragging it across the floor and knocking off a couple of the remaining boxes. The pain rushed in, but she knew it would be temporary. Soon she would figure out a better escape route.

Later that evening, after the storage room was completely cleared out, bare walls and a cot mattress, Kaylee lay silently. Wearing four cable restraints, her body curled up on the mattress without freedom of movement.

Her mind raced with new ideas to succeed against these inferior enemies. She recalled the gas tanker truck parked beside the gym. The tank held enough high-octane fuel to flood the whole building and ignite it in one massive fireball. If she could just escape while they slept, she could use the tanker's own hose to pump the gym full of gasoline. By the time anyone noticed it would be too late, and the explosion would consume everyone. Kaylee could destroy the entire school with one well-placed action.

But how to get out of these binds and past that locked steel door?

The situation seemed pretty bleak from Kaylee's point of view. Before she could flood the school with gasoline and ignite it, she needed to work her way out of four knots, each of them tougher than the first one she had escaped, plus get past the steel door barrier and then her father. The plan held a very low probability of success.

Twenty-Three

Kaylee awoke from a dark and dismal nightmare. Her body ached all over, as did her brain.

"Ow! What the hell? What's going on?"

Her body wracked with pain, and she could barely move. Unable to free her arms or legs, she rolled angrily on the floor. She suddenly felt very frightened, not knowing where she was or how she had gotten there.

"Help!" she screamed. "Help! What the hell are you people doing?"

Finally, she heard activity through the sealed steel door. Something scratched and scraped the metal. Then the door opened with a whoosh. Her father stood alone in the opening, bracing himself in the door jamb. His face seemed curious yet desperate.

"Ow. Ow. Daddy? They got me tied up!"

"Kaylee! You're back?" Her dad snapped to attention, and he rushed forward, hobbling on his injured foot.

"What do you mean I'm 'back? I'm tied up like a piece of meat. Get me outta here!"

She squirmed in her panic and hyperventilated. Her father dropped to her cot and untied her cords.

"Okay, okay. Don't struggle. I'm getting them off." Her father worked at her binds, but it was taking forever.

Kaylee ground her teeth. "Dammit. What is wrong with you people? What the hell?"

Her father whipped the first black cord off from around her wrist.

"Yeah, exactly," he murmured.

"Ow, ow, ow, my back. What happened?" She couldn't help but squirm and attempt to stretch out against her restraints. Cramps tensed along her back and legs.

Dad continued working the cords free until Kaylee could stretch. Her knees creaked and joints popped.

"You don't remember?" When he finished freeing her ankles, he sat beside her on the linoleum floor. "It was so terrible," he said. "You were just... like a machine. A killing machine. I don't have the words."

"What are you talking about?" said Kaylee. "I was asleep."

"No, angel. You were... scary."

Kaylee felt a plummeting terror at what she was hearing. "I don't remember how I got here."

Her father sighed. "There's a little girl upstairs I don't think I will ever forget."

Kaylee tried to recall anything she could. "Who? What are you saying? Where are we?" Her mind was a big blank slate. She felt lost like a hole had been blasted through her mind. "What girl?"

Kaylee's dad released a tear, which disturbed her greatly.

"Dad?"

He shook his head. "I don't know. Her name is Sally or something, with an S."

Kaylee fell inside, in the grip of something she couldn't understand.

"Did something happen to Sara?"

Dad shook his head emotionally. "She's-she'll be all right."

"Did I do something?"

He turned to her and somberly looked into her eyes. "Yeah, but, it's all over now."

Kaylee shook. "What do you mean? What did I do?"

"Shh. Shh. It's best we just go show them that you're okay. You're all better. Just be your old self."

She closed her eyes, and she shook her head, lying back on the wet, filthy cot. "I don't even know if I have an old self."

On the cusp of a breakdown, Kaylee held her face in her hands. Her father held onto her for comfort. "It'll be okay. We're going to get through this."

The green steel door hung open out into the hallway. Soft footsteps intruded. Kaylee lifted her head. Carrying a cafeteria tray with two plates on it, Melanie peeked into their closet, wearing a baffled expression.

Her dad said, "Hi there. What have you brought?"

Kaylee looked on tensely. "Hello, Melanie."

"She's? You're... normal again? I-I didn't realize that you could speak. I'm sorry." Flabbergasted, Melanie bobbed awkwardly with her tray as if unsure how to respond.

"Kaylee's back with us, and she's recovering. Thank you so much for bringing us breakfast."

"Oh, yeah. Sure." Melanie rushed to deliver the contents of the trays. "Here you go!"

As Melanie handed her a plate, Kaylee was so disoriented that she didn't know how to behave.

"What happened last night?" Kaylee stared up to capture Melanie's attention. "Did you see?"

"Me?" She blushed. "I only saw a little. You probably want to ask someone else, like your dad! Hi. I'm Melanie. I work in the library, which is like the HQ around here." With a casual grin she shook Dad's hand vigorously.

Kaylee twisted away. "Melanie? What did I do?"

Dad petted her hair softly. "Honey, it wasn't you. Just, don't dwell on it."

Kaylee's eyes drizzled again, and she obscured her face from them both. "What did I do? I wanna know!"

"I'll tell her," said her father. "Thank you again, Mel-?"

"Melanie. Or Melly. I'm glad to see you're better now, Kaylee. And hear your voice."

Kaylee nodded, still concealing her face.

"I'll see you later," said Melanie, and she was gone.

"Tell me!" Kaylee buried her head into the old, stinky mattress.

"Okay, okay. After we returned home, you went and looked in that car. You know? The car that crashed. The one that hit me."

"Yeah." Kaylee's memory flashed with Sean's image, the last thing she could remember. Sean lay dead in the driver's seat, after Dustin's arrow had pierced his heart.

"Well, inside the car," said her dad, "we think there was a booby trap, a screen. And you saw it."

"All right." Kaylee couldn't visualize the signal, but felt only a queasy sickness pulling at her abdomen.

"That's all it takes."

"And then what?"

"You went after that boy, whats-his-face?"

"Dustin?"

"The one who drove."

"Yeah, Dustin. What did I do to Dustin?"

"Now remember, it wasn't you. It was them. It wasn't you, Kaylee."

"And?" She turned her face from the mattress for a breath of fresher air, and she sat up, inhaling deeply.

"Well, you kicked his ass pretty good. And I think you might have bit him."

"Oh God."

"And then I heard you two fighting in the middle of our street, and I ran out. We broke it up."

"Oh, Dad. What happened with Sara?" Kaylee cringed with every nerve of her body.

"You really need to apologize to that little girl." He paused, but Kaylee glared at him.

"You grabbed her... with the cord... around her throat. It was horrible. I couldn't—I don't know."

"Was she scared?"

"She was, yeah." Dad wiped his brow with his wrist. "Yeah, and you pulled her across the yard, trying to get away. And you were choking her."

"Oh my God."

"We stopped you! We ended it. We let her go."

Kaylee lay back down to sob. Attempting to remember was futile, and her brain didn't seem to recall anything, as if none of those memories were stored in the first place.

"I don't remember."

"Good," said her dad. "Good."

Suddenly, Dustin jumped across the doorway and pointed a handgun at them both. "Freeze! Why's it open? What she doin'?"

"Easy, easy." Dad raised his hands slowly. "She's fixed now, okay, son? Dustin?"

"No way?" Dustin relaxed the revolver to his side. "What do you mean *fixed*?"

"Kaylee? Tell him."

Kaylee sat up contritely. "I'm sorry I attacked you, Dustin. I don't want you to hold that against me."

Dustin guffawed. "I can't get over hearin' you talk. This is so weird." He laughed in Dad's direction. "Ain't it?"

Her dad wouldn't get it.

Dustin led Kaylee and her father toward the cafeteria. It was still breakfast time, no dupes massed outside, and the large space was packed. The entire cafeteria deadened as the three stepped in through the door. Whispers shot across the tables. Curious teens gawked.

"Holy," Lucas jumped up to intercept them. "I thought I said not to let her out-"

"It's all cool," said Dustin, leading the parade.

A gaggle of onlookers collected at a safe distance. Rory snatched his shotgun, and he stormed over, chest out, full of machismo. The barrel of the gun bobbed in Kaylee's direction.

"Hey! Hey!" Dad moved his body to shield Kaylee. "Put that gun down! What do you think you're doing?"

"She's a robot," yelled Rory so that everyone would focus on him. "She's a God damn Terminator. You saw her! With your own eyes!"

Kaylee called back, "Screw you, dork."

The cafeteria silenced again, like a church at three a.m. No one had ever heard Kaylee speak before. They swarmed to get a better view of her.

Lucas said, "Everybody just chill. Put that shotgun down. What's the matter with you?"

"I ain't turnin' my back on that dupe bitch." Rory lowered the barrel but remained confrontational.

Kaylee stepped out. "I'm not a dupe!"

"You talk," said Caroline with a frown. "Where was your voice all this time when we could have used it?"

Kaylee huffed out, deflated.

Rory jolted forward. "She's a dupe spy!"

The mass of teenagers searched each other's faces, confused.

"Stop it," said her father. "She's not a spy. She's not under the influence of *them* anymore. End of story."

Rory flopped the shotgun back over his shoulder. "Oh yeah? As soon as she sees that video again, she'll cut all our throats. You too, guy."

Lucas shook his head. "That's for any-Look, if anybody sees that transmission, they're toast. Not just Colton. We saw it happen right here in the yard. You remember."

Rory danced around, having received some sympathetic looks from the crowd. "No! No! This is how it's gonna be! Listen to me!"

Dustin shouted, "Oh shut up, man! Just shut up!" He stepped forward to stare down Rory. Caroline shushed loudly, and others joined her, including Melanie.

"Calm down, people!" Lucas stepped forward to stand beside Kaylee. "She's okay now? Right?"

Kaylee's heart beat rapidly, her face in a cold sweat. She nodded. "I'm fine... My back is killing me."

Her dad slid to the other side of her. "You see? Everything's okay now."

The animosity of the mob dissipated somewhat. Lucas gave Kaylee a thorough inspection, up and down, for effect. "She seems to be okay now."

Rory marched away broodingly. "I don't trust her."

Kaylee sneered. "I don't trust you either, jerk!"

Lucas breathed easier. "So it's settled? Colton is back, one hundred percent on our side." He turned and gazed down into her green eyes. "Aren't ya?"

"One hundred and ten percent." Kaylee stood firm. Several admirers in the crowd clapped.

"All right," said Lucas. "That's what I want to hear."

The gathering dispersed.

Little Sara strolled in to the cafeteria, talking to a small, bulbous-headed doll, which someone must have crafted in the art room. Simultaneously Sara saw Kaylee, and Kaylee saw her. A convulsive, involuntary scream pierced the room. Sara peed down her legs.

Before Kaylee could say or do anything, Sara raced out to the hallway shrieking. Kaylee felt like Frankenstein's monster, reanimated from sewn-together pieces of corpses, as frigid as she had ever felt in her life. She knew something was so wrong that it needed to be dealt with right now. As Sara had fled into the school, terrified and with post-traumatic shock, Kaylee knew better than to pursue her. It would only make things worse, much worse.

Isolated in the cafeteria, alone despite the bustling crowd around her, Kaylee had to figure a new way to reach out to Sara without hurting her in the process. In a blurry daze, Kaylee spun and tried to think of an answer. The ceiling tiles flew by, the white wall clock above the door, then the mounted brown speaker box.

***

Jefferson's administrative office was occupied by Caroline Anderson, who lived in there by herself. It held convenient little rooms that locked. Caroline was the solitary type who preferred to be left alone after her shifts ended, but she wasn't there this morning.

The main reception area featured an open lobby. That's where Kaylee investigated. Opening cabinets and peeking under counters, eventually she located the school's public address amplifier. A microphone sat in a cabinet attached to the metal box by a long, coiled cord. Kaylee inspected it. Her finger clicked on a power button with a pop. Tapping on the microphone a couple of times, nothing happened. Then she flicked a second switch on the microphone's body, and suddenly she could feel the hot, tingly sensation that it was alive. Speakers all over the campus crackled simultaneously to life and teased the air with throbbing pulsations.

Now that Kaylee faced the big microphone alone, a sinking feeling in the pit of her guts reminded her that she had no idea what she was going to say. Her own voice still seemed unfamiliar, like a disembodied spirit floating away from her mouth every time she opened it. But this was too crucial. Sara was desperately hurting inside and off hiding by herself, and it was all her fault somehow.

Kaylee gasped, still in a flustered daze. She needed to believe that Sara could hear her, and that she would listen.

"Sara? It's Kaylee." Pausing to hear herself echo through the hallways, she knew that she couldn't stop now.

"Sara? It's really me again. Yesterday the dupes got me, and that wasn't me. It wasn't me, Sara. You have to believe me. I would never hurt you..."

Kaylee worried from every conceivable angle how she would be perceived with her soul laid out for the entire school to hear. There was no way to reach Sara without also reaching all of Jefferson High's population.

"You don't have to be afraid of me, Sara. I'm not going to hurt you. I swear. And I promise. I promise that I'll help you find your parents again. Okay? We're gonna find your mom and dad. I swear. Even if they're dupes, I know they can be saved. Everybody can be saved. All we have to do is turn off their signal. It's really the way to win. We can win! We can end this. I know we can."

Kaylee knew not to talk for too long, because everyone hated that. And she knew she had said what she wanted to, but still she couldn't be sure if Sara had actually heard.

"Please, Sara. Forgive me. You don't have to run away. That's all over now. I am so sorry I hurt you. I'm sorry."

Kaylee powered down the amplifier. The static in the air dissipated, and she sat back in the soft secretary's chair. Contemplating, she breathed just to hear herself.

The wall clock said two minutes to noon. Early still, and the dupes were out there somewhere, probably sleeping.

Twenty-Four

Kaylee marched out to the school's yard and searched for Lucas. Back inside the gym, she found him asleep. She had never seen Lucas sleep before. Lingering, she knew waking him could be a bad idea, but pleasantries and manners were for peacetime. Her hand shook Lucas's shoulder hard.

"Lucas. We need to move."

"What? What!" He jerked awake. "Dammit, Colton. What's going on? Status?"

"We need to move now. They're asleep. We need to cut their signal."

"Oh my God. It's so weird hearing you talk." Lucas rubbed his eyes and sat up. "What are you saying? You know where they are?"

"No."

He sat up and looked about the gym. "You don't. So, what *are* we doing?"

"Well, we have to find them and kill their transmission. Duh."

"And we have to do it right now?"

"Yeah." Kaylee squatted closer. "Before they wake up and get reprogrammed again. They're like vampires. We have to go when they're asleep."

"All right. I get it." Lucas looked to the gym's ceiling. "I'm never going to get any sleep. And you're sure they're all sleeping at the same time?"

"I'm not *positive*." Kaylee nibbled at her lower lip.

"Well. You're talking about risking our asses out there. What do you actually think you know?"

"Okay," she said emphatically. "Okay. I know they aren't dupes when they first wake up. They're people."

"All right. What else?"

Kaylee's face contorted. "Um... That's it."

Before Lucas could speak again, Kaylee yanked him up onto his feet.

"Come on. We need to move."

***

Their platoon of eight kids, plus Kaylee's dad, who hobbled along behind the group, darted up the sidewalk in a single file line. In a rush her father had fashioned a crutch out of a mop handle. Kaylee told him to stay back at Jefferson, but he was adamant. Although he couldn't keep up, he remained determined to fight off the pain in his swollen feet and lower legs, even if it killed him. He told her that he couldn't have her out of his sight again.

Their squad rushed in the direction suspected by the wall guards, who seemed to think the dupes retreated toward Martin Luther King Boulevard down the tranquil side streets. Kaylee, Dustin, and Lucas led the column, on the lookout for anything that moved. At the next cross street Dustin pointed his thumb to the right toward M.L.K., and the others silently followed, a line of ants on a straight trajectory toward trouble.

Kaylee panted. Her pack weighed her down. Since she carried no weapons, they made her haul several gallons of water and snacks for the group. Energized from her second wind, she bobbed up and down on each step ahead.

The air crackled subtly. Kaylee sensed the micro disturbances, and she felt she was suddenly being watched, like an eye in the sky stared down on them all. The air itself spied and tingled with barely perceptible vibrations.

At first Kaylee couldn't form a word, still jogging to keep pace with the group. "Huh, ahuh, huh, hey... Hey!" Signaling the others, she stopped in her tracks.

"What?" Lucas spun, searching, as did Dustin.

"Where?" Dustin fumbled, dropping an arrow. As he grabbed at the aluminum rod falling down near his knees, he attempted to strike a pose as if he had done it intentionally.

"Do you hear that?" Kaylee studied the street and looked up to the trees.

"No."

"I don't hear anything."

She said, "It's there. It's soft. Listen!"

The group silenced themselves. Her father eventually shuffled up to the front. He bore a semi-automatic handgun, which they'd retrieved from a dead dupe two days before.

Kaylee pointed diagonally across the street. "It's coming from that way. It's their signal." The boys appeared pensive. She made a beeline toward the sound.

"Everybody be ready," said Lucas. "Ready to run for it."

Around a house wall at the corner, she continued on toward the wide boulevard at the end of the block. Now she heard the signal more clearly. It didn't emanate from one loudspeaker, but it was more subliminal, like dozens of little televisions playing the same noise at the same time.

When Kaylee arrived at a white concrete business that faced onto Martin Luther King Boulevard, she instantly knew this was the place. All the dupes must be holed up nearby, so close that she could hear them.

Unseen speakers buzzed and rippled together in unison. Their sickening, computer-guided assault reminded her how easy it was to succumb to the dupe's grand bargain.

Knowing that if she looked out it could be the end of her, Kaylee tried to summon up enough courage to complete what she had started. The boys caught up to her, more cautious and suspicious of the situation than she was. She knew they really didn't trust her, that they thought she was leading them into a trap. And she knew that if she looked out into that signal and became again what she was yesterday, they would shoot her dead on the spot. Her father, lagging far behind, would be powerless to stop them.

Kaylee clung on to the corner of that white brick building, and she hoped that her mind wasn't deceiving her. Finally Dustin arrived beside her, and Kaylee felt so comforted that she could finally relax.

"They're right around the corner," she whispered.

"Got it," he said, as Lucas stepped up.

"How are we doing?"

Kaylee couldn't bring herself to take that next step out and look. "They're close."

Their line rattled to nervous attention, like an electrical charge racing down a wire. Kaylee said to Dustin, "Don't let me stare into the signal."

"Right." He nodded for reassurance. Then he placed a hand on Kaylee's shoulder, and she got ready to peek beyond the wall.

Kaylee scrunched up her face, and she squinted. When she leaned out, the waves of sound attacked her in bursts. She could feel their pull as they entered her mind. The building across the boulevard was a tan apartment complex, three floors high with wide cement steps.

Kaylee jumped back. "Dupes!"

Lucas raised his pistol. "Where? How many?"

Kaylee shook, but quickly controlled herself. "I saw two, one in each window on either side of the door."

"How far?"

"Across the street." She thought about what she had seen. "I think," she began, "that I can crawl behind the car here without being seen." She crouched down to peek out again. Several vehicles sat abandoned in the small corner parking lot.

Dustin wore his sniper rifle on his back next to his quiver of arrows, and he held the bow in his hands. Lucas tapped Dustin's shoulder.

"I'm a better shot with that rifle. May I?"

"Knock yourself out." Dustin wiggled the weapon off his shoulder, and Lucas grabbed it and checked its readiness.

"Kaylee, binoculars." Lucas adjusted the sight on the rifle, and he cleaned the glass.

Kaylee retrieved her binoculars from her backpack when her father finally pushed up to the front of the group.

"What's going on?" He sounded frail, as if each step were a struggle.

"Shh."

"They're out there," said Lucas. "Kaylee sniffed them out."

She hung a pair of small binoculars around her neck, and she crawled down on all fours at the corner. Her dad seemed horrified.

"Kaylee what are you doing now?"

"Just recon," she said.

Her father rushed to the corner, grabbing his own weapon and pushing Dustin and Lucas out of the way.

"Wait."

Kaylee crawled out into the open toward the parked cars.

Lucas said, "If you'll excuse me?" He crouched low, and then he lay right down on the asphalt with the hunting rifle laid across his two arms. Like a caterpillar he followed Kaylee to a spot beside a small sedan. The two of them settled in beneath the car, spying out across the boulevard from the dark shadows beneath.

Lucas whispered, "What have you got, Colton?"

"Still just two. They have machine guns, I think." Gazing through her binoculars, Kaylee slid deeper underneath the car to get a better view of the apartment's upper floors.

"Wait," whispered Kaylee. "There's more." She watched as two more dupes emerged from the side alley together on some sort of rounds. Her heart skipped as they stopped at the front stairs and searched the avenue with their own binoculars. She held up four fingers for Lucas and the others to consider.

The guards spent a couple of minutes at the steps before moving on down the block together and out of sight.

Lucas retreated. "Come on, back."

Kaylee wiggled out from under the car and they crawled back around the corner to meet up with the group. She said, "There's at least four awake. But the rest are probably sleeping."

Lucas pointed up to where the building would be, if not for the wall. "Satellite dish, and a couple TV antennas."

Dustin yawned. "How do we get up there?"

Lucas said, "There's fire escapes in the alley. Somebody's got to get around back when the guards aren't there. It looks like they keep walking around the block."

Dustin nodded. "Sounds good. Let's do it."

Kaylee raised her hand. "I'll go."

Her dad immediately tried to veto her. "No, Kaylee. That's for someone else." He shook his head hard, and he put his hand on her shoulder.

Kaylee stared sternly up into his face. "I have to do this. It's my plan, Dad."

"Come on," said her father. "This is for the boys."

She wrenched her arm free. "I'm going with my partner." She slid from his range and around to the other side of Dustin.

Their group divided up and set their plan in motion. Kaylee's raiders were to hike around several blocks and find the back way into the apartment building. Someone would need to climb onto the rooftop and disable the signal. If anything happened, the first group would cover the front and take out the guards holding the machine guns.

This plan didn't sit right with Kaylee, however. She moved into Lucas's face, in front of the entire group.

"Don't shoot the people, just their guns."

"Are you crazy?" said Lucas in disbelief.

Kaylee sneered. "If you're that good, like you say, you should be able to shoot their weapons." She scowled forcefully up at him. "They're people! Just like me. And you."

"I know, Colton. I know." Lucas softened his tone. "Look. We can try."

"What if they were your family?" she said. "Would you still just want to kill them all?"

Lucas rolled his eyes. "All right. You've made your point."

Her dad smiled. Unable to continue hiking with them, he opted to stay put at the corner of Martin Luther King Boulevard. The skin on his right calve appeared like a blue balloon full of blood. Kaylee started to worry that it might get infected if he didn't find medical attention soon.

The squad dashed back down the block. Dustin and Kaylee scoped out a route. Two other boys tried to keep up behind them.

Kaylee slammed into a tree and peeked left and right with her binoculars. With the wide M.L.K. Boulevard straight ahead, they needed to make triply sure that it was clear before risking everything.

Their squad took longer than expected to find a way around the back of the apartment building. Climbing fences, falling awkwardly, and freezing in terror at the passing of a stray dog, eventually they homed in on their target on the opposite side of a chain link fence. Here it was decided to wait for the dupe guards to pass on their rounds. Dustin produced the walkie-talkie from his backpack, which Kaylee knew was problematic.

"We're not supposed to," she said.

"It's a gamble," responded Dustin.

"You could give us away." Kaylee nervously considered snatching the device away from him again.

"Look. What good is havin' Lucas out front watching if he ain't gonna warn us when they're comin'?"

Kaylee thought hard over the choice. "Dammit."

Dustin made a decision, and he clicked on the radio and pressed the transmitter.

"L-dog, this is Dee-structo. Over."

"Radio silence, dipshit."

Kaylee rolled her eyes and stared smugly up at Dustin.

"No man. Not this time. We're gonna wait on dumb and dumber to take a stroll. You need to tip us if they come back. Over."

"Got it. Now shut up! Over."

"I love you, bro. Over." Dustin laughed to himself, prompting snickers from the other two boys. When he noticed them relaxing, he said, "Hey! Look sharp. They could be anywhere."

He pointed up at the surrounding buildings, the windows, the alley from which they had entered. The two younger boys immediately lost their smiles and took cover. Kaylee and Dustin hid themselves in the bushes to the side of the chain-link fence.

The radio squawked for an instant. "Incoming," said Lucas. Everyone clung to their hiding spots, motionless.

On the apartment building-side of the chain-link fence, two figures entered the alley, inspecting every nook of the rear yard. Each guard carried an assault rifle and a handgun. They mimicked one another, militarily precise in their movements. Neither dupe blinked. Methodically, the two dupes finished their tasks, turned about, and exited the alley.

"I think we're good," said Dustin. "Gimme a boost. Me and you, Kaylee."

The swirling electronic hum of the dupe signal filtered out through the apartment's windows as the two boys helped Dustin and Kaylee climb up over the fence.

Dustin dumped his supplies out of his backpack below the fire escape.

After descending the fence Kaylee sprinted to catch up with him.

Dustin's hands fiddled with a ball on a long string, and he kicked his backpack toward her. "You need the cutters and a crowbar. But that's it."

He threw the ball up and over the handle of the fire escape ladder above them. This pulled a string through, attached to a purple nylon rope.

"What am I doing?" Kaylee tried to slide the tools into her own backpack, but there was no room.

"Lose that stuff," said Dustin. "Come on!"

She dumped her food and water bottles out in the alley, and she shoved the tools in. Dustin was ready to send her airborne. He handed her the rope.

"Wrap it around your arms."

The rope felt rough and scratchy. Kaylee zipped her backpack and grabbed hold of the rope, gazing skyward with some dread. As she did, Dustin rushed away from the ladder, pulling her straight up toward the fire escape platform. The rope almost pulled her shoulder out of its socket, and she wanted to cry out. Dustin kept yanking her higher.

Kaylee fumbled about in mid air, trying to control herself and land on the railing of the rattling platform. It was high, twelve feet at least. Her fear of heights kicked in, and she became numb and useless.

Eventually, with a resounding clank she found herself lying dazed on the first level of the fire escape. Her arm throbbed as she released the rope. It slithered away and dropped.

With Dustin stuck down below, she knew it was all up to her. Kaylee attempted to climb the black iron ladder, which wobbled. This was quite a bit noisier than she imagined it would be.

Rung after rung, Kaylee ascended toward the next level, terrified to look down behind her. Dustin packed up their mess in the quiet alley below, and he headed back toward the chain link fence. Kaylee carefully wormed up the ladder to get some footing at the third level.

Two fat hands slammed against the inside window at the floor below, where she had first climbed up onto the fire escape. The window wrenched open, and a wide-eyed, middle-aged man stuck his bearded face out, peering up at Kaylee. His dark brown hair was patched with grey, as was his scraggly beard. Without pause, he emerged clunkily onto the iron fire escape below to pursue her.

Dustin called for his bow. "Come on, hurry up, hurry up." The boy on the other side of the fence fumbled with the weapon, pushing it up over the top of the fence, where the cable caught on a link.

Kaylee struggled higher on her way towards the rooftop. But the pursuing dupe man bounded up after her. A beast, he shook the entire structure with each rung. Her ladder jerked like an earthquake.

She tried to climb faster, but the man was already on the level below her. He leapt to the next ladder, and he yanked himself up at her feet.

Pulling up with all her strength, Kaylee saw the roof edge just above her face, but the big bearded dupe caught hold of her sneaker. He grabbed her hard, and he pulled her legs off away from the ladder, where she hung by her two hands.

Hanging on above the concrete alley, Kaylee battled to twist free of his steely grip on her ankle.

An arrow flew past and ricocheted off the side of the brick building with a spark. Dustin reloaded as Kaylee stomped down on the dupe's hairy face, but he held fast onto her other leg. Her right sneaker plummeted to the concrete below.

"Get away!"

Kicking wildly, Kaylee could feel him pulling her hands from the metal crossbar above. She let go with her right hand in order to move to the next rung down. The dupe man tossed her legs off the ladder to the side, trying to throw her off completely. Kaylee kicked at him, but he was just too strong and vicious.

Another arrow sailed right through the man's thigh. He howled and let go immediately to keep from falling off the ladder himself.

With the big dupe momentarily stunned, Kaylee's two feet flopped back onto the ladder.

"Oh my God!" Kaylee gasped, as she righted herself. Already exhausted from hanging on, she struggled upward and tumbled over the top of the ladder onto the flat rooftop.

The dupe man's beefy hand slammed onto the top rung of the ladder behind her. Kaylee rolled away on her back, but the steel tools dug into her.

Another arrow sailed off into the sky, and the crazed dupe continued his pursuit up onto the rooftop.

Jumping up to her knees, Kaylee saw the satellite dish and stumbled toward it, whipping off her backpack and removing several tools. With the crowbar, she whacked at the satellite dish's sensitive part in the middle.

The injured dupe fell over the roof lip, and he tried to crawl on one leg like some unstoppable zombie menace.

Kaylee wasn't satisfied with smashing the dish's middle. She opened the metal cutters and went to work on severing as many wires as possible.

Then she ran to the other side of the roof away from him to where the TV antennae were mounted. She grabbed hold and dove forward with the aluminum structure. The thin metal tubing gave way, and the device toppled completely. The big hairy dupe continued his crawling chase, leaking a trail of blood behind.

Kaylee wrenched the top of the antenna free. With this long multi-pronged spear, she readied herself to jab at the dupe's face. He seemed out of breath and struggling to stay up on his arms. She turned her attention to the other TV antenna. With cutters, she severed the wires. Then, with the crowbar, she worked the supporting clamps loose.

The dupe crawled toward her still.

Kaylee decided to just run to the other side of the roof again, where he would follow. At the street side of the roof she could see the white brick corner store building right across the boulevard. Lucas stuck his head out. She heard that the dupe's signal had quieted. It was silent. The air was free again. Kaylee held her thumb up, and Lucas acknowledged her with his own hand signal.

The bleeding dupe man kept himself coming despite its futility. Each crawl had less progress than the previous. His charge was so pathetic that Kaylee started to feel sorry for him. Once he arrived near the front of the roof, she simply ran around the side of him back to the final TV antenna, which she destroyed thoroughly. Her arms broke off every hollow aluminum branch. She smashed every little box with the crowbar, and she cut every kind of wire. For good measure, she returned to the satellite dish for a bit of extra sabotage, to make triply sure it wouldn't be returning to service.

That's when she heard the rifle shots echo across the faces of the downtown businesses. The bloodied, bearded dupe lay motionless on the rooftop. Kaylee approached to inspect him. Down below in the street, more gunshots rang out sporadically. So much blood had gushed from the bearded man's leg that it didn't look good for him. Suddenly hands slapped in between the rails of the ladder, where it curled up over the lip of the roof's edge.

Dustin popped his head up, his scruffy brown hair blowing in the breeze. Aiming his handgun sloppily, he located the unconscious heavyset dupe beside her.

Kaylee threw up her arms. "Don't! It's okay."

Dustin flung his body up and onto the roof. "You're takin' forever. Let's get."

"Wait." Kaylee stepped closer to the bloody body. With the pointed end of the iron crowbar she poked at him.

"I'm going to pull the arrow out," she said. Unscrewing the tip of the impaling arrow and dropping it, she pushed down with her foot and yanked at the aluminum rod until it slid out of the wound with a slurp. The leg bled even faster now.

"Give me something to tie it with!"

Dustin twitched, and he dug into his pack for a shirt. "Uh, here." He tossed it over.

Kaylee wrapped the dupe's leg with the T-shirt and tied a knot. It wasn't tight enough to stop the bleeding, so she took the bloody arrow, and she slid it through the knot in order to twist the rag tighter and stop the flow. After she felt pretty certain it was tight enough, she hooked the arrow in under the rag and secured it.

Gunshots hailed. The battle raged on below on the boulevard. Lucas' rifle thundered, while the dupes returned bursts of rapid-fire.

"We oughta look," said Dustin, and he snuck toward the street side of the rooftop with his revolver out in front.

Kaylee wiped the blood from her hands. They were stained with the sticky fluid, and they stuck to the metal tools. The gunshots silenced, and a general rumbling of voices and footsteps rose from below.

"Dustin? What's happening?" Kaylee gazed at him as he squatted down at the edge of the roof. She stalked closer.

"You're not gonna believe this," he said.

"What's going on?"

"The dupes inside, they all ganged up on the guys with the guns. They're awake. I think they're on our side."

Dustin turned back to her, astounded. Then he reached into his own pack and pulled out a couple of packages of rolled-up apricot fruit leather.

"Here." He handed one to her.

Kaylee opted to slide it into her own pack, with the sticky tools, and to get ready for the descent back to earth.

Down in the middle of the boulevard, the Jefferson fighters met with the crowd of dazed former dupes. At least forty of them, of all ages, poured onto the avenue. They celebrated as more emerged from the apartment.

"Hey," said Dustin, jumping to his feet. "Kaylee?"

She turned back and faced him.

"That was good. That was a good call." He smiled and extended his hand to help her up. Kaylee wasn't used to handshakes, and Dustin's paw was so rough and crushing it momentarily rattled her how strong he was. But he immediately softened his grip and gently moved it up and down.

Kaylee could feel her heart race. "We should get back down there," she said, trying to appear dutiful.

"Yeah. Just keep your eyes open. There could be more. Definitely."

She remembered the dupe lying on the roof near death. "What do we do about him?"

"I ain't a doctor," said Dustin. "Let's ask 'em down there."

"Good idea."

They carefully positioned themselves to descend the fire escape. Kaylee froze at the top, seeing how high it actually was all the way to the cold cement alley below. How had she gotten up there in the first place? Rejecting the ladder, she made a start to return up to the rooftop.

"You go first."

"What's the matter?" Dustin snickered. "Take off your backpack."

Kaylee nodded, not looking down, and she shook out of the straps. The navy blue backpack hung from her forearm as she clutched the horizontal iron bar.

"Now what?"

"Just drop it," he said.

Kaylee let the backpack slide off her wrist and plummet all the way down to the alley. She whined. "I don't actually like heights."

Dustin smirked at her expense, and he waited patiently as they both listened to the sounds of the crowd just around the corner.

Her father's voice bellowed, "Kaylee! Where are you?"

At the third level platform, Kaylee held on tightly to the rail, and she spotted her Dad down in the alley. Her father stumbled into the building's wall, and he sat on the ground.

"Dad! I'm here!"

He seemed relieved but in a lot of agony.

"What's the matter?"

Dad shook his head, and he held his face in his hands. "I can't," he said. "I can't go. I can't walk." Dad examined his feet, and he lay sideward in the dirty alley. He didn't seem capable of moving very well.

"I'm coming."

Kaylee and Dustin climbed down toward the earth. At the second floor platform, she inspected the ladder mechanism so as to have it drop down for them. They then heard an approaching jet plane. The engines sounded different than she remembered. This one was louder, flying low as it thundered on its approach over Martin Luther King Boulevard. They all saw it pass overhead, a twin engine military plane with one pilot. Everyone suddenly burst into an ecstatic cheer.

Kaylee raced down the alleyway to arrive at her father.

"Dad? I told you not to walk on it."

"I know. I know."

They each scrutinized the ballooning in his right foot, a dark, nightmarish swelling that had grown more severe. His legs no longer appeared human at the bottom, and they were so gorged with blood that they might burst.

"I'm gonna see if there's a doctor." Kaylee shot up, and she raced around and out onto the crowded avenue.

Her father called to her as she disappeared, "That plane-"

Twenty-Five

Kaylee maneuvered around all the dazed ex-dupes, some whom she recognized from their various attacks on the high school. It was shocking how they had returned to normalcy as if none of this had ever happened. They probably didn't even know about the war. Like lambs, they questioned one another, prodding for information to make sense of their predicament. It was as if they couldn't even understand why the streets were silent and cars were left abandoned as far as the eye could see.

Kaylee pushed past a couple of older ladies, and she looked for Lucas and her own people. A medical type man was working on one of the injured dupe guards at the steps of the apartment building.

Lucas popped out of the crowd in front of her holding two of the dupes' rectangular sub-machine guns. These were smashed with bullets, their casings shattered. He nodded arrogantly to make his announcement.

"This what you're talking about, Colton? Huh? Who's the man?"

"I need a doctor for my dad, and another man." She continued on past him.

"Yeah. Okay, but you know, I did what you wanted." Lucas dropped the broken weapons to his sides, still beaming.

Kaylee homed in on the man treating the injured dupe guard, and then she turned back around to Lucas.

"It's not about me, that you shouldn't kill other human beings, Lucas."

Leaving him without an opportunity for a comeback, she rushed to attract the attention of the doctor.

Everyone could hear that jet plane circling overhead, as it never flew off too far. It remained in a holding pattern not very high.

"I need a doctor," said Kaylee.

The young man, a stocky guy, about thirty and clean-shaven, said, "I'm a nurse."

Kaylee considered. "Well, I need somebody. Please? Will you look at him?"

"Yeah, yeah. In a minute." The nurse man patched up the injured dupe with tape and a bandage. Around them, the disoriented crowd searched for their bearings. The high school liberators shook hands with their former enemies. Everyone breathed easier and rejoiced in the victory.

Except Kaylee. With her new nurse acquaintance, the two rushed to the alley where her dad lay on his back, suffering. Dustin sat beside him, devouring another fruit snack.

"His feet," she said.

When the nurse man knelt down and peeked at the damage, he jerked back in surprise.

"Oh, that's bad. I've never seen a hematoma that bad." His face paled.

Kaylee looked closer at the ballooning foot. "He got hit by a car."

"I need to press hard and see if the bone feels broken."

Dad recoiled. "Just be careful, okay?"

Kaylee stared tensely down as the man poked at the purple part of the leg.

"Aah!" Dad yelled. "Easy! For God's sake!"

"Look, I'm sorry." The nurse paused. "What's your name?"

"Paul. Colton, and I have insurance." Dad tried to smile through his gritting teeth, but a tear fell out the corner of his eye.

"All right, Paul," said the nurse. "This looks like it could be broken. My name is Jesse, and I'm just trying to see how bad it is."

"I know. I know."

Jesse the nurse turned to Kaylee. "Can you find something for him to bite down on?"

Kaylee and Dustin produced a rolled-up sock, which was relatively clean. She handed it to her dad, who returned a look of absurdity.

"Thank you," he said sarcastically. Then he sniffed at it and stuck it into his mouth.

She grabbed her father's hand and squeezed it. Jesse ran his fingers down along the top of the shin, pushing it about. Suddenly Dad jerked back and roared into the sock.

Jesse said, "Okay, okay. Here. I think you have a problem." He poked at it further. "There. A piece of bone, a slab fracture off the tibia."

Kaylee stared back blankly. "Now what?"

The man breathed out to stall for a moment.

"Well, this is not good. He needs surgery, metal pins and a cast, an x-ray machine, antibiotics... and you need to drain that swelling. We need to get him to a medical facility."

Dad, Kaylee, and Dustin turned to him in disbelief. Kaylee attempted to understand Jesse's comprehension of the world. "There are no medical facilities. There's just you."

The nurse scoffed uneasily. "Of course there's emergency treatment centers. You have to find one."

Kaylee accepted his advice. "But what do we do right now?"

Jesse took another good look at her dad's leg, and he said, "Look, you've got to stay off it. I-I don't even know if it can be saved."

"What?" Dad snapped to attention.

"It might need... you know. Come off."

Kaylee gasped and shuddered. Dad sat forward to examine it more closely.

The nurse pointed along where the car had impacted. "See those dark areas? That's turning black. Look at it. That's just... That's real bad."

Kaylee jumped forward to see for herself, and to hound the nurse. "What can we do? Tell us."

"Keep it elevated and drain the blood out. You'll need a syringe. Do you people have any needles?"

After giving his best advice, Jesse the nurse set off for the rooftop to see what to do about the unconscious bearded dupe. Kaylee and her dad sat together in the alley. Dustin remained with them, pacing around for moral support.

"Kaylee, that aircraft," said her dad.

"What about it?"

"A-10. It could be bad news. We should leave the area immediately."

Dustin and Kaylee looked at one another.

Dustin spoke up. "I thought it was on our side?"

"Yeah?" said Dad. "And what gave you that idea?"

Kaylee reeled in frustration. "We can't move you, though."

"Honey, if that A-10 decides to open up, we are gonna have no choice in the matter."

It was too late. As they discussed the circling plane it had already come around, and its cannon strafed the people out on the boulevard. A massive barrage of shrapnel and fire erupted with a thousand fiery explosions.

The plane shot past overhead, but not before it released a bomb, which blew a massive crater in front of the apartment building. The deafening concussion knocked everyone over and blew out the windows of the stores. Shock waves shook the wall. Their little alley had been shielded from the devastation of the flying shrapnel.

That attacking plane wasn't finished yet, and it circled about for another pass over the area.

Smoke cleared, and Kaylee jumped up, pulling her father's arm, along with Dustin. The three of them hobbled to the alley entrance at the boulevard, where the scene was horrific in its totality. A dozen or more were now dead, some beyond identification. Another dozen people lay badly wounded. The lucky ones only had minor injuries. Lucas stumbled forward to them with a couple of his boys similarly dazed and bleeding from their faces and arms.

Kaylee scoped out the cross street.

"Come on, this way!" They headed for the nearest side street, and those who could move caught on to the plan. As they rushed across Martin Luther King Boulevard, a large military tank appeared in the distance. It turned onto the boulevard toward them. A turret fired an artillery shell, which instantly destroyed a nearby corner store in a fireball.

Kaylee felt the heat wash of the explosive ordnance on their backs. The three hobbled down a perpendicular side street. That gargantuan Abrams tank raced along the boulevard toward them. Its grinding tracks rattled windows as it built louder and more intimidating.

Her father panted. "Get inside here. We have to hide now. Just hide."

"There," Dustin pointed. They pushed ahead into a side yard, while the A-10's rapid cannon again thundered back at the apartment building. Hundreds of exploding rounds ignited in quick succession and deafened. The plane attempted to kill off the remaining wounded, while the rolling beast hunted for escaping fighters like Kaylee. After the aerial barrage faded, the tracks of the M-1 were heard grinding up the street surface. The tank smashed over cars and flattened parked autos.

Dad winced and groaned, his leg no longer to be ignored. This house was dark and dusty, the interior air so stagnant it induced coughing. Lucas, Rory, and a few of the high school's fighters rejoined them, pouring in through the back door.

Kaylee said, "Let's get him on the couch." The boys pitched in, and they arranged for her dad's legs to stay elevated.

Her father grunted in thanks.

Nearby, the assaulting tank fired another round, and an explosion echoed across town.

Kaylee looked around the room. Two of the boys peeked out the front window.

Her dad admonished them. "Everybody get down, and be silent."

The living room settled, and Kaylee crawled to the couch, resting her head on her father's arm. Time trickled, and her dad petted her hair, making her feel almost normal again.

Lucas shuffled over, patching his cuts with a first aid kit. "Mr. Colton?"

"Yes?"

"You have any ideas about all this?"

"What do you mean?"

"How long should we wait here?"

Her father tensed back into his pillow. "Let me... Let me think."

Kaylee snapped to attention. "We need to get syringes and antibiotics for my father as soon as possible." The tone of her voice was stern and commanding. Heads whipped toward her, and she glanced back at them unflinchingly.

Lucas sat. "All right. Where?"

Less self-assured, Kaylee asked, "Where's the nearest pharmacy?"

Rory chimed in. "I think that tank just blew it to hell. It's on King."

"Yeah, no. That wasn't the drug store," said Lucas. "The drug store's a block down."

Dad grabbed Kaylee's wrist before she could move. "Honey, no. Wait for that A-10 to go away. And the tanks."

"Tanks?" asked Lucas. "There's only one."

"I believe I heard two."

With that, the morale in the room dropped noticeably. The wounded returned to their peroxide, bandages and sterile tape. No one spoke for several minutes.

Kaylee returned her head back to her dad's shoulder, and they quietly passed the time. The tank receded into the distance, and life began to seep back inside the room with the orange glow of the sunset across the front windows.

Dad whispered to Kaylee, "I can still fly you out of here. We'll get to the Cessna. And we'll just go."

She looked up into his face, and she thought of escaping. "Where will we go?"

Her father hesitated. "We just have to find Sean. Where is that damned kid?"

Kaylee saw the image, Sean in the driver's seat. The arrow plunged through his chest, and the car crashed awkwardly and crushed in the impact. Sean's blood rolled over the edge of the leather seat like a waterfall. He sat motionless, his pale eyes staring, not seeing at all.

Kaylee looked at her father. "Sean's dead."

"What?" He jolted in place, his eyes suddenly alive with terror.

"He's dead, Daddy."

"No... No. Are you sure?"

Kaylee nodded, avoiding his eyes. So much pain. She could tell it overwhelmed him, and she couldn't do anything except hug him.

He started to cry. "How did it happen?"

Kaylee thought on it a minute. Deficient of words, she remained silent and scared of making her dad's condition any worse than it already was.

"He was a casualty," she said. "A part of the war."

"Oh God." Her father cried.

Kaylee comforted him as best she could. He seemed weaker now, physically as well as emotionally. If his fractured leg became infected, he could be in desperate trouble and even die. All the wounded were at risk of dying without medicine.

Kaylee lifted her head.

"The tank's gone. Time to go to that pharmacy." She sprang to action, the only response she could stomach at this point. Grabbing her backpack from the floor, she searched across their faces. She needed to know who would come with her.

"Dustin?"

"Yeah? Uh, okay," he said. "You just wanna make a quick run, right?"

She nodded, still soliciting more volunteers. Night had come, and the darkness could conceal their movements. None of the battered boys sprawled on the living room floor seemed eager to venture back out, not even Lucas. His own shrapnel wounds seemed significant now, and he looked exhausted.

"Anyone else?" said Kaylee, trying to sound inviting. Silence.

Dustin pulled himself to his feet, and he wrenched his pack up off the floor. "It's only just 'round the corner, right?"

Kaylee faced him. "We're good. It's just a quick trip to the store."

Lucas said, "Stay hidden. Don't lead anybody back here."

Dustin nodded in an obligatory manner. "All right."

Lucas shook himself to clarity. "If you're spotted, don't come back. Go the other direction."

"Got it," said Kaylee. "Anyone got a flashlight?"

***

In the stark, slicing shadows of Corner Drugs, Kaylee and Dustin stumbled on the debris, which lay all over the floor. The drug store had been ransacked, but many of the large, wide-mouthed plastic bottles had been left behind the pharmacist's counter. Kaylee read them in the blue glow of a tiny penlight.

"Aziromycin?" She called the names out to Dustin, who probably knew less about their meanings than she did.

"I dunno," he said, and he scavenged behind her in the racks of shelves. His face contorted, trying to figure out how to pronounce the various drugs.

"Amoxicillin?" Kaylee said, curious. "I think that's one."

"Just take all of it."

Kaylee felt stupid. She opened her sack and started throwing all the containers in.

"We still need needles."

"Right." He returned to search with his own flashlight, which kept cutting out. "Dammit!" He smacked at the plastic tube to get it to ignite again. "Piece a' crap."

Kaylee loaded her sack and wondered if it might be too heavy, filled with all those pill containers.

Hearing Dustin stop, behind her, she said, "Is there something?"

"Little needles, like it says, insulin injections and stuff."

She scooted over to see what he'd found. Shining her penlight, she took one of the plastic syringes in her hand and popped off the orange protector at the tip.

"Huh?" She looked it over carefully. "It's really small, and short."

"So?" he said. "It's a needle."

"But it's for draining out the blood. What if it's not big enough?"

"All right. I'll keep lookin'." Dustin twisted back in frustration.

Kaylee collected a full sack of pill containers, and it had grown so heavy that Dustin would need to haul it back. She turned to the drawers along the bottom of the pharmacist's counter. In the third drawer, she discovered a box of larger syringes.

"*Voilà!* Big needles."

"That's it," he said. "Let's roll."

Kaylee tried to yank the massive sack, but it would be impossible to walk with.

"I can't lift this."

Dustin nodded knowingly, and he snatched it up. The two snuck out through the back door. Streetlights ahead at the boulevard throbbed gently with soft orange pulsations. The pills inside the fat round sack rattled with each of Dustin's footsteps. Off in the distance, another artillery round exploded. A burning glow of firelight tickled the low-hanging clouds.

Kaylee thought back on the day's events, horrified how overwhelming these military attacks could be. Massive bombs obliterated entire buildings and streets.

"Dustin?" she said. "The school. We don't know what happened to them."

Dustin turned somberly, and then back to the mouth of the alley to recon the boulevard.

She pulled at the elbow of his shirt. "We need to go to the school."

Dustin held his index finger to his lips. "Shh." With a hand wave forward, the two bounded out over the sidewalk and across Martin Luther King to the other side. Kaylee scrambled to keep up with Dustin, who sprinted in a frenzy back to their safe house. Hauling the rattling canvas sack full of pills, like a skinny, unwashed Santa Claus, Dustin ran very fast when he wanted to. They both dashed around the next corner and up the side street, and they barreled into the backyard without even the thought of slowing down.

When they exploded in through the back door the injured were half-asleep and jolted from complacency. Lucas desperately grabbed for his gun as Dustin pushed inside with his flashlight glaring.

"It's us. It's us!"

Kaylee blurted, "We're back! We brought medicine."

Twenty-Six

The boys went to work digging through the new supplies. Kaylee's job was to attend to her father's mangled leg. With a kitchen pot to catch the excess bleeding, she attempted to jab a needle into his swollen leg and suck out the blood.

"It's gonna hurt, Dad. You don't want to look."

"It's okay. Just do it."

"I don't want to hurt you." Kaylee held fast, studying the business end of the hypodermic. Her hand trembled as she gingerly positioned it above her father's ballooning calf.

"I know it's going to be bad."

Her dad inhaled a deep breath. "It already hurts. Don't worry about it."

Kaylee searched above for inspiration. The needle slid in easily enough, as her father spasmed into the couch pillows. She retracted the plunger and filled the plastic tube with dark red liquid. "It's... I guess it's working," she said.

The boys stared over as she squirted the blood out into the pot. Then she was ready to harpoon the bloated leg again and draw out more.

"Ow!" Her father winced, but he kept his leg stationary. His words were barely decipherable through his gritting teeth as he growled, "You're doing good."

Kaylee jabbed into the wounded leg five times in various locations until she was satisfied that the swelling had ameliorated a bit. She patched the tiny holes with ointment and bandages. Then she stood to clean herself off and dispose of the blood waste.

"Is that better?"

"Yeah," he said. "I just need to lie here. I just want to go to sleep."

"Sure, Daddy." Kaylee petted his hair. Scanning around, she saw the guys had arranged all the medicine bottles in a row and made a list of what they had. She assessed the injured boys on the floor. They seemed to be in no immediate danger.

The high school had been left defenseless, and it weighed on her now like a block of cement.

"Guys?"

Several turned to her immediately, but not Rory or Lucas.

"The school, they're all alone. What if the dupes know about them?"

"Then they're probably toast," said Rory with his usual abrasiveness.

Kaylee stared at Lucas for a response. "They have to get out of there and hide."

Lucas probably knew she was right, but he was too sore, too exhausted, and too demoralized to come to a decision. He kept quiet. Down on the floor, his head rested back on a couch pillow propped against the wall.

Kaylee's dad scanned their faces, sympathetic to her plight. "Well, I can't go."

"Of course not," Kaylee snapped, "But I'm going. Is anybody coming with me this time?"

Lucas exhaled dramatically.

"Uh, Colton, I guess we can take a stroll back to Jefferson and grab supplies. There's nothing to eat in this damned house." He wiggled his body to awaken his lower regions. The motionless teens looked to him for a pass.

"That's very magnanimous of you, Lucas." Kaylee strapped on her backpack.

As he reached his feet, doubtlessly thinking on what magnanimous was supposed to mean, he looked down on the other teens in the dim streetlight that filtered in through the curtains.

"All right, you mutts. Don't think I'm carrying food back for you all."

The groans came audibly. Boys rustled to life again, and Kaylee retreated to the door at the rear of the house.

***

At Jefferson Avenue, on the far side, the pockmarked walls of the school came into view. Kaylee's group gathered behind tall red oleander, which formed a hedge at the corner yard.

Lucas took his flashlight, and he flicked a few flashing signals over the wall. It seemed quiet inside the school grounds, but Dustin started to grow noticeably nervous, fidgeting as if ready to run. Lucas flashed his light again, and then a dim head popped up over the wall. Lucas beamed the wall guard in the eyes.

"Psst. It's us," he called.

The reply came back, "How do I know it's still you?" The freshman on the wall sounded paranoid and scared.

Rory interjected, "Michael, you stupid prick. Of course it's us."

Several others shushed Rory in unison.

"All right," called the boy on the wall.

"Come on." Lucas waved them forward, and Kaylee marched out into the open across the four lanes of Jefferson Avenue with the others. They aimed their weapons toward the charred school bus gate.

Halfway across the avenue, Kaylee was suddenly hurled forward by Dustin, who screamed, "Run! Run!"

A second or two later, before Kaylee could think of anything else, Jefferson Avenue ignited in flames and smoke. Ripping apart the asphalt, hundreds of rounds showered the area with molten fragments, flames, and chunks of the road.

Dustin wrenched her arm, and they sprinted fast toward the school. Both slammed hard into the concrete wall, watching in horror as the avenue lit up in blinding violence. Hot, yellow reactions exploded in waves.

Incoming fire ripped everything in its path. Off on the horizon, from the blackness, white light flashed. The rapid-fire echoes, like a Gatling gun, arrived after the explosions.

The few teens who had progressed as far as the wall sidled toward the bus gate, trying to blend into the concrete.

Kaylee saw several fighters torn apart in the middle of Jefferson Avenue. Among them was Rory, whose leg was severed off at his thigh and lay ten feet away from him. Other kids were less fortunate. Little that remained of them even seemed human anymore.

Kaylee and Dustin slid sideward toward the school bus, and she suddenly yanked at Dustin's arm to stop him from entering. Rory screamed at the top of his lungs behind them. The shrieks haunted Kaylee, and she turned back to watch.

"Dustin, wait!"

"No!" He pulled ahead, dropping down to crawl beneath the school bus.

Kaylee followed. "Do you have your rope?"

"What?"

Another burst of fire rained down on the gymnasium building as several of their party raced to get inside there. They were sitting ducks, and the explosive rounds tore through everything like a blowtorch through butter.

Kaylee screamed, "We have to help him!" and she wedged herself beneath the bus. "Give me your rope," she said, grabbing at Dustin's backpack. Her fingers fumbled to unzip the pocket.

Rory squirmed in the center of the cratered avenue, holding the stump of his thigh. His pathetic cries rang out between bursts of enemy fire onto the school buildings. The dupe helicopter targeted vehicles next, the fire truck and the parked Mustang. Shards, splinters, and chunks of molten steel sprayed out in every direction.

Kaylee remained in her spot, wedged in at the tiny corner where the edge of the school's wall met the school bus. Out of sight of the predatory helicopter, she fiddled with Dustin's string.

A section of the gym's wall collapsed into a heap.

It seemed easy to toss the weighted beanbag at the end of the string. Kaylee got a quick feel for it, and she looked up.

"Uh, Rory?"

It wasn't clear if he could hear or see her as he grasped at his bleeding wound.

"Rory!"

His face turned up.

"I'm going to throw you a rope!"

Nodding frantically, he waited for the toss. Kaylee's first attempt flew far and wide.

"No, no over here!" Rory thrashed. More explosions ignited across the tops of the school buildings. Flames rose in intensity where the walls incinerated.

Kaylee threw the beanbag again, close enough for Rory to claw himself forward and snatch it.

"Pull it until the big rope comes," she shouted. Beneath the bus she yelled, "Guys! He has it!" She dashed under the bus with the rope in her hand as Rory yanked it from the opposite end.

Rory called, "What am I doing? What am I doing? Guys! Guys?"

Dustin called. "Tie it around you. Make a knot." Kaylee, Dustin, and Lucas readied themselves with the rope.

Lucas shouted, "Are you tied?"

"Yeah. Yeah. Do something!" Rory's hysteria frightened the other huddled teenagers.

They pulled Rory quickly, sliding him across the pockmarked wasteland that formerly was Jefferson

Avenue. Kaylee watched from beneath the bus as Rory twisted and rolled.

"Keep it going," she said. "Almost!"

Rory's skin scraped and his face was banged along the path, but they dragged him into the school's yard below the bus.

Lucas wrenched Rory the last several feet and turned him around to see his injury.

"Tie his leg off. Who's got a belt?"

Dustin shook his head.

"We'll use the rope."

Kaylee produced her knife, and she sliced a section of the purple rope to tie around Rory's thigh. He had lost so much blood that she worried it might be futile. His leg had singed so badly in the impact, however, that it might have cauterized the torn arteries and slowed the bleeding. They patched Rory's stump as best they could.

Rory looked from the boys and up to Kaylee.

"I owe you one," he said through his tears.

Kaylee nodded. "Or two or three."

Rory laughed, but the pain quickly altered his demeanor. They settled for stopping the bleeding, and Rory appeared destined to survive the night.

It seemed that the attack had stopped as quickly as it had begun. The explosions ceased, and only a few crackling flames inside the school provided background noise. Kaylee looked to the wall guard, Michael who was wedged in and hidden.

She said, "Is it gone?"

"I don't know." The boy remained half underneath the rear of the bus.

Lucas suddenly confronted Michael.

"Hey! You didn't think to tell us there was a God damned helicopter waiting for us?"

The boy rambled incoherently. "I-I didn't, you know-"

"Didn't you see it at all?"

"I-I thought it went away."

***

Kaylee stormed through the dark ruins of the gym. "Sara!"

She looked for signs of life. Turned toward the cafeteria, she could see movements, shadows in the slivers of light leaked onto the hallway floor. Bursting inside she found the bulk of the school sitting at cafeteria tables, chatting and eating. A stereo played pop dance music in the corner, and Kaylee thought it surreal with tanks and helicopters and planes hunting them down that music would be blaring out as if this was some different world entirely, an ordinary world where music was permitted. With the lights on and the tunes ringing, their cafeteria seemed almost normal.

Why is the power still on?

The dupes had done so much damage, taken so many lives, but they hadn't taken the electricity away.

Kaylee called out, "Is Sara here?"

Melanie responded, "She's with Caroline. Hi Kaylee. You guys are back!"

Kaylee felt overwhelmed and suffocated. She had to make a big announcement, but nobody seemed interested.

"Listen! We have to get out of here! They're gonna figure out where we are and come with more tanks! Grab all the food. We have to go hide!"

The mood in the cafeteria imploded with nervous ambiguity. Faces whipped uncertainly. Small talk ceased.

Lucas entered behind Kaylee, looking battered and scarred. "Hey. People! Pack up food. We need to move out. Is this everybody?"

Students scattered in a berserk flurry. Everyone raced to take something for themselves. The kitchen was overrun with grabbing hands and shoving bodies.

Caroline Anderson entered then with Sara beside her. "What's going on?"

"We have to leave," said Lucas. "We're all sitting ducks."

Caroline turned pale with dread. "Okay." She gazed over at the mob scene in the kitchen, and then she darted off to join in.

Kaylee spotted Sara, who was amused by this frenetic food panic. Sara hadn't yet noticed her, and Kaylee remained reluctant to spook her.

"Sara?"

Sara's eyes widened, and she held fast in place. "Huh."

Kaylee threw up her hands. "Sara, I'm not going to hurt you. I just want to help get you out of here before the dupes come back. We have to leave."

"We're going?" Sara suddenly turned giddy with excitement. "We get to go home!?" She danced about left and right, her little hands shaking with tension in front of her pint-sized body.

"No." Kaylee stepped closer. "We need to go hide somewhere else. Come on. Grab your stuff!" She approached, and the little girl flinched involuntarily.

Kaylee bent low to seem smaller. "We have to pack your stuff or you'll lose it. Okay? Hurry!"

"Okay." Sara played along, but Kaylee could tell that she remained suspicious. They both jogged back to the gym and to Sara's cot. There they packed a sack and a pink mini-backpack for Sara to wear. They tossed in clothes and her bulbous-headed doll, a small box of crayons and some coloring books.

"Is that everything?" said Kaylee.

"It's so weird." Sara stared, dumbfounded, her little freckled face full of wonder.

"What?"

"You know how to talk."

Kaylee smiled. "Yeah."

Sara said, "I like to talk. My mommy says girls are born talkers, and we talk a lot because we use our brains more than boys."

Kaylee giggled.

"She said boys can be pretty icky." Sara nodded with determination.

Kaylee laughed as she rose up. "We'll have to talk some more later. But right now, we better grab as much food as we can."

"Ooh. Little Paws!" Sara dove over her cot and held up a box in front of Kaylee, removing the lid.

"Ah, the kitty."

Sara reached in and took the cat in hand. "We need food for Little Paws too."

"Hmm." Kaylee led the way as Sara wriggled on her petite, cartoon-themed backpack. Kaylee carried a sack, while Sara brought the kitten in a shoe box.

"Come on, L.P.! We're goin' on a a'venture."

The night became silent except for the crackling flames, which smoldered in several of the classrooms on the second floor. No one knew if the helicopter still lingered about, hunting. No one could see into the black night to spot it. It was a military machine that could hover silently and strike from great distances. There was no safe place outside now, anywhere. Each step taken could be the last.

Jefferson High's surviving population waited in darkness, standing in the shadows near the gymnasium's crumbled side wall. Kaylee stood beside Sara in the middle of the bunch. All faces watched Lucas to learn if it was safe to emerge out of the darkness.

"We can't bunch up, okay?" Lucas called confidently from the gaping hole of the collapsed wall. "Go in pairs, and nobody get too close to the others. Don't give them a good target. Melanie?"

"Yes?" Melanie straightened up, carrying a box of important files.

"Are you coming?" Lucas called with his hand.

"First?" Her voice squeaked, and she looked around the group in confusion.

"Get ready to run for it."

Everyone held their breath. Lucas and Melanie bounded out toward the school bus. Dustin searched the horizon with his binoculars. A couple of boys dragged the injured Rory on an improvised stretcher fashioned from long poles and blankets pulled tightly across. Rory was in no shape to crack wise at them, and he seemed in urgent need of medical attention.

"I'm scared," said Sara.

"It's okay," said Kaylee. "You want to hold my hand?"

Sara thought it over and then nodded. Kaylee took her hand, and together they watched the exodus. The next pair made their mad dash for the bus. Lucas and Melanie had already disappeared into the night. Kaylee could feel Sara's hand squeezing harder and shaking. With a minute to spare, she knelt down to where Sara could see her face.

"Do you want a hug?"

Sara dropped her grip, and she stepped backwards shaking her head nervously. It was obvious she still harbored a deep fear of Kaylee.

Kaylee realized that she had gone too far, and so she backed away.

"It's okay. No worries." She stood up and watched the next pair make their desperate run toward freedom. Sara remained behind Kaylee several steps.

Kaylee wondered whether she should remind Sara to run, or wait until the last possible second. The pair ahead of them raced off together. Nothing bad had happened so far, and the air felt safe and still. But she could hear the distant rumble of another machine, a tank or a helicopter. She couldn't tell what it was, but it was definitely out there.

Kaylee and Sara were next in line. "Come on Sara!" Kaylee held out her hand, hoping Sara would just take it and flee with her. She waited another second, and then turned back.

The unseen machine rumbled more loudly.

"I'm not scared," announced Kaylee with an air of playful bravado. "Come on." She smiled, causing Sara to smile back involuntarily.

"Let's go. Go, go, go!"

With Sara's hand firmly in hers, the two began their rush toward the school bus.

"We're gonna crawl underneath. And then we're free." Kaylee dropped down to her knees and scooted under, listening for the rumbles of that machine, which sounded more and more like the massive tank from the afternoon. Kaylee reached the other side of the school bus's undercarriage while Sara gingerly tried to follow, sliding the shoe box in front of her.

Kaylee searched on Jefferson. To the right, where Jefferson met Martin Luther King Boulevard, she spotted it. The M-1 turned slowly toward their school.

"We can make it," said Kaylee. "But what about them?"

Sara struggled the last few feet beneath the bus, sliding Little Paws inside her shoe box. Meows sang out incessantly from within.

Kaylee suddenly changed her mind.

"Sara! We have to go back and warn the others!"

"What?" Sara gawked like a deer on the highway as Kaylee scooted past her, yanking her hand and turning her about face beneath the dirty bus.

"Come on. We'll go out a different way!"

Caroline and Ben ran up together and arrived at the bus as Kaylee emerged on the inside of the schoolyard. Caroline halted.

"What are you doing now?"

"There's a tank!" Kaylee yanked Sara up to her feet, and the two girls raced back into the ruins of the gymnasium. The unseen machine rumbled up the avenue just outside the walls.

Kaylee and Sara slammed back in through the rubble and right into the heart of the group.

"There's a tank out there." She pointed. "Let's go out another way."

She raced into the dark entrails of Jefferson to emerge at the football field. They all heard the tank maneuver to where the bus blocked the entrance. Their little squad of refugees followed Kaylee, and they all sprinted for the exterior wall on the opposite side of the complex, where tables and chairs had been propped as guard platforms.

Kaylee and Sara led the panicked charge.

Twenty-Seven

? massive detonation back at the front bus gate, and the tank motor revved. They could hear the tank smash its way into the school grounds. Kaylee flinched as the machine gun ripped apart the school buildings.

Kaylee yanked Sara to the top of the concrete wall, where both of them sat and examined the big drop down to the grass on the other side.

"Drop your backpack," said Kaylee. She and Sara tossed down their supplies. "Give me your hands. I'll lower you down."

"What about Little Paws?" Sara stared at the shoe box balancing precariously beside her.

Kaylee said, "I'll take him."

"Okay."

As Kaylee struggled to lower Sara down the outside of the sand-textured wall, more people climbed up onto their table to assist. Ben and Caroline came next. Ben's long arms were useful for lowering Sara all the way down to the ground before letting her go.

"You next," said Ben.

Kaylee nodded rapidly. Her hips and belly scraped against the rough exterior. Ben lowered Kaylee to where she dropped onto her butt in the damp grass.

"Little Paws!" Sara screeched.

Kaylee jumped back to her feet and called up to Ben. "The box! Hand it down." She accepted the kitten and handed her off to Sara. Now just the three of them, Kaylee gathered up their supplies. The others above negotiated how best to descend the wall.

"Come on, Sara. Let's go!" Kaylee wrenched Sara nearly off of her feet, and they rushed to the nearest side street in completely the wrong direction. These ghostly narrow streets remained deserted.

As they jogged together, they heard the military tank and its belligerent, destructive agenda. Artillery lit up the sky in flickering flashes above the school compound.

Sara couldn't keep up with Kaylee's crazed pace, so they slowed. Sara seemed ecstatic now to be free of the school prison. The kitten, sufficiently terrified, remained a constant source of meowing. Kaylee could hear her own breathing. She let go of Sara's hand.

The two slowed to a calm stroll, and Kaylee searched scrupulously for any signs of life.

"Sara, you know how we play hide and seek?"

"Yeah."

Kaylee scanned left and right on the lookout. "If we see anyone, we better go hide, okay?"

"Mmhm."

"And when you hide for real, you have to be very quiet."

"I know how to play," said Sara with self-assured smugness.

Kaylee smiled, examining a pair of yard gnomes on the lawn beside them. As they stepped down the sidewalk, a security floodlight suddenly painted over and startled them both.

"Come on, quickly!" Kaylee dashed for the end of the block. The light remained glaring. The streetlights remained bright as well.

Kaylee squinted into the dimness before sneaking onto the next quiet residential street. A thick canopy of leafage ensured deep shadows, nooks in which to hide.

"Where are we going?" said Sara. Her voice seemed less playful, slightly concerned.

"Um, I think it's this way."

"But what is it?"

"It's a house, where my dad is."

"Okay."

At Jefferson Avenue, Kaylee stopped and hid with Sara in the hedges against a house. The thought of crossing that wide, desolate expanse now felt horrifying. The tank, just down several blocks away, continued assaulting the empty school. Helicopters might have returned above, or even planes or men with machine guns.

"You see anything?" Kaylee asked Sara, as they both peered out.

"No."

"Me neither." Kaylee agonized over what to do. Turning to Sara, who waited patiently for news, she said, "All right. We'll run across, one at a time. Okay?"

"Not together?" The little girl seemed rightly concerned.

"Sara, listen to me, for reals. If something happens to me, I want you to turn around and sneak back where we came from." Kaylee pointed back down the street. "Don't cross the avenue. Find the others."

Sara seemed lost in her thoughts, suddenly overwhelmed.

"Promise me," said Kaylee. "If anything happens out there, just turn around and sneak back to find the rest of the school people."

"I don't want anything to happen to you, Kaylee."

"I know. I don't either."

The tank blasted another hole, and the two girls jolted. Kaylee stiffened.

"I'm gonna try for it!" With that, she ran out of the bushes and across the sidewalk into the wide avenue, carrying Sara's sack and a second bag of food. The running gave her a new sense of power and accomplishment. If she could only get all the way across that avenue, she knew it would be all right again. It seemed so easy, but it took so long to move each foot forward. Her legs floated in some kind of slow motion while she ran exposed to the eyes in the sky.

After she arrived, plunging up onto the nearest lawn and under a maple tree, she breathed easier again. She dropped her sacks and called to Sara, "Come on, it's clear! Run, Sara! Run!" She hoped that Sara would have the nerve to go now before anything unimaginably terrible showed up.

Sara hesitated for a couple of seconds, taking one last look left and right before bolting across Jefferson Avenue like a pee-wee soccer star racing down the field to kick her first goal. Kaylee opened her arms to call her in for a landing. Sara rushed step over step while explosions flared into the night clouds just down the avenue. She barreled into Kaylee, and they both fell back onto the damp grass, tumbling to a rest. There they huffed maniacally. Little Paws rolled clean out of her shoe box and screamed out in kitty disorientation.

"You're okay?" Kaylee checked Sara's head.

"We did it."

"We did it." Kaylee stared back into Sara's eyes. Wanting to squeeze her tightly, she restrained herself and sat up instead. The two girls gathered their meager belongings. Kaylee snatched Little Paws and returned her to the shoe box.

"There's a good kitty. Oh, sweet little kitty-cat."

***

Kaylee and Sara entered quietly through the back door. More and more of the school's teens had filled the modest dwelling, and the dark living room was packed. Kaylee saw instantly that her father was missing.

"Where's my dad?"

Most of the school survivors seemed to be accounted for. Dustin watched out of the front window. Lucas and Melanie read a map together at the kitchen table by the light of a flashlight. It was difficult to step over all the boys lying haphazardly on the floor. Kaylee led Sara down a hallway.

Her father had been relocated to a back bedroom. He lay on the bed, with pillows propping up his legs, and he seemed groggy, but alive. The girls dumped their supplies, and Kaylee approached the bed.

"How's your leg?"

"Better than my nerves," said her father. "You just stop leaving this house, and hide with the rest of us." He yanked Kaylee's arm, drawing her in to his chest. Squeezing her for a long time, he wouldn't let go.

Kaylee relaxed and rested.

Sara released Little Paws from her shoe box prison.

"Kaylee, I think she's hungry."

Kaylee lifted her head. "Did you bring her any food?"

"Tuna, remember!"

"Oh yeah. Why don't you go find a can opener in the kitchen?"

"Okay!" Sara tore off into the dark house on her mission.

Kaylee's eyes finally adjusted to the near darkness, and she could see her father's haggard face in the dim blue glow. His eyes seemed dark with sickly circles, and his cheeks drooped.

Her dad released his vice grip on her arm. "I've been listening to artillery shells all night. I can't have you running around in a war zone, Kaylee. What kind of a father would I be?"

Kaylee sat silently beside him.

"Listen, angel. The swelling is down a bit. I can fly us out of here. In the Cessna."

Kaylee recalled their airplane sitting strapped down to the airfield on the other side of the highway. It was a tiny white plane with four seats. She had flown with Dad a bunch of times on it, although the vertigo seized her every time they took off or landed. They would circle around the airport and follow the stream to the river. There she watched the bridges and the cars below. Across the river, in the skyscrapers and the massive buildings, a couple of million people worked. Their little play cars crawled like ants. That Cessna was their personal getaway vehicle. Her dad could spirit them away, and Kaylee could escape, but it only held four seats.

She considered for a while, her mind zipping through scenarios as her father argued for them to just run away, to fly off from it all and never come back. When it was clear that he had made up his mind already, Kaylee felt a cold streak inside her.

She decided that she wasn't on her father's wavelength at all.

"What about all of them?"

Her father tensed back. Flippantly he said, "There's a seat for your little friend, Sasha."

"Sara."

Her father threw up his hands, and he grasped for words. "And... And... even the boy... what's-his-name?"

"What about Sara's parents?"

"What about them?" Her father didn't seem to understand.

"I made a promise." Kaylee glared back, somewhat confused and somewhat emboldened. Her finger pointed into the house.

"What about all of them? What's going to happen to them?"

Her father snatched her hand and held it still. "This is war. War, Kaylee."

Kaylee yanked her hand free, and she retreated from the bed. "I know. I'm in it. What do you think I've been doing?"

"I'm getting you out of here tomorrow. The earlier the better."

"Where are we supposed to go?"

"Maybe Canada. Maybe Mexico."

The sum total of the conflict rushed back through her consciousness. So much human devastation that was beyond words... The flood of it just couldn't be articulated.

"It's not enough!"

"What do you mean?" Her dad twisted and adjusted his leg on the pillows.

"This is our country," said Kaylee. Suddenly she boiled over, on the edge of tears. "They killed my mother, turned my brother into a monster, and they almost killed you."

"Kaylee. They have armies. There could be millions."

"I don't care."

"Come here." Her dad opened his palms and exhaled softly. "Come here."

She stepped closer without returning to the bed. "What?"

"Revenge won't bring your mother back."

Now more than ever, his empty platitudes sounded like meaningless chatter.

"Justice."

She sneered, not a kid any longer. She'd rely on her own eyes and ears.

Sara popped into the doorway with a can opener in one hand and a cat in the other. When Kaylee spotted her in the corner of her eye, she blocked Sara from invading the bedroom.

"Sara, can you feed her in another room? Put her in the bathroom, please."

"Oh. Okay."

"And give her somewhere to do her business."

"Ew. Yeah." Sara grinned, and she turned about to take care of her kitty quandary.

Kaylee softly shut the bedroom door and locked it. Returning to face her father, she stepped up beside him again.

"I have an idea."

"Okay?" He stared blankly.

"What if we killed the power for the whole town?"

He seemed skeptical. "The electrical grid?"

"Yes." Kaylee nodded emotionally. "If we turn it off, then nobody can watch the signal. They'll all come back to our side."

"Maybe," he said. "There are generators and batt-"

"It'll work. Won't it?"

He hesitated before committing. "It could. Theoretically."

"Then it'll work."

***

Kaylee emerged from the back bedroom and stepped down the hallway, looking for Lucas.

He, Caroline, and Melanie organized their records and maps while helpers arranged cans and boxes. Others cooked for the group. All four burners blazed as a girl sipped at soup. Others snored sprawled on the floor. The smell was rising.

Kaylee entered their cluster, and she pulled up a chair to sit at the table. There she announced, "I have something to say."

Lucas smiled. "You always do."

He toasted his glass of apple cider in her direction. Small talk subsided, and Kaylee prepared to set her plan into motion.

Twenty-Eight

Kaylee and Dustin dashed from tree to tree. They decided to go on foot because of the helicopters. Stealing a car and racing around the streets would be too conspicuous. Their objective was only about a mile off, near Kaylee's neighborhood and adjacent to the freeway. She had fled right past the electrical sub-station on her frantic bike ride to escape her brother's killing spree.

Only Dustin volunteered to accompany her, and he brought along his hunting rifle with the scope attached. Kaylee didn't make a fuss when no one else stepped forward to take their chances out in the night. Even Dustin seemed pretty frightened, but he always agreed in the end whenever Kaylee came calling.

That evil helicopter changed the battlefield. Suddenly all were terrified to venture outside, except for Kaylee. For some reason she thought it was going to be okay. She had survived so many close calls that they were starting to become normalized, like an extreme sport or something.

Dustin hightailed it to another front yard and hid beneath a tree. Kaylee rushed to catch up. When they turned the next corner, they saw a sizable highway overpass and a black tunnel beneath it, where they would need to travel to reach the electrical complex.

Kaylee studied the terrain through her binoculars, and Dustin did likewise. They stood for a while and hunted blindly in the black sky for signs of activity. This was the last tree, the last bit of cover before they would charge out into the open and race toward the safety of the underpass.

"They don't know we're comin'," said Dustin.

"Nope."

"I like it that like that." Dustin returned his spy glasses to his backpack, and he produced a couple of chocolate bars. He handed one to Kaylee, and they unwrapped them and savored the caramel within.

The night air felt brisk, and Kaylee appreciated her chocolate vacation from the war.

"You're the only one who would come," she said.

Dustin nodded as he chewed rather loudly.

Kaylee looked up at his face, inquisitive. "You always come with me."

They finished off their energy bars, and Kaylee waited for a feeling to come over her that it was safe to venture out.

Dustin took a minute to gaze up at the stars. "You think they got satellites?"

"The dupes?" Kaylee turned her eyes up. "I guess they could."

Dustin seemed apprehensive. They both knew it wasn't safe beyond the neighborhood trees.

Kaylee dropped her gaze.

"You think it would be any better in the daytime?"

"No."

She glanced to the highway. "It's really close."

"How close?"

"Just on the other side."

Dustin thought it over.

"Screw it," he said. "Let's go." He marched out into the open at a steady gait, not quite running, not quite walking. Kaylee sprinted to catch up with him. As they charged together toward the highway underpass, she watched the right side and he the left. Dustin twisted his rifle off of his shoulder, positioned it in his hands, and clicked off the safety.

The two halted again, concealed in the shade of the overpass. They checked back behind them.

Kaylee said, "So far so good."

"We're good," said Dustin. "Don't worry."

"Yep."

"What do you think's gonna happen when we mess with the electricity?"

Kaylee dug into her pack and located a bottle of water. She offered it to Dustin, and he gulped down half the container.

"My dad said it might cause a big power failure across the region. A cascading blackout, it's called."

Dustin handed back the bottle. "Oh yeah?"

"Maybe." She wiped the mouth of the container with her sleeve, and she replaced the cap.

They plummeted into the darkness of the underpass. Neither was in any hurry to reach the other side, and their footsteps slowed considerably. Kaylee looked to Dustin in the black stillness, and she grinned.

"We're like Kurtz and Jasmine."

"What? Who?" Dustin snapped his head at her momentarily before he peered off into the shadows with his rifle at the ready.

"Did you ever read *Ghostly?*"

"Huh? No."

"It's a really popular book. Everyone reads it."

Dustin chuckled. "Not quite."

"Well, what *did* you do before all this?" Kaylee's eyes adjusted to the near absence of light. She wasn't sure whether to fear the darkness or to embrace it.

He relaxed his shoulders, and he rested his rifle against his chest. "Well...I helped my mom at the ranch. We've got a property down Wild Springs Road, and some horses, sheep, chickens. It's like a farm. Was."

"I see." Kaylee was at a loss. She knew next to nothing about farms or livestock. "You took care of the creatures?"

"Yep. Lotsa work, too."

"Dustin?"

"Yeah?"

"What happened to your mom?"

He froze at the edge of the underpass mouth and gazed at the road before them.

"We're here. Where do we go now?"

Kaylee felt a chill. "It's left."

"All right," said Dustin. "Let's do this quick and get the hell outta here, all right?"

"Fine by me."

The two poked their heads out to search in the tangerine streetlight. Dustin grabbed his binoculars again. They plotted a series of trees to leapfrog. On the left side of the road was a vacant lot full of oak trees and scraggly bushes, which Kaylee believed would take them directly to the power substation.

Dustin dashed first, and Kaylee followed more slowly. The two navigated through the wild brush, not finding any sort of trail but relieved that the pines towered enough above them to obscure the sky. The area seemed safe from the predatory choppers. Their mini-forest unfurled for a couple of acres until they stumbled upon a dark pile of dirt, a bulldozed embankment.

There the two stopped and beheld a field of high-voltage wires and metal towers, odd devices that linked them all together. An almost imperceptible buzz radiated from the massive electrical network. Dozens of thick steel cables entered the facility high above like industrial spiderwebs, which stretched across the landscape. The station glowed with perpetually burning yellow bulbs, perfect for targeting.

Kaylee said, "Figure out which ones are the transformers."

Dustin braced his rifle up against a tree, and he peeked around through the scope. "I don't know which one's which."

Kaylee dropped her backpack, and she produced her own binoculars to help Dustin. The metal boxes didn't look like anything in particular.

Dustin said, "Which one's the transformers?"

"Uh. I think the big tall one is."

"You sure?"

"No. But shoot it anyway."

Dustin flopped back, exasperated.

"You know? Every dupe within a mile is gonna hear these shots."

"Damn." Kaylee sat back in the dirt and leaves.

Dustin said, "What time is it?" The sky had lightened several shades of blue, from pitch-black. He checked the horizon for the sunrise.

She burrowed into the front pocket of her backpack to find her dad's wristwatch. "Five-forty."

"What time do you think they all head off to bed?"

"Six-thirty-ish."

"How 'bout we wait till seven?"

"But it'll be light out." She and Dustin peered into the woods desperately. Artificial yellow filtered in through the leaves and branches above, and the daylight quickly approached.

Dustin suddenly grabbed his rifle and aimed. "Screw it!"

Shots blasted. The concussions deafened Kaylee, and she held her ears. Dustin let four bullets fly into the power station. When he finished, she whipped her head about to try and reclaim her hearing, and she yawned. A few sparks sizzled out onto the cold concrete, but nothing much else happened. The lights remained bright.

"You missed?" she said, annoyed.

Dustin shook his head, and he grabbed the stock of the rifle again for another go. One of the transformers flared up with a brilliant white light. A searing flash blinded both of them, and they buried their faces in their arms. The electrical explosions continued, first subsiding a bit and then roaring up toward the sky. Another blast followed from another transformer, and then another. Each exploded as ferociously as the previous. As they shielded their faces from the blast waves, the power station lights cut out, and so did the lights in the surrounding neighborhood. Highway pole lights died. All the man-made sources in the vicinity ceased simultaneously.

Kaylee and Dustin uncovered their heads and jumped to their feet to flee. Pulsing white firelight clawed deeply into the surrounding forest. The town had gone black, and they couldn't see where they were rushing.

Awkwardly Kaylee smashed into tree branches and prickly bushes. She followed in Dustin's clumsy wake through the black soup as he navigated blindly back toward the highway underpass. Kaylee ran through without stopping and out the other side into the soft blue moonlight. She searched to see the limits of the darkness.

The blackout ended and the lights glowed still beyond the hills. The city's skyscrapers shone like massive beacons calling all in from the soupy night. There the lights streaked across the sky from helicopters and planes. The city at the end of the highway, across the river and a couple of miles to the east, overlooked their little suburb like the all-seeing eye on the pyramid on the back of the money. The metropolis jutted up from the quiet black sea like electric Himalayas.

Twenty-Nine

Kaylee Colton emerged from the back bedroom of the safe house. The dwelling chattered with incessant conversations from wall to wall. New people had joined, men mostly, and a few women fighters. Tough days had passed with their town under military occupation. Swift, brutal violence waited out the door as dupes patrolled in tanks, helicopters, and planes. Also above, and hiding in the clouds, robotic drones circled, ever on the hunt to execute hapless humans found wandering below.

Dupe forces shored up the big city and blocked off all access points. They prevented repeats of the electrical grid attacks that had undercut their control of the populace throughout the suburbs. Three-point-two million civilians lived within the city, each and every one of them a dupe.

Kaylee faced the room of fighters, armed only with a notebook and assorted words scratched down on pages. They all knew her by now, and she wondered what they were thinking as she scanned over their faces. Some ignored her, while others smiled with unintentionally goofy expressions of support. She navigated demurely toward the dining room table, where life and death plans were made and unmade nightly.

Kaylee accepted a seat beside Lucas and Melanie, and she laid her notebook down flat to pore over it.

"I made a list," she said.

Lucas nodded. "Hey, quiet down, everybody."

The room remained chaotic and distracted. So many frustrated people were living in such tight quarters that they bickered and argued most of the time now.

Caroline stepped to claim a closer spot, and Dustin hovered directly behind Kaylee, which she appreciated.

"We have to act," she said, "or they're going to wipe us out."

With that, the room fell to silence.

"I think the plan is solid. My father thinks it can work. So anyone who's going to be a part of it, we should strike tonight."

The room closed in almost imperceptibly. Haggard-looking veterans pressed up beside stone-faced, freckled teenagers. They shuffled to better listen.

With Kaylee's master plan explained, and some minor arguments which followed, it was decided to launch their most extreme operation to date.

Two men carried Kaylee's dad out of the bedroom on an improvised stretcher. The group checked their weapons and supplies and loaded up packs with tools. At the front door, as the operation was deemed ready, Kaylee faced her people one final time. The thirty-or-so determined warriors, in various states of injury, jammed in tight like sticks in a tinderbox.

Kaylee's hand remained on the doorknob, surprising them by not turning it.

"We should have a moment of silence."

Random grumbles shot out through the crowd like an ocean wave. After some clumsy repositioning, everyone stilled.

"Take a minute," said Kaylee, "to remember everybody who didn't make it. The people we've all lost."

She hung her head, visions of her mom dancing about within. She felt her mom's presence, and she knew those ghostly visions had all been true. They had to be. Her mother was looking out for her, even after her death. Kaylee would take this war to the ends of the earth in order to achieve justice for her beautiful mom, whom she had loved more than anyone else in her life. Kaylee didn't care if she failed, or if she was killed fighting back. She would never back down and never run away again.

After the minute of silence passed, she hoped that the others had used their moments to look inside themselves, like she had. She wanted them to be as committed and fearless as she was. They were a big team, and they followed her. Kaylee Colton was leading this revolution now.

She turned the knob and pulled back the front door. Her fighters had squashed forward, close to trampling her underfoot, and she had to maneuver around the swinging door while pushing the beefy guys the hell out of her way.

SUVs along the street were already hot-wired, gassed up, and checked. The rebels flooded out of the house and made straight for the vehicles. Kaylee jumped onto the lawn to wave them past and to meet up with her dad. As four men carefully lowered him down the front stairs, she stepped up.

"My dad's gonna ride with me in the black one. Can you put him in the back, please?"

The black SUV loaded up with Lucas, Dustin, Kaylee, and her dad stretched out across the rear compartment. With time ticking, the boys in front glared through the windshield at the slower-loading vehicles ahead.

Lucas sparked the ignition wire, and their car purred to life. "Let's go, let's go, let's go."

Dustin, beside him in the front seat, said, "They're good."

The car ahead twisted out of its spot and raced off. A third vehicle pulled out more cautiously, and then their own SUV joined the procession.

Kaylee's dad tapped her on the arm. "You know how I feel about you coming along on this."

She smiled noncommittally. "I know."

They whipped around a corner and down another quiet side street featuring many old trees, elms, and maples in full bloom and thick with overhanging leafy branches. They had decided to stay exclusively on side streets, on a route mapped out by Melanie, who had a knack for puzzles requiring meticulous detail.

Their trip through the dark pretzel maze took longer than anticipated. As the cars used no headlights, the streets were fraught with hazards from previous conflagrations, which hadn't been cleaned up in over a month of post-apocalyptic warfare. From shopping carts to trucks and buses, bullet casings to unexploded artillery shells, the streets were scrap wastelands.

Kaylee called up front to Lucas, "Does everyone know what they're doing?"

"I guess we'll find out." Lucas jerked the wheel, and they sped ahead to catch up.

Flying out and across another avenue, which crossed under the freeway, the cars exposed themselves momentarily, charging into new dark terrain. They turned in at a road sign and raced along rural roads and massive farm fields. The land was expansive and flat, acres of farmland ringed by thin rows of trees.

Another hard right turn and their column shot over a rough back road beside the local airfield. Runways poked deeply into overgrown weeds. The sprawling facility was too large for them to see beyond the landing strip. This road led to another road, which ran parallel to the runway. Suddenly their SUV jerked into a gravel lot, where they slid to a stop.

Lucas and Dustin jumped out of the SUV, leaving Kaylee and her father sitting in back. Dustin wielded a crowbar, and the two boys made a beeline for a one-story, corrugated tin building.

Her father suddenly barked at her in that intimidating tone, which made her stomach queasy.

"Get up there on that platform. I want to see a perfect PLF or forget it, I'm not takin' you."

"There's no time-" Kaylee snapped back from him to find the painted wooden platform, which poked up beyond the building.

"Knees together, butt tight, arms in by your chest, be a big spring. And if you fall forward, pick a side and drop onto your hip. Go."

Dustin and Lucas had already popped the lock off of the building's door and were inside. Kaylee growled, and she muscled open the SUV's back door. Running across the gravelly lot, she sized up the white wooden structure, with its crisscrossing supports and looming height. A simple wooden ladder at the rear shot up as on a high diving board. In front of the platform was a large sandbox to catch leapers. As Kaylee put hand over hand to ascend, she saw that the other team from the first SUV had cut through the chain-link fence and dismantled the cross bar.

At the top of the platform, the view looked terrifyingly tall and dangerous, at least ten feet in the air, plus her own height. She stared down over the flat terrain in the moonlight, and her hands began to shake. The feeling returned in all its debilitating force.

Kaylee's sneakers froze near the edge of the wood. Far below lay the sand box. Beyond that was the skydiving school's office, where Lucas and Dustin hauled parachutes out and stuffed them into the SUV beside her prone father. She really wanted to figure a way of avoiding this and climbing back down safely. The thought of hanging off the edge of the platform with her hands and dropping that way, entered her mind. Beside this ledge, another elevated section rose even taller. Kaylee rolled her eyes.

The boys had finished, and they were suddenly impatient.

"What are you doing?" Lucas shouted as Dustin snatched his rifle from the rear of the vehicle. Those who had opened a hole in the fence returned to their cars and were ready to move out. Suddenly, everyone's eyes turned to Kaylee. She whined, trying to remember.

"Knees together." She squatted down tightly. Squeezing her fists and curling up into a C, she let out a guttural, primal scream as she closed her eyes and jumped forward.

In midair, her eyes blew back open, and she saw only the sandy earth rushing to smack her body like it was a bug. She felt whacked by the entire planet. The thud resonated through her spine and skull when she hit the sand and fell forward onto her side.

Before she could even breathe again, Lucas was shouting at her.

"Come on! Let's go, Colton! Stop playing around!"

Kaylee stood up, wide awake but aching along her side. Her hands swatted the sand particles as she stumbled out of the sandbox to the SUV. The other vehicles were already crawling through the hole in the fence and onto the airport grounds.

Kaylee dove into the backseat, and Lucas floored the gas. In darkness the autos slithered through weeds beside the long fence. The only sound was of dried out crispy bushes crunching beneath their tires.

Her father gently punched her in her upper arm.

"That was good. Are you okay?"

Kaylee shrugged. She had to try and find an appropriate place to channel her anger. Glare leaked in through the dirt-streaked side windows. The airport operated, and cargo shipped on old mid-sized jet planes. The dupes shipped air freight to help in their war effort and communications. Planes departed nightly, which her father had taken note of. Here they were, loading up an old Boeing 737, with very little armed protection in sight. This target was too enticing for the rebels to ignore. Kaylee could only hope it wasn't some kind of a trap.

The SUVs halted. Spotters watched the big jet through binoculars and a telescope. Mid-sized trucks delivered pallets and large metal containers to the plane. A canvas-covered National Guard truck sat off to one side. Workmen drove specialized airport equipment to and from the airliner as they loaded it. There seemed to be fewer than twenty dupes involved, but more could easily be waiting inside the airport or keeping guard outside at the front entrance.

Their team was committed now, and they had the element of surprise on their side. Dupes didn't care much for surrendering, and no conflict with them could ever be considered easy.

Kaylee held the overhead handle as the SUVs raced ahead to start their attack. Bouncing violently over the dirt and bumps, they sped in toward the floodlights. Kaylee's SUV circled around the front of the jet airliner.

Dupe workmen were slow to respond. Most kept working, oblivious to the arrival of Kaylee's raiders. With a crash, the first SUV plowed into the rolling steel door leading to inside the warehouse. Their guys poured out, armed with lethal and non-lethal weapons alike. The men went for the controller to lower a rolling door and cut off access.

Dupes reacted individually as the other vehicles emptied out and the conflict began.

Kaylee's father tightly clutched a semi-automatic handgun as their SUV parked in the shadow of the 737. Kaylee jumped out with Lucas and Dustin, and they assessed the huge airliner before rushing up a ladder through the open cargo hold door.

Shots fired. Dupe soldiers exchanged bullets with their people.

Inside the plane, Kaylee, Dustin, and Lucas navigated around the pallets. A door separated the forward compartment from the rear bay. It was locked. Dustin yanked at it, but the sturdy metal hatch kept sealed.

"Crowbar," said Lucas, who dug into Dustin's backpack and wrenched out a long iron tool. The boys went to work jamming open the plane's interior door. After a couple of attempts, the lock broke apart and the door flew open. Straight ahead, down at the end of the narrow corridor, the cockpit door had been left open.

Silently, the three of them crept forward. Lucas held the crowbar, Dustin a pistol. Kaylee stepped gingerly behind them toward the cockpit.

Outside the plane, the battle escalated with sporadic assault rifle shots and shouts.

Without warning, two deafening explosions assaulted them. A large caliber handgun blasted massive magnum rounds out at them from the pilot's compartment. Holes ripped into the thin aluminum skin of the plane's walls as the three dove back toward the cargo hold.

A pilot remained holed up inside the cockpit, blindly shooting a .44 at them down the narrow corridor.

Kaylee couldn't hear anything, but she managed to crawl around the cargo bay.

Dustin shouted, "Now what?"

Kaylee sat with her back to the wall, listening in on the confused chaos outside the aircraft. Loading vehicles crashed and dropped their cargo. Screams echoed. Several more gunshots rang out. She felt sad that it was evolving into one giant mess. It seemed so easy on paper when she first thought about this and ran it by her father.

Dustin and Lucas held their handguns, and they took positions on either side of the cargo bay door. Kaylee watched helplessly as they cocked their weapons and made a plan to storm the front and kill the pilot.

"Hey!" she shouted. "Don't kill him."

"He's trying to kill us," said Dustin.

Kaylee frowned with ineffectualness. Another blast from the unseen .44 shocked her nervous system. Her body flailed back involuntarily into the metal wall of the cargo hold.

They had no way of knowing how many bullets the unseen dupe pilot had brought along. Time was swiftly running out. As soon as the military figured out what they were up to, it was over. The entire success of the mission— and their lives—depended on getting this plane in the air *now*.

Kaylee raised her Taser, which she had found at an abandoned police station in town that week.

"Stop!" she shouted as the boys set themselves to rush forward with guns blazing like psychos. They turned back to her, frustrated.

"What?"

"You can't shoot into the cockpit!" she yelled. "You'll mess up the plane! What are you doing?"

Lucas lowered his weapon, a bit embarrassed.

"Dammit!" said Dustin.

"What do we do, Colton?" Lucas stood beside the open doorway, and he spied at the cockpit.

Kaylee held up her Taser.

"We'll both go," she said. "After the bathroom we can split up. You go left and I'll go right."

"And me?" Dustin said sarcastically.

"You stay here and aim straight down the hallway in case he shows himself."

Dustin twisted up his face. "So, you *want* me to shoot into the cockpit now?"

"Only if you can't miss."

Dustin nodded, and he jumped across the doorway gap directly behind Lucas. "Hey, Kaylee?" he said.

"What?" She turned back nervously.

"Be careful, would ya?"

Kaylee stared down at the end of her Taser, determined as ever. With Lucas right behind her, she settled her mind. She watched the empty hallway, waiting for some unknown paranormal signal to finally spur her ahead. Lucas waited coolly for her to go first. It suddenly dawned on her that her father was alone out in the car below the plane. There was no time left. She had to do this.

Stepping forward into the doorway, Kaylee felt airy and ethereal, like her mom floating forward across the unknown.

Kaylee roared at the top of her lungs as she raced to dive to the side of the cockpit door in a cubby at the emergency hatch. Lucas followed her. Taking her cue, he shouted like a warring Viking as he dashed. He flew to the left, where he crashed to a stop opposite Kaylee.

The next bullet ripped into the metal corner above Lucas and drilled into the plane's bathroom. Kaylee poked her face out around her own corner, and she saw the arm, the handgun, the smoke rising and that concussive airwave pounding right through her brain.

She decided that a hand was as good a target as anything else, and she fired her Taser.

One of the filament wires struck the pilot's wrist, and his hand spasmed. His revolver dropped to the cockpit floor. Electrocuted, he stumbled forward a step onto his knees. Kaylee juiced him with clicking intensity so that he was brought down unconscious. The pilot was an older man with greying hair in a white captain's uniform. He rolled up into a convulsing ball beside his revolver. Kaylee stepped cautiously, and she wanted to take the weapon away from his reach before anyone did any more reckless shooting on her airplane.

Kaylee's father was delivered through the open cargo hold door. Lucas and Dustin carried him through the maze of pallets and containers to the pilot's chair. Kaylee lugged parachutes inside behind them. As they arrived at the front of the airliner Kaylee's dad started flicking switches, firing up engines and checking systems and gauges. Lucas backed out swiftly. Kaylee delivered the two parachutes.

"Stow those securely," her dad barked.

"Where?"

"There." He pointed back behind him, barely pausing in his system checks. The flaps on the wings flittered up and down, and the rudder left and right.

"All right. Get off this aircraft, people!"

Kaylee rushed back through the cargo hold, where the door remained open to allow Dustin and Lucas to exit. Lucas slid out and disappeared from sight.

Dustin, however, rotated back around with an uncharacteristic change of plans.

"I should stay," he said. The plane lunged forward, releasing its brake.

Kaylee stared back, dazed.

"Dustin, get off the plane!"

"You go," he said, looking determined as ever.

"No. Get out of here." She pushed at his arm until he stepped back to the wide-open hatch. They were already taxiing in an arc. Dustin lowered himself to slide out, halfway hanging from the side of the 737, but he refused to be cast out.

"Kaylee, I should do this."

"We'll be fine. Go!" She held her head, confused, now that the plane was rolling forward and turning about, with Dustin hanging out of the cargo door. He wouldn't release his grip as the jet rolled faster.

The intercom crackled.

"What's going on?" Her father's voice bellowed on the tinny speaker above her. Kaylee couldn't understand Dustin.

"I have to close the door." She pulled down at it, but Dustin remained in the way. Looking from the door mechanism back down to him, Kaylee suddenly saw a tear on Dustin's cheek. She froze in place as the aircraft lurched sideward in a sharp turn.

"Dustin?"

He didn't speak, but the look in his damp blue eyes told her how afraid he was that she wouldn't be coming back. The weight of it all flattened Kaylee's mind. Her hand shook on the door's locking handle.

"Goodbye," said Dustin. Then he jerked away and fell off down onto the tarmac.

Kaylee felt haunted, like she would never see him again, as she sealed the pressurized hatch and felt the plane jolt beneath her feet. The mission took top priority. She climbed about the pallets and through the cargo bay door and fought the acceleration as it threw her backward.

They were really going to do this. She suddenly felt so small and powerless with the thrusting of the jetliner's engines behind her. Clawing forward through the cockpit door, Kaylee pulled herself into the co-pilot's seat. The 737 moved rapidly now, her father whipping around the final turn to align them with the long runway.

"Strap in," he said tersely. "Quickly!"

With that, he pushed the accelerator forward, and Kaylee fumbled with her seat belt while being pinned back in a racing climb. She had been up in planes many times, but not like this. The runway remained dark, as did the plane's outer lights. Her father gave the engines every bit of thrust they could produce. It was no longer about doing it safely, and no passengers were going to complain as he wrenched them skyward at full speed and immediately rolled into a sharp turn.

Lining up the city lights, he closely monitored the plane's radar, and he kept them speeding so low that Kaylee felt like they were brushing the tops of the trees.

"Kaylee, the computer," he said, pointing. "Here. This is where you come in."

She studied the automatic flight navigation system, with its keypad of glowing red numbers.

"We'll set markers. You press enter and go to the next one. Press this."

"Okay." Kaylee was drawn to the front windscreen, feeling nauseous from the onrushing hills and houses they skipped over at four hundred miles an hour.

"Kaylee," said Dad in earnest. "I need exact points on the GPS. No delay. When I say *mark,* you hit it."

"I got it."

"First one coming up." They turned left and back right, swiftly approaching the river. "Mark!"

She pressed the button.

"That was late."

"What now?"

"Quicker next time. Move on to the next one."

Her father aligned the 737 with railroad tracks below. "Mark!"

Kaylee tapped the key and progressed to the third marker.

"It's at the end of the tracks, coming up." Her father watched the green radar scope, and he searched above in the night sky.

They had traveled so far without company. The old Boeing raced toward a facility with jutting smokestacks, massive industrial buildings and box cars. Kaylee stared at her index finger hovering just above the glowing red key. The smokestacks appeared right in their way.

"Three, two, one. Mark!"

She snapped the final marker into the computer and held fast. "Now what?"

He pulled up the plane vertical up away from the city, passing over tall buildings, and circling around to the right.

"I got it," he said.

As her father played with the computer, typing in data and flying the plane simultaneously, Kaylee didn't know where to look or what to look for. They had risen above the obstacles and were already approaching the powerless, black farmlands, which surrounded the city. On the radar, a couple of little green glowing dots were visible, meandering slowly.

"Dad?"

He typed several more coordinates.

"Are those dots getting closer?" The radar bothered her.

An explosive ordnance flared, impacted behind them, and tore through the cargo bay. The 737 took fire from those little green radar blips. Kaylee's dad lunged at the accelerator.

"Apaches, I think."

Evasively, their 737 dove back down toward the earth in a twisting, plummeting dash for safety along the ground.

Another explosion jolted the plane. One of their engines detonated.

"Dammit!" Dad cut the fuel to the destroyed engine and the plane jerked nearly out of control.

"What do we do?" Kaylee suddenly felt nauseous.

With one engine, their plane couldn't outrun the helicopters. Her father pulled back on the wheel.

"Hold on. New plan."

The 737 tilted up to the heavens, with full thrust pumped through its remaining engine. If Kaylee had felt sick before, she felt doubly so now that she couldn't even find the horizon. She closed her eyes as the pressure crushed her body.

When she found the strength to open them again, she saw her father frantically recalculating and reprogramming the computer. Their plane shot up and up. Suddenly they couldn't breathe.

Dad produced oxygen masks for them, and he seemed nearly as desperate as Kaylee felt. She strapped on her plastic mask and breathed deeply to fill her lungs with something breathable.

With acrobatic maneuvers, her father wrenched the airplane around in a corkscrew turn, and she caught momentary glimpses of the earth again.

"He can't follow," said her dad through his mask. "We're too high." Then he returned his attention to the onboard computer.

Kaylee panted into her mask to get enough air, rethinking her neat and easy plan to win the war. Frigid air seized the cockpit, and she shivered.

"We'll jump at fifteen thousand feet," said her dad through the muffles of his oxygen mask.

The idea of fifteen thousand feet.

How high is that? What's a mile again?

Five thousand, two hundred and eighty feet—everybody knew that. Jumping out of a plane three miles in the sky was not something she had ever desired to do.

The radar showed more blips in pursuit. The dupes had apparently gotten their act together. Now there were six.

"They're following us out here." he said. They turned in a gentle semi-circle through the black soup. "One more minute. Then we'll turn back."

Kaylee reached over and squeezed her father's hand. He took a few moments to hold her hand assuredly and look back at her.

"Daddy? I love you."

"Yeah, me too," he said. "It's working."

Studying the little blips, he wrenched the wheel to the right again, and they went rolling in a wide arc and back toward the glowing, white haze of the city off on the horizon. He checked their coordinates, making new corrections. With a button he engaged the plane's auto pilot system, and he studied the results.

"We're on automatic."

"Is it gonna work?"

"Of course it's gonna work." He chuckled.

Kaylee reached for the radio transmitter.

"Is this working?"

"Of course. Why?"

She pressed the send button. "This is the 737."

Her father stared, his jaw dropping slightly.

"Our target is the power generating plant, units one and two. Evacuate the workers. Evacuate everybody."

Her father jerked with intense aftershocks. "You just gave away our attack!"

Kaylee could see in his face that he was livid and suspicious of her. Perhaps he thought she was slipping into a relapse. That she was working for the other side like before. Her own dad suspected her of being some kind of dupe sleeper cell mole! She couldn't believe it.

In silence, he gawked over at her and yanked the microphone from her hand.

Kaylee responded with unflinching conviction, which was now her trademark. "Nobody else needs to die." The constant stream of oxygen felt refreshing, and emboldened her to see her plan through to the finish line. Nausea had passed now that the airliner had smoothed out and steadied.

"Kaylee. Two minutes." Dad sounded unsure about her, looking really pissy as he studied the radar screen.

Kaylee twisted back and assured herself that the parachutes remained secure behind them in the cubby.

"Listen," he said, striking a deathly serious tone. "When we jump, you don't pull your cord until you're stable, face down, looking at the ground."

"Okay."

"The last thing you want to do is pull that cord while you're out of control, rolling. Big no-no. There's no margin of error here."

"I got it."

"You remember how you land?"

"Yes."

"Square chutes, you pull the handles in as you touch down. It lifts you up and slows you down. Cushions the landing."

Kaylee nodded briskly as the two minute mark shot past. Their plane suddenly descended on its own, angling toward the city. The city's white, hazy glow grew larger and brighter. Dad focused on the radar signatures, and he monitored their flight path. Queasiness returned to her stomach as the g-forces took their toll.

"Seventeen thousand," he said. "Unbuckle your belt."

They unlatched their seat belts. Kaylee felt like she was on a massive roller coaster, close to falling right out of the coaster car.

"Fifteen-five," he said. "Get ready to grab those chutes."

The airliner whipped back up toward a more level position, and Kaylee could feel her guts sloshing about her abdomen.

"Now, Kaylee. Now!" Her dad twisted helplessly, still unable to stand on his damaged leg.

Kaylee jumped and climbed around the cockpit seat to retrieve the two heavy parachutes.

Her father made some last-second alterations to his computer. He snatched his parachute and he struggled to work it on in the cramped cockpit. Kaylee slid on her own parachute, and she locked it into place.

"Are you ready?" said Kaylee. She watched him snap his first strap shut. "Come on! Let's get out of here."

Taking her hand, her dad grabbed on tightly like a cub clinging onto its mother. He felt so heavy. Kaylee tried to pull him forward through the cockpit doorway. They each lumbered in their massive parachute packs, barely squeezing through. Dad paused at the doorway to check back on the looming city below them one last time.

"Keep going!" Kaylee pulled desperately, unable to yank him farther.

"They're closer than I thought."

"Dad!" Wrenching him away from the cockpit, she stumbled into him, and they fell back down the hallway together. Kaylee stopped at the plane's exit door, but her father kept going.

"Rear door," he said. "We're not jumping into the engine. Come on."

They fought their way back to the cargo bay door. Inside the massive hold, they saw the aircraft's skin was torn and gouged. Wind whistled shrilly through the jagged holes. Boxes and crates were blasted around everywhere haphazardly. Her father clicked shut his remaining parachute latch, and they navigated over the pallets and debris as best they could.

"Kaylee. Final descent any time now."

Kaylee yanked at his arm to help him over a crate. The two struggled toward the cargo bay door at the very rear of the airplane. It was across a wasteland of boxes and overturned pallets of merchandise.

Gravity shifted radically. So did the crates. Everything flowed violently in an unstable rush through the cavernous open space.

Kaylee fell back, and a loose box bulldozed her along the steel floor. She struggled to climb back up to her knees as the entire plane dove at a steep angle.

Her father was similarly thrown about, and he tumbled back toward the front.

"Dad!"

Kaylee twisted to her knees, and she pulled herself up. Her father struggled to yank his body back to where he had previously been. She stretched over the top of a crate and grabbed his hand. The two attempted to climb together back toward the cargo bay door. He was unable to stand up, and unable to crawl very well. Kaylee pulled as hard as she could to try and slide him back up toward the destination.

The exit was jammed with a tall pallet, which had shifted over during the aerial acrobatics. Kaylee pushed at it.

"What do I do?" Kaylee poked around to try and reach the door handle, but it was blocked with the stack of boxes sheathed tightly in plastic wrap.

"Cut off the wrapping," he said. He dug into his pocket and he retrieved a folding knife. "Here."

Kaylee caught the knife, opened it, and she sliced into the plastic. Her father climbed to his feet with support from some boxes, and they ripped into the pallet, tossing the contents out of the way.

The cargo hold around them suddenly ignited in flames and explosions. The plane took more incoming fire. Metal shrapnel shot in every direction. Holes popped along the sides with glowing fireballs. A piece of hot, searing metal blasted into Kaylee's shoulder, knocking her over.

She screamed and looked down at the bloody damage below her chin.

The plane dove steeper, on its final approach to crash into the coal-fired power plant that fed the city. The wayward pallet shifted a couple of feet to the right, freeing the door handle. Kaylee ignored her pain, and she used her good arm to pull herself up and go for the door handle. As it clicked, she felt pure terror.

The door whipped open to the air, on a pilot-less plane rocketing toward the ground on a kamikaze run. Three hundred mile-an-hour black icy winds raced past her face. Bright lights streaked below them, and Kaylee had lost track of her dad. He lay on his back, tilting back and forth on his parachute like a turtle. His body was wedged in between overturned boxes.

The edge of the outer door was more terrifying than she imagined it could be. She retreated from the hatch. Her dad saw that she had opened it, and he put up his palms to halt her.

"You go!" he yelled above the wind. "I'll follow you! Jump now!"

Kaylee turned to face the open hole but then turned back to him. Shaking her head, she rushed over to the boxes to grab for his arm. With newfound strength, Kaylee wrestled him up to his knees and stood him up.

"Don't forget what I told you," he said as they waddled forward together toward the open plane hatch.

"Let's get out of here!" she cried, desperate to overcome her sense of impending doom. At the opening, she stopped before the black void. The city below was unreal. The rushing wind was too much to bear. Thousands of feet to drop, and her body could move no more.

Her father kept on pushing, and he knocked her right out of the hatch into the night sky.

Kaylee screamed uncontrollably, thrown in a dizzying whiplash without any sense of control.

Thirty

Kaylee tumbled in the open air, and she spun end over end in the void. She couldn't hear herself shriek, and she was about to pass out from the violent g-forces. Her body sailed in a wild roll, gaining speed and trying to find some coherence in the blurry streaks of light spinning her toward unconsciousness. She couldn't breathe, as the impact of the winds flattened her chest and tossed her through the sky like a paper doll in a hurricane.

She realized that her screams were pointless. Instead, she clenched her jaw. With her arms held out like bird's wings, she attempted to stabilize herself. Dropping at a hundred and twenty miles per hour, Kaylee pointed herself down toward the streetlights and black rectangles below.

Her strong hand fumbled to snatch the metal ring on her chest, and she pulled the parachute cord. Her body catapulted back and crushed against the straps. Lacking air, she felt bludgeoned, on the verge of giving out.

Kaylee didn't have the energy required to throw up but simply bobbed about helplessly beneath the parachute. Her brain again slowly awakened.

Still a few thousand feet in the air, it seemed. Very high. Very nerve-wracking, and her dad was nowhere in sight.

Kaylee's neck had locked stiffly like rigor mortis, and she convinced her head to turn slightly in order to search the sky. Beyond her gaudy red parachute it was a dark, empty night, and she couldn't find him anywhere.

Her neck relaxed a bit, enough to crane around over her shoulder. Below cars parked in the street, and the headlights sliced ahead of them. Little figures scampered. Kaylee stared down at them, curious. She had fallen quite a bit lower, and still she could not see her dad.

The figures on the ground became more visible. Then she heard booms. Flashes of light poked up below her from the street. A whole series of booms rang out, louder and louder.

Her parachute suddenly jolted several times. Holes poked through the red sail above, and she felt the sting of bullets zinging up past her face. Helplessly Kaylee watched the dark forms on the ground target her while she fell closer and closer towards them.

It was then the 737 impacted the ground. The fireball was so gigantic and its effects so mighty that the entire city altered instantaneously. The airliner had made its scheduled landing into the coal-fired power generating station, setting off furnaces, steam, and fuel explosions all over the area.

The fiery glow washed over Kaylee as she descended from the clouds, supported only by her increasingly precarious Swiss cheese parachute.

When the city's power plant fell, so too did the power grid. Sectors fell dark one after the other in succession. Within moments, the entire world became pitch-black.

Kaylee plummeted toward the armed dupes below who wished to kill her. But they all stopped shooting when the jetliner struck. She watched the cars move out again and race off in the direction of the explosions, leaving her to fall alone.

Kaylee tried to remember how she was supposed to land. It was dark and dangerous. The ground rushed up with unseen hazards. Clinging to her handles, guiding the parachute this way and that, she floated wide of a large industrial building and toward an open street. Her body tensed. She could see grass in the moonlight smacking up toward her like a planet-sized fly swatter. With all her remaining strength, she pulled on her parachute guidelines and rejoined the earth. Both feet together, planting flatly on a patch of grass, she gently stood there while her chute deflated and relaxed behind her. A slight gust pulled it back, and her along with it.

"Aah!" She stumbled about, trying to yank at the massive blowing chute. Her hands grabbed clasps on her chest. These released the dragging chute. Dancing awkwardly to free herself, Kaylee wiggled out of her entanglement.

About a block over, she saw her father sail down and land hard, tumbling onto his side. She heard his groans. Feeling astoundingly strong, considering her shrapnel wound, bruises, and night of sheer terror, she ran to him.

"Daddy! Are you okay?"

Her father twisted in the middle of the asphalt to try and flip over. His hands fumbled to unclasp his straps. Kaylee pulled the ropes from his body, and she helped him sit up and extricate himself.

He said, "Was that what you had in mind?"

Kaylee could only laugh and smack him on the forehead.

The city lingered in true darkness. This lasted only several minutes as dawn rolled around on the planetary clock, and the sky lightened accordingly.

Kaylee assisted her dad, and they stumbled into the nearest car. She smashed the rear window with the end of a metal flashlight, and she proceeded to try and hot-wire it.

Thirty-One

Jasmine and Kurtz, the two wayward ghost hunters, did eventually find their way out of the secret passage beneath the Metropolitan Museum. They plunged into a narrow, snaking tube cut into the rock by water flowing over millennia. After crawling like moles, the two arrived in a cozy cavern, an oval chamber deep in the earth. A sliver of light beamed in, although they couldn't discern its source. Jasmine tingled with an overpowering presence like she had never experienced in all her previous paranormal encounters. Kurtz tripped over jutting stalagmites, and he tried to feel for a secret lever to open some kind of exit door.

Jasmine suddenly realized that Kurtz's efforts were in vain. The only way out of this subterranean death chamber was to go through the spirits themselves.

When she opened up her senses for full contact, the arrival was both colossal and beyond what ghost hunters were expected to experience during the normal course of their careers.

Kurtz had often visited the museum above them. There he marveled at the cultures of the past, all of which had disappeared forever, lost in time. Local tribes were no longer in existence, nor were the people of the jungles of the Americas, Neanderthals, Cro-Magnons, or Australopithecus peoples. Kurtz could not begin to say how many billions of individuals had lived and breathed and died off on planet Earth. Or how many babies had been born, all of them starting life pretty much in the same predicament. Or how many tribes and civilizations had vanished forever like droplets in the unceasing, unfeeling flow of history.

Kurtz turned to Jasmine, who swooned oddly in the center of the oval rocky space. As he approached her, she appeared to him oddly different, not herself. Intense flashes of lightning-like energy jolted out across the cavern from the rock walls themselves.

Indecipherable voices filtered in through the rock, a cacophony of vibrations not so much loud as pervasive and all-encompassing. A low-pitched roar enveloped the two. Kurtz froze in shock at Jasmine's possession. He quickly cleaned off his eyeglasses with his shirt tail, and placed them back on his nose as the glow intensified around her.

Jasmine reeled before Kurtz, contacted and consumed, overtaken by the discharging spiritual energies. Helpless and swallowed up whole by this intense spiritual bridge, Jasmine connected with all of the lost tribes like a conduit. Representatives from all the extinct peoples lived on in spirit form beneath the Earth's surface.

To Kurtz's shock, Jasmine's feet slowly left the cavern floor as she floated, and her body acted like a kind of circuit-breaker in the center of an increasingly bright, buzzing chamber. Electricity pulsed into her form and back out again. Lifted to the air by the barrage of electro-spiritual discharges, Jasmine's skin emitted white beams and sparkling lightning bolts. This sight rendered Kurtz more than a little disturbed. He jumped back up against the wall, terrified that they were both about to be cooked to a microwaved crisp. His glasses reflected back ethereal spirit-mists as they shot from the rock and right through Jasmine's helpless body. From her they danced and redirected back out again in a spiritual circuit. Her powers acted as a kind of paranormal capacitor, a semi-conductor that was now a major hub in Earth's inter-planar Internet.

Spirits zipped out from Jasmine's fingers and her black hair follicles, as well as her painted toenails. These strings of white energy melded into her and connected her directly to the Earth itself in a manner never before witnessed by any member of our human culture.

It was Kurtz, and Kurtz alone, who saw these connections. And it was Jasmine alone who became our

308

culture's single ambassador to the near-infinite line of predecessors who had lived and died before.

Jasmine hoped that these ancestors would find her acceptable as they absorbed her mind and experienced our modern civilization. But she found many of them to be confusing and steeped in their own contradictions. So much energy passed through Jasmine and her circuit bridge to the otherworld, and so quickly, that the amount of knowledge transferred defied human capacity for comprehension.

Jasmine eventually returned to the cave floor. Her feet floated back daintily and touched down on the moist dirt. With newfound wisdom, Jasmine could feel universality pulsing through her brain. Of interest to Kurtz, Jasmine also held the secret to getting them out of there.

The two epic ghost hunters ascended one of the rock walls, and they followed the narrow light shaft to its source inside the basement of the Metropolitan Museum.

Covered in dirty smears and caked in mud, the two teenagers emerged from several plastic sheets hanging at the entrance of an archaeological dig. Jasmine and Kurtz acted nonchalant as they tiptoed down a hallway and past several scientists, who were drinking coffee in the museum's break room.

On the way out, Jasmine explained to Kurtz about the numerous cultures and places she had visited and the various tribal practices she had witnessed. That spiritual conduit had transported her back through time and space. Her receptivity was all she needed to reconnect with those long-extinct societies, the peoples who had lived before. The spirits of the tribes lived on, said Jasmine, assembled from the total soul energy of their members. Collectively, their spiritual energy filtered down into Mother Earth and fanned out on invisible superhighways below the surface. Jasmine had never conceived of anything so infinite before. Kurtz concluded that this solved all of their mysteries at once.

As the two young spiritualists wrapped up their loose ends, Kaylee Colton smiled. She suspected *Ghostliest* might have some new tricks up its sleeve with such an audacious title. This really was the greatest ghost hunter book she had ever come upon, but she was open to finding another even better one in the future. What threw her for a loop, though, was not so much the source of modern spiritual discord as it was the very last line of the book.

From out of nowhere, Jasmine and Kurtz decided to take a break and go over their notes again, just to be sure about certain clues before agreeing to publish an extensive research paper in *Paranormal Archaeology Today*. That's when Jasmine licked her finger and stood before Kurtz admonishingly.

"There's still dirt on your nose, doofus," she said. Reaching her moist index finger, Jasmine flicked the specks off of Kurtz's crinkling nose.

"Is it all gone?" said Kurtz.

Jasmine leaned in close to inspect him. *Kurtz could sure use a bath,* she thought. He was passable enough to be seen in public, barely. From a distance, she could accept maybe being associated with him.

But suddenly Jasmine was overcome again, a mental pull not unlike that of the spirit bridge, which had lifted her clean up into the air. When she looked into Kurtz's face, she no longer felt the same about him. They had nearly died together down there in that mucky catacomb, after all. Dead.

She said, "Close your eyes."

"Huh?"

"Just do it."

With Kurtz blind and motionless before her, Jasmine leaned in and kissed him on his lips.

The End.

"What!" Kaylee shouted. Would there be a *More Ghostliest* to explain this? It was just insane.

***

Kaylee had driven her father back to town at dawn, from out of the dupe-occupied city, her first actual driving lesson on a street. Dad remained quite terrorized with Kaylee behind the wheel, but since his right foot was about to fall off he didn't have much of a choice.

She didn't crash the car. Neither did they face the dupes, who were now completely lost in chaos and disarray. The city effectively fell the moment that airliner had impacted its power-generating station. So many circuits tripped in rapid succession that a blackout wave fanned out across the greater region.

Back at their safe house, Kaylee had them patch up her shoulder. Caroline Anderson tweezered out a sliver of airplane skin. Kaylee kept the fragment as a souvenir. Caroline finished up with ointment and sterile bandages. While she patched, she told Kaylee some of the recent news items, but Kaylee couldn't keep her eyes open any longer.

For the next entire day Kaylee slept. She couldn't go on anymore without a deep rest, the kind that lasted so long that you couldn't even remember when it started.

Over the course of that very first day, day one, the dupes' stranglehold on the city and the region was smashed. Reports filtered in, slowly but surely, of military units fighting other military units for control. Doctors and nurses were located, and the practice of medicine returned at their local hospital. Video screens were removed and destroyed. A basement diesel generator provided temporary energy for surgery and specialized medical equipment.

Kaylee's father was operated on that day. The hospital returned to life and filled with injured patients. A bubble of freedom and ordinariness took root inside their hostile and unsure world.

At any moment a video screen could flash to life, and the entire ordeal would begin again.

***

Kaylee awakened eventually on the morning of the second day. She found Dustin Hafstead outside playing with Sara and her kitten Little Paws. Their neighborhood bustled with people returning to their houses. Others headed out on quests to find loved ones and to reclaim their own homes.

Kaylee noticed Dustin's foot set in a cast. He too had found medical help. He hobbled around impatiently, trying his best to ignore his handicap, but the cast raised his foot off the ground so that he couldn't walk properly, one leg longer than the other.

"Hey?" Kaylee called out to Dustin.

"You're up," he said. Limping, he bounded along as casually as ever.

Kaylee bent down to take a look at his foot.

"What happened to you?"

"Hospital's back," he said. "That's where we took your pa."

She pointed at his leg. "How did you do that?"

"Oh." Dustin seemed evasive.

Kaylee stared at him, expecting a response. His face twisted like a little boy, as if scheming an excuse that would please her.

She could tell that he didn't want to say.

"Dustin, what did you do?"

He huffed out in surrender. "Remember when I got out the plane? Musta been movin' faster than I thought."

Kaylee's eyes almost popped. She didn't want to laugh. It surely wasn't funny.

Why do people laugh when other people hurt themselves?

It was weird.

The streets were safe again, and they boxed up Little Paws and upgraded his accommodations to a proper kitty carrier, which they found in an abandoned department store. Once the cat was set up nicely, Kaylee, Dustin and Sara set off to locate Sara's parent's house.

Dustin drove the SUV, and Kaylee coaxed Sara to give them some useful hints. "What's it near?"

"My kindergarten. It's awound the corner."

Dustin drove the streets randomly. They never got much of a sense of their destination. In the back seat, Sara stared out the windows but remained silent.

Kaylee twisted around backwards.

"Do you remember the name of your kindergarten?"

"That's the name! Kindergarten. Look it up."

Kaylee's head drooped down onto the top of the seat. "Sara, there's lots of kindergartens."

"All you gotta do is look it up."

Kaylee rolled her eyes at the roof of the SUV. "Where!"

"In the telephone book. Duh."

She almost slapped herself in the forehead. They soon acquired an old yellow phone book from a filthy, out-of-service pay phone. Sure enough, the kindergarten schools were listed in order. In short time, they drove past a school that Sara recognized.

"That's my school!"

Dustin slammed the brakes.

"Yeah? So where's your house at little lady?"

Sara looked out the various car windows.

"Um, not yet."

Kaylee said, "Let's read the street signs." The first one said *Maple*.

"Is it Maple?"

"Yes! That's it!" Sara jumped up and down on the seat like a monkey. Dustin laughed as he pulled into the street.

Kaylee said, "Which house?"

Sara swiveled her head around and scrutinized each dwelling.

"It's sorta like that! Sorta. Ya-ya-ya, where is it?"

Kaylee looked to Dustin.

"Let's try back the other way."

Dustin nodded, and he turned the big vehicle around. After doubling back and continuing a ways, Sara chimed up softly, "I think it's a that one."

Dustin slowed to almost zero. "Are you sure?" he said.

Sara nodded, but not as enthusiastically as they had expected.

Kaylee said, "Okay. Let's get out."

The three investigated the exterior of the pastel blue, ranch-styled house. It seemed untouched by the chaos. Plants grew healthily with automatic sprinklers to thank. Sara seemed cautious, and Kaylee remained at her side for support. It occurred to her that Sara feared her parents had become dupes, like Kaylee had once become.

With each step toward her porch, Sara's dread heightened. Her little hands started to shake. Kaylee watched with concern as Sara slowed, unwilling to step to the front door herself. With Sara icy in her tracks, frozen in apoplexy, Kaylee knew that she had to do something. She was pretty sure this was the right address. Kaylee knelt down on the porch.

"Sara? You want me to knock?"

Sara's eyes drifted over, and she nodded.

"Okay. They might be home. Come on, relax."

Sara's eyes started to tear up. Kaylee knocked, and she adjusted her hair. The three waited together in a row on the porch.

Then the front door yanked open.

A man stood in the doorway. "Oh my God!" He dove down to his knees to greet Sara with a massive hug, swallowing her up.

Sara's mother shrieked from within the house.

"Is it Sara?" Her mother ran out to them, and they all nearly went tumbling down the porch staircase like a giant snowball.

Kaylee stepped back off the porch to stand beside Dustin on the concrete walkway. Dustin seemed happy now. Kaylee thought that he wasn't such a bad person, and he had a rugged, bad boy kind of thing with his scruffy hair and stubble and the way he dressed.

Sara broke off from her parents.

"Kaylee! You gotta meet my mom and dad!" She smashed into Kaylee and shared some of that excess affection. Then she grappled her wrist to pull her up the stairs again.

Sara's mother and father thanked Kaylee effusively, as well as Dustin. Sara wanted Kaylee to come live with them. Kaylee told them about her own father, whom she needed to go see at the hospital. After pleasantries, she and Dustin returned to the SUV.

On the drive to the hospital, Dustin slid a CD into the car's stereo. Kaylee didn't know what music it was, but it sounded very good. She was amazed that Dustin might know a thing about music. Then she remembered that he'd stolen somebody's guitar and all that other stuff.

Dustin piloted the SUV onto the hospital's street. They found a nearby parking spot in the half-empty lot. As he parked, his hand wavered above the ignition wires.

"Do you want me to come in?" he said. "Should I wait?"

Kaylee stiffened.

Do I want him to come into the hospital?
Why would he come in?
Why wouldn't he?

It was actually baffling, as she couldn't think of all the reasons why simultaneously.

"Uhh..." Kaylee looked up into Dustin's deep blue eyes. They were very beautiful, but she could never tell him anything like that. But they were. She stared motionlessly at Dustin's face. Now that the rest of the world had settled somewhat from the aftershocks, she found that she was no longer in any kind of a hurry.

Dustin was so pretty but so clueless. There was no way he could be thinking anything other than what she was thinking and what they were supposed to be thinking, but he looked so blank and expressionless.

What is wrong with him anyway?

She leaned forward a few inches, twisting her face up with determination. This seemed to confuse Dustin even further. He shrugged.

"What?"

With some sense of inevitability and courage, she finally said, "Dustin, close your eyes."

When he did, Kaylee bit down on her lip.

"Keep them closed. Completely."

"Why?" said Dustin.

"Just don't open them."

"Okay. They're closed," he said, not at all expecting what came next.

THE END

A Note to Readers

Thank you sincerely for taking a chance and reading *Transfixion*.

I wrote Kaylee Colton's story because I believe this is an important tale of war and peace, violence and non-violence. Also, I wrote an action-packed plot so that it could be adapted to the big silver screen.

That, however, is up to you. It's the readers who hold the real power. Only they can build the kind of momentum required to transform a novel into a movie. So write your own honest reviews. Post them to Facebook and wherever you hang out online, such as Amazon, Barnes & Noble, and Goodreads. Tell your friends—without any spoilers, of course. When the readers really want it, Hollywood listens.

Have a great day.

J. GIAMBRONE
@TransfixionBook
July 7, 2014

About the Author:

Novelist and screenwriter J. Giambrone has taken on the Sisyphean task of confronting the dominant American culture where it lives through storytelling, satire and the airing of uncomfortable truths. In an age of perpetual warfare, he has chosen an uncompromising endorsement of peace through understanding and justice. With *Transfixion,* the goal is to challenge readers of all ages to confront their own concepts of conflict, of resolution, and of the myriad tenuous threads that connect all of us. He also has a kid, a wife, a cat and two guitars.

Social Media Links:

Email: jgiambrone@live.com
Website: http://jgiambrone.wordpress.com/
Facebook: https://www.facebook.com/TransfixionBook
Twitter: https://twitter.com/TransfixionBook
Readwave: http://www.readwave.com/j.giambrone/